CLOTEL

broadview editions
series editor: Martin R. Boyne

CLOTEL;
or,
THE PRESIDENT'S DAUGHTER

William Wells Brown

edited by Geoffrey Sanborn

broadview editions

BROADVIEW PRESS – www.broadviewpress.com
Peterborough, Ontario, Canada

Founded in 1985, Broadview Press remains a wholly independent publishing house. Broadview's focus is on academic publishing; our titles are accessible to university and college students as well as scholars and general readers. With over 600 titles in print, Broadview has become a leading international publisher in the humanities, with world-wide distribution. Broadview is committed to environmentally responsible publishing and fair business practices.

The interior of this book is printed on 100% recycled paper.

© 2016 Geoffrey Sanborn

Library and Archives Canada Cataloguing in Publication

Brown, William Wells, 1814?-1884
[Clotel]
    Clotel, or, The president's daughter / William Wells Brown ; edited by Geoffrey Sanborn.

(Broadview editions)
Includes bibliographical references.
ISBN 978-1-55481-289-9 (paperback)

    1. Jefferson, Thomas, 1743-1826–Relations with women–Fiction.
2. African American families–Fiction. 3. Children of presidents–Fiction.
4. Racially mixed people–Fiction. 5. Illegitimate children–Fiction.
6. Women slaves–Fiction. 7. Domestic fiction. I. Sanborn, Geoffrey,
editor II. Title. III. Title: President's daughter. IV. Series: Broadview editions

PS1139.B9C53 2016   813'.4   C2016-900269-1

Broadview Editions
The Broadview Editions series is an effort to represent the ever-evolving canon of texts in the disciplines of literary studies, history, philosophy, and political theory. A distinguishing feature of the series is the inclusion of primary source documents contemporaneous with the work.

Advisory editor for this volume: Colleen Humbert

Broadview Press handles its own distribution in North America
PO Box 1243, Peterborough, Ontario K9J 7H5, Canada
555 Riverwalk Parkway, Tonawanda, NY 14150, USA
Tel: (705) 743-8990; Fax: (705) 743-8353
email: customerservice@broadviewpress.com

Distribution is handled by Eurospan Group in the UK, Europe, Central Asia, Middle East, Africa, India, Southeast Asia, Central America, South America, and the Caribbean. Distribution is handled by Footprint Books in Australia and New Zealand.

Broadview Press acknowledges the financial support of the Government of Canada through the Canada Book Fund for our publishing activities.

Typesetting by Aldo Fierro
Cover design by Aldo Fierro

PRINTED IN CANADA

Contents

Acknowledgements

I would like to thank the Louis Round Wilson Special Collections Library at the University of North Carolina at Chapel Hill for allowing me to use the text of *Clotel* on the website *Documenting the American South* as the basis of the present text. Thanks as well to Amherst College for the sabbatical that helped to make my work on this edition possible. And thanks above all to my wife, Sarah, and my children, Colin, Eli, and Calvy, who make all things possible.

Introduction

The Aesthetic of Attractions

In an article entitled "Christmas Festivities" that was published on 24 December 1861, a writer for the *Paterson Daily Guardian* announces that "at three o'clock on Christmas Day ... [t]he celebrated WM. WELLS BROWN will give a humorous and highly entertaining lecture, calculated to send everybody away with a broad grin however ruefully they appear on entering. Don't fail to hear this man; for he is no Artemus Ward"—a lecturer whose performance in Paterson, New Jersey, had just been panned—"but a regular genius in his way and worth your while to study as a character." Accompanying the article is a "programme of the entertainment," headlined "Great Attractions at Continental Hall," which promises not only an afternoon's worth of "classical, humorous, and sentimental recitations by the celebrated Elocutionist and Orator, Wm. Wells Brown," but also a "comic and sentimental" evening concert with "intervals [that] ... will be filled by Mr. Brown, with his unequalled attractive powers."[1]

Nowhere in the article or the program is it mentioned that Brown is black. Neither is it mentioned that he had been, for over a decade, one of the country's leading abolitionists. To all appearances, the "celebrated WM. WELLS BROWN" is first and foremost a showman—a rival less of Frederick Douglass than of P.T. Barnum,[2] whose holiday exhibitions were favorably reviewed just two columns to the right of the item on Brown. Like Barnum, who was currently displaying in his American Museum a white whale, a hippopotamus, an elephant turtle, the "mammoth bear Samson," 12 sea-horses, "monster snakes," and "Signor Pietro D'Olivera, the celebrated Rat tamer, with his famed 200 Indian white rats and mice, which he has tamed and trained to perform amusing tricks and feats, which no one had ever supposed rats could be taught," Brown offered up an array of attractions: stylized recitations, raconteurish interludes, and,

---

1 "Christmas Festivities," *Paterson Daily Guardian*, 24 December 1861, 3.
2 Frederick Douglass (1818–95) was the country's most famous black abolitionist; Phineas Taylor Barnum (1810–91) was the country's most famous mass-entertainment entrepreneur.

in his written work, wildly heterogeneous set-pieces—set-pieces whose only apparent organizational logic was, in the immortal words of Monty Python's Flying Circus, "and now for something completely different."[1]

Witness *Clotel*. As nearly all of its reviewers pointed out (see Appendix A), *Clotel* was an audience-minded performance, an effort to capitalize on the post–*Uncle Tom's Cabin* "mania" for abolitionist fiction in Great Britain, where Brown lived, lectured, and wrote between 1849 and 1854.[2] Just as the success of Douglass's 1845 *Narrative* had prompted Brown to write his own autobiography (*Narrative of the Life of William W. Brown* [1847]); just as the success of anti-slavery songbooks like George W. Clark's *The Liberty Minstrel* (1844) had prompted Brown to publish his own compilation of abolitionist lyrics (*The Anti-Slavery Harp* [1848]); just as the success of panorama exhibitions like John Banvard's *Mississippi from the Mouth of the Missouri to New Orleans* had prompted Brown to commission and exhibit a panorama of slavery-related scenes in the early 1850s; and just as the success of touristic travel narratives like Nathaniel Parker Willis's *People I Have Met; or, Pictures of Society and People of Mark* (1850) had prompted Brown to write a touristic travel narrative of his own (*Three Years in Europe; or, Places I Have Seen and People I Have Met* [1852]), so did Harriet Beecher Stowe's world-beating novel prompt Brown to compose *Clotel*. But whereas the disparate elements of *Uncle Tom's Cabin* are, in Stowe's words, "grouped together with reference to a general result, in the same manner that the mosaic artist groups his fragments of various stones into one general picture,"[3] the even more disparate elements of *Clotel* are simply exploded, one after another, in a fictional night-sky. The material of *Clotel* is Stowe-like; the aesthetic of its deployment is Barnumesque.

The name that the film historian Tom Gunning gives to that aesthetic is "the aesthetic of attractions."[4] For Gunning, an at-

---

1 "Barnum's Great Fairy Spectacle for the Holidays," *Paterson Daily Guardian*, 24 December 1861, 3.

2 The *London Athenaeum*, to take only one example, characterized *Clotel* as "a voice to swell the chorus which Mrs. Beecher Stowe has raised" ("American Books," 21 January 1854, 86). Harriet Beecher Stowe (1811–96) was the author of *Uncle Tom's Cabin* (1851–52).

3 Harriet Beecher Stowe, *A Key to Uncle Tom's Cabin* (Boston: Jewett, 1853), 5.

4 For more on the aesthetic of attractions, see Appendix C.

traction is "something that appears, attracts attention, and then disappears without either developing a narrative trajectory or a coherent diegetic world. Attractions work by interruption and constant change rather than steady development."[1] In the cultural environments where attractions are most often found—fairgrounds, circuses, amusement parks—the spectator's "delight comes from the unpredictability of the instant, a succession of excitements and frustrations whose order cannot be predicted by narrative logic and whose pleasures are never sure of being prolonged."[2] Although he focuses on the presence of the aesthetic of attractions in early cinema, Gunning conceives of that aesthetic as a fundamental aspect of the culture of modernity, capable of being traced backwards and forwards in time into all kinds of media. And indeed, in novels as well as films, in the mid-nineteenth century as well as the early twentieth century, one discovers again and again a "drive towards display, rather than creation of a fictional world; a tendency towards punctual temporality, rather than extended development; a lack of interest in character 'psychology' or the development of motivation; and a direct, often marked, address to the spectator at the expense of the creation of a diegetic coherence ... along with [an] ability to be attention-grabbing (usually by being exotic, unusual, unexpected, novel)."[3] The orientation toward coherence and closure is never entirely absent, of course. Nevertheless, throughout the visual and textual archive of modernity, there is a powerful counter-orientation toward irresolution and distraction, toward an unpredictable succession of "shows."

More than any other novel of its era, *Clotel* swings in the latter direction. Other novels of the 1850s have out-of-nowhere chapters, pull-out-the-stops passages, and sudden stylistic transitions: Herman Melville's *Moby-Dick* (1851), Nathaniel Hawthorne's *The House of the Seven Gables* (1851), and Fanny Fern's *Ruth*

---

1 Tom Gunning, "The Whole Town's Gawking: Early Cinema and the Visual Experience of Modernity," *Yale Journal of Criticism* 7 (1994): 193. The "diegetic world" is the interior world of a story, the time and space in which a narrative unfolds.

2 Tom Gunning, "'Now You See It, Now You Don't': The Temporality of the Cinema of Attractions," *Velvet Light Trap* 32 (Fall 1993): 10–11.

3 Tom Gunning, "Attractions: How They Came Into the World," in *The Cinema of Attractions Reloaded*, ed. Wanda Strauven (Amsterdam: Amsterdam UP, 2006), 36.

Hall (1854) come immediately to mind. But no other mid-nineteenth-century novel is so obviously meant to be a string on which attractions are strung—that is, to be the textual equivalent of a variety show. Before composing *Clotel*, Brown had drawn huge crowds all across England to his exhibition of a moving panorama of 24 non-continuous "views" of scenes related—sometimes quite distantly—to slavery, and he had enjoyed similar success with a magic lantern show consisting of images drawn from *Uncle Tom's Cabin*, his autobiography, and his panorama paintings. Tableaux supplemented by commentaries, commentaries broken off by the appearance of new tableaux—this was the formula for a series of performances that Brown describes in an 1851 letter as "*a paying concern.*"[1] It is not hard to see why a similar formula came to mind when he sat down to write *Clotel*.

The main object of the present edition is to make it possible to read *Clotel* in something like its original pop-cultural context, with some version of that historically specific formula in mind. Previous editions of the novel have contextualized, in valuable ways, Brown's use of the widespread rumor—since verified—that Thomas Jefferson (1743–1826) had children with his slave and mistress Sally Hemings (c. 1773–1835) and that at least one of those children, a girl, was sold at auction. Other aspects of the novel's content have been contextualized as well: its undermining of the logic of "scientific racism," for instance, and its allusions to the Compromise of 1850, which reaffirmed the provision of the constitution requiring Northerners to return fugitive slaves to their owners.[2] What has been left relatively unelaborated is the context of *Clotel*'s form. Why, wonders the critic J. Noel Heermance, did Brown construct a "skeleton of a plot on which ... anecdotes, stories, advertisements, and Virginia legislature speeches" are hung? Why does "the narrative mind behind the book's movement never [attempt] to signal who is important and who is not, where we are ultimately going and where we are not"?[3] The answer, at least in

---

1   Brown, letter to Wendell Phillips, 24 January 1851, quoted in Ezra Greenspan, *William Wells Brown: An African-American Life* (New York: Norton, 2014), 249; emphasis in original.
2   I am referring to some of the materials included in Robert S. Levine's landmark 2000 and 2011 editions of *Clotel*, published by Bedford/St. Martin's Press.
3   J. Noel Heermance, *William Wells Brown and Clotelle: A Portrait of the Artist in the First Negro Novel* (Hamden, CT: Archon, 1969), 164–65, 181.

part, is that Brown wanted to offer his readers a version of the experience that he offered so many of the audiences for his lectures and exhibitions: an experience in which one goes nowhere—or repeatedly goes over the same ground—but does so in animated company. As Mark Twain writes in an 1871 letter, "*Any* lecture of mine ought to be a running narrative-plank, with square holes in it, six inches apart, all the length of it, and then in my mental shop I ought to have plugs (half marked 'serious' and the others marked 'humorous') to select from and jam into their holes, according to the temper of the audiences."[1] *Clotel* is a similarly constructed performance, conceived of and elaborated with the temper of the audience in mind.

Of course, the audience for a work of literature is not present in the same way that an audience for a lecture is. Neither, crucially, is its master of ceremonies. Although authors and audiences alike cannot help but be implied by works of literature, they can *only* be implied. An author can't watch the faces and gauge the tempers of his or her readership as he or she writes; a reader can't watch the face and gauge the temper of an author as he or she reads. In certain contexts—especially the context of the aesthetic of attractions—that annihilation of presence can lead a writer to select his or her Twain-style plugs with great abandon and jam them into his or her plankholes with great force. It certainly seems to have had that effect on Brown. As I have shown elsewhere, *Clotel* contains at least 102 plagiarized passages, totaling roughly 12,232 words or 23 per cent of the novel. It contains, in addition, 54 explicit quotations totaling roughly 6,833 words, or 12 per cent of the novel.[2] Although Brown had plagiarized and hyper-quoted before, most notably in *Three Years in Europe*, those practices had never been as central to his compositional aesthetic as they are in *Clotel*. Out of a desire to be a hit—a culturally and politically significant hit—with an audience that he couldn't see and that couldn't see him, Brown draws without scruple on white writers and black writers, male writers and female writers, novels and newspapers, stories and sermons, speeches and songs. He

---

1   Mark Twain, letter to Olivia Langdon Clemens, 27 November 1871, in *Mark Twain's Letters, Vol. 4, 1870–1871*, ed. Victor Fischer and Michael B. Frank (Berkeley: U of California P, 1995), 498; emphasis in original.

2   Geoffrey Sanborn, *Plagiarama! William Wells Brown and the Aesthetic of Attractions* (New York: Columbia UP, 2015). For more on plagiarism, see Appendix E.

also breaks up the text of the novel with four plate images and prefaces it with a high-artifice, low-continuity memoir, in which he speaks of himself in the third person, interrupts himself with self-quotations and snatches of songs, and inserts a large number of press clippings and testimonials. Working with the materials and structures at his disposal, Brown creates a delivery system for attractions in an effort to draw as many readers as possible toward the anti-slavery cause. "You may be angry with him," he writes of Alexandre Dumas (1802–70) in *The Black Man* (1862), in a sentence plagiarized from an essay on that famously plagiaristic writer, "but you will confess that he is the opposite of tedious."[1]

Slavery and the Culture of Modernity

One might imagine that Brown didn't become a subject of modernity until sometime after 1 January 1834, when he escaped from his last owner, Enoch Price, into Ohio. As several recent historians have shown, however, modernity and slavery are not mutually exclusive. In the wake of the 1808 ban on importing slaves from Africa, the demand for slaves on the brutal plantations of the lower South began to be supplied on a large scale by the states of the upper South: Virginia, Maryland, Kentucky, and Missouri. This internal slave trade dramatically transformed American life, both inside and outside slavery (if, that is, after the Compromise of 1850, there can be said to have been any place "outside slavery" on American soil). Between 1820 and 1860, over 500,000 men, women, and children were purchased and transported to the plantations of the lower South. By 1860, the value of the slave population was conservatively estimated at $3 billion, or $86.7 billion in 2013 dollars. According to the historian Stephen Deyle, this was "roughly three times greater than the total amount of all capital, North and South combined, invested in manufacturing, almost three times the amount invested in railroads, and seven times the amount invested in banks. It was also equal to about seven times the total value of

---

1 William Wells Brown, *Clotel and Other Writings*, ed. Ezra Greenspan (New York: Library of America, 2014), 544. After being exposed, Dumas brazenly declared that "[t]he man of genius does not steal, he conquers" (quoted in Henry Breen, *Modern English Literature: Its Blemishes and Defects* [London: Longman, 1857], 218).

all currency in circulation in the country." No matter how loudly Southern apologists for slavery may have insisted that "their world was radically different from, not to mention far superior to, the increasingly modern, capitalistic society that was emerging in the north," their "premodern" society was in fact "propped up internally by a modern and market-driven domestic trade in slaves."[1]

One of the effects of the internal slave trade was that owners increasingly conceived of the value of their slaves not in relation to their productivity but in relation to what the market would bear. To an extraordinary degree, slaves became fungible, one step removed from cash. "Every slave know what, 'I'll put you in my pocket, sir!' mean," the ex-slave Isaiah Butler told an interviewer.[2] As a result, slavery became inseparable from the theater of market capitalism, in which value is, in the critic Gustavus Stadler's words, "the product of manipulations of the visible."[3] This may help to explain why, in the minds of white Southerners and Northerners alike, the slave trade was so often condensed into the scenario of an attractive young woman for sale. Because this woman-for-sale was, in accordance with the era's racist standards of beauty, very often imagined to be phenotypically white, many modern critics have seen her as a figuration of the desirability of whiteness. In the context of the above discussion, however, it might be worth conceiving of her as, in addition, an icon of the modern American economy. If the vibrancy of American markets was dependent on the attractiveness of slaves, then few scenarios could have given concrete form to the notoriously abstract Economy as effectively as a light-skinned woman's public sale. The swiftness with which buyers acquire this archetypically attractive commodity points not only to the forces of racism and rape culture, but also to the acceleration of turnover in modern capitalist economies; the reiterations of

---

1 Stephen Deyle, *Carry Me Back: The Domestic Slave Trade in American Life* (New York: Oxford UP, 2005), 7, 44, 59, 60. See also Edward E. Baptist, *The Half Has Never Been Told: Slavery and the Making of American Capitalism* (New York: Basic Books, 2014) and Walter Johnson, *Soul by Soul: Life Inside the Antebellum Slave Market* (Cambridge, MA: Harvard UP, 2001).

2 Quoted in Deyle, *Carry Me Back*, 233.

3 Gustavus Stadler, *Troubling Minds: The Cultural Politics of Genius in the United States, 1840–1890* (Minneapolis: U of Minnesota P, 2006), 82.

the scenario of her sale point not only to slavery's reality and anti-slavery's strategy, but also to the seemingly endless renewability of whatever buyers demand. She is an index both of white/male supremacist horrors and of the consumerist pleasures on which the Economy depends (see Appendix B).

By the time of his escape from slavery, Brown had come to know the internal slave trade inside out. He was born in one Upper South state (Kentucky), was transported to another (Missouri), and, once his owner John Young moved from rural Marthasville to St. Louis, was repeatedly hired out. One of the men who leased him was the slave trader William Walker. Over the course of a year, Walker and Brown made multiple trips between St. Louis and New Orleans to buy and sell slaves. Brown, who was then known as Sandford (his birth name, William, had been changed because it coincided with the name of his master's adopted son; "Wells Brown" would come from a white Ohioan who sheltered him after his escape), repeatedly prepped Walker's slaves for their market appearances, making them seem younger and happier than they actually were. "I have often set them to dancing when their cheeks were wet with tears," he writes in his 1847 *Narrative*.[1] By these painful means, he acquired what Stadler describes as "a behind-the-scenes view of the theater of value that slave capitalism, like capitalism generally, becomes in the market setting."[2] Well before leaving the South, Brown knew that the economy ran on the theatrical manipulation of appearances.

When he began to seek out ways of supporting himself—and, by 1839, a wife and two daughters—that knowledge was one of his primary resources. If we can believe the stories that he tells in the "Narrative of the Life and Escape of William Wells Brown," it was what made it possible for him to obtain writing lessons on false pretenses, to draw customers into his barber shop with misleading advertisements, and to circulate home-made currency in the absence of reserves. Far from concealing these and other self-advancing deceptions, Brown flaunts them, as if he has reason to believe that his audiences won't mind, and might actually enjoy, a certain amount of shiftiness. In *My Southern Home* (1880), Brown's narrator observes that Mrs. Gaines, the mistress of a plantation, "took peculiar pleasure in being misled by [the slaves]" and that Dr. Gaines, the master, "would allow

---

1 Brown, *Clotel and Other Writings*, ed. Greenspan, 24.
2 Stadler, *Troubling Minds*, 85.

himself to be carried off upon almost any pretext."[1] To all appearances, most of Brown's audience members felt much the same way. "Friend Brown, perhaps, throws too much humor in his subject, and is too rhetoric[al] for some," observes a writer for the *Pennsylvania Freeman* in 1849, "but to draw out an audience and to interest and enlighten the public, he is the man."[2] "He tells such ridiculous stories," Charlotte Forten-Grimké wrote in her journal in 1858, "that although I believe as little as I please—I can't help being amused."[3]

White abolitionists have never been known for their tolerance or enjoyment of "ridiculous stories." Neither have they been known for their openness to the unrestrained energies of the capitalist marketplace. Yet Brown, a celebrant of what the critic Stephen Best calls "the festal market whimsy of speculation," enjoyed an enormous popularity in abolitionist circles.[4] By peppering his lectures and publications with spirited anecdotes that might or might not be true, Brown tells us as much about his audiences, abolitionist and otherwise, as he tells us about himself. Instead of thinking of him simply as an object of cultural analysis—a source of information about slavery, racism, and African-American experience—we should think of him, in addition, as an agent of cultural analysis, someone whose work can tell us a great deal about the preferences and tolerances of his white contemporaries. Unquestionably, many mid-nineteenth-century Americans feared that "the self's moral and intellectual gyroscope would spin out of control as it entered the magnetic field of market relations."[5] Nevertheless, the "country that added bluffing to poker remained fascinated by the art of cool deception."[6] For his part, Brown remained fascinated, however ambivalently, by that country. "I love America," he told a British audience in 1849. "I admire her enterprising and industrious people ... but

1 Brown, *Clotel and Other Writings*, ed. Greenspan, 716.
2 *Pennsylvania Freeman*, 25 January 1849, 2; quoted in Greenspan, *William Wells Brown*, 185.
3 Charlotte Forten-Grimké, *The Journals of Charlotte Forten-Grimké*, ed. Brenda Stevenson (New York: Oxford UP, 2004), 330.
4 Stephen Best, *The Fugitive's Properties: Law and the Poetics of Possession* (Chicago: U of Chicago P, 2004), 183.
5 Jackson Lears, *Fables of Abundance: A Cultural History of Advertising in America* (Boston: Basic, 1994), 73.
6 Jackson Lears, *Something for Nothing: Luck in America* (New York: Viking, 2003), 100.

I hate her hideous institution, which has robbed me of a dear mother, which has plundered me of a beloved sister and three dear brothers, and which institution has doomed them to suffer, as they are now suffering, in chains and slavery."[1]

Attacking slavery while admiring enterprise might not seem logically coherent, given the degree to which slavery and the culture of modernity were intertwined. As the critic Nyong'o Tavia points out, however, "[t]he uneven ground of history ensures that social struggles are usually pitched not in terms of opposing discourses but in competitions over a single vernacular and improvisations upon a common repertoire."[2] Instead of opposing himself to the vernacular of racial modernity, Brown learned how to speak it fluently; instead of turning his back on the repertoire of white American stories, he riffed endlessly on its contents. As a result, it is often hard to know how to take him. Is his anecdote about a slave pulling the wrong tooth out of another slave's mouth an instance of minstrelsy or a parody of it? Is his representation of the dialect speech of slaves a reinforcement of racist stereotypes or a celebration of inventiveness? But the problem may ultimately lie in the framing of such problems. If we think of Brown as someone who competed over and improvised on the same materials as his white contemporaries, materials that emerged from the overlapping cultures of anti-slavery, racism, anti-racism, and modernity, then to isolate a single manifestation of those materials—to do a close reading of a single passage—is to miss the point. The art of *Clotel* is the art of the pop-cultural assemblage, the art of making something new out of materials drawn from common pools. Accordingly, the challenge for modern readers of *Clotel* is the challenge of what might be called a middle-distance reading, in which one steps back from traditional close-reading methodologies but not so far back that one is seeing only large-scale historical and cultural processes. From that middle distance, where one can see the bits and pieces out of which the novel was made, it is possible to perceive not the process of word-by-word composition but the process of block-by-block construction. It may be true that one cannot use the master's tools to dismantle the master's house, as Audre Lorde

---

1 "Public Reception of Wm. W. Brown in the Metropolis of England," *Liberator*, 2 November 1849, 1.

2 Nyong'o Tavia, *The Amalgamation Waltz: Race, Performance, and the Ruses of Memory* (Minneapolis: U of Minnesota P, 2009), 103.

once wrote.[1] But out of the lumber that the master has left lying around, one might be able to build a theater of one's own.

Clotel's Shows

Clotel begins with a prolonged series of set-ups: a preface, a memoir of the author, and an essayistic attack on slavery. Just as the narrative itself seems about to get going, however, its momentum is arrested by a show-stopping attraction: the sale of Clotel at auction. Throughout the antebellum period, the representations of such sales were extremely popular with abolitionists, as Brown well knew. His description of the sale is based on a short story called "An Auction," which was published in the *Utica Liberty Press*, reprinted in several newspapers as a true story, turned by a writer named Arzelia into a poem called "The Slave Auction—A Fact," and, shortly before the publication of *Clotel*, fictionalized by Brown himself in the first published African-American short story, "A True Story of Slave Life."[2] Instead of serving as a point of entry into an immersive fictional world, the description of Clotel's sale points us back to the print-cultural world from which it comes. It invites us not to merge, in private, with a lyrically expressed subjectivity, but to watch, in public, a familiar, spectacular show.

Other shows swiftly follow: a race between steamboats on the Mississippi River, which leads to an explosion; a poker game in which a slave owner bets and loses one of his slaves; the pursuit of runaway slaves by a pack of dogs; a sentimental evocation of a couple's love-filled cottage; a comic rendering of the deceptiveness of traders in the New Orleans slave market; dueling speeches and sermons on a Mississippi plantation; and comic anecdotes involving poor white Southerners. In most other novels, such set-pieces would be distractions from the main event. In *Clotel*, however, they *are* the main event, as the titles of the first seven chapters should suggest: "The Negro Sale," "Going to the

---

1 Audre Lorde, "The Master's Tools Will Never Dismantle the Master's House," in *Sister Outsider: Essays and Speeches* (New York: Crown, 2007), 110–13.

2 H.S.D., "An Auction," *National Anti-Slavery Standard*, 20 March 1845, 165 (see Appendix B2); Arzelia, "The Slave Auction—A Fact," *The Friend of Virtue*, 1 October 1847, 302; William Wells Brown, "A True Story of Slave Life," *Anti-Slavery Advocate* 1 (December 1852): 23.

South," "The Negro Chase," "The Quadroon's Home," "The Slave Market," "The Religious Teacher," "The Poor Whites, South." Stylistically, as well, the basic principle is variety: we veer from minstrelsy ("Dis nigger is no countefit; he is de genwine artekil" [p. 82]) to sweaty feature-writing ("Nearer and nearer the whimpering pack presses on; the delusion begins to dispel; all at once the truth flashes upon them like a glare of light; their hair stands on end; 'tis Tabor with his dogs" [p. 89]) to polished word-painting ("The iris of her large dark eye had the melting mezzotinto, which remains the last vestige of African ancestry, and gives that plaintive expression, so often observed, and so appropriate to that docile and injured race" [p. 92]) to sermonic flourishes ("Can that then be right, be well doing—can that obey God's behest, which makes a man a slave? which dooms him and all his posterity, in limitless generations, to bondage, to unrequited toil through life?" [p. 100]) to backwoods humor ("Clar out the pigs and ducks, and sweep up the floor; this is a preacher" [p. 108]). And what is true of the opening chapters is true of the book as a whole. "This little narrative occupies less than 200 pages, but it offers to the reader's attention a quantity of incident quite remarkable in these days of book-spinning," observes a reviewer of *Clotel* in the *Anti-Slavery Advocate*. "It is not too much to say that the book contains material amply sufficient, if artistically treated, to fill a three volume novel."[1]

The heterogeneity of *Clotel* is closely related to the heterogeneity of nineteenth-century plays, which were often "vehicles for startling special effects" like "fires, waterfalls, volcanoes, or shipwrecks" and were typically accompanied by interludes, after-pieces, and orchestral music.[2] It is related, as well, to the heterogeneity of non-theatrical entertainments, such as panoramas, pantomimes, puppet shows, fireworks, freak shows, museums, and circuses. In none of these theatrical or extra-theatrical

---

1 "*Clotel*," *Anti-Slavery Advocate* 2 (January 1854): 125; see Appendix A4. In the three relatively streamlined novels that Brown subsequently constructed out of the same set of materials—the serialized *Miralda; or, the Beautiful Quadroon* (1860–61), the 104-page *Clotelle: A Tale of the Southern States* (1864), and the 114-page *Clotelle: or, The Colored Heroine* (1867)—this quality is much less evident.

2 Robert Lewis, "Introduction: From Celebration to Show Business," in *From Traveling Show to Vaudeville: Theatrical Spectacle in America, 1830–1910* (Baltimore: Johns Hopkins UP, 2003), 9.

venues did customers expect the displays to be painstakingly elaborated and finished expressions of a distinctive personal vision. Then as now, on both sides of the Atlantic, mass-cultural audiences preferred variety and speed: a series of rapidly produced and rapidly consumable events (see Appendix C). Instead of seeing *Clotel* as a poorly executed novel, as so many modern critics have, we should see it as an experimental adaptation to a mass-cultural environment, an effort to generate the literary equivalent of "a phantasmagoria which a person enters in order to be distracted."[1]

Part of Brown's reason for putting on this kind of show is fairly obvious: to keep abolition's momentum going. In November 1857, when he was alternating between giving conventional anti-slavery lectures and staging one-man performances of his first play, *Experience; or, How to Give a Northern Man a Backbone* (1856), Brown told a fellow abolitionist that "there are some places where [the play] would take better than a lecture. People will pay to hear the Drama that would not give a cent in an anti-slavery meeting. We had meetings in Hartford last Sunday, and after three speeches, took up *Ninety Five Cents*. On Wednesday Evening I read the Drama in the same place, charged 10 cents at the door, paid $2.00 for the Hall, and had 5.00 over all expenses. Now, this is more than Mrs. Coleman, Mr. Howland and myself have taken up in Collections for the last ten days."[2] As far as Brown was concerned, the best way of getting the anti-slavery message out was by getting as many people as possible into the seats, even if that meant blurring the line between abolitionism and entertainment. In a cultural environment in which most white people were, as he put it in an 1847 lecture, "perfectly dead" to the "cries, shrieks, and groans of the Slave," he was willing to risk an approximation of Barnumesque amusement if it held out the prospect of bringing the masses to life on the subject of slavery.[3]

---

1 Walter Benjamin, "Grandville, or the World Exhibitions," in *The Arcades Project* (Cambridge, MA: Harvard UP, 1999), 7.

2 William Wells Brown, letter to Marius Robinson, 29 November 1857, repr. in *Speak Out in Thunder Tones: Letters and Other Writings by Black Northerners, 1787–1865*, ed. Dorothy Sterling (New York: Doubleday, 1973), 127.

3 William Wells Brown, *A Lecture Delivered Before the Female Anti-Slavery Society of Salem*, in *William Wells Brown: A Reader*, ed. Ezra Greenspan (Athens: U of Georgia P, 2008), 120.

In addition to working to end slavery, however, Brown was working to end racism, or "colorphobia," as it was called at the time. In *Clotel*, Brown mounts not only an immediate, practical effort to arouse abolitionist feelings by turning anti-slavery documents and arguments into variety-show attractions, but a more utopian effort to project a representational space that pretty much everything, everyone, and every part of everyone might enter. In *Three Years in Europe*, Brown writes that the white abolitionist James N. Buffum is the man he would choose if he were "sent out to find a man who should excel all others in collecting together new facts and anecdotes, and varnishing up old ones so that they would appear new, and bringing them into a meeting and emptying out, good or bad, the whole contents of his sack, to the delight and admiration of the audience." Buffum may not be a "great speaker," Brown acknowledges, but he knows how to delight an audience with the new and the new-seeming, the good and the bad, strewn about in profusion. Moreover, Brown notes, just as Buffum's speeches are open to otherness and seriality, so is his home open to a series of others: "If the fugitive slave, fresh from the cotton-field, should make his appearance in the town of Lynn, in Massachusetts, and should need a night's lodging or refreshments, he need go no farther than the hospitable door of James N. Buffum."[1] In *Clotel*, Brown aspires to be, like Buffum, hospitable in the broadest sense—to conjure up for his readers a representational space that is open to a democratically inclusive range of identities and experiences. Readers of *Clotel* are not meant to enjoy how well the elements in that space cohere; they are meant to enjoy how spiritedly they don't.

"How does one acquire a taste for democracy, a desire for democratic values?" asks the psychoanalytic theorist Adam Phillips.[2] Maybe, Brown thinks, one does it like this: by means of a politically urgent work of fiction shot through with a bumptious, generous unseriousness about oneself and others. In this form, anti-racism, still so often stereotyped and resisted as a joyless reformism, is capable of providing windfalls of psychic pleasure. Although the world that is brought into view by that pleasure—or, more exactly, by the desire to repeat it—has not yet been brought into existence, we are closer to it now than Brown and his audience were in 1853, at least in part because Brown

---

1   William Wells Brown, *Three Years in Europe* (London: Gilpin, 1852), 267.

2   Adam Phillips, *Equals* (New York: Basic Books, 2002), 24.

and other "black culture-nauts" were willing to take the first, risky steps in its direction.[1] Rough, studded with caricatures, intimate with the racism it ironizes—see, for instance, "My Little Nig" [p. 000]—*Clotel* is still capable of creating a potent mix of discomfort and delight. It is, in this sense, a forerunner of some of the most recent venues for antiracist entertainment, such as *Chappelle's Show*, the landmark 2004–06 television series hosted by the African-American comedian Dave Chappelle (b. 1973). "It may be said of us, that we have used very strong language," Brown says in an 1854 speech. "Why, sir, has not the time come for strong language? ... People want something strong,—they are willing to hear it; then I say, why not give it them?"[2] "This is like the greatest country in the world by default," Chappelle says in a 2006 interview. "But we could actually be the greatest country that ever existed if we were just honest about who we are ... and where we want to go, and if we learn how to have that discourse."[3] Like Chappelle, Brown senses in mass-cultural entertainment the potential for a truly democratic sociability, one that is grounded in a penchant for fabrication and an ability to take pleasure in it (see Appendix D). Who are we? Something other than what we appear to be. Where do we want to go? Somewhere other than where we are supposed to be. This, for Brown, is not the source of the great American problem. It is the beginning of that problem's solution.

1 Kennell Jackson, "Introduction: Traveling While Black," in *Black Cultural Traffic: Crossroads in Global Performance and Popular Culture*, ed. Harry J. Elam Jr. and Kennell Jackson (Ann Arbor: U of Michigan P, 2005), 30.

2 Brown, "Speech at Town Hall, Manchester, England," *Clotel and Other Writings*, ed. Ezra Greenspan, 891.

3 Dave Chappelle, "Inside the Actor's Studio Interview," http://genius.com/Dave-chappelle-inside-the-actors-studio-interview-annotated/.

William Wells Brown:
A Brief Chronology

1814?	Born outside Mt. Sterling, Kentucky, the child of Elizabeth, a slave, and George Higgins, the cousin of Elizabeth's master, Dr. John Young.
1817	Moves with his mother and six older siblings to a settlement in the Missouri Territory.
1825	Moves to St. Louis.
1828–32	Hired out to a series of different masters, including the slave trader William Walker, with whom he travels on the Mississippi River, bringing slaves to Southern markets.
1832	Escapes with mother into Illinois. Captured, brought back to St. Louis, and jailed. Sold to a tailor named Samuel Willi. Mother sold to a slave trader.
1833	Sold to a steamboat owner and pilot named Enoch Price. In November, accompanies Price's family to New Orleans; on the return trip, the steamboat continues past St. Louis to Cincinnati.
1834	Escapes in Cincinnati on New Year's Day and travels northeast through Ohio. Temporarily sheltered by a Quaker couple; subsequently adds the name of the man, Wells Brown, to his own. Settles in Cleveland, begins working on Lake Erie steamships, and meets and marries Elizabeth (Betsey) Schooner.
1836	Daughter Clarissa born. Moves to Buffalo.
1839	Daughter Josephine born.
1842	Daughter Henrietta born. Writes a letter to the editor of a black newspaper in Albany, his first known published work.
1843	Begins working as an agent of the Western New York Anti-Slavery Society.
1844	Daughter Henrietta dies. Officials of the Western New York Anti-Slavery Society raise funds to support his family.
1845	Discovers that Betsey is having an affair. Moves family to Farmington, New York.

1847	Separates from Betsey and moves to Boston. Arranges for Clarissa and Josephine to be taken in by a black family in New Bedford. Begins working as a lecturer with the Massachusetts Anti-Slavery Society. Publishes *Narrative of William W. Brown* and *A Lecture Delivered before the Female Anti-Slavery Society of Salem*.
1848	Publishes *The Anti-Slavery Harp*, a collection of antislavery songs.
1849	Sails to Great Britain in July. Attends International Peace Congress in Paris in September. Settles in London.
1850	Passage of Fugitive Slave Law strands him in Great Britain. Arranges for printings of *Narrative of William W. Brown* and *The Anti-Slavery Harp*. Commissions the painting of a panorama, which he subsequently exhibits in England, Scotland, and Wales. Publishes *A Description of William Wells Brown's Original Panoramic Views of the Scenes in the Life of an American Slave*.
1851	Arranges for Clarissa and Josephine to attend boarding school in France. Continues to lecture extensively.
1852	Publishes *Three Years in Europe*, the first African-American travel narrative. Publishes "A True Story of Slave Life," the first African-American short story. Arranges for Clarissa and Josephine to attend the Home and Colonial School in London. Betsey dies.
1853	Publishes *Clotel*, the first African-American novel.
1854	Friends in England purchase his freedom papers. Returns to the United States, settles in Boston, and resumes lecturing.
1855	Publishes *The American Fugitive in Europe*, an expanded version of *Three Years in Europe*. Publishes *St. Domingo: Its Revolution and Its Patriots*, the text of a lecture he had recently delivered. Clarissa marries Fritz Alcide Humbert in London. Josephine returns to the United States and joins him on the lecture circuit. Memoir entitled *Biography of an American Bondman*, almost certainly written by him, appears under Josephine's name.
1856	Josephine's enmeshment in a sexual scandal leads him to cut her out of his life. Begins offering dra-

matic readings of a play, *Experience; or, How to Get a Backbone*, the text of which has not survived.

1857   Popularity of *Experience* leads him to begin offering dramatic readings of a second play, *The Escape; or, A Leap for Freedom*.

1858   Publishes *The Escape*, the earliest surviving African-American play.

1859   Publishes *Memoir of William Wells Brown, an American Bondman*, a rewriting of *Biography of an American Bondman*.

1860   Marries Annie Elizabeth Gray and moves with her to Cambridge. Begins serializing *Miralda; or, The Beautiful Quadroon* in the *Weekly Anglo-African*.

1861   Son William Wells Brown Jr. is born in February and dies of cholera in July.

1862   Daughter Clotelle born. Publishes *The Black Man: His Antecedents, His Genius, and His Achievements*.

1864   Publishes *Clotelle: A Tale of the Southern States*, a revised version of *Miralda*.

1865   Begins practicing medicine in Boston. After the Civil War ends, turns to lecturing on temperance, civil rights, and education.

1867   Publishes *The Negro in the American Rebellion: His Heroism and His Fidelity* and *Clotelle: or, The Colored Heroine*, a slightly expanded version of *Clotelle: A Tale of the Southern States*.

1870   Clotelle dies.

1871   Clarissa, widowed ten years earlier, marries George Wainwright Sylvestre in Yorkshire.

1874   Josephine dies. Clarissa dies. Publishes *The Rising Son; or, The Antecedents and Advancement of the Colored Race*.

1877   Visits Great Britain, where he lectures on racial divisions in the temperance movement.

1878   Moves from Cambridge to Boston.

1879   Travels through the upper South lecturing on temperance and education.

1880   Publishes *My Southern Home; or, The South and Its People*.

1884   Dies on 6 November of bladder cancer. Buried in Cambridge Cemetery.

A Note on the Text

There are no real textual problems presented by *Clotel*, insofar as the only edition to appear in Brown's lifetime was the one published in London by Partridge and Oakey in 1853. (Brown does make use of parts of *Clotel* in *Miralda* and *Clotelle*, but each of those later works is a distinctive novel in its own right, not a new edition of *Clotel*.) The present text is a reproduction of the 1853 text. Obvious typographical errors and omissions have been silently corrected.

CLOTEL;

OR,

THE PRESIDENT'S DAUGHTER:

A Narrative of Slave Life

IN

THE UNITED STATES.

"We hold these truths to be self-evident: that all men are created equal; that they are endowed by their Creator with certain
inalienable rights, and that among these are LIFE, LIBERTY,
and the PURSUIT OF HAPPINESS."
—*Declaration of American Independence.*

PREFACE.

More than two hundred years have elapsed since the first cargo of slaves was landed on the banks of the James River, in the colony of Virginia, from the West coast of Africa. From the introduction of slaves in 1620, down to the period of the separation of the Colonies from the British Crown, the number had increased to five hundred thousand; now there are nearly four million. In fifteen of the thirty-one States, Slavery is made lawful by the Constitution, which binds the several States into one confederacy.

On every foot of soil, over which *Stars* and *Stripes* wave, the negro is considered common property, on which any white man may lay his hand with perfect impunity. The entire white population of the United States, North and South, are bound by their oath to the constitution, and their adhesion to the Fugitive Slave Law, to hunt down the runaway slave and return him to his claimant, and to suppress any effort that may be made by the slaves to gain their freedom by physical force. Twenty-five millions of whites have banded themselves in solemn conclave to keep four millions of blacks in their chains. In all grades of society are to be found men who either hold, buy, or sell slaves, from the statesmen and doctors of divinity, who can own their hundreds, down to the person who can purchase but one.

Were it not for persons in high places owning slaves, and thereby giving the system a reputation, and especially professed Christians, Slavery would long since have been abolished. The influence of the great "honours the corruption, and chastisement doth therefore hide his head."[1] The great aim of the true friends of the slave should be to lay bare the institution, so that the gaze of the world may be upon it, and cause the wise, the prudent, and the pious to withdraw their support from it, and leave it to its own fate. It does the cause of emancipation but little good to cry out in tones of execration against the traders, the kidnappers, the hireling overseers, and brutal drivers, so long as nothing is said to fasten the guilt on those who move in a higher circle.

The fact that slavery was introduced into the American colonies, while they were under the control of the British Crown, is a sufficient reason why Englishmen should feel a lively interest in its abolition; and now that the genius of mechanical invention has brought the two countries so near together, and both having one language and one literature, the influence of British public

---

1 Shakespeare, *Julius Caesar*, 4.3.15–16.

opinion is very great on the people of the New World.

If the incidents set forth in the following pages should add anything new to the information already given to the Public through similar publications, and should thereby aid in bringing British influence to bear upon American slavery, the main object for which this work was written will have been accomplished.

W. WELLS BROWN

22, Cecil Street, Strand, London.

CONTENTS.

NARRATIVE OF THE LIFE AND ESCAPE OF WILLIAM WELLS BROWN.[1]

"Shall tongues be mute when deeds are wrought
Which well might shame extremest Hell?
Shall freemen lack th' indignant thought?
Shall Mercy's bosom cease to swell?
Shall Honour bleed?—shall Truth succumb?
Shall pen, and press, and soul be dumb?"—*Whittier.*[2]

William Wells Brown, the subject of this narrative, was born a slave in Lexington, Kentucky, not far from the residence of the late Hon. Henry Clay.[3] His mother was the slave of Doctor John Young. His father was a slaveholder, and, besides being a near relation of his master, was connected with the Wicklief family, one of the oldest, wealthiest, and most aristocratic of the Kentucky planters. Dr. Young was the owner of forty or fifty slaves, whose chief employment was in cultivating tobacco, hemp, corn, and flax. The Doctor removed from Lexington, when William was five or six years old, to the state of Missouri, and commenced farming in a beautiful and fertile valley, within a mile of the Missouri river.

Here the slaves were put to work under a harsh and cruel overseer named Cook. A finer situation for a farm could not have been selected in the state. With climate favourable to agriculture, and soil rich, the products came in abundance. At an early age William was separated from his mother, she being worked in the field, and he as a servant in his master's medical department. When about ten years of age, the young slave's feelings were

---

1 Because the "Narrative of the Life and Escape of William Wells Brown" is stylistically continuous with Brown's other writings and because no one other than Brown is credited with its authorship—the prefatory biographies in *Three Years in Europe* (1852) and *The Rising Son* (1874) were openly credited to other writers—it is generally assumed that Brown wrote it. In the table of contents, it is identified as the "Memoir of the Author."

2 John Greenleaf Whittier, "Stanzas for the Times," lines 25–30. See the Select Bibliography for a full listing of the source-texts from which Brown plagiarizes or quotes. Whittier (1807–92) was a Quaker poet and abolitionist.

3 Henry Clay (1777–1852) was a Whig congressman from Kentucky who played an influential role in the passage of the Compromise of 1850, which mandated the enforcement of the Fugitive Slave Law.

much hurt at hearing the cries of his mother, while being flogged by the negro driver for being a few minutes behind the other hands in reaching the field. He heard her cry, "Oh, pray! oh, pray! oh, pray!" These are the words which slaves generally utter when imploring mercy at the hands of their oppressors.[1] The son heard it, though he was some way off. He heard the crack of the whip and the groans of his poor mother. The cold chill ran over him, and he wept aloud; but he was a slave like his mother, and could render her no assistance. He was taught by the most bitter experience, that nothing could be more heart-rending than to see a dear and beloved mother or sister tortured by unfeeling men, and to hear her cries, and not be able to render the least aid. When William was twelve years of age, his master left his farm and took up his residence near St. Louis. The Doctor having more hands than he wanted for his own use, William was let out to a Mr. Freeland, an innkeeper. Here the young slave found himself in the hands of a most cruel and heartless master. Freeland was one of the real chivalry of the South; besides being himself a slaveholder, he was a horse-racer, cock-fighter, gambler, and, to crown the whole, an inveterate drunkard. What else but bad treatment could be expected from such a character? After enduring the tyrannical and inhuman usage of this man for five or six months, William resolved to stand it no longer, and therefore ran away, like other slaves who leave their masters, owing to severe treatment; and not knowing where to flee, the young fugitive went into the forest, a few miles from St. Louis. He had been in the woods but a short time, when he heard the barking and howling of dogs, and was soon satisfied that he was pursued by the negro dogs; and, aware of their ferocious nature, the fugitive climbed a tree, to save himself from being torn to pieces. The hounds were soon at the trunk of the tree, and remained there, howling and barking, until those in whose charge they were came up. The slave was ordered down, tied, and taken home. Immediately on his arrival there, he was, as he expected, tied up in the smoke-house, and whipped till Freeland was satisfied, and then smoked with tobacco stems. This the slaveholder

---

1   The ex-slave William Grimes (1784–1865) similarly observes
    that he was used to hearing "the sound of Oh pray! Oh pray!
    which came from those poor slaves, then in preparation for being
    whipped, or experiencing then at the same time, the smart of
    the lash which was so often used without mercy" (*Life of William
    Grimes, the Runaway Slave* [New York, 1825], 36).

called "*Virginia play.*" After being well whipped and smoked, he was again set to work. William remained with this monster a few months longer, and was then let out to Elijah P. Lovejoy, who years after became the editor of an abolition newspaper, and was murdered at Alton, Illinois, by a mob of slaveholders from the adjoining state of Missouri.[1] The system of letting out slaves is one among the worst of the evils of slavery. The man who hires a slave, looks upon him in the same light as does the man who hires a horse for a limited period; he feels no interest in him, only to get the worth of his money. Not so with the man who owns the slave; he regards him as so much property, of which care should be taken. After being let out to a steamer as an under-steward, William was hired by James Walker, a slave-trader.[2] Here the subject of our memoir was made superintendent of the gangs of slaves that were taken to the New Orleans market. In this capacity, William had opportunities, far greater than most slaves, of acquiring knowledge of the different phases of the "*peculiar institution.*" Walker was a negro speculator, who was amassing a fortune by trading in the bones, blood, and nerves, of God's children. The thoughts of such a traffic causes us to exclaim with the poet,

"—Is there not some chosen curse,
Some hidden thunder in the stores of heaven,
Red with uncommon wrath, to blast the man
Who gains his fortune from the blood of souls?"[3]

Between fifty and sixty slaves were chained together, put on board a steam-boat bound for New Orleans, and started on the voyage. New and strange scenes began to inspire the young slave with the hope of escaping to a land of freedom. There was in the boat a large room on the lower deck in which the slaves were kept, men and women promiscuously, all chained two and two together, not even leaving the poor slaves the privilege of choos-

---

1   The murder of Elijah P. Lovejoy (1802–37), a native of Maine, galvanized anti-slavery sentiment in the North.
2   The reference is apparently to William Walker, a notorious Missourian slave-trader.
3   A much-circulated rewriting of lines from Joseph Addison's *Cato* (1712). Among the places where it appears is the frontispiece of George Bourne's *Picture of Slavery in the United States of America* (Middletown, CT: Hunt, 1834).

ing their partners. A strict watch was kept over them, so that they had no chance of escape. Cases had occurred in which slaves had got off their chains and made their escape at the landing-places, while the boat stopped to take in wood. But with all their care they lost one woman who had been taken from her husband and children, and having no desire to live without them, in the agony of her soul jumped overboard and drowned herself. Her sorrows were greater than she could bear; slavery and its cruel inflictions had broken her heart. She, like William, sighed for freedom, but not the freedom which even British soil confers and inspires, but freedom from torturing pangs, and overwhelming grief.

At the end of the week they arrived at New Orleans, the place of their destination. Here the slaves were placed in a negro pen, where those who wished to purchase could call and examine them. The negro pen is a small yard surrounded by buildings, from fifteen to twenty feet wide, with the exception of a large gate with iron bars. The slaves are kept in the buildings during the night, and turned into the pen during the day. After the best of the gang were sold off, the balance was taken to the Exchange coffee-house auction-rooms, and sold at public auction. After the sale of the last slave, William and Mr. Walker left New Orleans for St. Louis.

After they had been at St. Louis a few weeks another cargo of human flesh was made up. There were amongst the lot several old men and women, some of whom had grey locks. On their way down to New Orleans William had to prepare the old slaves for market. He was ordered to shave off the old men's whiskers, and to pluck out the grey hairs where they were not too numerous; where they were, he coloured them with a preparation of blacking with a blacking brush.[1] After having gone through the blacking process, they looked ten or fifteen years younger. William, though not well skilled in the use of scissors and razor, performed the office of the barber tolerably. After the sale of this gang of negroes they returned to St. Louis, and a second cargo was made up. In this lot was a woman who had a child at the breast, yet was compelled to travel through the interior of the country on foot with the other slaves. In a published memoir of his life, William says, "The child cried during the most of the day, which displeased Mr. Walker, and he told the mother that if her child did not stop crying, he would stop its mouth. After

---

1 Before being polished with blacking brushes, shoes and boots were darkened with a homemade substance called blacking.

a long and weary journey under a burning sun, we put up for the night at a country inn. The following morning, just as they were about to start, the child again commenced crying. Walker stepped up to her and told her to give the child to him. The mother tremblingly obeyed. He took the child by one arm, as any one would a cat by the leg, and walked into the house where they had been staying, and said to the lady, 'Madam, I will make you a present of this little nigger; it keeps making such a noise that I can't bear it.' 'Thank you, sir,' said the lady. The mother, as soon as she saw that her child was to be left, ran up to Mr. Walker, and falling on her knees, begged of him in an agony of despair, to let her have her child. She clung round his legs so closely, that for some time he could not kick her off; and she cried, 'O my child, my child. Master, do let me have my dear, dear child. Oh! do, do. I will stop its crying, and love you for ever if you will only let me have my child again.' But her prayers were not heeded, they passed on, and the mother was separated from her child for ever.

"After the woman's child had been given away, Mr. Walker rudely commanded her to retire into the ranks with the other slaves. Women who had children were not chained, but those who had none were. As soon as her child was taken she was chained to the gang."[1]

Some time after this, Walker bought a woman who had a blind child; it being considered worthless, it was given to the trader by the former owner of the woman on the score of humanity, he saying that he wished to keep mother and child together. At first Walker declined taking the child, saying that it would be too much trouble, but the mother wishing to have her boy with her, begged him to take it, promising to carry it the whole distance in her arms. Consequently he took the child, and the gang started on their route to the nearest steamboat landing, which was above one hundred miles. As might have been expected, the woman was unable to carry the boy and keep up with the rest of the gang. They put up at night at a small town, and the next morning, when about to start, Walker took the little boy from its mother and sold it to the innkeeper for the small sum of *one dollar*. The poor woman was so frantic at the idea of being separated from her only child, that it seemed impossible to get her to leave it. Not until the chains were put upon her limbs, and

---

1 The "published memoir" that Brown quotes from here and elsewhere in the preface is *Narrative of the Life of William W. Brown* (Boston: Anti-Slavery Society, 1847).

she fastened to the other slaves, could they get her to leave the spot. By main force this slave mother was compelled to go on and leave her child behind. Some days after, a lady from one of the free states was travelling the same road and put up at the same inn: she saw the child the morning after her arrival, and heard its history from one of the slaves, which was confirmed by the innkeeper's wife. A few days after, the following poem appeared in one of the newspapers, from the pen of the lady who had seen the blind child:—

"Come back to me, mother! why linger away
From thy poor little blind boy, the long weary day!
I mark every footstep, I list to each tone,
And wonder my mother should leave me alone!
There are voices of sorrow and voices of glee,
But there's no one to joy or to sorrow with me:
For each hath of pleasure and trouble his share,
And none for the poor little blind boy will care.

"My mother, come back to me! close to thy breast
Once more let thy poor little blind one be pressed;
Once more let me feel thy warm breath on my cheek,
And hear thee in accents of tenderness speak!
O mother! I've no one to love me—no heart
Can bear like thy own in my sorrows a part;
No hand is so gentle, no voice is so kind!
Oh! none like a mother can cherish the blind!

"Poor blind one! no mother thy wailing can hear,
No mother can hasten to banish thy fear;
For the slave-owner drives her, o'er mountain and wild,
And for one paltry dollar hath sold thee, poor child!
Ah! who can in language of mortals reveal
The anguish that none but a mother can feel,
When man in his vile lust of mammon[1] hath trod
On her child, who is stricken and smitten of God!

"Blind, helpless, forsaken, with strangers alone,
She hears in her anguish his piteous moan,
As he eagerly listens—but listens in vain,

---

1 Mammon is the name given to the devil of covetousness, i.e., wealth.

To catch the loved tones of his mother again!
The curse of the broken in spirit shall fall
On the wretch who hath mingled this wormwood and gall,
And his gain like a mildew shall blight and destroy,
Who hath torn from his mother the little blind boy."[1]

The thought that man can so debase himself as to treat a fel-low-creature as here represented, is enough to cause one to blush at the idea that such men are members of a civilised and Christian nation.

Nothing was more grievous to the sensitive feelings of William, than seeing the separation of families by the slave-trader: hus-bands taken from their wives, and mothers from their children, without the least appearance of feeling on the part of those who separated them. While at New Orleans, on one occasion, William saw a slave murdered. The circumstances were as fol-lows:—In the evening, between seven and eight o'clock, a slave came running down the levee, followed by several men and boys. The whites were crying out, "Stop that nigger! stop that nigger!" while the poor panting slave, in almost breathless accents, was repeating, "I did not steal the meat—I did not steal the meat." The poor man at last took refuge in the river. The whites who were in pursuit of him, ran on board of one of the boats to see if they could discover him. They finally espied him under the bow of the steamboat "Trenton." They got a pike-pole, and tried to drive him from his hiding-place. When they struck at him he would dive under the water. The water was so cold, that it soon became evident that he must come out or be drowned.

While they were trying to drive him from under the boat or drown him, he in broken and imploring accents said, "I did not steal the meat; I did not steal the meat. My master lives up the riv-er. I want to see my master. I did not steal the meat. Do let me go home to master." After punching and striking him over the head for some time, he at last sunk in the water, to rise no more alive.

On the end of the pike-pole with which they had been striking him was a hook, which caught in his clothing, and they hauled him up on the bow of the boat. Some said he was dead; others said he was "playing 'possum;" while others kicked him to make him get up; but it was of no use—he was dead.

As soon as they became satisfied of this they commenced leaving one after another. One of the hands on the boat informed

---

1 Margaret Bailey, "The Blind Slave Boy," lines 1–32.

the captain that they had killed the man, and that the dead body was lying on the deck. The captain, whose name was Hart, came on deck, and said to those who were remaining, "You have killed this nigger; now take him off my boat."[1] The dead body was dragged on shore and left there. William went on board of the boat where the gang of slaves were, and during the whole night his mind was occupied with what he had seen. Early in the morning he went on shore to see if the dead body remained there. He found it in the same position that it was left the night before. He watched to see what they would do with it. It was left there until between eight and nine o'clock, when a cart, which took up the trash from the streets, came along, and the body was thrown in, and in a few minutes more was covered over with dirt, which they were removing from the streets.

At the expiration of the period of his hiring with Walker, William returned to his master, rejoiced to have escaped an employment as much against his own feelings as it was repugnant to human nature. But this joy was of short duration. The Doctor wanted money, and resolved to sell William's sister and two brothers. The mother had been previously sold to a gentleman residing in the city of St. Louis. William's master now informed him that he intended to sell him, and, as he was his own nephew, he gave him the privilege of finding some one to purchase him who would treat him better than if he was sold on the auction block. William tried to make some arrangement by which he could purchase his own freedom, but the old Doctor would hear nothing of the kind. If there is one thing more revolting in the trade of human flesh than another, it is the selling of one's own blood relations.

He accordingly set out for the city in search of a new master. When he arrived there, he proceeded to the gaol with the hope of seeing his sister, but was again disappointed. On the following morning he made another attempt, and was allowed to see her once, for the last time. When he entered the room where she was seated in one corner, alone and disconsolate, there were four other women in the room, belonging to the same man, who were bought, the gaoler said, for the master's own use.

William's sister was seated with her face towards the door

---

1 Up to this point, Brown's account of this incident loosely follows the Rev. James Thome's account of a slave killed in New Orleans in December 1833 (Theodore Weld, *American Slavery as It Is*, 158–59).

when he entered, but her gaze was transfixed on nothingness, and she did not look up when he walked up to her; but as soon as she observed him she sprang up, threw her arms around his neck, leaned her head upon his breast, and without uttering a word, in silent, indescribable sorrow, burst into tears. She remained so for some minutes, but when she recovered herself sufficiently to speak, she urged him to take his mother immediately, and try to get to the land of freedom. She said there was no hope for herself, she must live and die a slave. After giving her some advice, and taking a ring from his finger, he bade her farewell for ever.

Reader, did ever a fair sister of thine go down to the grave prematurely, if so, perchance, thou hast drank deeply from the cup of sorrow? But how infinitely better is it for a sister to "go into the silent land"[1] with her honour untarnished, but with bright hopes, than for her to be sold to sensual slave-holders.

William had been in the city now two days, and as he was to be absent for only a week, it was well that he should make the best use of his time if he intended to escape. In conversing with his mother, he found her unwilling to make the attempt to reach the land of liberty, but she advised him by all means to get there himself if he possibly could. She said, as all her children were in slavery, she did not wish to leave them; but he loved his mother so intensely, that he could not think of leaving without her. He consequently used all his simple eloquence to induce her to fly with him, and at last he prevailed. They consequently fixed upon the next night as the time for their departure. The time at length arrived, and they left the city just as the clock struck nine. Having found a boat, they crossed the river in it. Whose boat it was he did not know; neither did he care: when it had served his purpose, he turned it adrift, and when he saw it last, it was going at a good speed down the river. After walking in the main road as fast as they could all night, when the morning came they made for the woods, and remained there during the day, but when night came again, they proceeded on their journey with nothing but the North Star to guide them. They continued to travel by night, and to bury themselves in the silent solitudes of the forest by day. Hunger and fatigue could not stop them, for the prospect of freedom at the end of the journey nerved them up. The very thought of leaving slavery, with its democratic whips, republican chains, and bloodhounds, caused the hearts of the weary fugi-

---

1 A common metaphor for the realm of the dead, drawn from Psalms.

tives to leap with joy. After travelling ten nights and hiding in the woods during the day for fear of being arrested and taken back, they thought they might with safety go the rest of their way by daylight. In nearly all the free states there are men who make a business of catching runaway slaves and returning them to their owners for the reward that may be offered; some of these were on the alert for William and his mother, for they had already seen the runaways advertised in the St. Louis newspapers.

All at once they heard the click of a horse's hoof, and looking back saw three men on horseback galloping towards them. They soon came up, and demanded them to stop. The three men dismounted, arrested them on a warrant, and showed them a handbill, offering two hundred dollars for their apprehension and delivery to Dr. Young and Isaac Mansfield in St. Louis.

While they were reading the handbill, William's mother looked him in the face, and burst into tears. "A cold chill ran over me," says he, "and such a sensation I never experienced before, and I trust I never shall again." They took out a rope and tied him, and they were taken back to the house of the individual who appeared to be the leader. They then had something given them to eat, and were separated. Each of them was watched over by two men during the night. The religious characteristic of the American slaveholder soon manifested itself, as before the family retired to rest they were all called together to attend prayers; and the very man who, but a few hours before, had arrested poor panting, fugitive slaves, now read a chapter from the Bible and offered a prayer to God; as if that benignant and omnipotent One consecrated the infernal act he had just committed.

The next morning they were chained and handcuffed, and started back to St. Louis. A journey of three days brought the fugitives again to the place they had left twelve days previously with the hope that they would never return. They were put in prison to await the orders of their owners. When a slave attempts to escape and fails, he feels sure of either being severely punished, or sold to the negro traders and taken to the far south, there to be worked up on a cotton, sugar, or rice plantation. This William and his mother dreaded. While they were in suspense as to what would be their fate, news came to them that the mother had been sold to a slave speculator. William was soon sold to a merchant residing in the city, and removed to his new owner's dwelling. In a few days the gang of slaves, of which William's mother was one, were taken on board a steamer to be carried to the New Orleans market. The young slave obtained permission from his new owner to go and take a last farewell of his mother. He went to the boat, and found her there, chained to another woman, and the whole number of slaves, amounting to some fifty or sixty, chained in the same manner. As the son approached his mother she moved not, neither did she weep; her emotions were too deep for tears. William approached her, threw his arms around her neck, kissed her, fell upon his knees begging her forgiveness, for he thought he was to blame for her sad condition, and if he had not persuaded her to accompany him she might not have been in chains then.

She remained for some time apparently unimpressionable, tearless, sighless, but in the innermost depths of her heart moved mighty passions. William says, "She finally raised her head, looked me in the face, and such a look none but an angel can give, and said, 'My dear son, you are not to blame for my being here. You have done nothing more nor less than your duty. Do not, I pray you, weep for me; I cannot last long upon a cotton plantation. I feel that my heavenly Master will soon call me home, and then I shall be out of the hands of the slaveholders.' I could hear no more—my heart struggled to free itself from the human form. In a moment she saw Mr. Mansfield, her master, coming toward that part of the boat, and she whispered in my ear, 'My child, we must soon part to meet no more on this side of the grave. You have ever said that you would not die a slave; that you would be a freeman. Now try to get your liberty! You will soon have no one to look after but yourself!' and just as she whispered the last sentence into my ear, Mansfield came up to me, and with an oath said, 'Leave here this instant; you have been the means of my losing one hundred dollars to get this wench back'—at the same time kicking me with a heavy pair of boots. As I left her she gave one shriek, saying, 'God be with you!' It was the last time that I saw her, and the last word I heard her utter.

"I walked on shore. The bell was tolling. The boat was about to start. I stood with a heavy heart, waiting to see her leave the wharf. As I thought of my mother, I could but feel that I had lost

> 'The glory of my life,
> My blessing and my pride!
> I half forgot the name of slave,
> When she was by my side.'[1]

---

1 Margaret Chandler, "The Bereaved Father," lines 25–28. Chandler (1807–34) was an abolitionist poet.

"The love of liberty that had been burning in my bosom had well-nigh gone out. I felt as though I was ready to die. The boat moved gently from the wharf, and while she glided down the river, I realised that my mother was indeed

'Gone—gone—sold and gone,
To the rice swamp, dark and lone!'[1]

"After the boat was out of sight I returned home; but my thoughts were so absorbed in what I had witnessed, that I knew not what I was about. Night came, but it brought no sleep to my eyes." When once the love of freedom is born in the slave's mind, it always increases and brightens, and William having heard so much about Canada, where a number of his acquaintances had found a refuge and a home, he heartily desired to join them. Building castles in the air in the daytime; incessantly thinking of freedom, he would dream of the land of liberty, but on waking in the morning would weep to find it but a dream.

"He would dream of Victoria's domain,[2]
And in a moment he seemed to be there;
But the fear of being taken again,
Soon hurried him back to despair."[3]

Having been for some time employed as a servant in an hotel, and being of a very active turn, William's new owner resolved to let him out on board a steamboat. Consequently the young slave was hired out to the steamer St. Louis, and soon after sold to Captain Enoch Price, the owner of that boat. Here he was destined to remain but a short period, as Mrs. Price wanted a carriage-driver, and had set her heart upon William for that purpose.

Scarcely three months had elapsed from the time that William became the property of Captain Price, ere that gentleman's family took a pleasure trip to New Orleans, and William accompanied them. From New Orleans the family proceeded to Louisville. The hope of escape again dawned upon the slave's mind, and the trials of the past were lost in hopes for the future. The love of liberty, which had been burning in his bosom for years, and which

---

1 John Greenleaf Whittier, "The Farewell of a Virginia Slave Mother to Her Daughters," lines 1–2.
2 I.e., Canada.
3 "I Am Monarch of Nought I Survey," lines 29–32.

at times had been well nigh extinguished, was now resuscitated. Hopes nurtured in childhood, and strengthened as manhood dawned, now spread their sails to the gales of his imagination. At night, when all around was peaceful, and in the mystic presence of the everlasting starlight, he would walk the steamer's decks, meditating on his happy prospects, and summoning up gloomy reminiscences of the dear hearts he was leaving behind him. When not thinking of the future his mind would dwell on the past. The love of a dear mother, a dear and affectionate sister, and three brothers yet living, caused him to shed many tears. If he could only be assured of their being dead, he would have been comparatively happy; but he saw in imagination his mother in the cotton-field, followed by a monster task-master, and no one to speak a consoling word to her. He beheld his sister in the hands of the slave-driver, compelled to submit to his cruelty, or, what was unutterably worse, his lust; but still he was far away from them, and could not do anything for them if he remained in slavery; consequently he resolved, and consecrated the resolve with a prayer, that he would start on the first opportunity.

That opportunity soon presented itself. When the boat got to the wharf where it had to stay for some time, at the first convenient moment Brown made towards the woods, where he remained until night-time. He dared not walk during the day, even in the state of Ohio; he had seen so much of the perfidy of white men, and resolved, if possible, not to get into their hands. After darkness covered the world, he emerged from his hiding-place; but he did not know east from west, or north from south; clouds hid the North Star from his view. In this desolate condition he remained for some hours, when the clouds rolled away, and his friend, with its shining face—the North Star—welcomed his sight. True as the needle to the pole he obeyed its attractive beauty, and walked on till daylight dawned.

It was winter-time; the day on which he started was the 1st of January, and, as it might be expected, it was intensely cold; he had no overcoat, no food, no friend, save the North Star, and the God which made it. How ardently must the love of freedom burn in the poor slave's bosom, when he will pass through so many difficulties, and even look death in the face, in winning his birth-right, freedom. But what crushed the poor slave's heart in his flight most was, not the want of food or clothing, but the thought that every white man was his deadly enemy. Even in the free states the prejudice against colour is so strong, that there appears to exist a deadly antagonism between the white and coloured races.

William in his flight carried a tinder-box[1] with him, and when he got very cold he would gather together dry leaves and stubble and make a fire, or certainly he would have perished. He was determined to enter into no house, fearing that he might meet a betrayer.

It must have been a picture which would have inspired an artist, to see the fugitive roasting the ears of corn that he found or took from barns during the night, at solitary fires in the deep solitudes of woods.

The suffering of the fugitive was greatly increased by the cold, from the fact of his having just come from the warm climate of New Orleans. Slaves seldom have more than one name, and William was not an exception to this, and the fugitive began to think of an additional name. A heavy rain of three days, in which it froze as fast as it fell, and by which the poor fugitive was completely drenched, and still more chilled, added to the depression of his spirits already created by his weary journey. Nothing but the fire of hope burning within his breast could have sustained him under such overwhelming trials,

> "Behind he left the whip and chains,
> Before him were sweet Freedom's plains."[2]

Through cold and hunger, William was now ill, and he could go no further. The poor fugitive resolved to seek protection, and accordingly hid himself in the woods near the road, until some one should pass. Soon a traveller came along, but the slave dared not speak. A few moments more and a second passed, the fugitive attempted to speak, but fear deprived him of voice. A third made his appearance. He wore a broad-brimmed hat and a long coat, and was evidently walking only for exercise.

William scanned him well, and though not much skilled in physiognomy, he concluded he was the man. William approached him, and asked him if he knew any one who would help him, as he was sick? The gentleman asked whether he was not a slave. The poor slave hesitated; but, on being told that he had nothing to fear, he answered, "Yes." The gentleman told him he was in a pro-slaving neighbourhood, but, if he would wait a little, he would go and get a covered waggon, and convey him to his house. After he had gone, the fugitive meditated whether he should stay or not,

---

1 A box containing items for kindling fires.
2 "The Flying Slave," lines 13–14.

being apprehensive that the broad-brimmed gentleman had gone for some one to assist him: he however concluded to remain.

After waiting about an hour—an hour big with fate to him— he saw the covered waggon making its appearance, and no one on it but the person he before accosted. Trembling with hope and fear, he entered the waggon, and was carried to the person's house. When he got there, he still halted between two opinions, whether he should enter or take to his heels; but he soon decided after seeing the glowing face of the wife. He saw something in her that bid him welcome, something that told him he would not be betrayed.

He soon found that he was under the shed of a Quaker, and a Quaker of the George Fox stamp.[1] He had heard of Quakers and their kindness; but was not prepared to meet with such hospitality as now greeted him. He saw nothing but kind looks, and heard nothing but tender words. He began to feel the pulsations of a new existence. White men always scorned him, but now a white benevolent woman felt glad to wait on him; it was a revolution in his experience. The table was loaded with good things, but he could not eat. If he were allowed the privilege of sitting in the kitchen, he thought he could do justice to the viands. The surprise being over his appetite soon returned.

"I have frequently been asked," says William, "how I felt upon finding myself regarded as a man by a white family; especially having just run away from one. I cannot say that I have ever answered the question yet. The fact that I was, in all probability, a freeman, sounded in my ears like a charm. I am satisfied that none but a slave could place such an appreciation upon liberty as I did at that time. I wanted to see my mother and sister, that I might tell them that "I was free!" I wanted to see my fellow-slaves in St. Louis, and let them know that the chains were no longer upon my limbs. I wanted to see Captain Price, and let him learn from my own lips that I was no more a chattel, but a MAN. I was anxious, too, thus to inform Mrs. Price that she must get another coachman, and I wanted to see Eliza more than I did Mr. Price or Mrs. Price. The fact that I was a freeman—could walk, talk, eat, and sleep as a man, and no one to stand over me with the blood-clotted cow-hide—all this made me feel that I was not myself."

---

1 George Fox (1624–91) was a founder of the Religious Society of Friends, a Christian sect whose adherents are usually referred to as Quakers.

The kind Quaker, who so hospitably entertained William, was called Wells Brown. He remained with him about a fortnight, during which time he was well fed and clothed. Before leaving, the Quaker asked him what was his name besides William? The fugitive told him he had no other. "Well," said he, "thee must have another name. Since thee has got out of slavery, thee has become a man, and men always have two names."

William told him that as he was the first man to extend the hand of friendship to him, he would give him the privilege of naming him.

"If I name thee," said he, "I shall call thee Wells Brown, like myself."

"But," said he, "I am not willing to lose my name of William. It was taken from me once against my will, and I am not willing to part with it on any terms."[1]

"Then," said the benevolent man, "I will call thee William Wells Brown."

"So be it," said William Wells Brown, and he has been known by this name ever since.

After giving the newly-christened freeman "a name," the Quaker gave him something to aid him to get "a local habitation."[2] So, after giving him some money, Brown again started for Canada. In four days he reached a public-house, and went in to warm himself. He soon found that he was not out of the reach of his enemies. While warming himself, he heard some men in an adjoining bar-room talking about some runaway slaves. He thought it was time to be off, and, suiting the action to the thought, he was soon in the woods out of sight. When night came, he returned to the road and walked on; and so, for two days and two nights, till he was faint and ready to perish of hunger.

In this condition he arrived in the town of Cleveland, Ohio, on the banks of Lake Erie, where he determined to remain until the spring of the year, and then to try and reach Canada. Here he was compelled to work merely for his food. "Having lived in that way," said he in a speech at a public meeting in Exeter Hall,

---

1 When Brown was about six years old, his master, John Young, adopted a nephew named William. As a result, Brown was forced to change his name to Sandford.
2 The allusion is to Shakespeare's *A Midsummer Night's Dream*, 5.1.18.

"for some weeks, I obtained a job, for which I received a shilling.[1] This was not only the only shilling I had, but it was the first I had received after obtaining my freedom, and that shilling made me feel, indeed, as if I had a considerable stock in hand. What to do with my shilling I did not know. I would not put it into the bankers' hands, because, if they would have received it, I would not trust them. I would not lend it out, because I was afraid I should not get it back again. I carried the shilling in my pocket for some time, and finally resolved to lay it out; and after considerable thinking upon the subject, I laid out 6d.[2] for a spelling-book, and the other 6d. for sugar candy or barley sugar.[3] Well, now, you will all say that the one 6d. for the spelling-book was well laid out; and I am of opinion that the other was well laid out too; for the family in which I worked for my bread had two little boys, who attended the school every day, and I wanted to convert them into teachers; so I thought that nothing would act like a charm so much as a little barley sugar. The first day I got my book and stock in trade, I put the book into my bosom, and went to saw wood in the wood-house on a very cold day. One of the boys, a little after four o'clock, passed through the wood-house with a bag of books. I called to him, and I said to him, 'Johnny, do you see this?' taking a stick of barley sugar from my pocket and showing it to him. Says he, 'Yes; give me a taste of it.' Said I, 'I have got a spellingbook too,' and I showed that to him. 'Now,' said I, 'if you come to me in my room, and teach me my A, B, C, I will give you a whole stick.' 'Very well,' said he, 'I will; but let me taste it.' 'No; I can't.' 'Let me have it now.' Well, I thought I had better give him a little taste, until the right time came; and I marked the barley sugar about a quarter of an inch down, and told him to bite that far and no farther. He made a grab, and bit half the stick, and ran off laughing. I put the other piece in my pocket, and after a little while the other boy, little David, came through the wood-house with his books. I said nothing about the barley sugar, or my wish to get education. I knew the other lad would communicate the news to him. In a little while he returned, and said, 'Bill, John says you have got some barley sugar.' 'Well,' I said, 'what of that?' 'He said you gave him some; give me a little taste.' 'Well, if you come to-night and help me to learn

---

1 A shilling was equal to 12 pence, or one-twentieth of a British pound.
2 An abbreviation for sixpence.
3 A hard candy shaped into small sticks.

my letters, I will give you a whole stick.' 'Yes; but let me taste it.' 'Ah! but you want to bite it.' 'No, I don't, but just let me taste it.' Well, I thought I had better show it to him. 'Now,' said he, 'let me touch my tongue against it.' I thought then that I had better give him a taste, but I would not trust him so far as I trusted John; so I called him to me, and got his head under my arm, and took him by the chin, and told him to hold out his tongue; and as he did so, I drew the barley sugar over very lightly. He said, 'That's very nice; just draw it over again.' 'I could stand here and let you draw it across my tongue all day.' The night came on; the two boys came out of their room up into the attic where I was lodging, and there they commenced teaching me the letters of the alphabet. We all laid down upon the floor, covered with the same blanket; and first one would teach me a letter, and then the other, and I would pass the barley sugar from one side to the other. I kept those two boys on my sixpenny worth of barley sugar for about three weeks. Of course I did not let them know how much I had. I first dealt it out to them a quarter of a stick at a time. I worked along in that way, and before I left that place where I was working for my bread, I got so that I could spell. I had a book that had the word *baker* in it, and the boys used to think that when they got so far as that, they were getting on pretty well. I had often passed by the school-house, and stood and listened at the window to hear them spell, and I knew that when they could spell *baker* they thought something of themselves; and I was glad when I got that far. Before I left that place I could read. Finally, from that I went on until I could write. How do you suppose I first commenced writing? for you will understand that up to the present time I never spent a day in school in my life, for I had no money to pay for schooling, so that I had to get my learning first from one and then from another. I carried a piece of chalk in my pocket, and whenever I met a boy I would stop him and take out my chalk and get at a board fence and then commence. First I made some flourishes with no meaning, and called a boy up, and said, 'Do you see that? Can you beat that writing?' Said he, 'That's not writing.' Well, I wanted to get so as to write my own name. I had got out of slavery with only one name. While escaping, I received the hospitality of a very good man, who had spared part of his name to me, and finally my name got pretty long, and I wanted to be able to write it. 'Now, what do you call that?' said the boy, looking at my flourishes. I said, 'Is not that *William Wells Brown*?' 'Give me the chalk,' says he, and he wrote out in large letters '*William Wells Brown*,' and I marked up the fence for nearly a quarter of a mile, trying to copy, till I got so that I could write my name. Then I went on with my chalking, and, in fact, all board fences within half a mile of where I lived were marked over with some kind of figures I had made, in trying to learn how to write. I next obtained an arithmetic, and then a grammar, and I stand here to-night, without having had a day's schooling in my life." Such were some of the efforts made by a fugitive slave to obtain for himself an education. Soon after his escape, Brown was married to a free coloured woman, by whom he has had three daughters, one of whom died in infancy. Having tasted the sweets of freedom himself, his great desire was to extend its blessing to his race, and in the language of the poet he would ask himself,

> "Is true freedom but to break
> Fetters for our own dear sake
> And with leathern hearts forget
> That we owe mankind a debt?
>
> "No! true freedom is to share
> All the chains our brothers wear,
> And with heart and hand to be
> Earnest to make others free."[1]

While acting as a servant to one of the steamers on Lake Erie, Brown often took fugitives from Cleveland and other ports to Buffalo, or Detroit, from either of which places they could cross to Canada in an hour. During the season of 1842, this fugitive slave conveyed no less than *sixty-nine* runaway slaves across Lake Erie, and placed them safe on the soil of Canada. The following interesting account of Brown's first going into business for himself, which we transcribe from his "Three Years in Europe," will show the energy of the man. He says, "In the autumn of 1835, having been cheated out of the previous summer's earnings by the captain of the steamer in which I had been employed running away with the money, I was, like the rest of the men, left without any means of support during the winter, and therefore had to seek employment in the neighbouring towns. I went to the town of Monroe in the state of Michigan, and while going through the principal streets looking for work, I passed the door of the

---

1 James Russell Lowell, "Are Ye Truly Free?" lines 17–24. Lowell (1819–91) was a poet, critic, and diplomat.

only barber in the town, whose shop appeared to be filled with persons waiting to be shaved. As there was but one man at work, and as I had, while employed in the steamer, occasionally shaved a gentleman who could not perform that office himself, it occurred to me that I might get employment here as a journeyman barber. I therefore made immediate application for work, but the barber told me he did not need a hand. But I was not to be put off so easily, and after making several offers to work cheap, I frankly told him, that if he would not employ me, I would get a room near him, and set up an opposition establishment. This threat, however, made no impression on the barber; and as I was leaving, one of the men, who were waiting to be shaved, said, 'If you want a room in which to commence business, I have one on the opposite side of the street.' This man followed me out; we went over, and I looked at the room. He strongly urged me to set up, at the same time promising to give me his influence. I took the room, purchased an old table, two chairs, got a pole with a red stripe painted around it, and the next day opened, with a sign over the door, 'Fashionable Hair-dresser from New York, Emperor of the West.' I need not add that my enterprise was very annoying to the 'shop over the way,' especially my sign, which happened to be the most extensive part of the concern. Of course I had to tell all who came in, that my neighbour on the opposite side did not keep clean towels, that his razors were dull, and, above all, he never had been to New York to see the fashions. Neither had I. In a few weeks I had the entire business of the town, to the great discomfiture of the other barber. At this time, money matters in the Western States were in a sad condition. Any person who could raise a small amount of money was permitted to establish a bank, and allowed to issue notes for four times the sum raised. This being the case, many persons borrowed money merely long enough to exhibit to the bank inspectors, and the borrowed money was returned, and the bank left without a dollar in its vaults, if, indeed, it had a vault about its premises. The result was, that banks were started all over the Western States, and the country flooded with worthless paper. These were known as the 'Wild Cat Banks.' Silver coin being very scarce, and the banks not being allowed to issue notes for a smaller amount than one dollar, several persons put out notes of from 6 to 75 cents in value; these were called 'Shinplasters.' The Shinplaster was in the shape of a promissory note, made payable on demand. I have often seen persons with large rolls of these bills, the whole not amounting to more than five dollars. Some weeks after I had commenced business on my 'own hook,' I was one evening very much crowded with customers; and while they were talking over the events of the day, one of them said to me, 'Emperor, you seem to be doing a thriving business. You should do as other business men, issue your Shinplasters.' This of course, as it was intended, created a laugh; but with me it was no laughing matter, for from that moment I began to think seriously of becoming a banker. I accordingly went a few days after to a printer, and he, wishing to get the job of printing, urged me to put out my notes, and showed me some specimens of engravings that he had just received from Detroit. My head being already filled with the idea of the bank, I needed but little persuasion to set the thing finally afloat. Before I left the printer the notes were partly in type, and I studying how I should keep the public from counterfeiting them. The next day, my Shinplasters were handed to me, the whole amount being twenty dollars; and, after being duly signed, were ready for circulation. The first night I had my money, my head was so turned and dizzy, that I could not sleep. In fact, I slept but little for weeks after the issuing of my bills. This fact satisfied me, that people of wealth pass many sleepless hours. At first my notes did not take well; they were too new, and viewed with a suspicious eye. But through the assistance of my customers, and a good deal of exertion on my part, my bills were soon in circulation; and nearly all the money received in return for my notes was spent in fitting up and decorating my shop. Few bankers get through this world without their difficulties, and I was not to be an exception. A short time after my money had been out, a party of young men, either wishing to pull down my vanity, or to try the soundness of my bank, determined to give it 'a run.' After collecting together a number of my bills, they came one at a time to demand other money for them; and I, not being aware of what was going on, was taken by surprise. One day as I was sitting at my table, stropping some new razors I had just purchased with the avails of my Shinplasters, one of the men entered and said, 'Emperor, you will oblige me if you will give me some other money for these notes of yours.' I immediately cashed the notes with the most worthless of the Wild Cat money that I had on hand, but which was a lawful tender. The young man had scarcely left, when a second appeared with a similar amount, and demanded payment. These were cashed, and soon a third came with his roll of notes. I paid these with an air of triumph, although I had but half a dollar left. I began now to think seriously what I should do, or how to act, provided another demand should be made. While I was thus engaged in thought, I saw the fourth man crossing the street, with a handful of notes, evidently my Shinplasters. I instantaneously shut the door, and looking out of the window said, 'I have closed business for to-day: come to-morrow and I will see you.' In looking across the street, I saw my rival standing at his shopdoor, grinning and clapping his hands at my apparent downfall. I was completely 'done *Brown*' for the day.[1] However, I was not to be 'used up'[2] in this way; so I escaped by the back door, and went in search of my friend, who had first suggested to me the idea of issuing my notes. I found him, told him of the difficulty I was in, and wished him to point out a way by which I might extricate myself. He laughed heartily at my sad position, and then said, 'You must act as all bankers do in this part of the country.' I inquired how they did; and he said, 'when your notes are brought to you, you must redeem them, and then send them out and get other money for them; and, with the latter, you can keep cashing your own Shinplasters.' This was, indeed, a new idea for me. I immediately commenced putting in circulation the notes which I had just redeemed, and my efforts were crowned with such success, that, together with the aid of my friend, who, like a philanthropist and Western Christian as he was, before I slept that night, my Shinplasters were again in circulation, and my bank once more on a sound basis."

In proportion as his mind expanded under the more favourable circumstances in which Brown was placed, he became anxious, not merely for the redemption of his race from personal slavery, but for the moral and religious elevation of those who were free. Finding that habits of intoxication were too prevalent among his coloured brethren, he, in conjunction with others, commenced a temperance reformation in their body.[3] Such was the success of their efforts that, in three years, in the city of Buffalo alone, a society of upwards of 500 members was raised out of a coloured population of less than 700. Of that society

---

1 Colloquial: bamboozled or fooled. By capitalizing "Brown," Brown emphasizes the pun on his last name.
2 Colloquial: depleted, worn out.
3 Temperance activism had taken on a newly sociable character just prior to Brown's formation of the Union Total Abstinence Society in 1842. The Washingtonian Total Abstinence Society, which began in Baltimore in 1840, had catalyzed the formation of thousands of groups similarly emphasizing total abstinence, the sharing of personal narratives of recovery, and the sponsorship of events that offered attractive alternatives to the pleasures of the saloon.

Mr. Brown was thrice elected president. The intellectual powers of our author, coupled with his intimate acquaintance with the workings of the slave system, early recommended him to the Abolitionists, as a man eminently qualified to arouse the attention of the people of the Northern States to the great national sin of America. In 1843, he was engaged by the Western New York Anti-Slavery Society as a lecturing agent. From 1844 to 1847, he laboured in the Anti-Slavery cause in connection with the American Anti-Slavery Society; and from that period up to the time of his departure for Europe, in 1849, he was an agent of the Massachusetts Anti-Slavery Society. The records of these societies furnish abundant evidence of the success of his labours. From the Massachusetts Anti-Slavery Society he early received the following testimonial. "Since Mr. Brown became an agent of this society, he has lectured in very many of the towns of this commonwealth, and gained for himself, the respect and esteem of all whom he met. Himself a fugitive slave, he can experimentally describe the situation of those in bonds as bound with them; and he powerfully illustrates the diabolism of that system which keeps in chains and darkness a host of minds, which, if free and enlightened, would shine among men like stars in the firmament." Another member of that society speaks thus of him:—"I need not attempt any description of the ability and efficiency which characterised the speeches of William Wells Brown throughout the meeting. To you who know him so well, it is enough to say that his lectures were worthy of himself. He has left an impression on the minds of the people, that few could have done. Cold indeed must be the hearts that could resist the appeals of so noble a specimen of humanity, in behalf of a crushed and despised race."

In 1847, Mr. Brown wrote a narrative of his life and escape from slavery, which rapidly ran through several editions. A copy of this he forwarded to his old master, from whom he had escaped, and soon after a friend of Mr. Brown's received the following letter:

"*St. Louis, Jan. 10th, 1848.*

"Sir,—I received a pamphlet, or a narrative, so called on the title-page, of the Life of William W. Brown, a fugitive slave, purporting to have been written by himself; and in his book I see a letter from you to the said William W. Brown. This said Brown is named William; he is a slave belonging to me, and ran away from me the first day of January, 1834.

"I purchased him of Mr. S. Willi, the last of September, 1833. I paid six hundred and fifty dollars for him. If I had wanted to speculate on him, I could have sold him for three times as much as I paid for him. I was offered two thousand dollars for him in New Orleans at one time, and fifteen hundred dollars for him at another time, in Louisville, Kentucky. But I would not sell him. I was told that he was going to run away, but I did not believe the man, for I had so much confidence in William. I want you to see him, and see if what I say is not the truth. I do not want him as a slave, but I think that his friends, who sustain him and give him the right hand of fellowship, or he himself, could afford to pay my agent in Boston three hundred and twenty five dollars, and I will give him free papers, so that he may go wherever he wishes to. Then he can visit St. Louis, or any other place he may wish.

"This amount is just half what I paid for him. Now, if this offer suits Mr. Brown, and the Anti-Slavery Society of Boston, or Massachusetts, let me know, and I will give you the name of my agent in Boston, and forward the papers, to be given to William W. Brown as soon as the money is paid.

"Yours respectfully,
"ENOCH PRICE."
"To Edmund Quincy, Esq."[1]

While Mr. Brown would most gladly have accepted manumission papers, relieving him from all future claim of the slaveholder, and thereby making his freedom more secure, he yet felt that he could not conscientiously purchase his liberty, because, by so doing, he would be putting money into the pockets of the manstealer which did not justly belong to him. He therefore refused the offer of Mr. Price. Notwithstanding the celebrity he had acquired in the North, as a man of genius and talent, and the general respect his high character had gained him, the slave spirit of America denied him the rights of a citizen. By the constitution of the United States he was every moment liable to be arrested, and returned to the slavery from which he had fled. His only protection from such a fate was the anomaly of the ascendancy of the public opinion over the law of the country.

It has been for years thought desirable and advantageous to the cause of Negro emancipation in America, to have some

---

1   Edmund Quincy (1808–77) was an abolitionist author and editor.

talented man of colour always in Great Britain, who should be a living refutation of the doctrine of the inferiority of the African race; and it was moreover felt that none could so powerfully advocate the cause of "those in bonds" as one who had actually been "bound with them."[1] Mr. Brown having received repeated invitations from distinguished English Abolitionists to visit Great Britain, and being chosen a delegate to the Paris Peace Congress of 1849[2] by the American Peace Society,[3] and also by a convention of the coloured people of Boston, he resolved to acquiesce in the wishes of his numerous friends, and accordingly sailed from the United States on the 18th of July, 1849.

On leaving America he bore with him the following testimony from the Board of Managers of the Massachusetts Anti-Slavery Society[4]:—

"In consequence of the departure for England of their esteemed friend and faithful co-labourer in the cause of the American slave, William W. Brown, the Board of Management of the Massachusetts Anti-Slavery Society would commend him to the confidence, respect, esteem, and hospitality of the friends of emancipation wherever he may travel:—

"1. Because he is a fugitive slave from the American house of bondage, and on the soil which gave him birth can find no spot on which he can stand in safety from his pursuers, protected by law.

"2. Because he is a man, and not a chattel; and while as the latter, he may at any time be sold at public vendue[5] under the American star-spangled banner, we rejoice to know that he will be recognised and protected as the former under the flag of England.

"3. Because, for several years past, he has nobly consecrated his time and talents, at great personal hazard, and under the most adverse circumstances, to the uncompromising advocacy of the cause of his enslaved countrymen.

"4. Because he visits England for the purpose of increasing,

---

1 Hebrews 13:3.
2 The 1849 Paris Peace Congress was the third of seven such congresses organized by the International Congress of the Friends of Peace between 1843 and 1853.
3 The American Peace Society, now based in Washington DC, was founded in 1828 by anti-war activist William Ladd (1778–1841).
4 The Massachusetts Anti-Slavery Society, founded in 1835, was an offshoot of the American Anti-Slavery Society.
5 Auction.

consolidating, and directing British humanity and piety against that horrible system of slavery in America, by which three millions of human beings, by creation the children of God, are ranked with four-footed beasts, and treated as marketable commodities.

"5. Because he has long been in their employment as a lecturing agent in Massachusetts, and has laboured with great acceptance and success; and from the acquaintance thus formed, they are enabled to certify that he has invariably conducted himself with great circumspection, and won for himself the sympathy, respect, and friendship of a very large circle of acquaintance."

The Coloured convention unanimously passed the following resolution:

"*Resolved*,—That we bid our brother, William Wells Brown, God speed in his mission to Europe, and commend him to the hospitality and encouragement of all true friends of humanity."

In a letter to an American journal, announcing his arrival at Liverpool, he speaks as follows:—

"No person of my complexion can visit this country without being struck with the marked difference between the English and the Americans. The prejudice which I have experienced on all and every occasion in the United States, and to some degree on board the *Canada*, vanished as soon as I set foot on the soil of Britain. In America I had been bought and sold as a slave, in the Southern States. In the so-called Free States I had been treated as one born to occupy an inferior position; in steamers, compelled to take my fare on the deck; in hotels, to take my meals in the kitchen; in coaches, to ride on the outside; in railways, to ride in the 'Negro car;' and in churches, to sit in the 'Negro pew.' But no sooner was I on British soil than I was recognised as a man and an equal. The very dogs in the streets appeared conscious of my manhood. Such is the difference, and such is the change that is brought about by a trip of nine days in an Atlantic steamer. * * * For the first time in my life, I can say 'I am truly free.' My old master may make his appearance here, with the constitution of the United States in his pocket, the fugitive slave law in one hand and the chains in the other, and claim me as his property; but all will avail him nothing. I can here stand and look the tyrant in the face, and tell him that I am his equal! England is, indeed, the 'land of the free, and the home of the brave.'"

The reception of Mr. Brown at the Peace Congress in Paris was most flattering. He admirably maintained his reputation as a public speaker. His brief address upon that "war spirit of America which holds in bondage nearly four millions of his brethren," produced a profound sensation. At its conclusion the speaker was warmly greeted by Victor Hugo, the Abbé Duguerry, Emile de Girardin, Richard Cobden,[1] and every man of note in the assembly. At the soirée given by M. de Tocquerelle, the Minister for Foreign Affairs,[2] and the other fêtes given to the members of the Congress, Mr. Brown was received with marked attention.

Having finished his Peace Mission in France, he returned to England, where he was received with a hearty welcome by some of the most influential abolitionists of this country. Most of the fugitive slaves, and in fact nearly all of the coloured men who have visited Great Britain from the United States, have come upon begging missions, either for some society or for themselves. Mr. Brown has been almost the only exception. With that independence of feeling, which those who are acquainted with him know to be one of his chief characteristics, he determined to maintain himself and family by his own exertions—by his literary labours, and the honourable profession of a public lecturer. From nearly all the cities and large provincial towns he received invitations to lecture or address public meetings. The mayors, or other citizens of note, presided over many of these meetings. At Newcastle-upon-Tyne a soirée was given him, and an address presented by the citizens. A large and influential meeting was held at Bolton, Lancashire, which was addressed by Mr. Brown, and at its close the ladies presented to him the following address:—

"An address, presented to Mr. William Wells Brown, the fugitive slave from America, by the ladies of Bolton, March 22nd, 1850:—

"Dear friend and brother,—We cannot permit you to depart from among us without giving expression to the feelings which we entertain towards yourself personally, and to the sympathy which you have awakened in our breasts for the three millions of our sisters and brothers who still suffer and groan in the prison-house of American bondage. You came among us an entire stranger; we received you for the sake of your mission; and having heard the story of your personal wrongs, and gazed with horror on the atrocities of slavery as seen through the medium

---

1 Victor Hugo (1802–85) was a well-known French author; the Abbé Duguerry (1797–1871) was a Parisian priest; Émile de Girardin (1802–81) was a French journalist and politician; Richard Cobden (1804–65) was an influential member of the British parliament.

2 Brown is referring to the writer and statesman Alexis de Tocqueville (1805–59).

of your touching descriptions, we are resolved, henceforward, in reliance on divine assistance, to render what aid we can to the cause which you have so eloquently pleaded in our presence.

"We have no words to express our detestation of the crimes which, in the name of liberty, are committed in the country which gave you birth. Language fails to tell our deep abhorrence of the impiety of those who, in the still more sacred name of religion, rob immortal beings not only of an earthly citizenship, but do much to prevent them from obtaining a heavenly one; and, as mothers and daughters, we embrace this opportunity of giving utterance to our utmost indignation at the cruelties perpetrated upon our sex, by a people professedly acknowledging the equality of all mankind. Carry with you, on your return to the land of your nativity, this our solemn protest against the wicked institution which, like a dark and baleful cloud, hangs over it; and ask the unfeeling enslavers, as best you can, to open the prison doors to them that are bound, and let the oppressed go free.

"Allow us to assure you that your brief sojourn in our town has been to ourselves, and to vast multitudes, of a character long to be remembered; and when you are far removed from us, and toiling, as we hope you may be long spared to do, in this righteous enterprise, it may be some solace to your mind to know that your name is cherished with affectionate regard, and that the blessing of the Most High is earnestly supplicated in behalf of yourself, your family, and the cause to which you have consecrated your distinguished talents."

A most respectable and enthusiastic public meeting was held at Sheffield, to welcome Mr. Brown, and the next day he was invited to inspect several of the large establishments there. While going through the manufactory of Messrs. Broadhead and Atkin, silver and electroplaters, &c., in Love-street, and whilst he was being shown through the works, a subscription was hastily set on foot on his behalf, by the workmen and women of the establishment, which was presented to Mr. Brown in the counting-house by a deputation of the subscribers. The spokesman (the designer to Messrs. Broadhead and Atkin) addressing Mr. Brown on behalf of the workpeople, begged his acceptance of the present as a token of esteem, as well as an expression of their sympathy in the cause he advocates, viz. that of the American slave. Mr. Brown briefly thanked the parties for their spontaneous free will offering, accompanied as it was by a generous expression of sympathy for his afflicted brethren and sisters in bondage.

Mr. Brown has been in England nearly four years, and

since his arrival he has travelled above twenty thousand miles through Great Britain, addressed one hundred and thirty public meetings, lectured in twenty-three mechanics and literary institutions, and given his services to many of the benevolent and religious societies on the occasion of their anniversary meetings. After a lecture, which he delivered before the Whittington Club, he received from the managers of that institution the following testimonial:

"*Whittington Club and Metropolitan Athenæum,*
"*189, Strand, June 21, 1850.*

"My dear sir,

I have much pleasure in conveying to you the best thanks of the Managing Committee of this institution for the excellent lecture you gave here last evening, and also in presenting you in their names with an honorary membership of the club. It is hoped that you will often avail yourself of its privileges by coming amongst us. You will then see, by the cordial welcome of the members, that they protest against the odious distinctions made between man and man, and the abominable traffic of which you have been the victim.

"For my own part, I shall be happy to be serviceable to you in any way, and at all times be glad to place the advantages of the institution at your disposal.

"I am, my dear sir,
"Yours truly,
"WILLIAM STRUDWICKE,
"Mr. W. Wells Brown."   "Secretary."

On the 1st of August, 1851, a meeting of the most novel character was held at the Hall of Commerce, London, the chief actors being American fugitive slaves. That meeting was most ably presided over by Mr. Brown, and the speeches made on the occasion by fugitive slaves were of the most interesting and creditable description. Although a residence in Canada is infinitely preferable to slavery in America, yet the climate of that country is uncongenial to the constitutions of the Negroes, and their lack of education is an almost insuperable barrier to their social progress. The latter evil Mr. Brown attempted to remedy by the establishment of Manual Labour Schools in Canada for fugitive slaves. A public meeting, attended by between 3,000 and 4,000 persons, was held on the 6th of January 1851, in the City Hall, Glasgow, which was presided over by Alexander Hastie, Esq., M.P., at which resolutions were unanimously passed, approving of Mr. Brown's scheme; which scheme, however, never received that amount of support which would have enabled him to bring it into practice; and the plan at present only remains as an evidence of its author's ingenuity and desire for the elevation of his oppressed and injured race. Mr. Brown subsequently made, through the columns of the *Times*, a proposition for the emigration of American fugitive slaves, under fair and honourable terms, from Canada to the West Indies, where there is a great lack of that labour which they are so capable of undertaking. These efforts all show the willingness of this fugitive slave to aid those of his race. Last year Mr. Brown published his "Three Years in Europe; or, Places I have seen and People I have met." And his literary abilities may be partly judged of from the following commendations of that ably written work:—

"The extraordinary excitement produced by 'Uncle Tom's Cabin'[1] will, we hope, prepare the public of Great Britain and America for this lively book of travels by a real fugitive slave. Though he never had a day's schooling in his life, he has produced a literary work not unworthy of a highly educated gentleman. Our readers will find in these letters much instruction, not a little entertainment, and the beatings of a manly heart, on behalf of a down-trodden race, with which they will not fail to sympathise."—*The Eclectic*.

"When he writes on the wrongs of his race, or the events of his own career, he is always interesting or amusing."—*The Athenæum*.

"The appearance of this book is too remarkable a literary event to pass without a notice. At the moment when attention in this country is directed to the state of the coloured people in America, the book appears with additional advantage; if nothing else were attained by its publication, it is well to have another proof of the capability of the Negro intellect. Altogether Mr. Brown has written a pleasing and amusing volume. Contrasted with the caricature and bombast of his white countrymen, Mr. Willis's description of 'People he has met,' a comparison suggest-

---

1 *Uncle Tom's Cabin* (1852), by Harriet Beecher Stowe (1811–96), was an immediate sensation in America and England. It would become the best-selling novel of the nineteenth century.

ed by the similarity of the title, it is both in intellect and in style a superior performance, and we are glad to bear this testimony to the literary merit of a work by a Negro author."—*The Literary Gazette.*

"That a man who was a slave for the first twenty years of his life, and who has never had a day's schooling, should produce such a book as this, cannot but astonish those who speak disparagingly of the African race."—*The Weekly News and Chronicle.*

"This remarkable book of a remarkable man cannot fail to add to the practical protests already entered in Britain against the absolute bondage of 3,000,000 of our fellow creatures. The impression of a self-educated son of slavery here set forth, must hasten the period when the senseless and impious denial of common claims to a common humanity, on the score of colour, shall be scouted with scorn in every civilised and Christian country. And when this shall be attained, among the means of destruction of the hideous abomination, his compatriots will remember with respect and gratitude the doings and sayings of William Wells Brown. The volume consists of a sufficient variety of scenes, persons, arguments, inferences, speculations, and opinions, to satisfy and amuse the most *exigeant* of those who read *pour se desennuyer*;[1] while those who look deeper into things, and view with anxious hope the progress of nations and of mankind, will feel that the good cause of humanity and freedom, of Christianity, enlightenment, and brotherhood, cannot fail to be served by such a book as this."—*Morning Advertiser.*

"He writes with ease and ability, and his intelligent observations upon the great question to which he has devoted, and is devoting his life, will be read with interest, and will command influence and respect."—*Daily News.*

Mr. Brown is most assiduous in his studies even at the present time. The following extract from his writings will show how he spends most of his leisure hours:—

"It was eight o'clock before I reached my lodgings. Although fatigued by the day's exertions, I again resumed the reading of Roscoe's 'Leo X.,'[2] and had nearly finished seventy-three pages, when the clock on St. Martin's Church apprised me that it was

---

1 *Exigeant*: hard to please; *pour se desennuyer*: to entertain themselves (French).

2 A reference to William Roscoe's *The Life and Pontificate of Leo the Tenth* (1805).

two. He who escapes from slavery at the age of twenty years without any education, as did the writer of this letter, must read when others are asleep, if he would catch up with the rest of the world. 'To be wise,' says Pope, 'is but to know how little can be known.'[1] The true searcher after truth and knowledge is always like a child; although gaining strength from year to year, he still 'learns to labour and to wait.'[2] The field of labour is ever expanding before him, reminding him that he has yet more to learn; teaching him that he is nothing more than a child in knowledge, and inviting him onward with a thousand varied charms. The son may take possession of the father's goods at his death, but he cannot inherit with the property the father's cultivated mind. He may put on the father's old coat, but that is all; the immortal mind of the first wearer has gone to the tomb. Property may be bequeathed but knowledge cannot. Then let him who would be useful in his generation be up and doing. Like the Chinese student who learned perseverance from the woman whom he saw trying to rub a crowbar into a needle, so should we take the experience of the past to lighten our feet through the paths of the future."

The following testimonial to Mr. Brown's abilities, from an American journal of which Frederick Douglass is editor,[3] shows that his talents are highly appreciated in that country:—

"We have the pleasure to lay before our readers another interesting letter from W. Wells Brown. We rejoice to find our friend still persevering in the pursuit of knowledge, and still more do we rejoice to find such marked evidence of his rapid progress as his several letters afford. But a few years ago he was a despised, degraded, whip-scarred slave, knowing nothing of letters; and now we find him writing accounts of his travels in a distant land, of which a man reared under the most favourable educational advantages might be proud."

We should have said that it was Mr. Brown's intention to have returned to the United States to his family ere this. But

---

1 Alexander Pope, *An Essay on Man* (1733–34), Epistle IV, 260–61.
2 Henry Wadsworth Longfellow, "A Psalm of Life" (1838), 36.
3 Frederick Douglass (1818–95) was the country's most famous black abolitionist. He edited the newspaper *The North Star* from 1847–51; the article from which Brown quotes appeared there on 17 April 1851.

the passage of the infamous "Fugitive Slave Law"[1] prevented his returning.

Mr. Brown's wife died in Buffalo N.Y. in Jan. 1851. He has two daughters who are now in this country, being trained for teachers. Of course we need not add that for their education they are entirely dependent on their father's exertions. During last year, the Rev. Edward Hore, of Ramsgate, through a willingness to assist Mr. Brown in returning to the United States, wrote to his former owner, and offered him £50, if he would relinquish all claim to him, and furnish the fugitive with papers of emancipation, but the following note from the slaveowner speaks for itself:

"*St. Louis, Feb. 16th, 1852.*

"Rev. sir,—I received your note, dated Jan. 6th, concerning a runaway slave of mine now known by the name of William Wells Brown. You state that I offered to take three hundred and twenty five dollars for him, and give him free papers, in 1848. I did so then, but since that time the laws of the United States are materially changed. The Fugitive Slave Bill has passed since then. I can now take him anywhere in the United States, and I have everything arranged for his arrest if he lands at any port in the United States. But I will give him papers of emancipation, properly authenticated by our statutes, for the sum of five hundred dollars (or £100) that will make him as free as any white person. If this suits your views, you can let me know, and I will have the papers made out and forwarded to Boston, to Joseph Gruley, of the firm of Charles Wilkins and Co., 33, Long Wharf. The money must be paid before the papers are handed over to your agent.

"Respectfully your obedient servant,
"To the Rev. Edward Hore."   "ENOCH PRICE."[2]

---

1   The Fugitive Slave Act or Law was passed by Congress on 18 September 1850. It required the return of all runaway slaves to their masters. The Act amended the earlier Fugitive Slave Act of 1793.

2   Two years later, Price accepted $300 in exchange for Brown's manumission.

CLOTEL;

OR,

THE PRESIDENT'S DAUGHTER

CHAPTER I.

THE NEGRO SALE.

"Why stands she near the auction stand,
    That girl so young and fair?
What brings her to this dismal place,
    Why stands she weeping there?"[1]

With the growing population of slaves in the Southern States of America, there is a fearful increase of half whites, most of whose fathers are slaveowners, and their mothers slaves. Society does not frown upon the man who sits with his mulatto child upon his knee, whilst its mother stands a slave behind his chair. The late Henry Clay, some years since, predicted that the abolition of negro slavery would be brought about by the amalgamation of the races. John Randolph, a distinguished slaveholder of Virginia, and a prominent statesman, said in a speech in the legislature of his native state, that "the blood of the first American statesmen coursed through the veins of the slave of the South."[2] In all the cities and towns of the slave states, the real negro, or clear black, does not amount to more than one in every four of the slave population. This fact is, of itself, the best evidence of the degraded and immoral condition of the relation of master and slave in the United States of America.

In all the slave states, the law says:—"Slaves shall be deemed, sold, taken, reputed, and adjudged in law to be chattels personal in the hands of their owners and possessors, and their executors, administrators and assigns, to all intents, constructions, and purposes whatsoever. A slave is one who is in the power of a master to whom he belongs. The master may sell him, dispose of his person, his industry, and his labour. He can do nothing, possess nothing, nor acquire anything, but what must belong to his master. The slave is entirely subject to the will of his master, who may correct and chastise him, though not with unusual rigour, or so as to maim and mutilate him, or expose him to the danger

---

1   Arzelia, "The Slave Auction—A Fact," 1–4.
2   John Randolph (1773–1833) was a Virginian slaveholder and
    politician.

of loss of life, or to cause his death.[1] The slave, to remain a slave, must be sensible that there is no appeal from his master."[2] Where the slave is placed by law entirely under the control of the man who claims him, body and soul, as property, what else could be expected than the most depraved social condition? The marriage relation, the oldest and most sacred institution given to man by his Creator, is unknown and unrecognised in the slave laws of the United States. Would that we could say, that the moral and religious teaching in the slave states were better than the laws; but, alas! we cannot. A few years since, some slaveholders became a little uneasy in their minds about the rightfulness of permitting slaves to take to themselves husbands and wives, while they still had others living, and applied to their religious teachers for advice; and the following will show how this grave and important subject was treated:—

> "Is a servant, whose husband or wife has been sold by his or her master into a distant country, to be permitted to marry again?"

The query was referred to a committee, who made the following report; which, after discussion, was adopted:—

> "That, in view of the circumstances in which servants in this country are placed, the committee are unanimous in the opinion, that it is better to permit servants thus circumstanced to take another husband or wife."[3]

---

1 "*Slaves shall be deemed, sold ... cause his death*": quoted in William Goodell, *The American Slave Code in Theory and Practice*, 25. Goodell (1792–1878) was a reformer, abolitionist, politician, pastor, and editor who led the American Temperance Society and helped form the American Anti-Slavery Society. Future references to quotations and plagiarisms will follow the above format: the passage in question will be identified by its opening and closing words, where necessary, and the source will be identified. Full bibliographic references to the sources of Brown's plagiarisms and quotations, including references to the databases from which they were retrieved, may be found in the Select Bibliography.

2 "*The slave, to remain a slave ... from his master*": quoted in Goodell, *American Slave Code*, 126.

3 "*Is a servant, whose husband or wife has been sold ... husband or wife*": "Ecclesiastical Action," *Emancipator*, 9 May 1839, 8; quoted in William I. Bowditch, *Slavery and the Constitution*, 62.

Such was the answer from a committee of the "Shiloh Baptist Association;" and instead of receiving light, those who asked the question were plunged into deeper darkness!

A similar question was put to the "Savannah River Association," and the answer, as the following will show, did not materially differ from the one we have already given:—

> "Whether, in a case of involuntary separation, of such a character as to preclude all prospect of future inter-course, the parties ought to be allowed to marry again."

Answer—

> "That such separation among persons situated as our slaves are, is civilly a separation by death; and they believe that, in the sight of God, it would be so viewed. To forbid second marriages in such cases would be to expose the parties, not only to stronger hardships and strong temptation, but to church-censure for acting in obedience to their masters, who cannot be expected to acquiesce in a regulation at variance with justice to the slaves, and to the spirit of that command which regulates marriage among Christians. The slaves are not free agents; and a dissolution by death is not more entirely without their consent, and beyond their con-trol, than by such separation."[1]

Although marriage, as the above indicates, is a matter which the slaveholders do not think is of any importance, or of any binding force with their slaves; yet it would be doing that degrad-ed class an injustice, not to acknowledge that many of them do regard it as a sacred obligation, and show a willingness to obey the commands of God on this subject. Marriage is, indeed, the first and most important institution of human existence—the foundation of all civilisation and culture—the root of church and state. It is the most intimate covenant of heart formed among mankind; and for many persons the only relation in which they feel the true sentiments of humanity. It gives scope for every human virtue, since each of these is developed from the love and confidence which here predominate. It unites all which enno-

---

1 "*Whether, in a case of involuntary separation ... by such separation*": "A Doctrine of Devils," 10; quoted in Bowditch, *Slavery*, 62.

bles and beautifies, life,—sympathy, kindness of will and deed, gratitude, devotion, and every delicate, intimate feeling. As the only asylum for true education, it is the first and last sanctuary of human culture. As husband and wife through each other become conscious of complete humanity, and every human feeling, and every human virtue; so children, at their first awakening in the fond covenant of love between parents, both of whom are tenderly concerned for the same object, find an image of complete humanity leagued in free love. The spirit of love which prevails between them acts with creative power upon the young mind, and awakens every germ of goodness within it. This invisible and incalculable influence of parental life acts more upon the child than all the efforts of education, whether by means of instruction, precept, or exhortation.[1] If this be a true picture of the vast influence for good of the institution of marriage, what must be the moral degradation of that people to whom marriage is denied? Not content with depriving them of all the higher and holier enjoyments of this relation, by degrading and darkening their souls, the slaveholder denies to his victim even that slight alleviation of his misery, which would result from the marriage relation being protected by law and public opinion.[2] Such is the influence of slavery in the United States, that the ministers of religion, even in the so-called free states, are the mere echoes, instead of the correctors, of public sentiment.

We have thought it advisable to show that the present system of chattel slavery in America undermines the entire social condition of man, so as to prepare the reader for the following narrative of slave life, in that otherwise happy and prosperous country.

In all the large towns in the Southern States, there is a class of slaves who are permitted to hire their time of their owners, and for which they pay a high price. These are mulatto women, or quadroons, as they are familiarly known, and are distinguished for their fascinating beauty. The handsomest usually pays the highest price for her time. Many of these women are the favourites of persons who furnish them with the means of paying their owners, and not a few are dressed in the most extravagant manner.

---

1 *"Marriage is, indeed, the first and most important ... precept, or exhortation"*: German theologian Wilhelm de Wette (1780–1849); quoted in Bowditch, *Slavery*, 56–57.

2 *"If this be a true picture of the vast influence ... relation being protected"*: Bowditch, *Slavery*, 57.

Reader, when you take into consideration the fact, that amongst the slave population no safeguard is thrown around virtue, and no inducement held out to slave women to be chaste, you will not be surprised when we tell you that immorality and vice pervade the cities of the Southern States in a manner unknown in the cities and towns of the Northern States. Indeed most of the slave women have no higher aspiration than that of becoming the finely-dressed mistress of some white man. And at negro balls and parties, this class of women usually cut the greatest figure.

At the close of the year—the following advertisement appeared in a newspaper published in Richmond, the capital of the state of Virginia:—"Notice: Thirty-eight negroes will be offered for sale on Monday, November 10th, at twelve o'clock, being the entire stock of the late John Graves, Esq. The negroes are in good condition, some of them very prime; among them are several mechanics, able-bodied field hands, plough-boys, and women with children at the breast, and some of them very prolific in their generating qualities, affording a rare opportunity to any one who wishes to raise a strong and healthy lot of servants for their own use. Also several mulatto girls of rare personal qualities: two of them very superior. Any gentleman or lady wishing to purchase, can take any of the above slaves on trial for a week, for which no charge will be made."[1] Amongst the above slaves to be sold were Currer and her two daughters, Clotel and Althesa; the latter were the girls spoken of in the advertisement as "very superior." Currer was a bright mulatto,[2] and of prepossessing appearance, though then nearly forty years of age. She had hired her time for more than twenty years, during which time she had lived in Richmond. In her younger days Currer had been the housekeeper of a young slave-holder; but of later years had been a laundress or washerwoman, and was considered to be a woman of great taste in getting up linen. The gentleman for whom she had kept house was Thomas Jefferson, by whom she had two daughters.[3] Jefferson being called to Washington to fill a government appointment, Currer was left behind, and thus she took herself to the business of washing, by which means she paid

---

1 Adapted from "Negroes for Sale," *Charleston Mercury*, 16 May 1838; quoted in Weld, *American Slavery*, 175.

2 A light-skinned mixed-race woman.

3 It was widely rumored in the early nineteenth century that Thomas Jefferson (1743–1826) was the father of the children of his slave Sally Hemings (c. 1773–1835), and that one of his daughters had been sold at auction. Thanks in part to DNA testing, it is now generally accepted that Jefferson was indeed the father of Hemings's children.

her master, Mr. Graves, and supported herself and two children. At the time of the decease of her master, Currer's daughters, Clotel and Althesa, were aged respectively sixteen and fourteen years, and both, like most of their own sex in America, were well grown. Currer early resolved to bring her daughters up as ladies, as she termed it, and therefore imposed little or no work upon them. As her daughters grew older, Currer had to pay a stipulated price for them; yet her notoriety as a laundress of the first class enabled her to put an extra price upon her charges, and thus she and her daughters lived in comparative luxury. To bring up Clotel and Althesa to attract attention, and especially at balls and parties, was the great aim of Currer. Although the term "negro ball" is applied to most of these gatherings, yet a majority of the attendants are often whites. Nearly all the negro parties in the cities and towns of the Southern States are made up of quadroon[1] and mulatto girls, and white men. These are democratic gatherings, where gentlemen, shopkeepers, and their clerks, all appear upon terms of perfect equality. And there is a degree of gentility and decorum in these companies that is not surpassed by similar gatherings of white people in the Slave States. It was at one of these parties that Horatio Green, the son of a wealthy gentleman of Richmond, was first introduced to Clotel. The young man had just returned from college, and was in his twenty-second year. Clotel was sixteen, and was admitted by all to be the most beautiful girl, coloured or white, in the city. So attentive was the young man to the quadroon during the evening that it was noticed by all, and became a matter of general conversation; while Currer appeared delighted beyond measure at her daughter's conquest. From that evening, young Green became the favourite visitor at Currer's house. He soon promised to purchase Clotel, as speedily as it could be effected, and make her mistress of her own dwelling; and Currer looked forward with pride to the time when she should see her daughter emancipated and free. It was a beautiful moonlight night in August, when all who reside in tropical climes are eagerly gasping for a breath of fresh air, that Horatio Green was seated in the small garden behind Currer's cottage, with the object of his affections by his side. And it was here that Horatio drew from his pocket the newspaper, wet from the press, and read the advertisement for the sale of the slaves to which we have alluded; Currer and her two daughters being of the number. At the close of the evening's visit, and as the young man was leaving, he said to the girl, "You shall soon be free and your own mistress."

---

1 Someone whose ancestry is one-quarter African and three-quarters white.

As might have been expected, the day of sale brought an unusual large number together to compete for the property to be sold. Farmers who make a business of raising slaves for the market were there; slave-traders and speculators were also numerously represented; and in the midst of this throng was one who felt a deeper interest in the result of the sale than any other of the bystanders; this was young Green. True to his promise, he was there with a blank bank check in his pocket, awaiting with impatience to enter the list as a bidder for the beautiful slave. The less valuable slaves were first placed upon the auction block, one after another, and sold to the highest bidder. Husbands and wives were separated with a degree of indifference that is unknown in any other relation of life, except that of slavery. Brothers and sisters were torn from each other; and mothers saw their children leave them for the last time on this earth.

It was late in the day, when the greatest number of persons were thought to be present, that Currer and her daughters were brought forward to the place of sale. Currer was first ordered to ascend the auction stand, which she did with a trembling step. The slave mother was sold to a trader. Althesa, the youngest, and who was scarcely less beautiful than her sister, was sold to the same trader for one thousand dollars. Clotel was the last, and, as was expected, commanded a higher price than any that had been offered for sale that day. The appearance of Clotel on the auction block created a deep sensation amongst the crowd. There she stood, with a complexion as white as most of those who were waiting with a wish to become her purchasers; her features as finely defined as any of her sex of pure Anglo-Saxon; her long black wavy hair done up in the neatest manner; her form tall and graceful, and her whole appearance indicating one superior to her position. The auctioneer commenced by saying, that "Miss Clotel had been reserved for the last, because she was the most valuable. How much gentlemen? Real Albino, fit for a fancy girl for any one.[1] She enjoys good health, and has a sweet temper. How much do you say?" "Five hundred dollars." "Only five hundred for such a girl as this? Gentlemen, she is worth a deal more than that sum; you certainly don't know the value of the article you are bidding upon. Here, gentlemen, I hold in my hand a paper certifying that she has a good moral character." "Seven hundred." "Ah, gentlemen, that is something like. This paper also states

---

1 *"How much gentlemen? ... girl for any one"*: H.S.D., "An Auction," 165 (see Appendix B2).

that she is very intelligent." "Eight hundred." "She is a devoted Christian, and perfectly trustworthy." "Nine hundred." "Nine fifty." "Ten." "Eleven." "Twelve hundred." Here the sale came to a dead stand. The auctioneer stopped, looked around, and began in a rough manner to relate some anecdotes relative to the sale of slaves, which, he said, had come under his own observation. At this juncture the scene was indeed strange. Laughing, joking, swearing, smoking, spitting, and talking kept up a continual hum and noise amongst the crowd; while the slave-girl stood with tears in her eyes, at one time looking towards her mother and sister, and at another towards the young man whom she hoped would become her purchaser. "The chastity of this girl is pure; she has never been from under her mother's care, she is a virtuous creature." "Thirteen." "Fourteen." "Fifteen." "Fifteen hundred dollars," cried the auctioneer, and the maiden was struck for that sum. This was a Southern auction, at which the bones, muscles, sinews, blood, and nerves of a young lady of sixteen were sold for five hundred dollars; her moral character for two hundred; her improved intellect for one hundred; her Christianity for three hundred; and her chastity and virtue for four hundred dollars more.[1] And this, too, in a city thronged with churches, whose tall spires look like so many signals pointing to heaven, and whose ministers preach that slavery is a God-ordained institution!

What words can tell the inhumanity, the atrocity, and the immorality of that doctrine which, from exalted office, commends such a crime to the favour of enlightened and Christian people? What indignation from all the world is not due to the government and people who put forth all their strength and power to keep in existence such an institution? Nature abhors it; the age repels it; and Christianity needs all her meekness to forgive it.[2]

Clotel was sold for fifteen hundred dollars, but her purchaser was Horatio Green. Thus closed a negro sale, at which two daughters of Thomas Jefferson, the writer of the Declaration of American Independence, and one of the presidents of the great republic, were disposed of to the highest bidder!

---

1 "*This was a Southern auction ... hundred dollars more*": H.S.D., "An Auction," 165.
2 "*What words can tell the inhumanity ... to forgive it*": George Allen, *Resistance to Slavery Every Man's Duty*, 15–16.

"O God! my every heart-string cries,
Dost thou these scenes behold
In this our boasted Christian land,
And must the truth be told?

"Blush, Christian, blush! for e'en the dark,
Untutored heathen see
Thy inconsistency; and, lo!
They scorn thy God, and thee!"[1]

CHAPTER II.

GOING TO THE SOUTH.

"My country, shall thy honoured name,
Be as a bye-word through the world?
Rouse! for, as if to blast thy fame,
This keen reproach is at thee hurled;
The banner that above thee waves,
Is floating o'er three million slaves."[2]

Dick Walker, the slave speculator, who had purchased Currer and
Althesa, put them in prison until his gang was made up, and then,
with his forty slaves, started for the New Orleans market. As many
of the slaves had been brought up in Richmond, and had relations
residing there, the slave trader determined to leave the city early in
the morning, so as not to witness any of those scenes so common
where slaves are separated from their relatives and friends, when
about departing for the Southern market. This plan was successful; for not even Clotel, who had been every day at the prison to
see her mother and sister, knew of their departure. A march of
eight days through the interior of the state, and they arrived on
the banks of the Ohio river, where they were all put on board a
steamer, and then speedily sailed for the place of their destination.

Walker had already advertised in the New Orleans papers, that
he would be there at a stated time with "a prime lot of able-bodied
slaves ready for field service; together with a few extra ones, between
the ages of fifteen and twenty-five." But, like most who make a business of buying and selling slaves for gain, he often bought some who

---

1 Arzelia, "The Slave Auction—A Fact," 25–32.
2 Robert C. Waterston, "Freedom's Banner," 1–6.

were far advanced in years, and would always try to sell them for five or ten years younger than they actually were. Few persons can arrive at anything like the age of a negro, by mere observation, unless they are well acquainted with the race. Therefore the slavetrader very frequently carried out this deception with perfect impunity. After the steamer had left the wharf, and was fairly on the bosom of the Father of Waters, Walker called his servant Pompey to him, and instructed him as to "getting the negroes ready for market." Amongst the forty negroes were several whose appearance indicated that they had seen some years, and had gone through some services. Their grey hair and whiskers at once pronounced them to be above the ages set down in the trader's advertisement. Pompey had long been with the trader, and knew his business; and if he did not take delight in discharging his duty, he did it with a degree of alacrity, so that he might receive the approbation of his master. "Pomp," as Walker usually called him, was of real negro blood, and would often say, when alluding to himself, "Dis nigger is no countefit; he is de genewine artekil." Pompey was of low stature, round face, and, like most of his race, had a set of teeth, which for whiteness and beauty could not be surpassed; his eyes large, lips thick, and hair short and woolly. Pompey had been with Walker so long, and had seen so much of the buying and selling of slaves, that he appeared perfectly indifferent to the heartrending scenes which daily occurred in his presence. It was on the second day of the steamer's voyage that Pompey selected five of the old slaves, took them into a room by themselves, and commenced preparing them for the market. "Well," said Pompey, addressing himself to the company, "I is de gentman dat is to get you ready, so dat you will bring marser a good price in de Orleans market. How old is you?" addressing himself to a man who, from appearance, was not less than forty. "If I live to see next corn-planting time I will either be forty-five or fifty-five, I don't know which." "Dat may be," replied Pompey; "But now you is only thirty years old; dat is what marser says you is to be." "I know I is more den dat," responded the man. "I knows nothing about dat," said Pompey; "but when you get in de market, an anybody axe you how old you is, an you tell 'em forty-five, marser will tie you up an gib you de whip like smoke. But if you tell 'em dat you is only thirty, den he wont." "Well den, I guess I will only be thirty when dey axe me," replied the chattel.

"What your name?" inquired Pompey. "Geemes," answered the man. "Oh, Uncle Jim, is it?" "Yes." "Den you must have off dem dare whiskers of yours, an when you get to Orleans you must grease dat face an make it look shiney." This was all said by Pompey in a manner which clearly showed that he knew what he was about.

"How old is you?" asked Pompey of a tall, strong-looking man. "I was twenty-nine last potato-digging time," said the man. "What's your name?" "My name is Tobias, but dey call me 'Toby.'" "Well, Toby, or Mr. Tobias, if dat will suit you better, you is now twenty-three years old, an no more. Dus you hear dat?" "Yes," responded Toby. Pompey gave each to understand how old he was to be when asked by persons who wished to purchase, and then reported to his master that the "old boys" were all right. At eight o'clock on the evening of the third day, the lights of another steamer were seen in the distance, and apparently coming up very fast. This was a signal for a general commotion on the Patriot, and everything indicated that a steamboat race was at hand. Nothing can exceed the excitement attendant upon a steamboat on the Mississippi river. By the time the boats had reached Memphis, they were side by side, and each exerting itself to keep the ascendancy in point of speed. The night was clear, the moon shining brightly, and the boats so near to each other that the passengers were calling out from one boat to the other. On board the Patriot, the firemen were using oil, lard, butter, and even bacon, with the wood, for the purpose of raising the steam to its highest pitch. The blaze, mingled with the black smoke, showed plainly that the other boat was burning more than wood. The two boats soon locked, so that the hands of the boats were passing from vessel to vessel, and the wildest excitement prevailed throughout amongst both passengers and crew. At this moment the engineer of the Patriot was seen to fasten down the safety-valve, so that no steam should escape. This was, indeed, a dangerous resort. A few of the boat hands who saw what had taken place, left that end of the boat for more secure quarters.

The Patriot stopped to take in passengers, and still no steam was permitted to escape. At the starting of the boat cold water was forced into the boilers by the machinery, and, as might have been expected, one of the boilers immediately exploded. One dense fog of steam filled every part of the vessel, while shrieks, groans, and cries were heard on every hand. The saloons and cabins soon had the appearance of a hospital. By this time the boat had landed, and the Columbia, the other boat, had come alongside to render assistance to the disabled steamer. The killed and scalded (nineteen in number) were put on shore, and the Patriot, taken in tow by the Columbia, was soon again on its way.

It was now twelve o'clock at night, and instead of the passengers being asleep the majority were gambling in the saloons. Thousands of dollars change hands during a passage from Louisville or St. Louis to New Orleans on a Mississippi steamer, and many men, and even ladies, are completely ruined. "Go call my boy, steward," said Mr. Smith, as he took his cards one by one from the table. In a few moments a fine looking, bright-eyed mulatto boy, apparently about fifteen years of age, was standing by his master's side at the table. "I will see you, and five hundred dollars better," said Smith, as his servant Jerry approached the table. "What price do you set on that boy?" asked Johnson, as he took a roll of bills from his pocket. "He will bring a thousand dollars, any day, in the New Orleans market," replied Smith. "Then you bet the whole of the boy, do you?" "Yes." "I call you, then," said Johnson, at the same time spreading his cards out upon the table. "You have beat me," said Smith, as soon as he saw the cards. Jerry, who was standing on top of the table, with the bank notes and silver dollars round his feet, was now ordered to descend from the table. "You will not forget that you belong to me," said Johnson, as the young slave was stepping from the table to a chair. "No, sir," replied the chattel. "Now go back to your bed, and be up in time to-morrow morning to brush my clothes and clean my boots, do you hear?" "Yes, sir," responded Jerry, as he wiped the tears from his eyes.

Smith took from his pocket the bill of sale and handed it to Johnson; at the same time saying, "I claim the right of redeeming that boy, Mr. Johnson. My father gave him to me when I came of age, and I promised not to part with him." "Most certainly, sir, the boy shall be yours, whenever you hand me over a cool thousand," replied Johnson. The next morning, as the passengers were assembling in the breakfast saloons and upon the guards of the vessel, and the servants were seen running about waiting upon or looking for their masters, poor Jerry was entering his new master's state-room with his boots. "Who do you belong to?" said a gentleman to an old black man, who came along leading a fine dog that he had been feeding. "When I went to sleep last night, I belonged to Governor Lucas; but I understand dat he is bin gambling all night, so I don't know who owns me dis morning." Such is the uncertainty of a slave's position. He goes to bed at night the property of the man with whom he has lived for years, and gets up in the morning the slave of some one whom he has never seen before! To behold five or six tables in a steamboat's cabin, with half-a-dozen men playing at cards, and money, pistols, bowie-knives, &c. all in confusion on the tables, is what may be seen at almost any time on the Mississippi river.

On the fourth day, while at Natchez, taking in freight and passengers, Walker, who had been on shore to see some of his old customers, returned, accompanied by a tall, thin-faced man, dressed in black, with a white neckcloth, which immediately proclaimed him to be a clergyman. "I want a good, trusty woman for house service," said the stranger, as they entered the cabin where Walker's slaves were kept. "Here she is, and no mistake," replied the trader. "Stand up, Currer, my gal; here's a gentleman who wishes to see if you will suit him." Althesa clung to her mother's side, as the latter rose from her seat. "She is a rare cook, a good washer, and will suit you to a T, I am sure." "If you buy me, I hope you will buy my daughter too," said the woman, in rather an excited manner. "I only want one for my own use, and would not need another," said the man in black, as he and the trader left the room. Walker and the parson went into the saloon, talked over the matter, the bill of sale was made out, the money paid over, and the clergyman left, with the understanding that the woman should be delivered to him at his house. It seemed as if poor Althesa would have wept herself to death, for the first two days after her mother had been torn from her side by the hand of the ruthless trafficker in human flesh. On the arrival of the boat at Baton Rouge, an additional number of passengers were taken on board; and, amongst them, several persons who had been attending the races. Gambling and drinking were now the order of the day. Just as the ladies and gentlemen were assembling at the supper-table, the report of a pistol was heard in the direction of the Social Hall, which caused great uneasiness to the ladies, and took the gentlemen to that part of the cabin. However, nothing serious had occurred. A man at one of the tables where they were gambling had been seen attempting to conceal a card in his sleeve, and one of the party seized his pistol and fired; but fortunately the barrel of the pistol was knocked up, just as it was about to be discharged, and the ball passed through the upper deck, instead of the man's head, as intended. Order was soon restored; all went on well the remainder of the night, and the next day, at ten o'clock, the boat arrived at New Orleans, and the passengers went to the hotels and the slaves to the market!

"Our eyes are yet on Afric's shores,
Her thousand wrongs we still deplore;
We see the grim slave trader there;
We hear his fettered victim's prayer;
And hasten to the sufferer's aid,
Forgetful of *our own 'slave trade.'*

"The Ocean 'Pirate's' fiend-like form
Shall sink beneath the vengeance-storm;
His heart of steel shall quake before
The battle-din and havoc roar:
The knave shall die, the Law hath said,
While it protects our own *'slave trade.'*

"What earthly eye presumes to scan
The wily Proteus-heart[1] of man?—
What potent hand will e'er unroll
The mantled treachery of his soul!—
O where is he who hath surveyed
The horrors of *our own 'slave trade'?*

"There is an eye that wakes in light,
There is a hand of peerless might;
Which, soon or late, shall yet assail
And rend dissimulation's veil:
Which *will* unfold the masquerade
Which justifies *our own 'slave trade.'*"[2]

---

1 A heart that is, like the Greek god Proteus, changeable.
2 Edwin, "Our Own 'Slave Trade,'" lines 1–24.

CHAPTER III.

THE NEGRO CHASE.

We shall now return to Natchez, where we left Currer in the hands of the Methodist parson. For many years, Natchez has enjoyed a notoriety for the inhumanity and barbarity of its inhabitants, and the cruel deeds perpetrated there, which have not been equalled in any other city in the Southern States. The following advertisements, which we take from a newspaper published in the vicinity, will show how they catch their negroes who believe in the doctrine that "all men are created free."

"NEGRO DOGS.—The undersigned, having bought the entire pack of negro dogs (of the Hay and Allen stock), *he now proposes to catch runaway negroes.* His charges will be three dollars a day for hunting, and fifteen dollars for catching a runaway. He resides three and one half miles north of Livingston, near the lower Jones' Bluff Road.

"WILLIAM GAMBREL."

"Nov. 6, 1845."[1]

"NOTICE.—The subscriber, living on Carroway Lake, on Hoe's Bayou, in Carroll parish, sixteen miles on the road leading from Bayou Mason to Lake Providence, is ready with a pack of dogs to hunt runaway negroes at any time. These dogs are well trained, and are known throughout the parish. Letters addressed to me at Providence will secure immediate attention. My terms are five dollars per day for hunting the trails, whether the negro is caught or not. Where a twelve hours' trail is shown, and the negro not taken, no charge is made. For taking a negro, twenty-five dollars, and no charge made for hunting.

"JAMES W. HALL."

"Nov. 26, 1847."[2]

These dogs will attack a negro at their master's bidding and cling to him as the bull-dog will cling to a beast. Many are the speculations, as to whether the negro will be secured alive or dead, when these dogs once get on his track. A slave hunt took

---

1 *"NEGRO DOGS—The undersigned ... Nov. 6, 1845"*: "Negro Dogs"; quoted in Bowditch, *Slavery*, 101.

2 *"NOTICE.—The subscriber ... Nov. 26, 1847"*: "Notice"; quoted in Bowditch 101.

place near Natchez, a few days after Currer's arrival, which was calculated to give her no favourable opinion of the people. Two slaves had run off owing to severe punishment. The dogs were put upon their trail. The slaves went into the swamps, with the hope that the dogs when put on their scent would be unable to follow them through the water. The dogs soon took to the swamp, which lies between the highlands, which was now covered with water, waist deep: here these faithful animals, *swimming* nearly all the time, followed the zigzag course, the tortuous twistings and windings of these two fugitives, who, it was afterwards discovered, were lost; sometimes scenting the tree wherein they had found a temporary refuge from the mud and water; at other places where the deep mud had pulled off a shoe, and they had not taken time to put it on again. For two hours and a half, for four or five miles, did men and dogs wade through this bushy, dismal swamp, surrounded with grim-visaged alligators, who seemed to look on with jealous eye at this encroachment of their hereditary domain; now losing the trail—then slowly and dubiously taking it off again, until they triumphantly threaded it out, bringing them back to the river, where it was found that the negroes had crossed their own trail, near the place of starting. In the meantime a heavy shower had taken place, putting out the trail. The negroes were now at least four miles ahead.

It is well known to hunters that it requires the keenest scent and best blood to overcome such obstacles, and yet these persevering and sagacious animals conquered every difficulty. The slaves now made a straight course for the Baton Rouge and Bayou Sara road, about four miles distant.

Feeling hungry now, after their morning walk, and perhaps thirsty, too, they went about half a mile off the road, and ate a good, hearty, substantial breakfast. Negroes must eat, as well as other people, but the dogs will tell on them. Here, for a moment, the dogs are at fault, but soon unravel the mystery, and bring them back to the road again; and now what before was wonderful, becomes almost a miracle. Here, in this common highway—the thoroughfare for the whole country around—through mud and through mire, meeting waggons and teams, and different solitary wayfarers, and, what above all is most astonishing, actually running through a gang of negroes, their favourite game, who were working on the road, they pursue the track of the two negroes; they even ran for eight miles to the very edge of the plain—the slaves near them for the last mile. At first they would fain believe it some hunter chasing deer. Nearer and nearer the whimpering pack presses on; the delusion begins to dispel; all at once the truth flashes upon them like a glare of light; their hair stands on end; 'tis Tabor with his dogs. The scent becomes warmer and warmer. What was an irregular cry, now deepens into one ceaseless roar, as the relentless pack rolls on after its human prey. It puts one in mind of Actæon[1] and his dogs. They grow desperate and leave the road, in the vain hope of shaking them off. Vain hope, indeed! The momentary cessation only adds new zest to the chase. The cry grows louder and louder; the yelp grows short and quick, sure indication that the game is at hand. It is a perfect rush upon the part of the hunters, while the negroes call upon their weary and jaded limbs to do their best, but they falter and stagger beneath them. The breath of the hounds is almost upon their very heels, and yet they have a vain hope of escaping these sagacious animals. They can run no longer; the dogs are upon them; they hastily attempt to climb a tree, and as the last one is nearly out of reach, the catch-dog seizes him by the leg, and brings him to the ground; he sings out lustily and the dogs are called off.[2] After this man was secured, the one in the tree was ordered to come down; this, however, he refused to do, but a gun being pointed at him, soon caused him to change his mind. On reaching the ground, the fugitive made one more bound, and the chase again commenced. But it was of no use to run and he soon yielded. While being tied, he committed an unpardonable offence: he resisted, and for that he must be made an example on their arrival home. A mob was collected together, and a Lynch court was held, to determine what was best to be done with the negro who had had the impudence to raise his hand against a white man. The Lynch court decided that the negro should be burnt at the stake. A Natchez newspaper, the *Free Trader*, giving an account of it says,

"The body was taken and chained to a tree immediately on the banks of the Mississippi, on what is called Union Point. Faggots were then collected and piled around him, to which he appeared quite indifferent. When the work was completed, he was asked what he had to say. He then warned all to take example by him, and asked the prayers of all around; he then called for a drink of water, which was handed to him; he drank

---

1 In Greek mythology, a hunter who was turned into a stag and killed by his own hounds.

2 "*The dogs soon took to the swamp, which lies between ... are called off*": "Hunting Robbers with Bloodhounds," 1.

it, and said, 'Now set fire—I am ready to go in peace!' The torches were lighted, and placed in the pile, which soon ignited. He watched unmoved the curling flame that grew, until it began to entwine itself around and feed upon his body; then he sent forth cries of agony painful to the ear, begging some one to blow his brains out; at the same time surging with almost superhuman strength, until the staple with which the chain was fastened to the tree (not being well secured) drew out, and he leaped from the burning pile. At that moment the sharp ringing of several rifles was heard: the body of the negro fell a corpse on the ground. He was picked up by some two or three, and again thrown into the fire, and consumed, not a vestige remaining to show that such a being ever existed."[1]

Nearly 4,000 slaves were collected from the plantations in the neighbourhood to witness this scene. Numerous speeches were made by the magistrates and ministers of religion to the large concourse of slaves, warning them, and telling them that the same fate awaited them, if they should prove rebellious to their owners. There are hundreds of negroes who run away and live in the woods. Some take refuge in the swamps, because they are less frequented by human beings. A Natchez newspaper gave the following account of the hiding-place of a slave who had been captured:—

"A runaway's den was discovered on Sunday, near the Washington Spring, in a little patch of woods, where it had been for several months so artfully concealed under ground, that it was detected only by accident, though in sight of two or three houses, and near the road and fields where there has been constant daily passing. The entrance was concealed by a pile of pine straw, representing a hog-bed, which being removed, discovered a trap-door and steps that led to a room about six feet square, comfortably ceiled with plank, containing a small fire place, the flue of which was ingeniously conducted above ground and concealed by the straw. The inmates took the alarm, and made their escape; but Mr. Adams and his excellent dogs being put upon the trail, soon run down and secured one of them, which proved to be a negro-fellow who had been out about a year. He stated

1   "The body was taken and chained to a tree ... being ever existed":
    "Horrible Murders by Negroes," 2.

that the other occupant was a woman, who had been a runaway a still longer time. In the den was found a quantity of meal, bacon, corn, potatoes, &c. and various cooking utensils and wearing apparel."—*Vicksburgh Sentinel*, Dec. 6th, 1838.[1]

Currer was one of those who witnessed the execution of the slave at the stake, and it gave her no very exalted opinion of the people of the cotton growing district.

CHAPTER IV.

THE QUADROON'S HOME.

"How sweetly on the hill side sleeps
The sunlight with its quickening rays!
The verdant trees that crown the steeps,
Grow greener in its quivering blaze."[2]

About three miles from Richmond is a pleasant plain, with here and there a beautiful cottage surrounded by trees so as scarcely to be seen. Among them was one far retired from the public roads, and almost hidden among the trees. It was a perfect model of rural beauty. The piazzas that surrounded it were covered with clematis and passion flower. The pride of China mixed its oriental looking foliage with the majestic magnolia, and the air was redolent with the fragrance of flowers, peeping out of every nook and nodding upon you with a most unexpected welcome. The tasteful hand of art had not learned to imitate the lavish beauty and harmonious disorder of nature, but they lived together in loving amity, and spoke in accordant tones. The gateway rose in a gothic arch, with graceful tracery in iron work, surmounted by a cross, round which fluttered and played the mountain fringe, that lightest and most fragile of vines.[3] This cottage was hired by Horatio Green for Clotel, and the quadroon girl soon found herself in her new home.

---

1 "*A runaway's den was discovered on Sunday ... wearing apparel*": "Macon," 2; quoted in Bowditch, *Slavery*, 103.

2 William H. Burleigh, "A Summer Morning in the Country," lines 1–4.

3 "*Among them was one far retired ... vines*": Lydia Maria Child, "The Quadroons," 115–16. Child (1802–80) was an abolitionist, activist, and novelist.

The tenderness of Clotel's conscience, together with the care her mother had with her and the high value she placed upon virtue, required an outward marriage; though she well knew that a union with her proscribed race was unrecognised by law, and therefore the ceremony would give her no legal hold on Horatio's constancy. But her high poetic nature regarded reality rather than the semblance of things; and when he playfully asked how she could keep him if he wished to run away, she replied, "If the mutual love we have for each other, and the dictates of your own conscience do not cause you to remain my husband, and your affections fall from me, I would not, if I could, hold you by a single fetter." It was indeed a marriage sanctioned by heaven, although unrecognised on earth.[1] There the young couple lived secluded from the world, and passed their time as happily as circumstances would permit. It was Clotel's wish that Horatio should purchase her mother and sister, but the young man pleaded that he was unable, owing to the fact that he had not come into possession of his share of property, yet he promised that when he did, he would seek them out and purchase them. Their first-born was named Mary, and her complexion was still lighter than her mother. Indeed she was not darker than other white children. As the child grew older, it more and more resembled its mother. The iris of her large dark eye had the melting mezzotinto,[2] which remains the last vestige of African ancestry, and gives that plaintive expression, so often observed, and so appropriate to that docile and injured race.[3] Clotel was still happier after the birth of her dear child; for Horatio, as might have been expected, was often absent day and night with his friends in the city, and the edicts of society had built up a wall of separation between the quadroon and them.[4] Happy as Clotel was in Horatio's love, and surrounded by an outward environment of beauty, so well adapted to her poetic spirit, she felt these incidents with inexpressible pain. For herself she cared but

---

1 "*The tenderness of Clotel's conscience ... unrecognised on earth*": Child, "The Quadroons," 117–18.

2 Rich and deep tone. From mezzotint, a printmaking process that produces mid-tones between black and white.

3 "*The iris of her large dark eye ... injured race*": Child, "The Quadroons," 118–19.

4 "*the edicts of society had built ... wall of separation*": Child, "The Quadroons," 116.

little; for she had found a sheltered home in Horatio's heart, which the world might ridicule, but had no power to profane. But when she looked at her beloved Mary, and reflected upon the unavoidable and dangerous position which the tyranny of society had awarded her, her soul was filled with anguish. The rare loveliness of the child increased daily, and was evidently ripening into most marvellous beauty. The father seemed to rejoice in it with unmingled pride; but in the deep tenderness of the mother's eye, there was an indwelling sadness that spoke of anxious thoughts and fearful foreboding. Clotel now urged Horatio to remove to France or England, where both her and her child would be free, and where colour was not a crime. This request excited but little opposition, and was so attractive to his imagination, that he might have overcome all intervening obstacles, had not "a change come over the spirit of his dreams." He still loved Clotel; but he was now becoming engaged in political and other affairs which kept him oftener and longer from the young mother; and ambition to become a statesman was slowly gaining the ascendancy over him.[1]

Among those on whom Horatio's political success most depended was a very popular and wealthy man, who had an only daughter. His visits to the house were at first purely of a political nature; but the young lady was pleasing, and he fancied he discovered in her a sort of timid preference for himself. This excited his vanity, and awakened thoughts of the great worldly advantages connected with a union. Reminiscences of his first love kept these vague ideas in check for several months; for with it was associated the idea of restraint. Moreover, Gertrude, though inferior in beauty, was yet a pretty contrast to her rival. Her light hair fell in silken ringlets down her shoulders, her blue eyes were gentle though inexpressive, and her healthy cheeks were like opening rosebuds. He had already become accustomed to the dangerous experiment of resisting his own inward convictions; and this new impulse to ambition, combined with the strong temptation of variety in love, met the ardent young man weakened in moral principle, and unfettered by laws of the land. The change wrought upon him was soon noticed by Clotel.[2]

---

1 "*Happy as Clotel was in Horatio's ... ascendancy over him*": Child, "The Quadroons," 119–20.

2 "*Among those on whom Horatio's political success ... noticed by Clotel*": Child, "The Quadroons," 121–23.

CHAPTER V.

THE SLAVE MARKET.

"What! mothers from their children riven!
What! God's own image bought and sold!
Americans to market driven,
And barter'd as the brute for gold."—*Whittier.*[1]

Not far from Canal-street, in the city of New Orleans, stands a large two story flat building surrounded by a stone wall twelve feet high, the top of which is covered with bits of glass, and so constructed as to prevent even the possibility of any one's passing over it without sustaining great injury. Many of the rooms resemble cells in a prison. In a small room near the "office" are to be seen any number of iron collars, hobbles, handcuffs, thumbscrews, cowhides, whips, chains, gags, and yokes. A back yard inclosed by a high wall looks something like the playground attached to one of our large New England schools, and in which are rows of benches and swings. Attached to the back premises is a good-sized kitchen, where two old negresses are at work, stewing, boiling, and baking, and occasionally wiping the sweat from their furrowed and swarthy brows.

The slave-trader Walker, on his arrival in New Orleans, took up his quarters at this slave pen with his gang of human cattle; and the morning after, at ten o'clock, they were exhibited for sale. There, first of all, was the beautiful Althesa, whose pale countenance and dejected look told how many sad hours she had passed since parting with her mother at Natchez. There was a poor woman who had been separated from her husband and five children. Another woman, whose looks and manner were expressive of deep anguish, sat by her side.[2] There, too, was "Uncle Geemes," with his whiskers off, his face shaved clean, and the grey hair plucked out, and ready to be sold for ten years younger than he was. Toby was also there, with his face shaved and greased, ready for inspection. The examination commenced, and was carried on in a manner calculated to shock the feelings of any one not devoid of the milk of human kindness. "What are you wiping your eyes for?" inquired a fat, red-faced man, with a white hat set on one side of his head, and a cigar in his mouth, of a woman who sat on one of the stools. "I s'pose I have been crying."

---

1   John Greenleaf Whittier, "Our Countrymen in Chains," lines 21–24.
2   "*Another woman, whose looks and manner … by her side*": John Greenleaf Whittier, "The Great Slave Market," 120.

"Why do you cry?" "Because I have left my man behind." "Oh, if I buy you I will furnish you with a better man than you left. I have lots of young bucks on my farm." "I don't want, and will never have, any other man," replied the woman. "What's your name?" asked a man in a straw hat of a tall negro man, who stood with his arms folded across his breast, and leaning against the wall. "My name is Aaron, sir." "How old are you?" "Twenty-five." "Where were you raised?" "In old Virginny, sir." "How many men have owned you?" "Four." "Do you enjoy good health?" "Yes, sir." "How long did you live with your first owner?" "Twenty years." "Did you ever run away?" "No, sir." "Did you ever strike your master." "No, sir." "Were you ever whipped much?" "No, sir, I s'pose I did not deserve it." "How long did you live with your second master?" "Ten years, sir." "Have you a good appetite?" "Yes, sir." "Can you eat your allowance?" "Yes, sir, when I can get it." "What were you employed at in Virginia?" "I worked in de terbacar feel." "In the tobacco field?" "Yes, sir." "How old did you say you were?" "I will be twenty-five if I live to see next sweet potater-digging time." "I am a cotton planter, and if I buy you, you will have to work in the cotton field. My men pick one hundred and fifty pounds a day, and the women one hundred and forty, and those who fail to pick their task receive five stripes from the cat for each pound that is wanting. Now, do you think you could keep up with the rest of the hands?" "I don't know, sir, I 'spec I'd have to." "How long did you live with your third master?" "Three years, sir." "Why, this makes you thirty-three, I thought you told me you was only twenty-five?" Aaron now looked first at the planter, then at the trader, and seemed perfectly bewildered. He had forgotten the lesson given him by Pompey as to his age, and the planter's circuitous talk (doubtless to find out the slave's real age) had the negro off his guard. "I must see your back, so as to know how much you have been whipped, before I think of buying," said the planter. Pompey, who had been standing by during the examination, thought that his services were now required, and stepping forward with a degree of officiousness, said to Aaron, "Don't you hear de gentman tell you he want to zamon your limbs. Come, unharness yeself, old boy, an don't be standing dar." Aaron was soon examined and pronounced "sound;" yet the conflicting statement about the age was not satisfactory.

Fortunate for Althesa she was spared the pain of undergoing such an examination, Mr. Crawford, a teller in one of the banks, had just been married, and wanted a maid-servant for his wife; and passing through the market in the early part of the day, was pleased with the young slave's appearance and purchased her, and in his dwelling the quadroon found a much better home than often falls to the lot of a slave sold in the New Orleans market. The heart-rending and cruel traffic in slaves which has been so often described, is not confined to any particular class of persons. No one forfeits his or her character or standing in society, by buying or selling slaves; or even raising slaves for the market. The precise number of slaves carried from the slave-raising to the slave-consuming states, we have no means of knowing. But it must be very great, as more than forty thousand were sold and taken out of the state of Virginia in one year. Known to God only is the amount of human agony and suffering which sends its cry from the slave markets and negro pens, unheard and unheeded by man, up to his ear; mothers weeping for their children, breaking the night-silence with the shrieks of their breaking hearts.[1] From some you will hear the burst of bitter lamentation, while from others the loud hysteric laugh, denoting still deeper agony.[2] Most of them leave the market for cotton or rice plantations,

> "Where the slave-whip ceaseless swings,
> Where the noisome insect stings,
> Where the fever demon strews
> Poison with the falling dews,
> Where the sickly sunbeams glare
> Through the hot and misty air."[3]

CHAPTER VI.

THE RELIGIOUS TEACHER.

> "What! preach and enslave men?
> Give thanks—and rob thy own afflicted poor?
> Talk of thy glorious liberty, and then
> Bolt hard the captive's door?"—*Whittier.*[4]

The Rev. John Peck was a native of the state of Connecticut, where he was educated for the ministry, in the Methodist per-

---

1 *"Known to God only is the amount ... their breaking hearts"*: Whittier, "Great Slave Market," 120.
2 *"From some you will hear the burst ... still deeper agony"*: "Views of the Benevolent Society of Alexandria," 2.
3 Whittier, "The Farewell of a Virginia Slave Mother to Her Daughters," lines 3–8.
4 John Greenleaf Whittier, "Clerical Oppressors," lines 5–8.

suasion. His father was a strict follower of John Wesley, and spared no pains in his son's education, with the hope that he would one. day be as renowned as the great leader of his sect.[1] John had scarcely finished his education at New Haven, when he was invited by an uncle, then on a visit to his father, to spend a few months at Natchez in the state of Mississippi. Young Peck accepted his uncle's invitation, and accompanied him to the South. Few young men, and especially clergymen, going fresh from a college to the South, but are looked upon as geniuses in a small way, and who are not invited to all the parties in the neighbourhood. Mr. Peck was not an exception to this rule. The society into which he was thrown on his arrival at Natchez was too brilliant for him not to be captivated by it; and, as might have been expected, he succeeded in captivating a plantation with seventy slaves, if not the heart of the lady to whom it belonged. Added to this, he became a popular preacher, had a large congregation with a snug salary. Like other planters, Mr. Peck confided the care of his farm to Ned Huckelby, an overseer of high reputation in his way. The Poplar Farm, as it was called, was situated in a beautiful valley nine miles from Natchez, and near the river Mississippi. The once unshorn face of nature had given way, and now the farm blossomed with a splendid harvest, the neat cottage stood in a grove where Lombardy poplars lift their tufted tops almost to prop the skies; the willow, locust, and horse-chestnut spread their branches, and flowers never cease to blossom.[2] This was the parson's country house, where the family spent only two months during the year.

The town residence was a fine villa, seated upon the brow of a hill at the edge of the city. It was in the kitchen of this house that Currer found her new home. Mr. Peck was, every inch of him, a democrat, and early resolved that his "people," as he called his slaves, should be well fed and not overworked, and therefore laid down the law and gospel to the overseer as well as the slaves.

"It is my wish," said he to Mr. Carlton, an old school-fellow, who was spending a few days with him, "it is my wish that a new system be adopted on the plantations in this estate. I believe that

---

1 John Wesley (1703–91) was the founder of Methodism and an opponent of slavery.

2 *The once unshorn face of nature ... a splendid harvest*": "Prospects of Slavery," 65; "*where Lombardy poplars lift their tufted ... cease to blossom*": [Helen de Kroyft], "Beautiful Letter," 4.

the sons of Ham[1] should have the gospel, and I intend that my negroes shall. The gospel is calculated to make mankind better, and none should be without it." "What say you," replied Carlton, "about the right of man to his liberty?" "Now, Carlton, you have begun again to harp about man's rights; I really wish you could see this matter as I do. I have searched in vain for any authority for man's natural rights; if he had any, they existed before the fall. That is, Adam and Eve may have had some rights which God gave them, and which modern philosophy, in its pretended reverence for the name of God, prefers to call natural rights. I can imagine they had the right to eat of the fruit of the trees of the garden; they were restricted even in this by the prohibition of one. As far as I know without positive assertion, their liberty of action was confined to the garden. These were not 'inalienable rights,' however, for they forfeited both them and life with the first act of disobedience. Had they, after this, any rights? We cannot imagine them; they were condemned beings; they could have no rights, but by Christ's gift as king. These are the only rights man can have as an independent isolated being, if we choose to consider him in this impossible position, in which so many theorists have placed him. If he had no rights, he could suffer no wrongs. Rights and wrongs are therefore necessarily the creatures of society, such as man would establish himself in his gregarious state. They are, in this state, both artificial and voluntary. Though man has no rights, as thus considered, undoubtedly he has the power, by such arbitrary rules of right and wrong as his necessity enforces."[2] "I regret I cannot see eye to eye with you," said Carlton. "I am a disciple of Rousseau,[3] and have for years made the rights of man my study; and I must confess to you that I can see no difference between white men and black men as it regards liberty." "Now, my dear Carlton, would you really have the negroes enjoy the same rights with ourselves?" "I would, most certainly. Look at our great Declaration of Independence; look even at the con-

---

1   In retribution for his son Ham's transgression, Noah curses Ham's son Canaan, saying "a servant of servants shall he be unto his brethren" (Genesis 9:25). The story was frequently used as a justification for the enslavement of black people, who were thought—without biblical justification—to be descended from Ham.

2   "*I have searched in vain for any authority ... his necessity enforces*": [William F. Hutson], "The *History of the Girondists*," 401–02.

3   Jean-Jacques Rousseau (1712–78) was an Enlightenment writer and philosopher.

stitution of our own Connecticut, and see what is said in these about liberty." "I regard all this talk about rights as mere humbug. The Bible is older than the Declaration of Independence, and there I take my stand. The Bible furnishes to us the armour of proof, weapons of heavenly temper and mould, whereby we can maintain our ground against all attacks. But this is true only when we obey its directions, as well as employ its sanctions. Our rights are there established, but it is always in connection with our duties. If we neglect the one we cannot make good the other. Our domestic institutions can be maintained against the world, if we but allow Christianity to throw its broad shield over them. But if we so act as to array the Bible against our social economy, they must fall. Nothing ever yet stood long against Christianity. Those who say that religious instruction is inconsistent with our peculiar civil polity, are the worst enemies of that polity. They would drive religious men from its defence. Sooner or later, if those views prevail, they will separate the religious portion of our community from the rest, and thus divided we shall become an easy prey.[1] Why, is it not better that Christian men should hold slaves than unbelievers? We know how to value the bread of life, and will not keep it from our slaves."

"Well, every one to his own way of thinking," said Carlton, as he changed his position. "I confess," added he, "that I am no great admirer of either the Bible or slavery. My heart is my guide: my conscience is my Bible. I wish for nothing further to satisfy me of my duty to man. If I act rightly to mankind, I shall fear nothing." Carlton had drunk too deeply of the bitter waters of infidelity, and had spent too many hours over the writings of Rousseau, Voltaire, and Thomas Paine,[2] to place that appreciation upon the Bible and its teachings that it demands. During this conversation there was another person in the room, seated by the window, who, although at work upon a fine piece of lace, paid every attention to what was said. This was Georgiana, the only daughter of the parson. She had just returned from Connecticut, where she had finished her education. She had had the opportunity of contrasting the spirit of Christianity and liberty in New England with that of slavery in her native state,

---

1 *"The Bible furnishes to us the armour of proof ... an easy prey"*: [James Thornwell], "The Religious Instruction of the Black Population," 108.
2 Voltaire (1694–1778) and Thomas Paine (1737–1809) were, like Rousseau, associated with the rationalism and political radicalism of the Enlightenment.

and had learned to feel deeply for the injured negro. Georgiana was in her nineteenth year, and had been much benefited by a residence of five years at the North. Her form was tall and graceful; her features regular and well defined; and her complexion was illuminated by the freshness of youth, beauty, and health.[1] The daughter differed from both the father and his visitor upon the subject which they had been discussing, and as soon as an opportunity offered, she gave it as her opinion, that the Bible was both the bulwark of Christianity and of liberty. With a smile she said, "Of course, papa will overlook my differing from him, for although I am a native of the South, I am by education and sympathy a Northerner." Mr. Peck laughed and appeared pleased, rather than otherwise, at the manner in which his daughter had expressed herself.

From this Georgiana took courage and said, "We must try the character of slavery, and our duty in regard to it, as we should try any other question of character and duty. To judge justly of the character of anything, we must know what it does. That which is good does good, and that which is evil does evil. And as to duty, God's designs indicate his claims. That which accomplishes the manifest design of God is right; that which counteracts it, wrong. Whatever, in its proper tendency and general effect, produces, secures, or extends human welfare, is according to the will of God, and is good; and our duty is to favour and promote, according to our power, that which God favours and promotes by the general law of his providence. On the other hand, whatever in its proper tendency and general effect destroys, abridges, or renders insecure, human welfare, is opposed to God's will, and is evil. And as whatever accords with the will of God, in any manifestation of it should be done and persisted in, so whatever opposes that will should not be done, and if done, should be abandoned. Can that then be right, be well doing—can that obey God's behest, which makes a man a slave? which dooms him and all his posterity, in limitless generations, to bondage, to unrequited toil through life?[2] 'Thou shalt love thy neighbour as thyself.'[3] This single passage of Scripture should cause us to have respect to the rights of the slave. True Christian love is of an enlarged, disinterested nature. It loves all who love the Lord Jesus Christ in sincerity, without regard

---

1 "*Her form was tall and graceful ... beauty, and health*": "Charlotte Corday," 275.

2 "*We must try the character of slavery ... toil through life*": Allen, *Resistance to Slavery*, 13.

3 Matthew 22:39.

to colour or condition."[1] "Georgiana, my dear, you are an abolitionist; your talk is fanaticism," said Mr. Peck in rather a sharp tone; but the subdued look of the girl, and the presence of Carlton, caused the father to soften his language. Mr. Peck having lost his wife by consumption, and Georgiana being his only child, he loved her too dearly to say more, even if he felt displeased. A silence followed this exhortation from the young Christian. But her remarks had done a noble work. The father's heart was touched; and the sceptic, for the first time, was viewing Christianity in its true light.

"I think I must go out to your farm," said Carlton, as if to break the silence. "I shall be pleased to have you go," returned Mr. Peck. "I am sorry I can't go myself, but Huckelby will show you every attention; and I feel confident that when you return to Connecticut, you will do me the justice to say, that I am one who looks after my people, in a moral, social, and religious point of view." "Well, what do you say to my spending next Sunday there?" "Why, I think that a good move; you will then meet with Snyder, our missionary." "Oh, you have missionaries in these parts, have you?" "Yes," replied Mr. Peck; "Snyder is from New York, and is our missionary to the poor, and preaches to our 'people' on Sunday; you will no doubt like him; he is a capital fellow." "Then I shall go," said Carlton, "but only wish I had company." This last remark was intended for Miss Peck, for whom he had the highest admiration.

It was on a warm Sunday morning, in the month of May, that Miles Carlton found himself seated beneath a fine old apple tree, whose thick leaves entirely shaded the ground for some distance round. Under similar trees and near by, were gathered together all the "people" belonging to the plantation. Hontz Snyder was a man of about forty years of age, exceedingly low in stature, but of a large frame. He had been brought up in the Mohawk Valley, in the state of New York, and claimed relationship with the oldest Dutch families in that vicinity. He had once been a sailor, and had all the roughness of character that a sea-faring man might expect to possess; together with the half-Yankee, half-German peculiarities of the people of the Mohawk Valley. It was nearly eleven o'clock when a one-horse waggon drove up in haste, and the low squatty preacher got out and took his place at the foot of one of the trees, where a sort of rough board table was placed, and took his books from his pocket and commenced.

---

1 *"True Christian love is of an enlarged ... colour or condition"*: Thomas Reade, *Christian Retirement* (1825); quoted in *Gleanings from Pious Authors*, 50.

"As it is rather late," said he, "we will leave the singing and praying for the last, and take our text, and commence immediately. I shall base my remarks on the following passage of Scripture, and hope to have that attention which is due to the cause of God:—'All things whatsoever ye would that men should do unto you, do ye even so unto them;' that is, do by all mankind just as you would desire they should do by you, if you were in their place and they in yours.

"Now, to suit this rule to your particular circumstances, suppose you were masters and mistresses, and had servants under you, would you not desire that your servants should do their business faithfully and honestly, as well when your back was turned as while you were looking over them? Would you not expect that they should take notice of what you said to them? that they should behave themselves with respect towards you and yours, and be as careful of every thing belonging to you as you would be yourselves? You are servants: do, therefore, as you would wish to be done by, and you will be both good servants to your masters and good servants to God, who requires this of you, and will reward you well for it, if you do it for the sake of conscience, in obedience to his commands.[1]

"You are not to be eye-servants. Now, eye-servants are such as will work hard, and seem mighty diligent, while they think anybody is taking notice of them; but, when their masters' and mistresses' backs are turned they are idle, and neglect their business. I am afraid there are a great many such eye-servants among you, and that you do not consider how great a sin it is to be so, and how severely God will punish you for it. You may easily deceive your owners, and make them have an opinion of you that you do not deserve, and get the praise of men by it; but remember that you cannot deceive Almighty God, who sees your wickedness and deceit, and will punish you accordingly. For the rule is, that you must obey your masters in all things, and do the work they set you about with fear and trembling, in singleness of heart as unto Christ; not with eye-service, as men-pleasers, but as the servants of Christ, doing the will of God from the heart; with good-will doing service as to the Lord, and not as to men.[2]

"Take care that you do not fret or murmur, grumble or repine at your condition; for this will not only make your life uneasy, but will

---

1 *"All things whatsoever ye would ... to his commands"*: William Meade, *Sermons Addressed to Masters and Servants* (1743); quoted in Bowditch, *Slavery*, 41–42. Meade (1789–1862) was an Episcopalian bishop.

2 *"You are not to be eye-servants ... as to men"*: Meade, *Sermons*; quoted in Bowditch, *Slavery*, 35.

greatly offend Almighty God. Consider that it is not yourselves, it is not the people that you belong to, it is not the men who have brought you to it, but *it is the will of God who hath by his providence made you servants, because, no doubt, he knew that condition would be best for you in this world, and help you the better towards heaven, if you would but do your duty in it.* So that any discontent at your not being free, or rich, or great, as you see some others, is quarrelling with your heavenly Master, and finding fault with God himself, who hath made you what you are, and hath promised you as large a share in the kingdom of heaven as the greatest man alive, if you will but behave yourself aright, and do the business he hath set you about in this world honestly and cheerfully. Riches and power have proved the ruin of many an unhappy soul, by drawing away the heart and affections from God, and fixing them on mean and sinful enjoyments; so that, when God, who knows our hearts better than we know them ourselves, sees that they would be hurtful to us, and therefore keeps them from us, it is the greatest mercy and kindness he could show us.

"You may perhaps fancy that, if you had riches and freedom, you could do your duty to God and man with greater pleasure than you can now. But pray consider that, if you can but save your souls through the mercy of God, you will have spent your time to the best of purposes in this world; and he that at last can get to heaven has performed a noble journey, let the road be ever so rugged and difficult. Besides, you really have a great advantage over most white people, who have not only the care of their daily labour upon their hands, but the care of looking forward and providing necessaries for to-morrow and next day, and of clothing and bringing up their children, and of getting food and raiment for as many of you as belong to their families, which often puts them to great difficulties, and distracts their minds so as to break their rest, and take off their thoughts from the affairs of another world. Whereas you are quite eased from all these cares, and have nothing but your daily labour to look after, and, when that is done, take your needful rest. Neither is it necessary for you to think of laying up anything against old age, as white people are obliged to do; for the laws of the country have provided that you shall not be turned off when you are past labour, but shall be maintained, while you live, by those you belong to, whether you are able to work or not.[1]

---

1 *"Take care that you do not fret ... work or not"*: Meade, *Sermons*; quoted in Bowditch, *Slavery*, 44–45.

"There is only one circumstance which may appear grievous, that I shall now take notice of, and that is correction.

"Now, when correction is given you, you either deserve it, or you do not deserve it. But whether you really deserve it or not, it is your duty, and Almighty God requires that you bear it patiently. You may perhaps think that this is hard doctrine; but, if you consider it right, you must needs think otherwise of it. Suppose, then, that you deserve correction, you cannot but say that it is just and right you should meet with it. Suppose you do not, or at least you do not deserve so much, or so severe a correction, for the fault you have committed, you perhaps have escaped a great many more, and are at last paid for all. Or suppose you are quite innocent of what is laid to your charge, and suffer wrongfully in that particular thing, is it not possible you may have done some other bad thing which was never discovered, and that Almighty God who saw you doing it would not let you escape without punishment one time or another? And ought you not, in such a case, to give glory to him, and be thankful that he would rather punish you in this life for your wickedness than destroy your souls for it in the next life? But suppose even this was not the case (a case hardly to be imagined), and that you have by no means, known or unknown, deserved the correction you suffered, there is this great comfort in it, that, if you bear it patiently, and leave your cause in the hands of God, he will reward you for it in heaven, and the punishment you suffer unjustly here shall turn to your exceeding great glory hereafter.[1]

"Lastly, you should serve your masters faithfully, because of their goodness to you. See to what trouble they have been on your account. Your fathers were poor ignorant and barbarous creatures in Africa, and the whites fitted out ships at great trouble and expense and brought you from that benighted land to Christian America, where you can sit under your own vine and fig tree and no one molest or make you afraid. Oh, my dear black brothers and sisters, you are indeed a fortunate and a blessed people. Your masters have many troubles that you know nothing about. If the banks break, your masters are sure to lose something. If the crops turn out poor, they lose by it. If one of you die, your master loses what he paid for you, while you lose nothing. Now let me exhort you once more to be faithful."

Often during the delivery of the sermon did Snyder cast an anxious look in the direction where Carlton was seated; no doubt

---

1 *"There is only one circumstance ... great glory hereafter"*: Meade, *Sermons*; quoted in Bowditch, *Slavery*, 47. The remainder of Snyder's sermon was apparently composed by Brown.

to see if he had found favour with the stranger. Huckelby, the overseer, was also there, seated near Carlton. With all Snyder's gesticulations, sonorous voice, and occasionally bringing his fist down upon the table with the force of a sledge hammer, he could not succeed in keeping the negroes all interested: four or five were fast asleep, leaning against the trees; as many more were nodding, while not a few were stealthily cracking and eating hazelnuts. "Uncle Simon, you may strike up a hymn," said the preacher as he closed his Bible. A moment more, and the whole company (Carlton excepted) had joined in the well known hymn, commencing with

"When I can read my title clear
To mansions in the sky."[1]

After the singing, Sandy closed with prayer, and the following questions and answers read, and the meeting was brought to a close.

"*Q.* What command has God given to servants concerning obedience to their masters?—*A.* 'Servants, obey in all things your masters according to the flesh, not with eye-service as men-pleasers, but in singleness of heart, fearing God.'

"*Q.* What does God mean by masters according to the flesh?—*A.* 'Masters in this world.'

"*Q.* What are servants to count their masters worthy of?—*A.* 'All honour.'

"*Q.* How are they to do the service of their masters?—*A.* '*With good will*, doing service as unto the Lord, and not unto men.'

"*Q.* How are they to try to please their masters?—*A.* 'Please him well in all things, not answering again.'

"*Q.* Is a servant who is an eye-servant to his earthly master an eye-servant to his heavenly master?—*A.* 'Yes.'

"*Q.* Is it right in a servant, when commanded to do any thing, to be sullen and slow, and answer his master again?—*A.* 'No.'

"*Q.* If the servant professes to be a Christian, ought he not to be *as a Christian servant*, an example to all other servants of love and obedience to his master?—*A.* 'Yes.'

"*Q.* And, should his master be a Christian also, ought he not on that account specially to love and obey him?—*A.* 'Yes.'

"*Q.* But suppose the master is hard to please, and threatens and punishes more than he ought, what is the servant to do?—*A.* 'Do his best to please him.'

---

1 Isaac Watts, "Hymn 65," lines 1–2.

"*Q.* When the servant suffers *wrongfully* at the hands of his master, and, to please God, takes it patiently, will God reward him for it?—*A.* 'Yes.'

"*Q.* Is it right for the servant to *run away*, or is it right to *harbour* a runaway?—*A.* 'No.'[1]

"*Q.* If a servant runs away, what should be done with him?—*A.* 'He should be caught and brought back.'

"*Q.* When he is brought back, what should be done with him?—*A.* 'Whip him well.'

"*Q.* Why may not the whites be slaves as well as the blacks?—*A.* 'Because the Lord intended the negroes for slaves.'

"*Q.* Are they better calculated for servants than the whites?—*A.* 'Yes, their hands are large, the skin thick and tough, and they can stand the sun better than the whites.'

"*Q.* Why should servants not complain when they are whipped?—*A.* 'Because the Lord has commanded that they should be whipped.'

"*Q.* Where has He commanded it?—*A.* 'He says, He that knoweth his master's will, and doeth it not, shall be beaten with many stripes.'

"*Q.* Then is the master to blame for whipping his servant?—*A.* 'Oh, no! he is only doing his duty as a Christian.'"

Snyder left the ground in company with Carlton and Huckelby, and the three dined together in the overseer's dwelling.

"Well," said Joe, after the three white men were out of hearing, "Marser Snyder bin try hesef today." "Yes," replied Ned; "he want to show de strange gentman how good he can preach." "Dat's a new sermon he gib us to-day," said Sandy. "Dees white fokes is de very dibble," said Dick; "and all dey whole study is to try to fool de black people." "Didn't you like de sermon?" asked Uncle Simon. "No," answered four or five voices. "He rared and pitched enough," continued Uncle Simon.

Now Uncle Simon was himself a preacher, or at least he thought so, and was rather pleased than otherwise, when he heard others spoken of in a disparaging manner. "Uncle Simon can beat dat sermon all to pieces," said Ned, as he was filling

---

1 "*Q. What command has God given ... runaway? A. 'No'*": Charles Colcock Jones, *A Catechism of Scripture Doctrine and Practice* (1837); quoted in Bowditch, *Slavery*, 50. The remainder of the catechism was apparently composed by Brown. Jones (1804–63) was a Presbyterian clergyman, plantation owner, and missionary.

his mouth with hazelnuts. "I got no notion of dees white fokes, no how," returned Aunt Dafney. "Dey all de time tellin' dat de Lord made us for to work for dem, and I don't believe a word of it." "Marser Peck give dat sermon to Snyder, I know," said Uncle Simon. "He jest de one for dat," replied Sandy. "I think de people dat made de Bible was great fools," said Ned. "Why?" asked Uncle Simon. "'Cause dey made such a great big book and put nuttin' in it, but servants obey yer masters." "Oh," replied Uncle Simon, "thars more in de Bible den dat, only Snyder never reads any other part to us; I use to hear it read in Maryland, and thar was more den what Snyder lets us hear." In the overseer's house there was another scene going on, and far different from what we have here described.

CHAPTER VII.

THE POOR WHITES, SOUTH.

"No seeming of logic can ever convince the American people, that thousands of our slave-holding brethren are not excellent, humane, and even Christian men, fearing God, and keeping His commandments."—*Rev. Dr. Joel Parker.*[1]

"You like these parts better than New York," said Carlton to Snyder, as they were sitting down to dinner in the overseer's dwelling. "I can't say that I do," was the reply; "I came here ten years ago as missionary, and Mr. Peck wanted me to stay, and I have remained. I travel among the poor whites during the week, and preach for the niggers on Sunday." "Are there many poor whites in this district?" "Not here, but about thirty miles from here, in the Sand Hill district; they are as ignorant as horses. Why it was no longer than last week I was up there, and really you would not believe it, that people were so poor off. In New England, and, I may say, in all the free states, they have free schools, and everybody gets educated. Not so here. In Connecticut there is only one out of every five hundred above twenty-one years that can neither read nor write. Here there is one out of every eight that can neither read nor write. There is

---

1 Joel Parker (1816–88), "A Discourse Delivered in the Clinton Street Church"; quoted in "Spirit of Colonization," 113. Parker, a Presbyterian minister, was the pastor of Philadelphia's Clinton Street Church.

not a single newspaper taken in five of the counties in this state. Last week I was at Sand Hill for the first time, and I called at a farmhouse. The man was out. It was a low log-hut, and yet it was the best house in that locality. The woman and nine children were there, and the geese, ducks, chickens, pigs, and children were all running about the floor. The woman seemed scared at me when I entered the house. I inquired if I could get a little dinner, and my horse fed. She said, yes, if I would only be good enough to feed him myself, as her 'gal,' as she called her daughter, would be afraid of the horse. When I returned into the house again from the stable, she kept her eyes upon me all the time. At last she said, 'I s'pose you aint never bin in these parts afore?' 'No,' said I. 'Is you gwine to stay here long?' 'Not very long,' I replied. 'On business I s'pose.' 'Yes,' said I, 'I am hunting up the lost sheep of the house of Israel.' 'Oh,' exclaimed she, 'hunting for lost sheep is you? Well, you have a hard time to find 'em here. My husband lost an old ram last week, and he aint found him yet, and he's hunted every day.' 'I am not looking for four-legged sheep,' said I, 'I am hunting for sinners.' 'Ah;' she said, 'then you are a preacher.' 'Yes,' said I. 'You are the first of that sort that's bin in these diggins for many a day.' Turning to her eldest daughter, she said in an excited tone, 'Clar out the pigs and ducks, and sweep up the floor; this is a preacher.' And it was some time before any of the children would come near me; one remained under the bed (which, by the by, was in the same room), all the while I was there. 'Well,' continued the woman, 'I was a tellin' my man only yesterday that I would like once more to go to meetin' before I died, and he said as he should like to do the same. But as you have come, it will save us the trouble of going out of the district.'"[1] "Then you found some of the lost sheep," said Carlton. "Yes," replied Snyder, "I did not find anything else up there. The state makes no provision for educating the poor: they are unable to do it themselves, and they grow up in a state of ignorance and degradation. The men hunt and the women have to go in the fields and labour." "What is the cause of it?" inquired Carlton; "Slavery," answered Snyder, "slavery,—and nothing else. Look at the city of Boston; it pays more taxes for the support of the government than this entire state. The people of Boston do more business than the whole population of Mississippi put together. I was told some very amusing things while at Sand Hill. A farmer there told me a story

---

1 "*Last week I was at Sand Hill ... the district*": loosely based on "Due Respect to a Clergyman," *New Orleans Times-Picayune*, 21 August 1842, 1.

about an old woman, who was very pious herself. She had a husband and three sons, who were sad characters, and she had often prayed for their conversion but to no effect. At last, one day while working in the corn-field, one of her sons was bitten by a rattlesnake. He had scarce reached home before he felt the poison, and in his agony called loudly on his Maker.

"The pious old woman, when she heard this, forgetful of her son's misery, and everything else but the glorious hope of his repentance, fell on her knees, and prayed as follows,—'Oh! Lord, I thank thee, that thou hast at last opened Jimmy's eyes to the error of his ways; and I pray that, in thy Divine mercy, thou wilt send a rattlesnake to bite the old man, and another to bite Tom, and another to bite Harry, for I am certain that nothing but a rattlesnake, or something of the kind, will ever turn them from their sinful ways, they are so hard-headed.'[1] When returning home, and before I got out of the Sand Hill district, I saw a funeral, and thought I would fasten my horse to a post and attend. The coffin was carried in a common horse cart, and followed by fifteen or twenty persons very shabbily dressed, and attended by a man whom I took to be the religious man of the place. After the coffin had been placed near the grave, he spoke as follows,—

> 'Friends and neighbours! you have congregated to see this lump of mortality put into a hole in the ground. You all know the deceased—a worthless, drunken, good-for-nothing vagabond. He lived in disgrace and infamy, and died in wretchedness. You all despised him—you all know his brother Joe, who lives on the hill? He's not a bit better, though he has scrap'd together a little property by cheating his neighbours. His end will be like that of this loathsome creature, whom you will please put into the hole as soon as possible. I wont ask you to drop a tear, but brother Bohow will please raise a hymn while we fill up the grave.'"[2]

"I am rather surprised to hear that any portion of the whites in this state are in so low a condition." "Yet it is true," returned Snyder. "These are very onpleasant facts to be related to ye, Mr. Carlton,"

---

1   "*A farmer there told me a story ... so hard-headed*": loosely based on "A Curious Prayer," *Boston Herald*, 6 May 1853, 1.

2   "*Friends and neighbours! you have congregated ... fill up the grave*": "Curious Funeral Service," 2.

said Huckelby; "but I can bear witness to what Mr. Snyder has told ye." Huckelby was from Maryland, where many of the poor whites are in as sad a condition as the Sand Hillers of Mississippi. He was a tall man, of iron constitution, and could neither read nor write, but was considered one of the best overseers in the country. When about to break a slave in, to do a heavy task, he would make him work by his side all day; and if the new hand kept up with him, he was set down as an able bodied man. Huckelby had neither moral, religious, or political principles, and often boasted that conscience was a matter that never "cost" him a thought. "Mr. Snyder aint told ye half about the folks in these parts;" continued he; "we who comes from more enlightened parts don't know how to put up with 'em down here. I find the people here knows mighty little indeed; in fact, I may say they are univarsaly onedicated. I goes out among none on 'em, 'cause they aint such as I have been used to 'sociate with. When I gits a little richer, so that I can stop work, I tend to go back to Maryland, and spend the rest of my days." "I wonder the negroes don't attempt to get their freedom by physical force." "It aint no use for 'em to try that, for if they do, we puts 'em through by daylight," replied Huckelby. "There are some desperate fellows among the slaves," said Snyder. "Indeed," remarked Carlton. "Oh, yes," replied the preacher. "A case has just taken place near here, where a neighbour of ours, Mr. J. Higgerson, attempted to correct a negro man in his employ, who resisted, drew a knife, and stabbed him (Mr. H.) in several places. Mr. J.C. Hobbs (a Tennessean) ran to his assistance. Mr. Hobbs stooped to pick up a stick to strike the negro, and, while in that position, the negro rushed upon him, and caused his immediate death. The negro then fled to the woods, but was pursued with dogs, and soon overtaken. He had stopped in a swamp to fight the dogs, when the party who were pursuing him came upon him, and commanded him to give up, which he refused to do. He then made several efforts to stab them. Mr. Roberson, one of the party, gave him several blows on the head with a rifle gun; but this, instead of subduing, only increased his desperate revenge. Mr. R. then discharged his gun at the negro, and missing him, the ball struck Mr. Boon in the face, and felled him to the ground. The negro, seeing Mr. Boon prostrated, attempted to rush up and stab him, but was prevented by the timely interference of some one of the party. He was then shot three times with a revolving pistol, and once with a rifle, and after having his throat cut, he still kept the knife firmly grasped in his hand, and tried to cut their legs when they approached to put an end to his life.[1] This chastisement was given because the negro grumbled, and found fault with his master for flogging his wife." "Well, this is a bad state of affairs indeed, and especially the condition of the poor whites," said Carlton. "You see," replied Snyder, "no white man is respectable in these slave states who works for a living. No community can be prosperous, where honest labour is not honoured. No society can be rightly constituted, where the intellect is not fed. Whatever institution reflects discredit on industry, whatever institution forbids the general culture of the understanding, is palpably hostile to individual rights, and to social well-being.[2] Slavery is the incubus that hangs over the Southern States." "Yes," interrupted Huckelby; "them's just my sentiments now, and no mistake. I think that, for the honour of our country, this slavery business should stop. I don't own any, no how, and I would not be an overseer if I wern't paid for it."

CHAPTER VIII.

THE SEPARATION.

"In many ways does the full heart reveal
The presence of the love it would conceal;
But in far more the estranged heart lets know
The absence of the love, which yet it fain would show."[3]

At length the news of the approaching marriage of Horatio met the ear of Clotel. Her head grew dizzy, and her heart fainted within her; but, with a strong effort at composure, she inquired all the particulars, and her pure mind at once took its resolution. Horatio came that evening, and though she would fain have met him as usual, her heart was too full not to throw a deep sadness over her looks and tones. She had never complained of his decreasing tenderness, or of her own lonely hours; but he felt that the mute appeal of her heart-broken looks was more terrible than words. He kissed the hand she offered, and with a countenance almost as sad as her own,

1   *"Mr. J. Higgerson, attempted to correct a negro man ... to his life"*: "Shocking Affair—Desperate Courage of a Slave," 76.
2   *"No community can be prosperous ... social well-being"*: John G. Palfrey, *Papers on the Slave Power*, 53.
3   Samuel Taylor Coleridge, *"Eros aei lalethros etairos,"* quoted in Child, "The Quadroons," 123.

led her to a window in the recess shadowed by a luxuriant passion flower. It was the same seat where they had spent the first evening in this beautiful cottage, consecrated to their first loves. The same calm, clear moonlight looked in through the trellis. The vine then planted had now a luxuriant growth; and many a time had Horatio fondly twined its sacred blossoms with the glossy ringlets of her raven hair. The rush of memory almost overpowered poor Clotel; and Horatio felt too much oppressed and ashamed to break the long deep silence. At length, in words scarcely audible, Clotel said: "Tell me, dear Horatio, are you to be married next week?" He dropped her hand as if a rifle ball had struck him; and it was not until after long hesitation, that he began to make some reply about the necessity of circumstances. Mildly but earnestly the poor girl begged him to spare apologies. It was enough that he no longer loved her, and that they must bid farewell. Trusting to the yielding tenderness of her character, he ventured, in the most soothing accents, to suggest that as he still loved her better than all the world, she would ever be his real wife, and they might see each other frequently. He was not prepared for the storm of indignant emotion his words excited. True, she was his slave; her bones, and sinews had been purchased by his gold, yet she had the heart of a true woman, and hers was a passion too deep and absorbing to admit of partnership, and her spirit was too pure to form a selfish league with crime.

At length this painful interview came to an end. They stood together by the Gothic gate, where they had so often met and parted in the moonlight. Old remembrances melted their souls. "Farewell, dearest Horatio," said Clotel. "Give me a parting kiss." Her voice was choked for utterance, and the tears flowed freely, as she bent her lips toward him. He folded her convulsively in his arms, and imprinted a long impassioned kiss on that mouth, which had never spoken to him but in love and blessing. With efforts like a death-pang she at length raised her head from his heaving bosom, and turning from him with bitter sobs, "It is our last. To meet thus is henceforth crime. God bless you. I would not have you so miserable as I am. Farewell. A last farewell." "The last?" exclaimed he, with a wild shriek. "Oh God, Clotel, do not say that;" and covering his face with his hands, he wept like a child. Recovering from his emotion, he found himself alone. The moon looked down upon him mild, but very sorrowfully; as the Madonna seems to gaze upon her worshipping children, bowed down with consciousness of sin. At that moment he would have given worlds to have disengaged himself from Gertrude, but he had gone so far, that blame, disgrace, and duels with angry relatives would now attend any effort to obtain his freedom. Oh, how the moonlight oppressed him with its friendly sadness! It was like the plaintive eye of his forsaken one, like the music of sorrow echoed from an unseen world. Long and earnestly he gazed at that cottage, where he had so long known earth's purest foretaste of heavenly bliss. Slowly he walked away; then turned again to look on that charmed spot, the nestling-place of his early affections. He caught a glimpse of Clotel, weeping beside a magnolia, which commanded a long view of the path leading to the public road. He would have sprung toward her but she darted from him, and entered the cottage. That graceful figure, weeping in the moonlight, haunted him for years. It stood before his closing eyes, and greeted him with the morning dawn. Poor Gertrude, had she known all, what a dreary lot would hers have been; but fortunately she could not miss the impassioned tenderness she never experienced; and Horatio was the more careful in his kindness, because he was deficient in love.[1] After Clotel had been separated from her mother and sister, she turned her attention to the subject of Christianity, and received that consolation from her Bible that is never denied to the children of God. Although it was against the laws of Virginia, for a slave to be taught to read, Currer had employed an old free negro, who lived near her, to teach her two daughters to read and write. She felt that the step she had taken in resolving never to meet Horatio again would no doubt expose her to his wrath, and probably cause her to be sold, yet her heart was too guileless for her to commit a crime, and therefore she had ten times rather have been sold as a slave than do wrong. Some months after the marriage of Horatio and Gertrude their barouche[2] rolled along a winding road that skirted the forest near Clotel's cottage, when the attention of Gertrude was suddenly attracted by two figures among the trees by the wayside; and touching Horatio's arm, she exclaimed, "Do look at that beautiful child." He turned and saw Clotel and Mary. His lips quivered, and his face became deadly pale. His young wife looked at him intently, but said nothing.[3] In returning home, he took another road; but his wife seeing this, expressed a wish to go back the way they had come. He objected, and suspicion was awakened in her heart, and she soon after learned that the mother

---

1 *"At length the news of the approaching marriage ... deficient in love"*: Child, "The Quadroons," 123–28.

2 Horse-drawn carriage with a retractable hood.

3 *"their barouche rolled along a winding road that skirted ... said nothing"*: Child, "The Quadroons," 128–29.

of that lovely child bore the name of Clotel, a name which she had often heard Horatio murmur in uneasy slumbers. From gossiping tongues she soon learned more than she wished to know. She wept, but not as poor Clotel had done; for she never had loved, and been beloved like her, and her nature was more proud: henceforth a change came over her feelings and her manners, and Horatio had no further occasion to assume a tenderness in return for hers. Changed as he was by ambition, he felt the wintry chill of her polite propriety, and sometimes, in agony of heart, compared it with the gushing love of her who was indeed his wife. But these and all his emotions were a sealed book to Clotel, of which she could only guess the contents. With remittances for her and her child's support, there sometimes came earnest pleadings that she would consent to see him again; but these she never answered, though her heart yearned to do so. She pitied his young bride, and would not be tempted to bring sorrow into her household by any fault of hers. Her earnest prayer was, that she might not know of her existence. She had not looked on Horatio since she watched him under the shadow of the magnolia, until his barouche passed her in her rambles some months after. She saw the deadly paleness of his countenance, and had he dared to look back, he would have seen her tottering with faintness. Mary brought water from a rivulet, and sprinkled her face. When she revived, she clasped the beloved child to her heart with a vehemence that made her scream. Soothingly she kissed away her fears, and gazed into her beautiful eyes with a deep, deep sadness of expression, which poor Mary never forgot. Wild were the thoughts that passed round her aching heart, and almost maddened her poor brain; thoughts which had almost driven her to suicide the night of that last farewell. For her child's sake she had conquered the fierce temptation then; and for her sake, she struggled with it now. But the gloomy atmosphere of their once happy home overclouded the morning of Mary's life. Clotel perceived this, and it gave her unutterable pain.[1]

> "'Tis ever thus with woman's love,
> True till life's storms have passed;
> And, like the vine around the tree,
> It braves them to the last."[2]

---

1 *"She wept, but not as poor … unutterable pain"*: Child, "The Quadroons," 129–31.
2 P.S. Badger, "The Wife," lines 17–20.

CHAPTER IX.

THE MAN OF HONOUR.

"My tongue could never learn sweet soothing words,
But now thy beauty is propos'd, my fee,
My proud heart sues, and prompts my tongue to speak."

Shakspeare.[1]

James Crawford, the purchaser of Althesa, was from the green mountains of Vermont, and his feelings were opposed to the holding of slaves. But his young wife persuaded him into the idea that it was no worse to own a slave than to hire one and pay the money to another. Hence it was that he had been induced to purchase Althesa. Henry Morton, a young physician from the same state, and who had just commenced the practice of his profession in New Orleans, was boarding with Crawford when Althesa was brought home. The young physician had been in New Orleans but a few weeks, and had seen very little of slavery. In his own mountain home he had been taught that the slaves of the Southern states were negroes, if not from the coast of Africa, the descendants of those who had been imported. He was unprepared to behold with composure a beautiful young white girl of fifteen in the degraded position of a chattel slave. The blood chilled in his young heart as he heard Crawford tell how, by bantering with the trader, he had bought her for two hundred dollars less than he first asked. His very looks showed that the slave girl had the deepest sympathy of his heart. Althesa had been brought up by her mother to look after the domestic concerns of her cottage in Virginia, and knew well the duties imposed upon her. Mrs. Crawford was much pleased with her new servant, and often made mention of her in presence of Morton. The young man's sympathy ripened into love, which was reciprocated by the friendless and injured child of sorrow. There was but one course left; that was, to purchase the young girl and make her his wife, which he did six months after her arrival in Crawford's family. The young physician and his wife immediately took lodgings in another part of the city; a private teacher was called in, and the young wife taught some of those accomplishments which are necessary for one's taking a position in society. Dr. Morton soon obtained a large practice in his profession, and with it increased

---

1 Shakespeare, *Richard III*, 1.2.169–71.

in wealth—but with all his wealth he never would own a slave. Mrs. Morton was now in a position to seek out and redeem her mother, whom she had not heard of since they parted at Natchez. An agent was immediately despatched to hunt out the mother and to see if she could be purchased. The agent had no trouble in finding out Mr. Peck: but all overtures were unavailing; he would not sell Currer. His excuse was, that she was such a good housekeeper that he could not spare her. Poor Althesa felt sad when she found that her mother could not be bought. However, she felt a consciousness of having done her duty in the matter, yet waited with the hope that the day might come when she should have her mother by her side.

CHAPTER X.

THE YOUNG CHRISTIAN.

"Here we see *God dealing in slaves*; giving them to his own favourite child [Abraham], a man of superlative worth, and as a reward for his eminent goodness."—*Rev. Theodore Clapp, of New Orleans.*[1]

On Carlton's return the next day from the farm, he was overwhelmed with questions from Mr. Peck, as to what he thought of the plantation, the condition of the negroes, Huckelby and Snyder; and especially how he liked the sermon of the latter. Mr. Peck was a kind of a patriarch in his own way. To begin with, he was a man of some talent. He not only had a good education, but was a man of great eloquence, and had a wonderful command of language. He too either had, or thought he had, poetical genius; and was often sending contributions to the *Natchez Free Trader*, and other periodicals. In the way of raising contributions for foreign missions, he took the lead of all others in his neighbourhood. Everything he did, he did for the "glory of God," as he said: he quoted Scripture for almost everything he did. Being in good circumstances, he was able to give to almost all benevolent causes to which he took a fancy. He was a most loving father, and his daughter exercised considerable influence over him, and, owing to her piety and judgment, that influence had a beneficial effect. Carlton, though a schoolfellow of the parson's,

---

1 "Clerical Blasphemy," 3; quoted in Bowditch, *Slavery*, 1.

was nevertheless nearly ten years his junior; and though not an avowed infidel, was, however, a free-thinker, and one who took no note of to-morrow. And for this reason Georgiana took peculiar interest in the young man, for Carlton was but little above thirty and unmarried. The young Christian felt that she would not be living up to that faith that she professed and believed in, if she did not exert herself to the utmost to save the thoughtless man from his downward career; and in this she succeeded to her most sanguine expectations. She not only converted him, but in placing the Scriptures before him in their true light, she redeemed those sacred writings from the charge of supporting the system of slavery, which her father had cast upon them in the discussion some days before.

Georgiana's first object, however, was to awaken in Carlton's breast a love for the Lord Jesus Christ. The young man had often sat under the sound of the gospel with perfect indifference. He had heard men talk who had grown grey bending over the Scriptures, and their conversation had passed by him unheeded; but when a young girl, much younger than himself, reasoned with him in that innocent and persuasive manner that woman is wont to use when she has entered with her whole soul upon an object, it was too much for his stout heart, and he yielded. Her next aim was to vindicate the Bible from sustaining the monstrous institution of slavery. She said, "'God has created of one blood all the nations of men, to dwell on all the face of the earth.'[1] To claim, hold, and treat a human being as property is felony against God and man.[2] The Christian religion is opposed to slaveholding in its spirit and its principles; it classes men-stealers among murderers; and it is the duty of all who wish to meet God in peace, to discharge that duty in spreading these principles.[3] Let us not deceive ourselves into the idea that slavery is right, because it is profitable to us. Slaveholding is the highest possible violation of the eighth commandment. To take from a man his earnings, is theft; but to take the earner is a compound, life-long theft; and we who profess to follow in the footsteps of our Redeemer, should do our utmost to extirpate slavery from the

---

1 Acts 17:26.

2 "To claim, hold, and treat a human being ... God and man": LaRoy Sunderland, Anti-Slavery Manual, 40.

3 "The Christian religion is opposed to slaveholding ... among murderers": Bishop Beilby Porteus (1731–1809); quoted in Sunderland, Anti-Slavery Manual, 140.

land.[1] For my own part, I shall do all I can. When the Redeemer was about to ascend to the bosom of the Father, and resume the glory which he had with him before the world was, he promised his disciples that the power of the Holy Ghost should come upon them, and that they should be witnesses for him to the uttermost parts of the earth. What was the effect upon their minds? 'They all continued with one accord in prayer and supplication with the women.' Stimulated by the confident expectation that Jesus would fulfil his gracious promise, they poured out their hearts in fervent supplications, probably for strength to do the work which he had appointed them unto, for they felt that without him they could do nothing, and they consecrated themselves on the altar of God, to the great and glorious enterprise of preaching the unsearchable riches of Christ to a lost and perishing world. Have we less precious promises in the Scriptures of truth? May we not claim of our God the blessing promised unto those who consider the poor: the Lord will preserve them and keep them alive, and they shall be blessed upon the earth? Does not the language, 'Inasmuch as ye did it unto one of the least of these my brethren, ye did it unto me,' belong to all who are rightly engaged in endeavouring to unloose the bondman's fetters? Shall we not then do as the apostles did? Shall we not, in view of the two millions of heathen in our very midst, in view of the souls that are going down in an almost unbroken phalanx to utter perdition, continue in prayer and supplication, that God will grant us the supplies of his Spirit to prepare us for that work which he has given us to do? Shall not the wail of the mother as she surrenders her only child to the grasp of the ruthless kidnapper, or the trader in human blood, animate our devotions? Shall not the manifold crimes and horrors of slavery excite more ardent outpourings at the throne of grace to grant repentance to our guilty country, and permit us to aid in preparing the way for the glorious second advent of the Messiah, by preaching deliverance to the captives, and the opening of the prison doors to those who are bound."[2]

Georgiana had succeeded in rivetting the attention of Carlton during her conversation, and as she was finishing her last sentence, she observed the silent tear stealing down the cheek of the newly born child of God. At this juncture her father entered, and

---

1 *"Slaveholding is the highest possible violation ... life-long theft"*:
   Theodore Weld, *The Bible Against Slavery*, 11.

2 *"When the Redeemer was about to ascend ... who are bound"*: [Sarah
   Grimké], *An Address to Free Colored Americans*, 24–25.

Carlton left the room. "Dear papa," said Georgiana, "will you grant me one favour; or, rather, make me a promise?" "I can't tell, my dear, till I know what it is," replied Mr. Peck. "If it is a reasonable request, I will comply with your wish," continued he. "I hope, my dear," answered she, "that papa would not think me capable of making an unreasonable request." "Well, well," returned he; "tell me what it is." "I hope," said she, "that in your future conversation with Mr. Carlton, on the subject of slavery, you will not speak of the Bible as sustaining it." "Why, Georgiana, my dear, you are mad, aint you?" exclaimed he, in an excited tone. The poor girl remained silent; the father saw in a moment that he had spoken too sharply; and taking her hand in his he said, "Now, my child, why do you make that request?" "Because," returned she, "I think he is on the stool of repentance, if he has not already been received among the elect. He, you know, was bordering upon infidelity, and if the Bible sanctions slavery, then he will naturally enough say that it is not from God; for the argument from internal evidence is not only refuted, but actually turned against the Bible.[1] If the Bible sanctions slavery, then it misrepresents the character of God.[2] Nothing would be more dangerous to the soul of a young convert than to satisfy him that the Scriptures favoured such a system of sin." "Don't you suppose that I understand the Scriptures better than you? I have been in the world longer." "Yes," said she, "you have been in the world longer, and amongst slaveholders so long that you do not regard it in the same light that those do who have not become so familiar with its every-day scenes as you. I once heard you say, that you were opposed to the institution, when you first came to the South." "Yes," answered he, "I did not know so much about it then." "With great deference to you, papa," replied Georgiana, "I don't think that the Bible sanctions slavery. The Old Testament contains this explicit condemnation of it, 'He that stealeth a man, and selleth him, or if he be found in his hand, he shall surely be put to death;' and 'Woe unto him that buildeth his house by unrighteousness, and his chambers by wrong; that useth his neighbour's service without

---

1 "*for the argument from internal evidence ... against the Bible*": William Weston Patton, *Slavery, the Bible, Infidelity: Pro-slavery Interpretations of the Bible*, 6. Patton (1821–89) was an abolitionist and academic who would later become the president of Howard University (1877–89).
2 "*If the Bible sanctions slavery ... character of God*": Patton, *Slavery*, 7.

wages, and giveth him not for his work;' when also the New
Testament exhibits such words of rebuke as these, 'Behold the
hire of the labourers who have reaped down your fields, which
is of you kept back by fraud, crieth; and the cries of them who
have reaped are entered into the ears of the Lord of Sabaoth.'
'The law is not made for a righteous man, but for the lawless
and disobedient, for the ungodly and for sinners, for unholy and
profane, for murderers of fathers and murderers of mothers, for
manslayers, for whoremongers, for them that defile themselves
with mankind, for *menstealers*, for liars, for perjured persons.' A
more scathing denunciation of the sin in question is surely to be
found on record in no other book.[1] I am afraid," continued the
daughter, "that the acts of the professed friends of Christianity
in the South do more to spread infidelity than the writings of all
the atheists which have ever been published. The infidel watches
the religious world. He surveys the church, and, lo! thousands
and tens of thousands of her accredited members actually hold
slaves. Members 'in good and regular standing,' fellowshipped
throughout Christendom except by a few anti-slavery churches
generally despised as ultra and radical, reduce their fellow men
to the condition of chattels, and by force keep them in that state
of degradation. Bishops, ministers, elders, and deacons are engaged in this awful business, and do not consider their conduct
as at all inconsistent with the precepts of either the Old or New
Testaments. Moreover, those ministers and churches who do
not themselves hold slaves, very generally defend the conduct
of those who do, and accord to them a fair Christian character,
and in the way of business frequently take mortgages and levy
executions on the bodies of their fellow men, and in some cases
of their fellow Christians.

"Now is it a wonder that infidels, beholding the practice and
listening to the theory of professing Christians, should conclude
that the Bible inculcates a morality not inconsistent with chattelis-
ing human beings? And must not this conclusion be strengthened,
when they hear ministers of talent and learning declare that the
Bible does sanction slaveholding, and that it ought not to be made
a disciplinable offence in churches? And must not all doubt be dis-
sipated, when one of the most learned professors in our theological
seminaries asserts that the Bible 'recognises that the relation may
still exist, *salva fide et salva ecclesia*' (without injury to the Christian

---

1   "*The Old Testament contains this explicit ... no other book*": Patton,
    Slavery, 5.

faith or church) and that only 'the *abuse* of it is the essential and fundamental wrong?' Are not infidels bound to believe that these professors, ministers, and churches understand their own Bible, and that, consequently, notwithstanding solitary passages which appear to condemn slaveholding, the Bible sanctions it?[1] When nothing can be further from the truth. And as for Christ, his whole life was a living testimony against slavery and all that it inculcates. When he designed to do us good, he took upon himself the form of a servant. He took his station at the bottom of society. He voluntarily identified himself with the poor and the despised.[2] The warning voices of Jeremiah and Ezekiel were raised in olden time, against sin. Let us not forget what followed. 'Therefore, thus saith the Lord—ye have not hearkened unto me in proclaiming liberty every one to his brother, and every one to his neighbour—behold I proclaim a liberty for you saith the Lord, to the sword, to the pestilence, and to the famine.' Are we not virtually as a nation adopting the same impious language, and are we not exposed to the same tremendous judgments? Shall we not, in view of those things, use every laudable means to awaken our beloved country from the slumbers of death, and baptize all our efforts with tears and with prayers, that God may bless them. Then, should our labour fail to accomplish the end for which we pray, we shall stand acquitted at the bar of Jehovah, and although we may share in the national calamities which await unrepented sins, yet that blessed approval will be ours.—'Well done good and faithful servants, enter ye into the joy of your Lord.'"[3]

"My dear Georgiana," said Mr. Peck, "I must be permitted to entertain my own views on this subject, and to exercise my own judgment."

"Believe me, dear papa," she replied, "I would not be understood as wishing to teach you, or to dictate to you in the least; but only grant my request, not to allude to the Bible as sanctioning slavery, when speaking with Mr. Carlton."

"Well," returned he, "I will comply with your wish."

The young Christian had indeed accomplished a noble work; and whether it was admitted by the father, or not, she was his superior and his teacher. Georgiana had viewed the right to enjoy

---

1   "*He surveys the church, and, lo! … Bible sanctions it?*": Patton, *Slavery*, 5–6.

2   "*When he designed to do us good … and the despised*": Grimké, *Address*, 14.

3   "*The warning voices of Jeremiah and Ezekiel … of your Lord*": Grimké, *Address*, 28.

perfect liberty as one of those inherent and inalienable rights which pertain to the whole human race, and of which they can never be divested, except by an act of gross injustice.[1] And no one was more able than herself to impress those views upon the hearts of all with whom she came in contact. Modest and self-possessed, with a voice of great sweetness, and a most winning manner, she could, with the greatest ease to herself, engage their attention.[2]

CHAPTER XI.

THE PARSON POET.

"Unbind, unbind my galling chain,
And set, oh! set me free:
No longer say that I'll disdain
The gift of liberty."[3]

Through the persuasion of Mr. Peck, and fascinated with the charms of Georgiana, Carlton had prolonged his stay two months with his old school-fellow. During the latter part of the time he had been almost as one of the family. If Miss Peck was invited out, Mr. Carlton was, as a matter of course. She seldom rode out, unless with him. If Mr. Peck was absent, he took the head of the table; and, to the delight of the young lady, he had on several occasions taken part in the family worship. "I am glad," said Mr. Peck, one evening while at the tea table, "I am glad, Mr. Carlton, that my neighbour Jones has invited you to visit him at his farm. He is a good neighbour, but a very ungodly man; I want that you should see his people, and then, when you return to the North, you can tell how much better a Christian's slaves are situated than one who does nothing for the cause of Christ." "I hope, Mr. Carlton," said Georgiana, "that you will spend the Sabbath with him, and have a religious interview with the negroes." "Yes," replied the parson, "that's well thought of, Georgy." "Well, I think I will go up on Thursday next, and stay till Monday," said Carlton; "and I shall act upon your suggestion,

---

1 *"the right to enjoy perfect liberty ... gross injustice"*: Virginia Congressman Samuel McDowell Moore (1796–1875); quoted in Grimké, *Address,* 5.
2 *"Modest and self-possessed, with a voice ... engage their attention"*: "Lucy Stone," 29.
3 Source unknown.

Miss Peck," continued he; "and try to get a religious interview with the blacks. By-the-by," remarked Carlton, "I saw an advertisement in the *Free Trader* to-day that rather puzzled me. Ah, here it is now; and," drawing the paper from his pocket, "I will read it, and then you can tell me what it means:

> 'TO PLANTERS AND OTHERS.—*Wanted fifty negroes.* Any person having *sick negroes*, considered *incurable* by their respective physicians, (their owners of course,) and wishing to dispose of them, Dr. Stillman will pay cash for negroes affected with scrofula or king's evil, confirmed hypochondriacism, apoplexy, or diseases of the brain, kidneys, spleen, stomach and intestines, bladder and its appendages, diarrhoea, dysentery, &c. *The highest cash price will be paid as above.*'[1]

When I read this to-day I thought that the advertiser must be a man of eminent skill as a physician, and that he intended to cure the sick negroes; but on second thought I find that some of the diseases enumerated are certainly incurable. What can he do with these sick negroes?" "You see," replied Mr. Peck, laughing, "that he is a doctor, and has use for them in his lectures. The doctor is connected with a small college. Look at his prospectus, where he invites students to attend, and that will explain the matter to you." Carlton turned to another column, and read the following:

> "Some advantages of a peculiar character are connected with this institution, which it may be proper to point out. No place in the United States offers as great opportunities for the acquisition of anatomical knowledge. Subjects being obtained from among the coloured population in sufficient numbers *for every purpose*, and proper dissections carried on *without offending any individuals in the community!*"[2]

"These are for dissection, then?" inquired Carlton with a trembling voice. "Yes," answered the parson. "Of course they wait till

---

1   *"TO PLANTERS AND OTHERS ... as above"*: advertisement, *Charleston Mercury*, 12 October 1838; quoted in Jonathan Walker, *A Brief View of American Chattelized Humanity*, 10.

2   *"Some advantages of a peculiar ... the community"*: prospectus of the South Carolina Medical College; quoted in Walker, *Brief View*, 11.

they die before they can use them." "They keep them on hand, and when they need one they bleed him to death," returned Mr. Peck. "Yes, but that's murder." "Oh, the doctors are licensed to commit murder, you know; and what's the difference, whether one dies owing to the loss of blood, or taking too many pills? For my own part, if I had to choose, I would rather submit to the former." "I have often heard what I considered hard stories in abolition meetings in New York about slavery; but now I shall begin to think that many of them are true." "The longer you remain here the more you will be convinced of the iniquity of the institution," remarked Georgiana. "Now, Georgy, my dear, don't give us another abolition lecture, if you please," said Mr. Peck. "Here, Carlton," continued the parson, "I have written a short poem for your sister's album, as you requested me; it is a domestic piece, as you will see." "She will prize it the more for that," remarked Carlton; and taking the sheet of paper, he laughed as his eyes glanced over it. "Read it out, Mr. Carlton," said Georgiana, "and let me hear what it is; I know papa gets off some very droll things at times." Carlton complied with the young lady's request, and read aloud the following rare specimen of poetical genius:

"MY LITTLE NIG.

"I have a little nigger, the blackest thing alive,
He'll be just four years old if he lives till forty-five;
His smooth cheek hath a glossy hue, like a new
    polished boot,
And his hair curls o'er his little head as black as any soot.
His lips bulge from his countenance—his little ivories
    shine—
His nose is what we call a little pug, but fashioned very fine:
Although not quite a fairy, he is comely to behold,
And I wouldn't sell him, 'pon my word, for a hundred
    all in gold.

"He gets up early in the morn, like all the other nigs,
And runs off to the hog-lot, where he squabbles with
    the pigs—
And when the sun gets out of bed, and mounts up in the sky,
The warmest corner of the yard is where my nig doth lie.
And there extended lazily, he contemplates and
    dreams,
(I cannot qualify to this, but plain enough it seems;)

Until 'tis time to take in grub, when you can't find
   him there,
For, like a politician, he has gone to hunt his share.

"I haven't said a single word concerning my plantation,
Though a prettier, I guess, cannot be found within the
   nation;
When he gets a little bigger, I'll take and to him show it,
And then I'll say, 'My little nig, now just prepare to go it!'
I'll put a hoe into his hand—he'll soon know what it means,
And every day for dinner, he shall have bacon and greens."[1]

CHAPTER XII.

A NIGHT IN THE PARSON'S KITCHEN.

"And see the servants met,
   Their daily labour's o'er;
And with the jest and song they set
   The kitchen in a roar."[2]

Mr. Peck kept around him four servants besides Currer, of whom
we have made mention: of these, Sam was considered the first. If a
dinner-party was in contemplation, or any company to be invited to
the parson's, after all the arrangements had been talked over by the
minister and his daughter, Sam was sure to be consulted upon the
subject by "Miss Georgy," as Miss Peck was called by the servants.
If furniture, crockery, or anything else was to be purchased, Sam felt
that he had been slighted if his opinion had not been asked. As to the
marketing, he did it all. At the servants' table in the kitchen, he sat
at the head, and was master of ceremonies. A single look from him
was enough to silence any conversation or noise in the kitchen, or any
other part of the premises. There is, in the Southern States, a great
amount of prejudice against colour amongst the negroes themselves.
The nearer the negro or mulatto approaches to the white, the more

---

1 . Thomas G. Key, "My Little Nig," 208. The poem first appeared
   in the *Hamburg* (SC) *Journal* and was reprinted in the *Liberator* as
   an example of "the value placed upon 'the nigs' by their miscreant
   owners."
2 Thomas Frean, "A Parody on 'Massachusetts vs. South Carolina,'"
   165.

he seems to feel his superiority over those of a darker hue. This is, no doubt, the result of the prejudice that exists on the part of the whites towards both mulattoes and blacks. Sam was originally from Kentucky, and through the instrumentality of one of his young masters whom he had to take to school he had learned to read so as to be well understood; and, owing to that fact, was considered a prodigy among the slaves, not only of his own master's, but those of the town who knew him. Sam had a great wish to follow in the footsteps of his master, and be a poet; and was, therefore, often heard singing doggerels of his own composition. But there was one great drawback to Sam, and that was his colour. He was one of the blackest of his race. This he evidently regarded as a great misfortune. However, he made up for this in his dress. Mr. Peck kept his house servants well dressed; and as for Sam, he was seldom seen except in a ruffled shirt. Indeed, the washerwoman feared him more than all others about the house.

Currer, as we have already stated, was chief of the kitchen department, and had a general supervision of the household affairs. Alfred the coachman, Peter, and Hetty made up the remainder of the house servants. Besides these, Mr. Peck owned eight slaves who were masons. These worked in the city. Being mechanics, they were let out to greater advantage than to keep them on the farm. However, every Sunday night, Peck's servants, including the bricklayers, usually assembled in the kitchen, when the events of the week were freely discussed and commented on. It was on a Sunday evening, in the month of June, that there was a party at Mr. Peck's, and, according to custom in the Southern States, the ladies had their maid-servants with them. Tea had been served in "the house," and the servants, including the strangers, had taken their seats at the tea table in the kitchen. Sam, being a "single gentleman," was unusually attentive to the "ladies" on this occasion. He seldom or ever let the day pass without spending at least an hour in combing and brushing up his "hair." Sam had an idea that fresh butter was better for his hair than any other kind of grease; and therefore, on churning days, half a pound of butter had always to be taken out before it was salted. When he wished to appear to great advantage, he would grease his face, to make it "shiny." On the evening of the party therefore, when all the servants were at the table, Sam cut a big figure. There he sat with his wool well combed and buttered, face nicely greased, and his ruffles extending five or six inches from his breast. The parson in his own drawing-room did not make a more imposing appearance than did his servant on this occasion. "I jist bin had my fortune told last Sunday night," said Sam, as he helped one of the girls to some sweet hash. "Indeed," cried half-a-dozen voices. "Yes," continued he; "Aunt Winny teld me I is to hab de prettiest yaller gal[1] in town, and dat I is to be free." All eyes were immediately turned toward Sally Johnson, who was seated near Sam. "I speck I see somebody blush at dat remark," said Alfred. "Pass dem pancakes and molasses up dis way, Mr. Alf, and none of your insinawaysion here," rejoined Sam. "Dat reminds me," said Currer, "dat Dorcas Simpson is gwine to git married." "Who to, I want to know?" inquired Peter. "To one of Mr. Darby's field-hands," answered Currer. "I should tink dat dat gal would not trow hersef away in dat manner," said Sally. "She good enough looking to get a house servant, and not to put up wid a fiel' nigger," continued she. "Yes," said Sam, "dat's a wery insensible remark of yours, Miss Sally. I admire your judgment wery much, I assure you. Dah's plenty of suspectible and well-dressed house servants dat a gal of her looks can get, wid out taken up wid dem common darkies." "Is de man black or a mulatto?" inquired one of the company. "He's nearly white," replied Currer. "Well den, dat's some exchuse for her," remarked Sam; "for I don't like to see dis malgemation of blacks and mulattoes, no how," continued Sam. "If I had my rights I would be a mulatto too, for my mother was almost as light-coloured as Miss Sally," said he. Although Sam was one of the blackest men living, he nevertheless contended that his mother was a mulatto, and no one was more prejudiced against the blacks than he. A good deal of work, and the free use of fresh butter, had no doubt done wonders for his "hare" in causing it to grow long, and to this he would always appeal when he wished to convince others that he was part of an Anglo-Saxon. "I always thought you was not clear black, Mr. Sam," said Agnes. "You are right dahr, Miss Agnes. My hare tells what company I belong to," answered Sam. Here the whole company joined in the conversation about colour, which lasted for some time, giving unmistakeable evidence that caste is owing to ignorance. The evening's entertainment concluded by Sam's relating a little of his own experience while with his first master in old Kentucky.

Sam's former master was a doctor, and had a large practice among his neighbours, doctoring both masters and slaves. When Sam was about fifteen years of age, his old master set him to grinding up the ointment, then to making pills. As the young student grew older and became more practised in his profession, his services were of more importance to the doctor. The physician having a good business, and a large number of his patients being slaves, the most of whom had to call on the doctor when ill, he put Sam to bleeding, pulling

---

1 Light-skinned mixed-race woman.

teeth, and administering medicine to the slaves. Sam soon acquired the name amongst the slaves of the "Black Doctor." With this appellation he was delighted, and no regular physician could possibly have put on more airs than did the black doctor when his services were required. In bleeding, he must have more bandages, and rub and smack the arm more than the doctor would have thought of. We once saw Sam taking out a tooth for one of his patients, and nothing appeared more amusing. He got the poor fellow down on his back, and he got a straddle of the man's chest, and getting the turnkeys on the wrong tooth, he shut both eyes and pulled for his life. The poor man screamed as loud as he could, but to no purpose. Sam had him fast. After a great effort, out came the sound grinder, and the young doctor saw his mistake; but consoled himself with the idea that as the wrong tooth was out of the way, there was more room to get at the right one. Bleeding and a dose of calomel was always considered indispensable by the "Old Boss;" and, as a matter of course, Sam followed in his footsteps.

On one occasion the old doctor was ill himself, so as to be unable to attend to his patients. A slave, with pass in hand, called to receive medical advice, and the master told Sam to examine him and see what he wanted. This delighted him beyond measure, for although he had been acting his part in the way of giving out medicine as the master ordered it, he had never been called upon by the latter to examine a patient, and this seemed to convince him that, after all, he was no sham doctor. As might have been expected, he cut a rare figure in his first examination, placing himself directly opposite his patient, and folding his arms across his breast, and looking very knowingly, he began, "What's de matter wid you?" "I is sick." "Where is you sick?" "Here," replied the man, putting his hand upon his stomach. "Put out your tongue," continued the doctor. The man run out his tongue at full length. "Let me feel your pulse," at the same time taking his patient's hand in his, placing his fingers on his pulse, he said, "Ah, your case is a bad one; if I don't do something for you, and dat pretty quick, you'll be a gone coon, and dat's sartin." At this the man appeared frightened and inquired what was the matter with him: in answer, Sam said, "I done told you dat your case is a bad one, and dat's enough." On Sam's returning to his master's bedside, the latter said, "Well, Sam, what do you think is the matter with him?" "His stomach is out of order, sir," he replied. "What do you think had best be done for him?" "I think I better bleed him and give him a dose of calomel," returned Sam. So to the latter's gratification the master let him have his own way. We need not further say, that the recital of Sam's experience as a physician gave him a high position amongst the servants that evening, and made him a decided favourite with the ladies, one of whom feigned illness, when the black doctor, to the delight of all, and certainly to himself, gave medical advice. Thus ended the evening amongst the servants in the parson's kitchen.

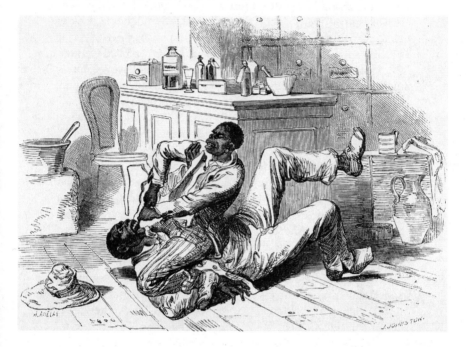

CHAPTER XIII.

A SLAVE HUNTING PARSON.

"'Tis too much prov'd—that with devotion's visage,
And pious action, we do sugar o'er the devil himself."
Shakspeare[1]

"You will, no doubt, be well pleased with neighbour Jones," said Mr. Peck, as Carlton stepped into the chaise to pay his promised visit to the "ungodly man." "Don't forget to have a religious interview with the negroes," remarked Georgiana, as she gave the last nod to her young convert. "I will do my best," returned Carlton, as the vehicle

---

1 Shakespeare, *Hamlet*, 3.1.47–49.

left the door. As might have been expected, Carlton met with a cordial reception at the hands of the proprietor of the Grove Farm. The servants in the "Great House" were well dressed, and appeared as if they did not want for food. Jones knew that Carlton was from the North, and a non-slaveholder, and therefore did everything in his power to make a favourable impression on his mind. "My negroes are well clothed, well fed, and not over worked," said the slaveholder to his visitor, after the latter had been with him nearly a week. "As far as I can see, your slaves appear to good advantage," replied Carlton. "But," continued he, "if it is a fair question, do you have preaching among your slaves on Sunday, Mr. Jones?" "No, no," returned he, "I think that's all nonsense; my negroes do their own preaching." "So you do permit them to have meetings." "Yes, when they wish. There's some very intelligent and clever chaps among them." "As to-morrow is the Sabbath," said Carlton, "if you have no objection, I will attend meeting with them." "Most certainly you shall, if you will do the preaching," returned the planter. Here the young man was about to decline, but he remembered the parting words of Georgiana, and he took courage and said, "Oh, I have no objection to give the negroes a short talk." It was then understood that Carlton was to have a religious interview with the blacks the next day, and the young man waited with a degree of impatience for the time.

In no part of the South are slaves in a more ignorant and degraded state than in the cotton, sugar, and rice districts.

If they are permitted to cease labour on the Sabbath, the time is spent in hunting, fishing, or lying beneath the shade of a tree, resting for the morrow. Religious instruction is unknown in the far South, except among such men as the Rev. C.C. Jones, John Peck, and some others who regard religious instruction, such as they impart to their slaves, as calculated to make them more trustworthy and valuable as property. Jones, aware that his slaves would make rather a bad show of intelligence if questioned by Carlton, resolved to have them ready for him, and therefore gave his driver orders with regard to their preparation. Consequently, after the day's labour was over, Dogget, the driver, assembled the negroes together and said, "Now, boys and gals, your master is coming down to the quarters to-morrow with his visitor, who is going to give you a preach, and I want you should understand what he says to you. Now many of you who came of Old Virginia and Kentuck, know what preaching is, and others who have been raised in these parts do not. Preaching is to tell you that you are mighty wicked and bad at heart. This, I suppose, you all know. But if the gentleman should ask you who made you, tell him the Lord; if he ask if you wish to go to heaven, tell him yes. Remember that you are all Christians, all love the Lord, all want to go to heaven, all love your masters, and all love me. Now, boys and gals, I want you to show yourselves smart to-morrow: be on your p's and q's, and, Monday morning, I will give you all a glass of whiskey bright and early." Agreeable to arrangement the slaves were assembled together on Sunday morning under the large trees near the great house, and after going through another drilling from the driver, Jones and Carlton made their appearance. "You see," said Jones to the negroes, as he approached them, "you see here's a gentleman that's come to talk to you about your souls, and I hope you'll all pay that attention that you ought." Jones then seated himself in one of the two chairs placed there for him and the stranger.

Carlton had already selected a chapter in the Bible to read to them, which he did, after first prefacing it with some remarks of his own. Not being accustomed to speak in public, he determined, after reading the Bible, to make it more of a conversational meeting than otherwise. He therefore began asking them questions. "Do you feel that you are a Christian?" asked he of a full-blooded negro that sat near him. "Yes, sir," was the response. "You feel, then, that you shall go to heaven." "Yes, sir." "Of course you know who made you?" The man put his hand to his head and began to scratch his wool; and, after a little hesitation, answered, "De overseer told us last night who made us, but indeed I forgot the gentman's name." This reply was almost too much for Carlton, and his gravity was not a little moved. However, he bit his tongue, and turned to another man, who appeared, from his looks, to be more intelligent. "Do you serve the Lord?" asked he. "No, sir, I don't serve anybody but Mr. Jones; I neber belong to anybody else." To hide his feelings at this juncture, Carlton turned and walked to another part of the grounds, to where the women were seated, and said to a mulatto woman who had rather an anxious countenance, "Did you ever hear of John the Baptist?" "Oh yes, marser, John de Baptist; I know dat nigger bery well indeed; he libs in Old Kentuck, where I come from." Carlton's gravity here gave way, and he looked at the planter and laughed right out. The old woman knew a slave near her old master's farm in Kentucky, and was ignorant enough to suppose that he was the John the Baptist inquired about. Carlton occupied the remainder of the time in reading Scripture and talking to them. "My niggers aint shown off very well to-day," said Jones, as he and his visitor left the grounds. "No," replied Carlton. "You did not get hold of the bright ones," continued the planter. "So it seems," remarked Carlton. The planter evidently felt that his neighbour, Parson Peck, would have a nut to crack over the account that Carlton would give of the ignorance of the slaves, and said and did all in his power to remove the bad impression already made; but to no purpose. The report made by Carlton, on his return, amused the parson very much. It appeared to him the best reason why professed Christians like himself should be slave-holders. Not so with Georgiana. She did not even smile when Carlton was telling his story, but seemed sore at heart that such ignorance should prevail in their midst. The question turned upon the heathen of other lands, and the parson began to expatiate upon his own efforts in foreign missions, when his daughter, with a child-like simplicity, said,

> "Send Bibles to the heathen;
> On every distant shore,
> From light that's beaming o'er us,
> Let streams increasing pour
> But keep it from the millions
> Down-trodden at our door.
>
> "Send Bibles to the heathen,
> Their famished spirits feed;
> Oh! haste, and join your efforts,
> The priceless gift to speed;
> Then flog the trembling negro
> If he should learn to read."[1]

"I saw a curiosity while at Mr. Jones's that I shall not forget soon," said Carlton. "What was it?" inquired the parson. "A kennel of bloodhounds; and such dogs I never saw before. They were of a species between the bloodhound and the foxhound, and were ferocious, gaunt, and savage-looking animals. They were part of a stock imported from Cuba, he informed me. They were kept in an iron cage, and fed on Indian corn bread. This kind of food, he said, made them eager for their business.[2] Sometimes they would give the dogs meat, but it was always after they had been chasing a negro." "Were those the dogs you had, papa, to hunt Harry?" asked Georgiana. "No, my dear," was the short reply: and the parson seemed anxious to change the conversation to something else. When Mr. Peck had left the room, Carlton spoke more freely of what he had seen, and

---

1   "Missionary Hymn, for the South," lines 7–18.
2   *"They were of a species between the bloodhound ... for their business"*:
    "A Visit to a Kennel of Blood-hounds, Kept for the Purpose of
    Hunting Slaves," 912.

spoke more pointedly against slavery; for he well knew that Miss Peck sympathised with him in all he felt and said.

"You mentioned about your father hunting a slave," said Carlton, in an under tone. "Yes," replied she; "papa went with some slave-catchers and a parcel of those nasty negro-dogs, to hunt poor Harry. He belonged to papa and lived on the farm. His wife lives in town, and Harry had been to see her, and did not return quite as early as he should; and Huckelby was flogging him, and he got away and came here. I wanted papa to keep him in town, so that he could see his wife more frequently; but he said they could not spare him from the farm, and flogged him again, and sent him back. The poor fellow knew that the overseer would punish him over again, and instead of going back he went into the woods." "Did they catch him?" asked Carlton. "Yes," replied she. "In chasing him through the woods, he attempted to escape by swimming across a river, and the dogs were sent in after him, and soon caught him. But Harry had great courage and fought the dogs with a big club; and papa seeing the negro would escape from the dogs, shot at him, as he says, only to wound him, that he might be caught; but the poor fellow was killed." Overcome by relating this incident, Georgiana burst into tears.

Although Mr. Peck fed and clothed his house servants well, and treated them with a degree of kindness, he was, nevertheless, a most cruel master. He encouraged his driver to work the field-hands from early dawn till late at night; and the good appearance of the house-servants, and the preaching of Snyder to the field negroes, was to cause himself to be regarded as a Christian master. Being on a visit one day at the farm, and having with him several persons from the Free States, and wishing to make them believe that his slaves were happy, satisfied, and contented, the parson got out the whiskey and gave each one a dram, who in return had to drink the master's health, or give a toast of some kind. The company were not a little amused at some of the sentiments given, and Peck was delighted at every indication of contentment on the part of the blacks. At last it came to Jack's turn to drink, and the master expected something good from him, because he was considered the cleverest and most witty slave on the farm.

"Now," said the master, as he handed Jack the cup of whiskey; "now, Jack, give us something rich. You know," continued he, "we have raised the finest crop of cotton that's been seen in these parts for many a day. Now give us a toast on cotton; come, Jack, give us something to laugh at." The negro felt not a little elated at being made the hero of the occasion, and taking the whiskey in his right hand, put his left to his head and began to scratch his wool, and said,

"The big bee flies high,
The little bee make the honey:
The black folks makes the cotton,
And the white folks gets the money."[1]

CHAPTER XIV.

A FREE WOMAN REDUCED TO SLAVERY.

Althesa found in Henry Morton a kind and affectionate husband; and his efforts to purchase her mother, although unsuccessful, had doubly endeared him to her. Having from the commencement resolved not to hold slaves, or rather not to own any, they were compelled to hire servants for their own use. Five years had passed away, and their happiness was increased by two lovely daughters. Mrs. Morton was seated, one bright afternoon, busily engaged with

---

1 "Sentimental," 165.

her needle, and near her sat Salome, a servant that she had just taken into her employ. The woman was perfectly white; so much so, that Mrs. Morton had expressed her apprehensions to her husband, when the woman first came, that she was not born a slave. The mistress watched the servant, as the latter sat sewing upon some coarse work, and saw the large silent tear in her eye. This caused an uneasiness to the mistress, and she said, "Salome, don't you like your situation here?" "Oh yes, madam," answered the woman in a quick tone, and then tried to force a smile. "Why is it that you often look sad, and with tears in your eyes?" The mistress saw that she had touched a tender chord, and continued, "I am your friend; tell me your sorrow, and, if I can, I will help you." As the last sentence was escaping the lips of the mistress, the slave woman put her check apron to her face and wept. Mrs. Morton saw plainly that there was cause for this expression of grief, and pressed the woman more closely. "Hear me, then," said the woman calming herself: "I will tell you why I sometimes weep. I was born in Germany, on the banks of the Rhine. Ten years ago my father came to this country, bringing with him my mother and myself. He was poor, and I, wishing to assist all I could, obtained a situation as nurse to a lady in this city. My father got employment as a labourer on the wharf, among the steamboats; but he was soon taken ill with the yellow fever, and died. My mother then got a situation for herself, while I remained with my first employer. When the hot season came on, my master, with his wife, left New Orleans until the hot season was over, and took me with them. They stopped at a town on the banks of the Mississippi river, and said they should remain there some weeks. One day they went out for a ride, and they had not been gone more than half an hour, when two men came into the room and told me that they had bought me, and that I was their slave. I was bound and taken to prison, and that night put on a steamboat and taken up the Yazoo river, and set to work on a farm. I was forced to take up with a negro, and by him had three children. A year since my master's daughter was married, and I was given to her. She came with her husband to this city, and I have ever since been hired out."

"Unhappy woman," whispered Althesa, "why did you not tell me this before?" "I was afraid," replied Salome, "for I was once severely flogged for telling a stranger that I was not born a slave." On Mr. Morton's return home, his wife communicated to him the story which the slave woman had told her an hour before, and begged that something might be done to rescue her from the situation she was then in. In Louisiana as well as many others of the slave states, great obstacles are thrown in the way of persons who have been wrongfully reduced to slavery regaining their freedom. A person claiming to be free must prove his right to his liberty. This, it will be seen, throws the burden of proof upon the slave, who, in all probability, finds it out of his power to procure such evidence. And if any free person shall attempt to aid a freeman in regaining his freedom, he is compelled to enter into security in the sum of one thousand dollars, and if the person claiming to be free shall fail to establish such fact, the thousand dollars are forfeited to the state. This cruel and oppressive law has kept many a freeman from espousing the cause of persons unjustly held as slaves. Mr. Morton inquired and found that the woman's story was true, as regarded the time she had lived with her present owner; but the latter not only denied that she was free, but immediately removed her from Morton's. Three months after Salome had been removed from Morton's and let out to another family, she was one morning cleaning the door steps, when a lady passing by, looked at the slave and thought she recognised some one that she had seen before. The lady stopped and asked the woman if she was a slave, "I am," said she. "Were you born a slave?" "No, I was born in Germany." "What's the name of the ship in which you came to this country?" inquired the lady. "I don't know," was the answer. "Was it the *Amazon?*" At the sound of this name, the slave woman was silent for a moment, and then the tears began to flow freely down her care-worn cheeks. "Would you know Mrs. Marshall, who was a passenger in the *Amazon*, if you should see her?" inquired the lady. At this the woman gazed at the lady with a degree of intensity that can be imagined better than described, and then fell at the lady's feet. The lady was Mrs. Marshall. She had crossed the Atlantic in the same ship with this poor woman. Salome, like many of her countrymen, was a beautiful singer, and had often entertained Mrs. Marshall and the other lady passengers on board the *Amazon*. The poor woman was raised from the ground by Mrs. Marshall, and placed upon the door step that she had a moment before been cleaning. "I will do my utmost to rescue you from the horrid life of a slave," exclaimed the lady, as she took from her pocket her pencil, and wrote down the number of the house, and the street in which the German woman was working as a slave.

After a long and tedious trial of many days, it was decided that Salome Miller was by birth a free woman, and she was set at liberty. The good and generous Althesa had contributed some of the money toward bringing about the trial, and had done much to cheer on Mrs. Marshall in her benevolent object. Salome

Miller is free, but where are her three children? They are still slaves, and in all human probability will die as such.

This, reader, is no fiction; if you think so, look over the files of the New Orleans newspapers of the years 1845–6, and you will there see reports of the trial.[1]

CHAPTER XV.

TO-DAY A MISTRESS, TO-MORROW A SLAVE.

"I promised thee a sister tale
Of man's perfidious cruelty;
Come, then, and hear what cruel wrong
Befel the dark ladie."—*Coleridge.*[2]

Let us return for a moment to the home of Clotel. While she was passing lonely and dreary hours with none but her darling child, Horatio Green was trying to find relief in that insidious enemy of man, the intoxicating cup. Defeated in politics, forsaken in love by his wife, he seemed to have lost all principle of honour, and was ready to nerve himself up to any deed, no matter how unprincipled. Clotel's existence was now well known to Horatio's wife, and both her and her father demanded that the beautiful quadroon and her child should be sold and sent out of the state. To this proposition he at first turned a deaf ear; but when he saw that his wife was about to return to her father's roof, he consented to leave the matter in the hands of his father-in-law. The result was, that Clotel was immediately sold to the slave-trader, Walker, who, a few years previous, had taken her mother and sister to the far South. But, as if to make her husband drink of the cup of humiliation to its very dregs, Mrs. Green resolved to take his child under her own roof for a servant. Mary was, therefore, put to the meanest work that could be found, and although only ten years of age, she was often compelled to perform labour, which, under ordinary circumstances, would have been thought too hard for one much older. One condition of the sale of Clotel to Walker was, that she should be taken out of the state,

---

1 Articles from the New Orleans newspapers on the Salome Muller/ Sally Miller case were reprinted throughout the northern states. See, for instance, "Sally Miller," *Albany Evening Journal*, 14 July 1845, 2.
2 Samuel Taylor Coleridge, "The Ballad of the Dark Ladie" (1798); quoted in Child 115.

which was accordingly done. Most quadroon women who are taken to the lower countries to be sold are either purchased by gentlemen for their own use, or sold for waiting-maids; and Clotel, like her sister, was fortunate enough to be bought for the latter purpose. The town of Vicksburgh stands on the left bank of the Mississippi, and is noted for the severity with which slaves are treated. It was here that Clotel was sold to Mr. James French, a merchant.

Mrs. French was severe in the extreme to her servants. Well dressed, but scantily fed, and overworked were all who found a home with her. The quadroon had been in her new home but a short time ere she found that her situation was far different from what it was in Virginia. What social virtues are possible in a society of which injustice is the primary characteristic? in a society which is divided into two classes, masters and slaves?[1] Every married woman in the far South looks upon her husband as unfaithful, and regards every quadroon servant as a rival. Clotel had been with her new mistress but a few days, when she was ordered to cut off her long hair. The negro, constitutionally, is fond of dress and outward appearance. He that has short, woolly hair, combs it and oils it to death. He that has long hair, would sooner have his teeth drawn than lose it. However painful it was to the quadroon, she was soon seen with her hair cut as short as any of the full-blooded negroes in the dwelling.

Even with her short hair, Clotel was handsome. Her life had been a secluded one, and though now nearly thirty years of age, she was still beautiful. At her short hair, the other servants laughed, "Miss Clo needn't strut round so big, she got short nappy har well as I," said Nell, with a broad grin that showed her teeth. "She tinks she white, when she come here wid dat long har of hers," replied Mill. "Yes," continued Nell; "missus make her take down her wool so she no put it up to-day."

The fairness of Clotel's complexion was regarded with envy as well by the other servants as by the mistress herself. This is one of the hard features of slavery. To-day the woman is mistress of her own cottage; to-morrow she is sold to one who aims to make her life as intolerable as possible. And be it remembered, that the house servant has the best situation which a slave can occupy. Some American writers have tried to make the world believe that the condition of the labouring classes of England is as bad as the slaves of the United States.

---

1 *"What social virtues are possible ... into two classes"*: Harriet Martineau, *Society in America*, 2:107. Martineau (1802–76) was an English social theorist.

The English labourer may be oppressed, he may be cheated, defrauded, swindled, and even starved; but it is not slavery under which he groans.[1] He cannot be sold; in point of law he is equal to the prime minister. "It is easy to captivate the unthinking and the prejudiced, by eloquent declamation about the oppression of English operatives being worse than that of American slaves, and by exaggerating the wrongs on one side and hiding them on the other. But all informed and reflecting minds, knowing that bad as are the social evils of England, those of Slavery are immeasurably worse."[2] But the degradation and harsh treatment that Clotel experienced in her new home was nothing compared with the grief she underwent at being separated from her dear child. Taken from her without scarcely a moment's warning, she knew not what had become of her. The deep and heartfelt grief of Clotel was soon perceived by her owners, and fearing that her refusal to take food would cause her death, they resolved to sell her. Mr. French found no difficulty in getting a purchaser for the quadroon woman, for such are usually the most marketable kind of property. Clotel was sold at private sale to a young man for a housekeeper; but even he had missed his aim.

CHAPTER XVI.

DEATH OF THE PARSON.

Carlton was above thirty years of age, standing on the last legs of a young man, and entering on the first of a bachelor. He had never dabbled in matters of love, and looked upon all women alike. Although he respected woman for her virtues, and often spoke of the goodness of heart of the sex, he had never dreamed of marriage. At first he looked upon Miss Peck as a pretty young woman, but after she became his religious teacher, he regarded her in that light, that every one will those whom they know to be their superiors. It was soon seen, however, that the young man not only respected and reverenced Georgiana for the incalculable service she had done him, in awakening him to a sense of duty to his soul, but he had learned to bow to the shrine of Cupid. He found, weeks after he had been in her company, that when he met her at table, or alone in the

---

1 *"The English labourer may be oppressed ... under which he groans"*: W. Tillinghast, "Chattel and Wages Laborers," 61.
2 Source unknown.

drawing-room, or on the piazza, he felt a shortness of breath, a palpitating of the heart, a kind of dizziness of the head; but he knew not its cause.

This was love in its first stage. Mr. Peck saw, or thought he saw, what would be the result of Carlton's visit, and held out every inducement in his power to prolong his stay. The hot season was just commencing, and the young Northerner was talking of his return home, when the parson was very suddenly taken ill. The disease was the cholera, and the physicians pronounced the case incurable. In less than five hours John Peck was a corpse. His love for Georgiana, and respect for her father, had induced Carlton to remain by the bedside of the dying man, although against the express orders of the physician. This act of kindness caused the young orphan henceforth to regard Carlton as her best friend. He now felt it his duty to remain with the young woman until some of her relations should be summoned from Connecticut. After the funeral, the family physician advised that Miss Peck should go to the farm, and spend the time at the country seat; and also advised Carlton to remain with her, which he did.

At the parson's death his negroes showed little or no signs of grief. This was noticed by both Carlton and Miss Peck, and caused no little pain to the latter. "They are ungrateful," said Carlton, as he and Georgiana were seated on the piazza. "What," asked she, "have they to be grateful for?" "Your father was kind, was he not?" "Yes, as kind as most men who own slaves; but the kindness meted out to blacks would be unkindness if given to whites. We would think so, should we not?" "Yes," replied he. "If we would not consider the best treatment which a slave receives good enough for us, we should not think he ought to be grateful for it. Everybody knows that slavery in its best and mildest form is wrong. Whoever denies this, his lips libel his heart. Try him! Clank the chains in his ears, and tell him they are for him; give him an hour to prepare his wife and children for a life of slavery; bid him make haste, and get ready their necks for the yoke, and their wrists for the coffle chains; then look at his pale lips and trembling knees, and you have nature's testimony against slavery."[1]

"Let's take a walk," said Carlton, as if to turn the conversation. The moon was just appearing through the tops of the trees, and

---

1 *"Whoever denies this, his lips ... testimony against slavery"*: Weld, *American Slavery*, 7.

the animals and insects in an adjoining wood kept up a continued din of music. The croaking of bull-frogs, buzzing of insects,
cooing of turtle-doves, and the sound from a thousand musical
instruments, pitched on as many different keys, made the welkin[1]
ring.[2] But even all this noise did not drown the singing of a party
of the slaves, who were seated near a spring that was sending up
its cooling waters. "How prettily the negroes sing," remarked
Carlton, as they were wending their way towards the place from
whence the sound of the voices came. "Yes," replied Georgiana;
"master Sam is there, I'll warrant you: he's always on hand when
there's any singing or dancing. We must not let them see us,
or they will stop singing." "Who makes their songs for them?"
inquired the young man. "Oh, they make them up as they sing
them; they are all impromptu songs." By this time they were near
enough to hear distinctly every word; and, true enough, Sam's
voice was heard above all others. At the conclusion of each song
they all joined in a hearty laugh, with an expression of "Dats de
song for me;" "Dems dems."

"Stop," said Carlton, as Georgiana was rising from the log upon
which she was seated; "stop, and let's hear this one." The piece was
sung by Sam, the others joining in the chorus, and was as follows:

Sam.

"Come, all my brethren, let us take a rest,
While the moon shines so brightly and clear;
Old master is dead, and left us at last,
And has gone at the Bar to appear.
Old master has died, and lying in his grave,
And our blood will awhile cease to flow;
For he's gone where the slaveholders go.

Chorus.

"Hang up the shovel and the hoe—
Take down the fiddle and the bow—
Old master has gone to the slaveholder's rest;
He has gone where they all ought to go.

---

1 Sky.

2 *"The croaking of bull-frogs, buzzing ... many different keys"*: "The
Dismal Swamp," 1.

Sam.

"I heard the old doctor say the other night,
As he passed by the dining-room door—
'Perhaps the old man may live through the night,
But I think he will die about four.'
Young mistress sent me, at the peril of my life,
For the parson to come down and pray,
For says she, 'Your old master is now about to die,'
And says I, 'God speed him on his way.'

"Hang up the shovel, &c.

"At four o'clock at morn the family was called
Around the old man's dying bed;
And oh! but I laughed to myself when I heard
That the old man's spirit had fled.
Mr. Carlton cried, and so did I pretend;
Young mistress very nearly went mad;
And the old parson's groans did the heavens fairly rend;
But I tell you I felt mighty glad.

"Hang up the shovel, &c.

"We'll no more be roused by the blowing of his horn,
Our backs no longer he will score;
He no more will feed us on cotton-seeds and corn;
For his reign of oppression now is o'er.
He no more will hang our children on the tree,
To be ate by the carrion crow;
He no more will send our wives to Tennessee;
For he's gone where the slaveholders go.

"Hang up the shovel and the hoe,
Take down the fiddle and the bow,
We'll dance and sing,
And make the forest ring,
With the fiddle and the old banjo."[1]

---

1 J. Mac C. Simpson, "The Slaveholder's Rest," 188.

The song was not half finished before Carlton regretted that he had caused the young lady to remain and hear what to her must be anything but pleasant reflections upon her deceased parent. "I think we will walk," said he, at the same time extending his arm to Georgiana. "No," said she "let's hear them out. It is from these unguarded expressions of the feelings of the negroes, that we should learn a lesson." At its conclusion they walked towards the house in silence: as they were ascending the steps, the young man said, "They are happy, after all. The negro, situated as yours are, is not aware that he is deprived of any just rights." "Yes, yes," answered Georgiana: "you may place the slave where you please; you may dry up to your utmost the fountains of his feelings, the springs of his thought; you may yoke him to your labour, as an ox which liveth only to work, and worketh only to live; you may put him under any process which, without destroying his value as a slave, will debase and crush him as a rational being; you may do this, and *the idea that he was born to be free will survive it all.* It is allied to his hope of immortality; it is the ethereal part of his nature, which oppression cannot reach; it is a torch lit up in his soul by the hand of Deity, and never meant to be extinguished by the hand of man."[1]

On reaching the drawing-room, they found Sam snuffing the candles, and looking as solemn and as dignified as if he had never sung a song or laughed in his life. "Will Miss Georgy have de supper got up now?" asked the negro. "Yes," she replied. "Well," remarked Carlton, "that beats anything I ever met with. Do you think that was Sam we heard singing?" "I am sure of it," was the answer. "I could not have believed that that fellow was capable of so much deception," continued he. "Our system of slavery is one of deception; and Sam, you see, has only been a good scholar. However, he is as honest a fellow as you will find among the slave population here. If we would have them more honest, we should give them their liberty, and then the inducement to be dishonest would be gone. I have resolved that these creatures shall all be free." "Indeed!" exclaimed Carlton. "Yes, I shall let them all go free, and set an example to those about me." "I honour your judgment," said he. "But will the state permit them to remain?" "If not, they can go where they can live in freedom. I will not be unjust because the state is."

---

1 *"you may place the slave where you please ... hand of man"*: James G. McDowell; quoted in "Emancipation in Maryland," 130.

CHAPTER XVII.

RETALIATION.

"I had a dream, a happy dream;
    I thought that I was free:
That in my own bright land again
    A home there was for me."[1]

With the deepest humiliation Horatio Green saw the daughter of Clotel, his own child, brought into his dwelling as a servant. His wife felt that she had been deceived, and determined to punish her deceiver. At first Mary was put to work in the kitchen, where she met with little or no sympathy from the other slaves, owing to the fairness of her complexion. The child was white, what should be done to make her look like other negroes, was the question Mrs. Green asked herself. At last she hit upon a plan: there was a garden at the back of the house over which Mrs. Green could look from her parlour window. Here the white slave-girl was put to work, without either bonnet or handkerchief upon her head. A hot sun poured its broiling rays on the naked face and neck of the girl, until she sank down in the corner of the garden, and was actually broiled to sleep. "Dat little nigger ain't working a bit, missus," said Dinah to Mrs. Green, as she entered the kitchen. "She's lying in the sun, seasoning; she will work better by and by," replied the mistress. "Dees white niggers always tink dey sef good as white folks," continued the cook. "Yes, but we will teach them better; won't we, Dinah?" "Yes, missus, I don't like dees mularter niggers, no how; dey always want to set dey sef up for something big." The cook was black, and was not without that prejudice which is to be found among the negroes, as well as among the whites of the Southern States. The sun had the desired effect, for in less than a fortnight Mary's fair complexion had disappeared, and she was but little whiter than any other mulatto children running about the yard. But the close resemblance between the father and child annoyed the mistress more than the mere whiteness of the child's complexion. Horatio made proposition after proposition to have the girl sent away, for every time he beheld her countenance it reminded him of the happy days he had spent with Clotel. But his wife had commenced, and determined to carry out her unfeeling and fiendish designs. This child was not only white, but she was the

---

1 "Phoebe Morel," lines 1–4.

granddaughter of Thomas Jefferson, the man who, when speaking against slavery in the legislature of Virginia, said,

> "The whole commerce between master and slave is a perpetual exercise of the most boisterous passions; *the most unremitting despotism on the one part, and degrading submission on the other.* With what execration should the statesman be loaded who, permitting one half the citizens thus to trample on the rights of the other, transforms those into despots and these into enemies, destroys the morals of the one part, and the *amor patriæ*[1] of the other! For if the slave can have a country in this world, it must be any other in preference to that in which he is born to live and labour for another; in which be must lock up the faculties of his nature, contribute as far as depends on his individual endeavours to the evanishment of the human race, or entail his own miserable condition on the endless generations proceeding from him. And can the liberties of a nation be thought secure when we have removed their only firm basis, a conviction in the minds of the people that these liberties are the gift of God? that they are not to be violated but with his wrath? Indeed, I tremble for my country when I reflect that God is just; that his justice cannot sleep for ever; that, considering numbers, nature, and natural means only, a revolution of the wheel of fortune, an exchange of situation, is among possible events; that it may become probable by supernatural interference! The Almighty has no attribute which can take side with us in such a contest.

> .   .   .   .

> "What an incomprehensible machine is man! Who can endure toil, famine, stripes, imprisonment, and death itself, in vindication of his own liberty, and the next moment be deaf to all those motives, whose power supported him through his trial, and inflict on his fellow men a bondage, *one hour of which is fraught with more misery than ages of that which he rose in rebellion to oppose!* But we must wait with patience the workings of an

---

1   Love of country (Latin).

overruling Providence, and hope that that is preparing the deliverance of these our suffering brethren. When the measure of their tears shall be full—when their tears shall have involved heaven itself in darkness—doubtless a God of justice will awaken to their distress, and by diffusing light and liberality among their oppressors, or at length by his exterminating thunder, manifest his attention to things of this world, and that they are not left to the guidance of blind fatality."[1]

The same man, speaking of the probability that the slaves might some day attempt to gain their liberties by a revolution, said,

"I tremble for my country, when I recollect that God is just, and that His justice cannot sleep for ever. The Almighty has no attribute that can take sides with us in such a struggle."[2]

But, sad to say, Jefferson is not the only American statesman who has spoken high-sounding words in favour of freedom, and then left his own children to die slaves.

CHAPTER XVIII.

THE LIBERATOR.

"We hold these truths to be self-evident, that all men are created free and equal; that they are endowed by their Creator with certain inalienable rights; among these are *life, liberty,* and the pursuit of happiness." —*Declaration of American Independence.*

The death of the parson was the commencement of a new era in the history of his slaves. Only a little more than eighteen years of age, Georgiana could not expect to carry out her own wishes in regard to the slaves, although she was sole heir to her father's estate. There were distant relations whose opinions she had at least to respect. And both law and public opinion in the state

---

1   Thomas Jefferson; quoted in William Lloyd Garrison, *Letter to Louis Kossuth*, 40.
2   This sentence appears in the passages from Jefferson, above.

were against any measure of emancipation that she might think of adopting; unless, perhaps, she might be permitted to send them to Liberia.[1] Her uncle in Connecticut had already been written to, to come down and aid in settling up the estate. He was a Northern man, but she knew him to be a tight-fisted yankee, whose whole counsel would go against liberating the negroes. Yet there was one way in which the thing could be done. She loved Carlton, and she well knew that he loved her; she read it in his countenance every time they met, yet the young man did not mention his wishes to her. There were many reasons why he should not. In the first place, her father was just deceased, and it seemed only right that he should wait a reasonable time. Again, Carlton was poor, and Georgiana was possessed of a large fortune; and his high spirit would not, for a moment, allow him to place himself in a position to be regarded as a fortune-hunter. The young girl hinted, as best she could, at the probable future; but all to no purpose. He took nothing to himself. True, she had read much of "woman's rights;" and had even attended a meeting, while at the North, which had been called to discuss the wrongs of woman; but she could not nerve herself up to the point of putting the question to Carlton, although she felt sure that she should not be rejected. She waited, but in vain. At last, one evening, she came out of her room rather late, and was walking on the piazza for fresh air. She passed near Carlton's room, and heard the voice of Sam. The negro had just come in to get the young man's boots, and had stopped, as he usually did, to have some talk. "I wish," said Sam, "dat Marser Carlton an Miss Georgy would get married; den, I 'spec, we'd have good times." "I don't think your mistress would have me," replied the young man. "What make tink dat, Marser Carlton?" "Your mistress would marry no one, Sam, unless she loved them." "Den I wish she would lub you, cause I tink we have good times den. All our folks is de same 'pinion like me," returned the negro, and then left the room with the boots in his hands. During the conversation between the Anglo-Saxon and the African, one word had been dropped by the former that haunted the young lady the remainder of the night—"Your mistress would marry no one unless she loved them." That word awoke her in the morning, and caused her to decide upon this important subject. Love

---

1 A country on the west coast of Africa. It was founded as a colony by the American Colonization Society in 1821 as part of a white supremacist effort to expatriate free black people. Liberia declared its independence in 1847.

and duty triumphed over the woman's timid nature, and that day Georgiana informed Carlton that she was ready to become his wife. The young man, with grateful tears, accepted and kissed the hand that was offered to him. The marriage of Carlton and Miss Peck was hailed with delight by both the servants in the house and the negroes on the farm. New rules were immediately announced for the working and general treatment of the slaves on the plantation. With this, Huckelby, the overseer, saw his reign coming to an end; and Snyder, the Dutch preacher, felt that his services would soon be dispensed with, for nothing was more repugnant to the feelings of Mrs. Carlton than the sermons preached by Snyder to the slaves. She regarded them as something intended to make them better satisfied with their condition, and more valuable as pieces of property, without preparing them for the world to come. Mrs. Carlton found in her husband a congenial spirit, who entered into all her wishes and plans for bettering the condition of their slaves. Mrs. Carlton's views and sympathies were all in favour of immediate emancipation; but then she saw, or thought she saw, a difficulty in that. If the slaves were liberated they must be sent out of the state. This, of course, would incur additional expense; and if they left the state, where had they better go? "Let's send them to Liberia," said Carlton. "Why should they go to Africa, any more than to the Free States or to Canada?" asked the wife. "They would be in their native land," he answered. "Is not this their native land? What right have we, more than the negro to the soil here, or to style ourselves native Americans? Indeed it is as much their homes as ours, and I have sometimes thought it was more theirs. The negro has cleared up the lands, built towns, and enriched the soil with his blood and tears; and in return, he is to be sent to a country of which he knows nothing. Who fought more bravely for American independence than the blacks? A negro, by the name of Attucks, was the first that fell in Boston at the commencement of the revolutionary war; and, throughout the whole of the struggles for liberty in this country, the negroes have contributed their share. In the last war with Great Britain, the country was mainly indebted to the blacks in New Orleans for the achievement of the victory at that place; and even General Jackson, the commander in chief, called the negroes together at the close of the war, and addressed them in the following terms:—

"'Soldiers!—When on the banks of the Mobile I called you to take up arms, inviting you to partake the perils and glory of your *white fellow citizens, I expected much from you*; for I was not ignorant that you possessed qualities most formidable to an invading enemy. I knew with what fortitude you could endure hunger and thirst, and all the fatigues of a campaign. *I knew well how you loved your native country*, and that you, as well as ourselves, had to defend what *man* holds most dear—his parents, wife, children, and property. *You have done more than I expected.* In addition to the previous qualities I before knew you to possess, I found among you a noble enthusiasm, which leads to the performance of great things.

"'Soldiers! The President of the United States shall hear how praiseworthy was your conduct in the hour of danger, and the representatives of the American people will give you the praise your exploits entitle you to. Your general anticipates them in applauding your noble ardour.'[1]

"And what did these noble men receive in return for their courage, their heroism? Chains and slavery. Their good deeds have been consecrated only in their own memories. Who rallied with more alacrity in response to the summons of danger? If in that hazardous hour, when our homes were menaced with the horrors of war, we did not disdain to call upon the negro to assist in repelling invasion, why should we, now that the danger is past, deny him a home in his native land?"[2] "I see," said Carlton, "you are right, but I fear you will have difficulty in persuading others to adopt your views." "We will set the example," replied she, "and then hope for the best; for I feel that the people of the Southern States will one day see their error. Liberty has always been our watchword, as far as profession is concerned. Nothing has been held so cheap as our common humanity, on a national average. If every man had his aliquot[3] proportion of the injustice done in this land, by law and violence, the present freemen of the northern section would many of them commit

---

1 Seventh US president (1829–37) Andrew Jackson (1767–1845); quoted in William Cooper Nell, *Services of Colored Americans, in the Wars of 1776 and 1812*, 21. Nell (1816–74) was an abolitionist, journalist, and author.
2 *"Their good deeds have been ... danger is past"*: "The Free Colored Veterans," 2; quoted in Nell, *Services*, 22.
3 Fractional.

suicide in self-defence, and would court the liberties awarded by Ali Pasha of Egypt to his subjects. Long ere this we should have tested, in behalf of our bleeding and crushed American brothers of every hue and complexion, every new constitution, custom, or practice, by which inhumanity was supposed to be upheld, the injustice and cruelty they contained, emblazoned before the great tribunal of mankind for condemnation; and the good and available power they possessed, for the relief, deliverance and elevation of oppressed men, permitted to shine forth from under the cloud, for the refreshment of the human race."[1]

Although Mr. and Mrs. Carlton felt that immediate emancipation was the right of the slave and the duty of the master, they resolved on a system of gradual emancipation, so as to give them time to accomplish their wish, and to prepare the negro for freedom. Huckelby was one morning told that his services would no longer be required. The negroes, ninety-eight in number, were called together and told that the whip would no longer be used, and that they would be allowed a certain sum for every bale of cotton produced. Sam, whose long experience in the cotton-field before he had been taken into the house, and whose general intelligence justly gave him the first place amongst the negroes on the Poplar Farm, was placed at their head. They were also given to understand that the money earned by them would be placed to their credit; and when it amounted to a certain sum, they should all be free.

The joy with which this news was received by the slaves, showed their grateful appreciation of the boon their benefactors were bestowing upon them. The house servants were called and told that wages would be allowed them, and what they earned set to their credit, and they too should be free. The next were the bricklayers. There were eight of these, who had paid their master two dollars per day, and boarded and clothed themselves. An arrangement was entered into with them, by which the money they earned should be placed to their credit; and they too should be free, when a certain amount should be accumulated; and great was the change amongst all these people. The bricklayers had been to work but a short time, before their increased industry was noticed by many. They were no longer apparently the same people. A sedateness, a care, an economy, an industry, took possession of them, to which there seemed to

---

1   "*Nothing has been held so cheap as our common humanity ... the human race*": Alvan Stewart (1790–1849), *A Legal Argument Before the Supreme Court of the State of New Jersey*, 7.

be no bounds but in their physical strength. They were never tired of labouring, and seemed as though they could never effect enough. They became temperate, moral, religious, setting an example of innocent, unoffending lives to the world around them, which was seen and admired by all.[1] Mr. Parker, a man who worked nearly forty slaves at the same business, was attracted by the manner in which these negroes laboured. He called on Mr. Carlton, some weeks after they had been acting on the new system, and offered 2,000 dollars for the head workman, Jim. The offer was, of course, refused. A few days after the same gentleman called again, and made an offer of double the sum that he had on the former occasion. Mr. Parker, finding that no money would purchase either of the negroes, said, "Now, Mr. Carlton, pray tell me what it is that makes your negroes work so? What kind of people are they?" "I suppose," observed Carlton, "that they are like other people, flesh and blood." "Why, sir," continued Parker, "I have never seen such people; building as they are next door to my residence, I see and have my eye on them from morning till night. You are never there, for I have never met you, or seen you once at the building. Why, sir, I am an early riser, getting up before day; and do you think that I am not awoke every morning in my life by the noise of their trowels at work, and their singing and noise before day; and do you suppose, sir, that they stop or leave off work at sundown? No, sir, but they work as long as they can see to lay a brick, and then they carry up brick and mortar for an hour or two afterward, to be ahead of their work the next morning. And again, sir, do you think that they walk at their work? No, sir, they run all day. You see, sir, those immensely long ladders, five stories in height; do you suppose they walk up them? No, sir, they run up and down them like so many monkeys all day long. I never saw such people as these in my life. I don't know what to make of them. Were a white man with them and over them with a whip, then I should see and understand the cause of the running and incessant labour; but I cannot comprehend it; there is something in it, sir. Great man, sir, that Jim; great man; I should like to own him."[2] Carlton here informed Parker that their liberties depended upon their work; when the latter replied, "If niggers can work so for the

---

1   *"They were no longer apparently the same people ... admired by all"*:
    John McDonogh, *Letter of John McDonogh, on African Colonization*,
    18. McDonogh (1779–1850), a Louisianian slaveholder, was active
    in the American Colonization Society.

2   *"What kind of people are they? ... to own him"*: McDonogh, *Letter*,
    24–25.

promise of freedom, they ought to be made to work without it." This last remark was in the true spirit of the slaveholder, and reminds us of the fact that, some years since, the overseer of General Wade Hampton offered the niggers under him a suit of clothes to the one that picked the most cotton in one day; and after that time that day's work was given as a task to the slaves on that plantation; and, after a while, was adopted by other planters.[1]

The negroes on the farm, under "Marser Sam," were also working in a manner that attracted the attention of the planters round about. They no longer feared Huckelby's whip, and no longer slept under the preaching of Snyder. On the Sabbath, Mr. and Mrs. Carlton read and explained the Scriptures to them; and the very great attention paid by the slaves showed plainly that they appreciated the gospel when given to them in its purity. The death of Currer, from yellow fever, was a great trial to Mrs. Carlton; for she had not only become much attached to her, but had heard with painful interest the story of her wrongs, and would, in all probability, have restored her to her daughter in New Orleans.

CHAPTER XIX.

ESCAPE OF CLOTEL.

"The fetters galled my weary soul—
A soul that seemed but thrown away;
I spurned the tyrant's base control,
Resolved at least the man to play."[2]

No country has produced so much heroism in so short a time, connected with escapes from peril and oppression, as has occurred in the United States among fugitive slaves, many of whom show great shrewdness in their endeavours to escape from this land of bondage. A slave was one day seen passing on the high road from a border town in the interior of the state of Virginia to the Ohio river. The man had neither hat upon his head or coat upon his back. He was driving before him a very nice fat pig, and

---

1 Wade Hampton (1752–1835) was a wealthy slaveholder and politician from South Carolina who served as a general in the War of 1812.

2 Elizur Wright, "The Fugitive Slave to the Christian," lines 1–4.

appeared to all who saw him to be a labourer employed on an adjoining farm. "No negro is permitted to go at large in the Slave States without a written pass from his or her master, except on business in the neighbourhood." "Where do you live, my boy?" asked a white man of the slave, as he passed a white house with green blinds. "Jist up de road, sir," was the answer. "That's a fine pig." "Yes, sir, marser like dis choat berry much." And the negro drove on as if he was in great haste. In this way he and the pig travelled more than fifty miles before they reached the Ohio river. Once at the river they crossed over; the pig was sold; and nine days after the runaway slave passed over the Niagara river, and, for the first time in his life, breathed the air of freedom. A few weeks later, and, on the same road, two slaves were seen passing; one was on horseback, the other was walking before him with his arms tightly bound, and a long rope leading from the man on foot to the one on horseback. "Oh, ho, that's a runaway rascal, I suppose," said a farmer, who met them on the road. "Yes, sir, he bin runaway, and I got him fast. Marser will tan his jacket for him nicely when he gets him." "You are a trustworthy fellow, I imagine," continued the farmer. "Oh yes, sir; marser puts a heap of confidence in dis nigger." And the slaves travelled on. When the one on foot was fatigued they would change positions, the other being tied and driven on foot. This they called "ride and tie." After a journey of more than two hundred miles they reached the Ohio river, turned the horse loose, told him to go home, and proceeded on their way to Canada. However they were not to have it all their own way. There are men in the Free States, and especially in the states adjacent to the Slave States, who make their living by catching the runaway slave, and returning him for the reward that may be offered. As the two slaves above mentioned were travelling on towards the land of freedom, led by the North Star, they were set upon by four of these slave-catchers, and one of them unfortunately captured. The other escaped. The captured fugitive was put under the torture, and compelled to reveal the name of his owner and his place of residence. Filled with delight, the kidnappers started back with their victim. Overjoyed with the prospect of receiving a large reward, they gave themselves up on the third night to pleasure. They put up at an inn. The negro was chained to the bed-post, in the same room with his captors. At dead of night, when all was still, the slave arose from the floor upon which he had been lying, looked around, and saw that the white men were fast asleep. The brandy punch had done its work. With palpitating heart and trembling limbs he viewed his position. The door was fast, but the warm weather had compelled them to leave the window open. If he could but get his chains off, he might escape through the window to the piazza, and reach the ground by one of the posts that supported the piazza. The sleeper's clothes hung upon chairs by the bedside; the slave thought of the padlock key, examined the pockets and found it. The chains were soon off, and the negro stealthily making his way to the window: he stopped and said to himself, "These men are villains, they are enemies to all who like me are trying to be free. Then why not I teach them a lesson?" He then undressed himself, took the clothes of one of the men, dressed himself in them, and escaped through the window, and, a moment more, he was on the high road to Canada. Fifteen days later, and the writer of this gave him a passage across Lake Erie, and saw him safe in her Britannic Majesty's dominions.

We have seen Clotel sold to Mr. French in Vicksburgh, her hair cut short, and everything done to make her realise her position as a servant. Then we have seen her re-sold, because her owners feared she would die through grief. As yet her new purchaser treated her with respectful gentleness, and sought to win her favour by flattery and presents, knowing that whatever he gave her he could take back again. But she dreaded every moment lest the scene should change, and trembled at the sound of every footfall.[1] At every interview with her new master Clotel stoutly maintained that she had left a husband in Virginia, and would never think of taking another. The gold watch and chain, and other glittering presents which he purchased for her, were all laid aside by the quadroon, as if they were of no value to her. In the same house with her was another servant, a man, who had from time to time hired himself from his master. William was his name. He could feel for Clotel, for he, like her, had been separated from near and dear relatives, and often tried to console the poor woman. One day the quadroon observed to him that her hair was growing out again. "Yes," replied William, "you look a good deal like a man with your short hair." "Oh," rejoined she, "I have often been told that I would make a better looking man than a woman. If I had the money," continued she, "I would bid farewell to this place." In a moment more she feared that she had said too much, and smilingly remarked, "I am always talking nonsense." William was a tall, full-bodied negro, whose very countenance beamed with intelligence. Being a mechanic, he had, by his own industry, made

---

1 *"As yet her new purchaser treated her ... of every footfall"*: Child, "The Quadroons," 138–39.

more than what he paid his owner; this he laid aside, with the hope that some day he might get enough to purchase his freedom. He had in his chest one hundred and fifty dollars. His was a heart that felt for others, and he had again and again wiped the tears from his eyes as he heard the story of Clotel as related by herself. "If she can get free with a little money, why not give her what I have?" thought he, and then he resolved to do it. An hour after, he came into the quadroon's room, and laid the money in her lap, and said, "There, Miss Clotel, you said if you had the means you would leave this place; there is money enough to take you to England, where you will be free. You are much fairer than many of the white women of the South, and can easily pass for a free white lady." At first Clotel feared that it was a plan by which the negro wished to try her fidelity to her owner; but she was soon convinced by his earnest manner, and the deep feeling with which he spoke, that he was honest. "I will take the money only on one condition," said she; "and that is, that I effect your escape as well as my own." "How can that be done?" he inquired. "I will assume the disguise of a gentleman and you that of a servant, and we will take passage on a steamboat and go to Cincinnati, and thence to Canada." Here William put in several objections to the plan. He feared detection, and he well knew that, when a slave is once caught when attempting to escape, if returned is sure to be worse treated than before. However, Clotel satisfied him that the plan could be carried out if he would only play his part.

The resolution was taken, the clothes for her disguise procured, and before night everything was in readiness for their departure. That night Mr. Cooper, their master, was to attend a party, and this was their opportunity. William went to the wharf to look out for a boat, and had scarcely reached the landing ere he heard the puffing of a steamer. He returned and reported the fact. Clotel had already packed her trunk, and had only to dress and all was ready. In less than an hour they were on board the boat. Under the assumed name of "Mr. Johnson," Clotel went to the clerk's office and took a private state room for herself, and paid her own and servant's fare. Besides being attired in a neat suit of black, she had a white silk handkerchief tied round her chin, as if she was an invalid. A pair of green glasses covered her eyes; and fearing that she would be talked to too much and thus render her liable to be detected, she assumed to be very ill. On the other hand, William was playing his part well in the servants' hall; he was talking loudly of his master's wealth. Nothing appeared as good on the boat as in his master's fine mansion. "I don't like dees steamboats no how," said William; "I hope when marser goes on a journey agin he will take de carriage and de hosses." Mr. Johnson (for such was the name by which Clotel now went) remained in his room, to avoid, as far as possible, conversation with others. After a passage of seven days they arrived at Louisville, and put up at Gough's Hotel. Here they had to await the departure of another boat for the North. They were now in their most critical position. They were still in a slave state, and John C. Calhoun, a distinguished slave-owner, was a guest at this hotel.[1] They feared, also, that trouble would attend their attempt to leave this place for the North, as all persons taking negroes with them have to give bail that such negroes are not runaway slaves. The law upon this point is very stringent: all steamboats and other public conveyances are liable to a fine for every slave that escapes by them, besides paying the full value for the slave. After a delay of four hours, Mr. Johnson and servant took passage on the steamer Rodolph, for Pittsburgh. It is usual, before the departure of the boats, for an officer to examine every part of the vessel to see that no slave secretes himself on board, "Where are you going?" asked the officer of William, as he was doing his duty on this occasion. "I am going with marser," was the quick reply. "Who is your master?" "Mr. Johnson, sir, a gentleman in the cabin." "You must take him to the office and satisfy that captain that all is right, or you can't go on this boat." William informed his master what the officer had said. The boat was on the eve of going, and no time could be lost, yet they knew not what to do. At last they went to the office, and Mr. Johnson, addressing the captain, said, "I am informed that my boy can't go with me unless I give security that he belongs to me." "Yes," replied the captain, "that is the law." "A very strange law indeed," rejoined Mr. Johnson, "that one can't take his property with him." After a conversation of some minutes, and a plea on the part of Johnson that he did not wish to be delayed owing to his illness, they were permitted to take their passage without farther trouble, and the boat was soon on its way up the river.[2] The fugitives had now passed the Rubicon,[3] and the next place at which they would

---

1   John Caldwell Calhoun (1782–1850) was an influential pro-slavery politician from South Carolina.
2   The story of the escape of William and Clotel is based on the escape of William and Ellen Craft from Macon, Georgia, in December 1848. Brown met the Crafts soon after their escape and lectured with them in the United States and Great Britain.
3   Boundary line, point of no return. A reference to Julius Caesar's insurrectionary crossing of the Rubicon River into Italy in 49 BCE.

land would be in a Free State. Clotel called William to her room, and said to him, "We are now free, you can go on your way to Canada, and I shall go to Virginia in search of my daughter." The announcement that she was going to risk her liberty in a Slave State was unwelcome news to William. With all the eloquence he could command, he tried to persuade Clotel that she could not escape detection, and was only throwing her freedom away. But she had counted the cost, and made up her mind for the worst. In return for the money he had furnished, she had secured for him his liberty, and their engagement was at an end.

After a quick passage the fugitives arrived at Cincinnati, and there separated. William proceeded on his way to Canada, and Clotel again resumed her own apparel, and prepared to start in search of her child. As might have been expected, the escape of those two valuable slaves created no little sensation in Vicksburgh. Advertisements and messages were sent in every direction in which the fugitives were thought to have gone. It was soon, however, known that they had left the town as master and servant; and many were the communications which appeared in the newspapers, in which the writers thought, or pretended, that they had seen the slaves in their disguise. One was to the effect that they had gone off in a chaise; one as master, and the other as servant. But the most probable was an account given by a correspondent of one of the Southern newspapers, who happened to be a passenger in the same steamer in which the slaves escaped, and which we here give:—

> "One bright starlight night, in the month of December last, I found myself in the cabin of the steamer Rodolph, then lying in the port of Vicksburgh, and bound to Louisville. I had gone early on board, in order to select a good berth, and having got tired of reading the papers, amused myself with watching the appearance of the passengers as they dropped in, one after another, and I being a believer in physiognomy, formed my own opinion of their characters.
>
> "The second bell rang, and as I yawningly returned my watch to my pocket, my attention was attracted by the appearance of a young man who entered the cabin supported by his servant, a strapping negro.
>
> "The man was bundled up in a capacious overcoat; his face was bandaged with a white handkerchief, and its expression entirely hid by a pair of enormous spectacles.

"There was something so mysterious and unusual about the young man as he sat restless in the corner, that curiosity led me to observe him more closely.

"He appeared anxious to avoid notice, and before the steamer had fairly left the wharf, requested, in a low, womanly voice, to be shown his berth, as he was an invalid, and must retire early: his name he gave as Mr. Johnson. His servant was called, and he was put quietly to bed. I paced the deck until Tybee light grew dim in the distance, and then went to my berth.

"I awoke in the morning with the sun shining in my face; we were then just passing St. Helena. It was a mild beautiful morning, and most of the passengers were on deck, enjoying the freshness of the air, and stimulating their appetites for breakfast. Mr. Johnson soon made his appearance, arrayed as on the night before, and took his seat quietly upon the guard of the boat.

"From the better opportunity afforded by daylight, I found that he was a slight built, apparently handsome young man, with black hair and eyes, and of a darkness of complexion that betokened Spanish extraction. Any notice from others seemed painful to him; so to satisfy my curiosity, I questioned his servant, who was standing near, and gained the following information.

"His master was an invalid—he had suffered for a long time under a complication of diseases, that had baffled the skill of the best physicians in Mississippi he was now suffering principally with the 'rheumatism,' and he was scarcely able to walk or help himself in any way. He came from Vicksburgh, and was now on his way to Philadelphia, at which place resided his uncle, a celebrated physician, and through whose means he hoped to be restored to perfect health.

"This information, communicated in a bold, off-hand manner, enlisted my sympathies for the sufferer, although it occurred to me that he walked rather too gingerly for a person afflicted with so many ailments."[1]

After thanking Clotel for the great service she had done him in bringing him out of slavery, William bade her farewell. The prejudice that exists in the Free States against coloured persons,

---

1 "An Incident at the South," 23.

on account of their colour, is attributable solely to the influence of slavery, and is but another form of slavery itself. And even the slave who escapes from the Southern plantations, is surprised when he reaches the North, at the amount and withering influence of this prejudice. William applied at the railway station for a ticket for the train going to Sandusky, and was told that if he went by that train he would have to ride in the luggage-van. "Why?" asked the astonished negro. "We don't send a Jim Crow carriage but once a day, and that went this morning." The "Jim Crow" carriage is the one in which the blacks have to ride. Slavery is a school in which its victims learn much shrewdness, and William had been an apt scholar. Without asking any more questions, the negro took his seat in one of the first-class carriages. He was soon seen and ordered out. Afraid to remain in the town longer, he resolved to go by that train; and consequently seated himself on a goods' box in the luggage-van. The train started at its proper time, and all went on well. Just before arriving at the end of the journey, the conductor called on William for his ticket. "I have none," was the reply. "Well, then, you can pay your fare to me," said the officer. "How much is it?" asked the black man. "Two dollars." "What do you charge those in the passenger-carriage?" "Two dollars." "And do you charge me the same as you do those who ride in the best carriages?" asked the negro. "Yes," was the answer. "I shan't pay it," returned the man. "You black scamp, do you think you can ride on this road without paying your fare?" "No, I don't want to ride for nothing; I only want to pay what's right." "Well, launch out two dollars, and that's right." "No, I shan't; I will pay what I ought, and won't pay any more." "Come, come, nigger, your fare and be done with it," said the conductor, in a manner that is never used except by Americans to blacks. "I won't pay you two dollars, and that enough," said William. "Well, as you have come all the way in the luggage-van, pay me a dollar and a half and you may go." "I shan't do any such thing." "Don't you mean to pay for riding?" "Yes, but I won't pay a dollar and a half for riding up here in the freight-van. If you had let me come in the carriage where others ride, I would have paid you two dollars." "Where were you raised? You seem to think yourself as good as white folks." "I want nothing more than my rights." "Well, give me a dollar, and I will let you off." "No, sir, I shan't do it." "What do you mean to do then—don't you wish to pay anything?" "Yes, sir, I want to pay you the full price." "What do you mean by full price?" "What do you charge per hundred-weight for goods?" inquired the negro with a degree of gravity that would have astonished Diogenes[1] himself. "A quarter of a dollar per hundred," answered the conductor. "I weight just one hundred and fifty pounds," returned William, "and will pay you three-eighths of a dollar." "Do you expect that you will pay only thirty-seven cents for your ride?" "This, sir, is your own price. I came in a luggage-van, and I'll pay for luggage." After a vain effort to get the negro to pay more, the conductor took the thirty-seven cents, and noted in his cash-book, "Received for one hundred and fifty pounds of luggage, thirty-seven cents." This, reader, is no fiction; it actually occurred in the railway above described.

Thomas Corwin, a member of the American Congress, is one of the blackest white men in the United States.[2] He was once on his way to Congress, and took passage in one of the Ohio river steamers. As he came just at the dinner hour, he immediately went into the dining saloon, and took his seat at the table. A gentleman with his whole party of five ladies at once left the table. "Where is the captain," cried the man in an angry tone. The captain soon appeared, and it was sometime before he could satisfy the old gent. that Governor Corwin was not a nigger. The newspapers often have notices of mistakes made by innkeepers and others who undertake to accommodate the public, one of which we give below.

On the 6th inst., the Hon. Daniel Webster and family entered Edgartown, on a visit for health and recreation.[3] Arriving at the hotel, without alighting from the coach, the landlord was sent for to see if suitable accommodation could be had. That dignitary appearing, and surveying Mr. Webster, while the hon. senator addressed him, seemed woefully to mistake the dark features of the traveller as he sat back in the corner of the carriage, and to suppose him a *coloured man*, particularly as there were two coloured servants of Mr. W. outside. So he promptly declared that there was no room for him and his family, and he could not be accommodated there—at the same time suggesting that he might perhaps find accommodation at some of the huts "up back," to which he pointed. So deeply did the prejudice of looks possess him, that he appeared not to notice that the stranger introduced himself to him as Daniel Webster, or

---

1 Diogenes the Cynic (c. 404–323 BCE) was a Greek philosopher. He is said to have gone about with a lamp in search of an honest man.
2 Thomas Corwin (1794–1865) served as governor of Ohio from 1840 to 1844 and as a US senator from 1845 to 1850.
3 Daniel Webster (1782–1852) was an influential lawyer and politician from New Hampshire who helped to negotiate the passage of the 1850 Fugitive Slave Law; *inst*: of this month (Latin).

to be so ignorant as not to have heard of such a personage; and turning away, he expressed to the driver his astonishment that he should bring *black* people there for *him* to take in. It was not till he had been repeatedly assured and made to understand that the said Daniel Webster was a real live senator of the United States, that he perceived his awkward mistake and the distinguished honour which he and his house were so near missing.[1]

In most of the Free States, the coloured people are disfranchised on account of their colour. The following scene, which we take from a newspaper in the state of Ohio, will give some idea of the extent to which this prejudice is carried.

> "The whole of Thursday last was occupied by the Court of Common Pleas for this county in trying to find out whether one Thomas West was of the VOTING CO-LOUR, as some had very *constitutional doubts* as to whether his colour was orthodox, and whether his hair was of the official crisp! Was it not a dignified business? Four profound judges, four acute lawyers, twelve grave jurors, and I don't know how many venerable witnesses, making in all about thirty men, perhaps, all engaged in the profound, laborious, and illustrious business, of finding out whether a man who pays tax, works on the road, and is an industrious farmer, has been born according to the republican, Christian constitution of Ohio—so that he can vote! And they wisely, gravely, and 'JUDGMATICAL-LY' decided that he should not vote! What wisdom—what research it must have required to evolve this truth! It was left for the Court of Common Pleas for Columbian county, Ohio, in the United States of North America, to find out what Solomon never dreamed of—the courts of all civilised, heathen, or Jewish countries, never contemplated. Lest the wisdom of our courts should be circumvented by some such men as might be named, who are so near being born constitutionally that they might be taken for white by sight, I would suggest that our court be invested with SMELLING powers, and that if a man don't exhale the constitutional smell, he shall not vote! This would be an additional security to our liberties."[2]

---

1 "Quite a Blunder," *Emancipator and Republican*, 16 August 1849, 1.
2 "Hurrah for the Nineteenth Century!" *Liberator*, 17 November 1843, 182.

William found, after all, that liberty in the so-called Free States was more a name than a reality; that prejudice followed the coloured man into every place that he might enter. The temples erected for the worship of the living God are no exception. The finest Baptist church in the city of Boston has the following paragraph in the deed that conveys its seats to pewholders:

> "And it is a further condition of these presents, that if the owner or owners of said pew shall determine hereafter to sell the same, it shall first be offered, in writing, to the standing committee of said society for the time being, at such price as might otherwise be obtained for it; and the said committee shall have the right, for ten days after such offer, to purchase said pew for said society, at that price, first deducting therefrom all taxes and assessments on said pew then remaining unpaid. And if the said committee shall not so complete such purchase within said ten days, then the pew may be sold by the owner or owners thereof (after payment of all such arrears) to any one respectable *white person*, but upon the same conditions as are contained in this instrument; and immediate notice of such sale shall be given in writing, by the vendor, to the treasurer of said society."

Such are the conditions upon which the Rowe Street Baptist Church, Boston, disposes of its seats. The writer of this is able to put that whole congregation, minister and all, to flight, by merely putting his coloured face in that church. We once visited a church in New York that had a place set apart for the sons of Ham. It was a dark, dismal looking place in one corner of the gallery, grated in front like a hen-coop, with a black border around it. It had two doors; over one was B.M.—black men; over the other B.W.—black women.

CHAPTER XX.

A TRUE DEMOCRAT.

"Who can, with patience, for a moment see
The medley mass of pride and misery,
Of whips and charters, manacles and rights,
Of slaving blacks and democratic whites,
And all the piebald policy that reigns

In free confusion o'er Columbia's plains?
To think that man, thou just and gentle God!
Should stand before thee with a tyrant's rod,
O'er creatures like himself, with souls from thee,
Yet dare to boast of perfect liberty!"—*Thomas Moore*.[1]

Educated in a free state, and marrying a wife who had been a victim to the institution of slavery, Henry Morton became strongly
opposed to the system. His two daughters, at the age of twelve
years, were sent to the North to finish their education, and to
receive that refinement that young ladies cannot obtain in the
Slave States. Although he did not publicly advocate the abolition
of slavery, he often made himself obnoxious to private circles,
owing to the denunciatory manner in which he condemned the
"peculiar institution." Being one evening at a party, and hearing
one of the company talking loudly of the glory and freedom of
American institutions, he gave it as his opinion that, unless slavery
was speedily abolished, it would be the ruin of the Union. "It is not
our boast of freedom," said he, "that will cause us to be respected
abroad. It is not our loud talk in favour of liberty that will cause us
to be regarded as friends of human freedom; but our acts will be
scrutinised by the people of other countries. We say much against
European despotism; let us look to ourselves. That government
is despotic where the rulers govern subjects by their own mere
will—by decrees and laws emanating from their uncontrolled
will, in the enactment and execution of which the ruled have no
voice, and under which they have no right except at the will of
the rulers. Despotism does not depend upon the number of the
rulers, or the number of the subjects. It may have one ruler or
many. Rome was a despotism under Nero; so she was under the
triumvirate. Athens was a despotism under Thirty Tyrants; under
her Four Hundred Tyrants; under her Three Thousand Tyrants.
It has been generally observed that despotism increases in severity
with the number of despots; the responsibility is more divided,
and the claims more numerous. The triumvirs each demanded his
victims. The smaller the number of subjects in proportion to the
tyrants, the more cruel the oppression, because the less danger
from rebellion. In this government, the free white citizens are the
rulers—the sovereigns, as we delight to be called. All others are
subjects. There are, perhaps, some sixteen or seventeen millions
of sovereigns, and four millions of subjects.

---

1 Thomas Moore, "To the Lord Viscount Forbes," lines 139–48.

"The rulers and the ruled are of all colours, from the clear white of the Caucasian tribes to the swarthy Ethiopian. The former, by courtesy, are all called white, the latter black. In this government the subject has no rights, social, political, or personal. He has no voice in the laws which govern him. He can hold no property. His very wife and children are not his. His labour is another's. He, and all that appertain to him, are the absolute property of his rulers. He is governed, bought, sold, punished, executed, by laws to which he never gave his assent, and by rulers whom he never chose. He is not a serf merely, with half the rights of men like the subjects of despotic Russia; but a native slave, stripped of every right which God and nature gave him, and which the high spirit of our revolution declared inalienable—which he himself could not surrender, and which man could not take from him. Is he not then the subject of despotic sway?

"The slaves of Athens and Rome were free in comparison. They had some rights—could acquire some property; could choose their own masters, and purchase their own freedom; and, when free, could rise in social and political life. The slaves of America, then, lie under the most absolute and grinding despotism that the world ever saw. But who are the despots? The rulers of the country—the sovereign people! Not merely the slaveholder who cracks the lash. He is but the instrument in the hands of despotism. That despotism is the government of the Slave States, and the United States, consisting of all its rulers—all the free citizens. Do not look upon this as a paradox, because you and I and the sixteen millions of rulers are free. The rulers of every despotism are free. Nicholas of Russia is free. The grand Sultan of Turkey is free. The butcher of Austria is free. Augustus, Anthony, and Lepidus were free, while they drenched Rome in blood. The Thirty Tyrants—the Four Hundred—the Three Thousand, were free while they bound their countrymen in chains. You, and I, and the sixteen millions are free, while we fasten iron chains, and rivet manacles on four millions of our fellow-men—tear their wives and children from them—separate them—sell them, and doom them to perpetual, eternal bondage. Are we not then despots—despots such as history will brand and God abhor?"[1]

"We, as individuals, are fast losing our reputation for honest dealing. Our nation is losing its character. The loss of a firm

---

1 *"That government is despotic where the rulers govern ... and God abhor?"*: Thaddeus Stevens, "The Slavery Question," 37.

national character, or the degradation of a nation's honour, is the inevitable prelude to her destruction. Behold the once proud fabric of a Roman empire—an empire carrying its arts and arms into every part of the Eastern continent; the monarchs of mighty kingdoms dragged at the wheels of her triumphal chariots; her eagle waving over the ruins of desolated countries;—where is her splendour, her wealth, her power, her glory? Extinguished for ever. Her mouldering temples, the mournful vestiges of her former grandeur, afford a shelter to her muttering monks. Where are her statesmen, her sages, her philosophers, her orators, generals? Go to their solitary tombs and inquire. She lost her national character, and her destruction followed. The ramparts of her national pride were broken down, and Vandalism desolated her classic fields.[1] Then let the people of our country take warning ere it is too late. But most of us say to ourselves,

> "'Who questions the right of mankind to be free?
> Yet, what are the rights of the *negro* to me?
> I'm well fed and clothed, I have plenty of pelf[2]—
> I'll care for the blacks when I turn black myself.'[3]

"New Orleans is doubtless the most immoral place in the United States. The theatres are open on the Sabbath. Bull-fights, horse-racing, and other cruel amusements are carried on in this city to an extent unknown in any other part of the Union. The most stringent laws have been passed in that city against negroes, yet a few years since the State Legislature passed a special act to enable a white man to marry a coloured woman, on account of her being possessed of a large fortune. And, very recently, the following paragraph appeared in the city papers:—

> "'There has been quite a stir recently in this city, in
> consequence of a marriage of a white man, named
> Buddington, a teller in the Canal Bank, to the negro
> daughter of one of the wealthiest merchants. Budding-
> ton, before he could be married, was obliged to swear
> that he had negro blood in his veins, and to do this he

---

1 "*The loss of a firm national character, or the degradation ... her classic fields*": Milton Maxcy, *An Oration, Delivered in the Dutch Church in Schenectady*, 19.

2 Money, especially when obtained dishonestly.

3 "Love Thy Neighbor," 128.

made an incision in his arm, and put some of her blood in the cut. The ceremony was performed by a Catholic clergyman, and the bridegroom has received with his wife a fortune of fifty or sixty thousand dollars.'[1]

"It seems that the fifty or sixty thousand dollars entirely covered the negro woman's black skin, and the law prohibiting marriage between blacks and whites was laid aside for the occasion."

Althesa felt proud, as well she might, at her husband's taking such high ground in a slaveholding city like New Orleans.

CHAPTER XXI.

THE CHRISTIAN'S DEATH.

"O weep, ye friends of freedom weep!
Your harps to mournful measures sweep."[2]

On the last day of November, 1620, on the confines of the Grand Bank of Newfoundland, lo! we behold one little solitary tempest-tost and weatherbeaten ship; it is all that can be seen on the length and breadth of the vast intervening solitudes, from the melancholy wilds of Labrador and New England's iron-bound shores, to the western coasts of Ireland and the rock-defended Hebrides, but one lonely ship greets the eye of angels or of men, on this great thoroughfare of nations in our age. Next in moral grandeur, was this ship, to the great discoverer's: Columbus[3] found a continent; the May-flower[4] brought the seed-wheat of states and empire. That is the May-flower, with its servants of the living God, their wives and little ones, hastening to lay the foundations of nations in the occidental lands of the setting-sun. Hear the voice of prayer to God for his protection, and the glorious music of praise, as it breaks into the wild tempest of the mighty deep, upon the ear of God. Here in this ship are great and good men. Justice, mercy, hu-

---

1 "Phlebotomy—Amalgamation!" 46.
2 D.H. Jaques, "Your Brother Is a Slave," lines 1, 3.
3 The Italian explorer Christopher Columbus (c. 1451–1506) landed in the Bahamas in 1492.
4 The *Mayflower* was the ship in which Protestant Separatists first traveled to New England.

manity, respect for the rights of all; each man honoured, as he was useful to himself and others; labour respected, law-abiding men, constitution-making and respecting men; men, whom no tyrant could conquer, or hardship overcome, with the high commission sealed by a Spirit divine, to establish religious and political liberty for all. This ship had the embryo elements of all that is useful, great, and grand in Northern institutions; it was the great type of goodness and wisdom, illustrated in two and a quarter centuries gone by; it was the good genius of America.

But look far in the South-east, and you behold on the same day, in 1620, a low rakish ship hastening from the tropics, solitary and alone, to the New World. What is she? She is freighted with the elements of unmixed evil. Hark! hear those rattling chains, hear that cry of despair and wail of anguish, as they die away in the un-pitying distance. Listen to those shocking oaths, the crack of that flesh-cutting whip. Ah! it is the first cargo of slaves on their way to Jamestown, Virginia.[1] Behold the Mayflower anchored at Plymouth Rock, the slave-ship in James River. Each a parent, one of the pros-perous, labour-honouring, law-sustaining institutions of the North; the other the mother of slavery, idleness, lynch-law, ignorance, un-paid labour, poverty, and duelling, despotism, the ceaseless swing of the whip, and the peculiar institutions of the South. These ships are the representation of good and evil in the New World, even to our day. When shall one of those parallel lines come to an end?[2]

The origin of American slavery is not lost in the obscurity of by-gone ages. It is a plain historical fact, that it owes its birth to the African slave trade, now pronounced by every civilised com-munity the greatest crime ever perpetrated against humanity.[3] Of all causes intended to benefit mankind, the abolition of chattel slavery must necessarily be placed amongst the first, and the ne-gro hails with joy every new advocate that appears in his cause. Commiseration for human suffering and human sacrifices awak-ened the capacious mind, and brought into action the enlarged benevolence, of Georgiana Carlton. With respect to her philos-

---

1 About 50 African men, women, and children, acquired through the capture of a Portuguese slave ship, were carried by English colonists to the Jamestown settlement in 1619.

2 *"On the last day of November, 1620 ... to an end"*: Stewart, *Legal Argument*, 9–10.

3 *"The origin of American slavery is not ... perpetrated against humanity"*: John Scoble, "American Slavery," 97. Scoble (1799–1877) was a British abolitionist.

ophy—it was of a noble cast. It was, that all men are by nature equal; that they are wisely and justly endowed by the Creator with certain rights, which are irrefragable; and that, however human pride and human avarice may depress and debase, still God is the author of good to man—and of evil, man is the artificer to himself and to his species. Unlike Plato and Socrates,[1] her mind was free from the gloom that surrounded theirs; her philosophy was founded in the school of Christianity; though a devoted member of her father's church, she was not a sectarian.[2]

We learn from Scripture, and it is a little remarkable that it is the only exact definition of religion found in the sacred volume, that "pure religion and undefiled before God, even the Father, is this, to visit the fatherless and widows in their affliction, and to keep oneself unspotted from the world." "Look not every man on his own things, but every man also on the things of others." "Remember them that are in bonds as bound with them." "Whatsoever ye would that others should do to you, do ye even so to them."[3]

This was her view of Christianity, and to this end she laboured with all her energies to convince her slaveholding neighbours that the negro could not only take care of himself, but that he also appreciated liberty, and was willing to work and redeem himself. Her most sanguine wishes were being realized when she suddenly fell into a decline. Her mother had died of consumption, and her physician pronounced this to be her disease. She was prepared for this sad intelligence, and received it with the utmost composure. Although she had confidence in her husband that he would carry out her wishes in freeing the negroes after her death, Mrs. Carlton resolved upon their immediate liberation. Consequently the slaves were all summoned before the noble woman, and informed that they were no longer bondsmen. "From this hour," said she, "you are free, and all eyes will be fixed upon you. I dare not predict how far your example may affect the welfare of your brethren yet in bondage. If you are temperate, industrious, peaceable, and pious,

---

1 Plato (c. 427–347 BCE) was a Greek philosopher; he studied with and wrote about the philosopher Socrates (c. 470–399 BCE).

2 *"Commiseration for human suffering ... school of Christianity"*: Benjamin F. Hughes, *Eulogium on the Life and Character of William Wilberforce*, 13. Wilberforce (1759–1833) was a British politician and abolitionist.

3 *"We learn from Scripture, and it is ... so to them"*: "Christianized Sensibility vs. Christianity," 58. The biblical quotations are from James 1:27, Philippians 2:4, Hebrews 13:3, and Matthew 7:12.

you will show to the world that slaves can be emancipated without danger.[1] Remember what a singular relation you sustain to society. The necessities of the case require not only that you should behave as well as the whites, but better than the whites; and for this reason: if you behave no better than they, your example will lose a great portion of its influence. Make the Lord Jesus Christ your refuge and exemplar. His is the only standard around which you can successfully rally. If ever there was a people who needed the consolations of religion to sustain them in their grievous afflictions, you are that people.[2] You had better trust in the Lord than to put confidence in man. Happy is that people whose God is the Lord.[3] Get as much education as possible for yourselves and your children. An ignorant people can never occupy any other than a degraded station in society; they can never be truly free until they are intelligent.[4] In a few days you will start for the state of Ohio, where land will be purchased for some of you who have families, and where I hope you will all prosper. We have been urged to send you to Liberia, but we think it wrong to send you from your native land. We did not wish to encourage the Colonization Society,[5] for it originated in hatred of the free coloured people. Its pretences are false, its doctrines odious, its means contemptible.[6] Now, whatever may be your situation in life, 'Remember those in bonds as bound with them.'[7] You must get ready as soon as you can for your journey to the North."

Seldom was there ever witnessed a more touching scene than this. There sat the liberator,—pale, feeble, emaciated, with death stamped upon her countenance, surrounded by the sons and daughters of Africa; some of whom had in former years been

---

1 *"I dare not predict how far ... emancipated without danger"*: William Lloyd Garrison, *An Address, Delivered Before the Free People of Color, in Philadelphia, New-York, and Other Cities, During the Month of June, 1831*, 5–6. Garrison (1805–79) was an abolitionist, journalist, and social reformer.

2 *"Remember what a singular relation ... are that people"*: Garrison, *Address*, 6–7.

3 *"You had better trust in the Lord ... is the Lord"*: Garrison, *Address*, 8.

4 *"Get as much education as possible ... they are intelligent"*: Garrison, *Address*, 10.

5 See p. 147, note 1.

6 *"Its pretences are false, its doctrines ... its means contemptible"*: Garrison, *Address*, 22.

7 Hebrews 13:3.

separated from all that they had held near and dear, and the most of whose backs had been torn and gashed by the negro whip. Some were upon their knees at the feet of their benefactress; others were standing round her weeping. Many begged that they might be permitted to remain on the farm and work for wages, for some had wives and some husbands on other plantations in the neighbourhood, and would rather remain with them.

But the laws of the state forbade any emancipated negroes remaining, under penalty of again being sold into slavery. Hence the necessity of sending them out of the state. Mrs. Carlton was urged by her friends to send the emancipated negroes to Africa. Extracts from the speeches of Henry Clay, and other distinguished Colonization Society men, were read to her to induce her to adopt this course. Some thought they should be sent away because the blacks are vicious; others because they would be missionaries to their brethren in Africa. "But," said she, "if we send away the negroes because they are profligate and vicious, what sort of missionaries will they make? Why not send away the vicious among the whites for the same reason, and the same purpose?"[1]

Death is a leveller, and neither age, sex, wealth, nor usefulness can avert when he is permitted to strike. The most beautiful flowers soon fade, and droop, and die; this is also the case with man; his days are uncertain as the passing breeze. This hour he glows in the blush of health and vigour, but the next he may be counted with the number no more known on earth.[2]

Although in a low state of health, Mrs. Carlton had the pleasure of seeing all her slaves, except Sam and three others, start for a land of freedom. The morning they were to go on board the steamer, bound for Louisville, they all assembled on the large grass plot, in front of the drawing-room window, and wept while they bid their mistress farewell. When they were on the boat, about leaving the wharf, they were heard giving the charge to those on shore—"Sam, take care of Misus, take care of Marser, as you love us, and hope to meet us in de Hio (Ohio), and in heben; be sure and take good care of Misus and Marser."[3]

---

1 "*if we send away the negroes because … the same purpose?*": Garrison, *Address*, 22.

2 "*The most beautiful flowers soon fade … known on earth*": Edmund Rack; quoted in *Gleanings*, 24.

3 "*they were heard giving the charge … Misus and Marser*": McDonogh, *Letter*, 26.

In less than a week after her emancipated people had started for Ohio, Mrs. Carlton was cold in death. Mr. Carlton felt deeply, as all husbands must who love their wives, the loss of her who had been a lamp to his feet, and a light to his path.[1] She had converted him from infidelity to Christianity; from the mere theory of liberty to practical freedom. He had looked upon the negro as an ill-treated distant link of the human family; he now regarded them as a part of God's children. Oh, what a silence pervaded the house when the Christian had been removed. His indeed was a lonesome position.

> "'Twas midnight, and he sat alone—
> The husband of the dead,
> That day the dark dust had been thrown
> Upon the buried head."[2]

In the midst of the buoyancy of youth, this cherished one had drooped and died. Deep were the sounds of grief and mourning heard in that stately dwelling, when the stricken friends, whose office it had been to nurse and soothe the weary sufferer, beheld her pale and motionless in the sleep of death.

Oh what a chill creeps through the breaking heart when we look upon the insensible form, and feel that it no longer contains the spirit we so dearly loved! How difficult to realise that the eye which always glowed with affection and intelligence—that the ear which had so often listened to the sounds of sorrow and gladness—that the voice whose accents had been to us like sweet music, and the heart, the habitation of benevolence and truth, are now powerless and insensate as the bier upon which the form rests. Though faith be strong enough to penetrate the cloud of gloom which hovers near, and to behold the freed spirit safe, *for ever*, safe in its home in heaven, yet the thoughts *will* linger sadly and cheerlessly upon the grave.[3]

Peace to her ashes! she fought the fight, obtained the Christian's victory, and wears the crown.[4] But if it were that departed spirits are permitted to note the occurrences of this world, with what a frown of disapprobation would hers view the effort being made

---

1 Paraphrase of Psalm 119:105.
2 Gillies, "Alone," lines 1–4.
3 "*In the midst of the buoyancy of youth ... upon the grave*": [Jane S. Welch], "Jairus's Daughter," 108.
4 Paraphrase of 2 Timothy 4:7.

in the United States to retard the work of emancipation for which she laboured and so wished to see brought about.

In what light would she consider that hypocritical priesthood who gave their aid and sanction to the infamous "Fugitive Slave Law."[1] If true greatness consists in doing good to mankind, then was Georgiana Carlton an ornament to human nature. Who can think of the broken hearts made whole, of sad and dejected countenances now beaming with contentment and joy, of the mother offering her free-born babe to heaven, and of the father whose cup of joy seems overflowing in the presence of his family, where none can molest or make him afraid.[2] Oh, that God may give more such persons to take the whip-scarred negro by the hand, and raise him to a level with our common humanity! May the professed lovers of freedom in the new world see that true liberty is freedom for all! and may every American continually hear it sounding in his ear:—

> "Shall every flap of England's flag
> Proclaim that all around are free,
> From 'farthest Ind' to each blue crag
> That beetles o'er the Western Sea?
> And shall we scoff at Europe's kings,
> When Freedom's fire is dim with us,
> The damning shade of Slavery's curse?"[3]

CHAPTER XXII.

A RIDE IN A STAGE-COACH.

We shall now return to Cincinnati, where we left Clotel preparing to go to Richmond in search of her daughter. Tired of the disguise in which she had escaped, she threw it off on her arrival at Cincinnati. But being assured that not a shadow of safety would attend her visit to a city in which she was well known, unless in some disguise, she again resumed men's apparel on leaving Cincinnati. This time she had more the appearance of an Italian

---

1 "*Peace to her ashes! ... who gave their aid*": Hughes, *Eulogium*, 13.
2 "*If true greatness consists in doing good ... make him afraid*": Robert Purvis, *A Tribute to the Memory of Thomas Shipley*, 8. Purvis (1810–98) was a wealthy African-American activist; Shipley (1784–1836) was a philanthropist and abolitionist.
3 Whittier, "Our Countrymen in Chains," 33–40.

or Spanish gentleman. In addition to the fine suit of black cloth, a splendid pair of dark false whiskers covered the sides of her face, while the curling moustache found its place upon the upper lip. From practice she had become accustomed to high-heeled boots, and could walk without creating any suspicion as regarded her sex. It was on a cold evening that Clotel arrived at Wheeling, and took a seat in the coach going to Richmond. She was already in the state of Virginia, yet a long distance from the place of her destination.

A ride in a stage-coach, over an American road, is unpleasant under the most favourable circumstances. But now that it was winter, and the roads unusually bad, the journey was still more dreary. However, there were eight passengers in the coach, and I need scarcely say that such a number of genuine Americans could not be together without whiling away the time somewhat pleasantly. Besides Clotel, there was an elderly gentleman with his two daughters—one apparently under twenty years, the other a shade above. The pale, spectacled face of another slim, tall man, with a white neckerchief, pointed him out as a minister. The rough featured, dark countenance of a stout looking man, with a white hat on one side of his head, told that he was from the sunny South. There was nothing remarkable about the other two, who might pass for ordinary American gentlemen. It was on the eve of a presidential election, when every man is thought to be a politician. Clay, Van Buren, and Harrison were the men who expected the indorsement of the Baltimore Convention.[1] "Who does this town go for?" asked the old gent. with the ladies, as the coach drove up to an inn, where groups of persons were waiting for the latest papers. "We are divided," cried the rough voice of one of the outsiders. "Well, who do you think will get the majority here?" continued the old gent. "Can't tell very well; I go for 'Old Tip,'"[2] was the answer from without. This brought up the subject fairly before the passengers, and when the coach again started a general discussion commenced, in which all took a part except Clotel and the young ladies. Some were for Clay, some for Van Buren, and others for "Old Tip." The coach stopped to take

1 At the 1840 Democratic convention in Baltimore, the incumbent president, Martin Van Buren (1782–1862) received the party's nomination; at the 1839 Whig convention in Harrisburg, William Henry Harrison (1773–1841) defeated Henry Clay for the nomination. Harrison won the 1840 presidential election but died shortly after taking office.
2 Nickname of William Henry Harrison.

in a real farmer-looking man, who no sooner entered than he was saluted with "Do you go for Clay?" "No," was the answer. "Do you go for Van Buren?" "No." "Well, then, of course you will go for Harrison." "No." "Why, don't you mean to work for any of them at the election?" "No." "Well, who will you work for?" asked one of the company. "I work for Betsy and the children, and I have a hard job of it at that," replied the farmer, without a smile. This answer, as a matter of course, set the new comer down as one upon whom the rest of the passengers could crack their jokes with the utmost impunity. "Are you an Odd Fellow?"[1] asked one. "No, sir, I've been married more than a month." "I mean, do you belong to the order of Odd Fellows?" "No, no; I belong to the order of married men." "Are you a mason?"[2] "No, I am a carpenter by trade." "Are you a Son of Temperance?"[3] "Bother you, no; I am a son of Mr. John Gosling."[4] After a hearty laugh in which all joined, the subject of Temperance became the theme for discussion. In this the spectacled gent. was at home. He soon showed that he was a New Englander, and went the whole length of the "Maine Law."[5] The minister was about having it all his own way, when the Southerner, in the white hat, took the opposite side of the question. "I don't bet a red cent on these teetotlars,"[6] said he, and at the same time looking round to see if he had the approbation of the rest of the company. "Why?" asked the minister. "Because they are a set who are afraid to spend a cent. They are a bad lot, the whole on 'em." It was evident that the white hat gent. was an uneducated man. The minister commenced in full earnest, and gave an interesting account of the progress of temperance in Connecticut, the state from which he came, proving, that a great portion of the prosperity of the state was attributable to the disuse of intoxicating drinks. Every one thought the white hat had got the worst of the argument, and that he was settled for the remainder of the night. But not he; he took fresh courage and began again. "Now," said he, "I have just

---

1 Odd Fellows are members of an exclusive fraternal organization.
2 Masons are members of the Free and Accepted Masons society, an exclusive fraternal organization.
3 Sons of Temperance were members of a fraternal organization founded in 1843.
4 *"Are you an Odd Fellow? ... Mr. John Gosling"*: "Smart Boy," 111.
5 In 1851, Maine's state legislature banned the sale and manufacture of alcoholic beverages.
6 Teetotalers abstained not only from distilled alcohol but from beer and wine as well.

been on a visit to my uncle's in Vermont, and I guess I knows a little about these here teetotlars. You see, I went up there to make a little stay of a fortnight. I got there at night, and they seemed glad to see me, but they didn't give me a bit of anything to drink. Well, thinks I to myself, the jig's up: I sha'n't get any more liquor till I get out of the state. We all sat up till twelve o'clock that night, and I heard nothing but talk about the 'Juvinal Temperance Army,' the 'Band of Hope,' the 'Rising Generation,' the 'Female Dorcas Temperance Society,' 'The None Such,' and I don't know how many other names they didn't have. As I had taken several pretty large 'Cock Tails' before I entered the state, I thought upon the whole that I would not spile for the want of liquor. The next morning, I commenced writing back to my friends, and telling them what's what. Aunt Polly said, 'Well, Johnny, I s'pose you are given 'em a pretty account of us all here.' 'Yes,' said I; 'I am tellin' 'em if they want anything to drink when they come up here, they had better bring it with 'em.' 'Oh,' said aunty, 'they would search their boxes; can't bring any spirits in the state.' Well, as I was saying, jist as I got my letters finished, and was going to the post office (for uncle's house was two miles from the town), aunty says, 'Johnny, I s'pose you'll try to get a little somthin' to drink in town won't you?' Says I, 'I s'pose it's no use.' 'No,' said she, 'you can't; it aint to be had no how, for love nor money.' So jist as I was puttin' on my hat, 'Johnny,' cries out aunty, 'What,' says I. 'Now I'll tell you, I don't want you to say nothin' about it, but I keeps a little rum to rub my head with, for I am troubled with the headache, now I don't want you to mention it for the world, but I'll give you a little taste, the old man is such a teetotaller, that I should never hear the last of it, and I would not like for the boys to know it, they are members of the "Cold Water Army."'[1]

"Aunty now brought out a black bottle and gave me a cup, and told me to help myself, which I assure you I did. I now felt ready to face the cold. As I was passing the barn I heard uncle thrashing oats, so I went to the door and spoke to him. 'Come in, John,' says he. 'No,' said I; 'I am goin' to post some letters,' for I was afraid that he would smell my breath if I went too near to him. 'Yes, yes, come in.' So I went in, and says he, 'It's now eleven o'clock; that's about the time you take your grog, I s'pose, when you are at home.' 'Yes,' said I. 'I am sorry for you, my lad; you can't get anything up here; you can't even get it at the

---

1 A young men's and women's temperance organization.

chemist's, except as medicine, and then you must let them mix it and you take it in their presence.' 'This is indeed hard,' replied I; 'Well, it can't be helped,' continued he: 'and it ought not to be if it could. It's best for society; people's better off without drink. I recollect when your father and I, thirty years ago, used to go out on a spree and spend more than half a dollar in a night. Then here's the rising generation; there's nothing like settin' a good example. Look how healthy your cousins are—there's Benjamin, he never tasted spirits in his life. Oh, John, I would you were a teetotaller.' 'I suppose,' said I, 'I'll have to be one till I leave the state.' 'Now,' said he, 'John, I don't want you to mention it, for your aunt would go into hysterics if she thought there was a drop of intoxicating liquor about the place, and I would not have the boys to know it for anything, but I keep a little brandy to rub my joints for the rheumatics, and being it's you, I'll give you a little dust.' So the old man went to one corner of the barn, took out a brown jug and handed it to me, and I must say it was a little the best cogniac that I had tasted for many a day. Says I, 'Uncle, you are a good judge of brandy.' 'Yes,' said he, 'I learned when I was young.' So off I started for the post office. In returnin' I thought I'd jist go through the woods where the boys were chopping wood, and wait and go to the house with them when they went to dinner. I found them hard at work, but as merry as crickets. 'Well, cousin John, are you done writing?' 'Yes,' answered I. 'Have you posted them?' 'Yes.' 'Hope you didn't go to any place inquiring for grog.' 'No, I knowed it was no good to do that.' 'I suppose a cock-tail would taste good now.' 'Well, I guess it would,' says I. The three boys then joined in a hearty laugh. 'I suppose you have told 'em that we are a dry set up here?' 'Well, I aint told 'em anything else.' 'Now, cousin John,' said Edward, 'if you wont say anything, we will give you a small taste. For mercy's sake don't let father or mother know it; they are such rabid teetotallers, that they would not sleep a wink to-night if they thought there was any spirits about the place.' 'I am mum,' says I. And the boys took a jug out of a hollow stump, and gave me some first-rate peach brandy. And during the fortnight that I was in Vermont, with my teetotal relations, I was kept about as well corned as if I had been among my hot water friends in Tennessee."

This narrative, given by the white hat man, was received with unbounded applause by all except the pale gent. in spectacles, who showed, by the way in which he was running his fingers between his cravat and throat, that he did not intend to "give it up so." The white hat gent was now the lion of the company.

"Oh, you did not get hold of the right kind of teetotallers," said the minister. "I can give you a tale worth a dozen of yours," continued he. "Look at society in the states where temperance views prevail, and you will there see real happiness. The people are taxed less, the poor houses are shut up for want of occupants, and extreme destitution is unknown. Every one who drinks at all is liable to become an habitual drunkard. Yes, I say boldly, that no man living who uses intoxicating drinks, is free from the danger of at least occasional, and if of occasional, ultimately of habitual excess. There seems to be no character, position, or circumstances that free men from the danger. *I have known* many young men of the finest promise, led by the drinking habit into vice, ruin, and early death. *I have known* many tradesmen whom it has made bankrupt. *I have known* Sunday scholars whom it has led to prison—teachers, and even superintendents, whom it has dragged down to profligacy. *I have known* ministers of high academic honours, of splendid eloquence, nay, of vast usefulness, whom it has fascinated, and hurried over the precipice of public infamy with their eyes open, and gazing with horror on their fate. *I have known* men of the strongest and clearest intellect and of vigorous resolution, whom it has made weaker than children and fools—gentlemen of refinement and taste whom it has debased into brutes—poets of high genius whom it has bound in a bondage worse than the galleys, and ultimately cut short their days. *I have known* statesmen, lawyers, and judges whom it has killed—kind husbands and fathers whom it has turned into monsters. *I have known* honest men whom it has made villains—elegant and Christian *ladies* whom it has *converted into bloated sots*."[1]

"But you talk too fast," replied the white hat man. "You don't give a feller a chance to say nothin'." "I heard you," continued the minister, "and now you hear me out. It is indeed wonderful how people become lovers of strong drink. Some years since, before I became a teetotaller I kept spirits about the house, and I had a servant who was much addicted to strong drink. He used to say that he could not make my boots shine, without mixing the blacking with whiskey. So to satisfy myself that the whiskey was put in the blacking, one morning I made him bring the dish in which he kept the blacking, and poured in the whiskey myself. And now, sir, what do you think?" "Why, I s'pose your boots

---

1 *"I say boldly, that no man living who uses intoxicating ... into bloated sots"*: Edward Baines, "Testimony and Appeal on the Effects of Total Abstinence," 10.

shined better than before," replied the white hat. "No," continued the minister. "He took the blacking out, and I watched him, and he drank down the whiskey, blacking, and all."

This turned the joke upon the advocate of strong drink, and he began to put his wits to work for arguments. "You are from Connecticut, are you?" asked the Southerner. "Yes, and we are an orderly, pious, peaceable people. Our holy religion is respected, and we do more for the cause of Christ than the whole Southern States put together." "I don't doubt it," said the white hat gent. "You sell wooden nutmegs[1] and other spurious articles enough to do some good. You talk of your 'holy religion;' but your robes' righteousness are woven at Lowell and Manchester;[2] your paradise is high per centum on factory stocks; your palms of victory and crowns of rejoicing are triumphs over a rival party in politics, on the questions of banks and tariffs. If you could, you would turn heaven into Birmingham,[3] make every angel a weaver, and with the eternal din of looms and spindles drown all the anthems of the morning stars.[4] Ah! I know you Connecticut people like a book. No, no, all hoss;[5] you can't come it on me." This last speech of the rough featured man again put him in the ascendant, and the spectacled gent. once more ran his fingers between his cravat and throat. "You live in Tennessee, I think," said the minister. "Yes," replied the Southerner, "I used to live in Orleans, but now I claim to be a Tennessean." "You people of New Orleans are the most ungodly set in the United States," said the minister. Taking a New Orleans newspaper from his pocket he continued, "Just look here, there are not less than three advertisements of bull fights to take place on the Sabbath. You people of the Slave States have no regard for the Sabbath, religion, morality or anything else intended to make mankind better." Here Clotel could have borne ample testimony, had she dared to have taken sides with the Connecticut man. Her residence in Vicksburgh had given her an opportunity of knowing something of the character of the inhabitants of the far

---

1 According to legend, peddlers from Connecticut sold wooden nutmegs in place of the genuine article; Connecticut's official nickname, "The Nutmeg State," is an allusion to this practice.

2 Lowell, Massachusetts, and Manchester, England, were well known for their textile factories.

3 City in England associated with manufacturing.

4 "*You talk of your 'holy religion;' ... the morning stars*": minister and abolitionist Parker Pillsbury (1809–98); quoted in "Worshippers of Mammon," 4.

5 Misprint for "ol' hoss," or old horse.

South. "Here is an account of a grand bull fight that took place in New Orleans a week ago last Sunday. I will read it to you." And the minister read aloud the following:

"Yesterday, pursuant to public notice, came off at Gretna, opposite the Fourth District, the long heralded fight between the famous grizzly bear, General Jackson (victor in fifty battles), and the Attakapas bull, Santa Anna.

"The fame of the coming conflict had gone forth to the four winds, and women and children, old men and boys, from all parts of the city, and from the breezy banks of Lake Pontchartrain and Borgne,[1] brushed up their Sunday suit, and prepared to see the fun. Long before the published hour, the quiet streets of the rural Gretna were filled with crowds of anxious denizens, flocking to the arena, and before the fight commenced, such a crowd had collected as Gretna had not seen, nor will be likely to see again.

"The arena for the sports was a cage, twenty feet square, built upon the ground, and constructed of heavy timbers and iron bars. Around it were seats, circularly placed, and intended to accommodate many thousands. About four or five thousand persons assembled, covering the seats as with a cloud, and crowding down around the cage, were within reach of the bars.

"The bull selected to sustain the honour and verify the pluck of Attakapas on this trying occasion was a black animal from the Opelousas, lithe and sinewy as a four year old courser, and with eyes like burning coals. His horns bore the appearance of having been filed at the tips, and wanted that keen and slashing appearance so common with others of his kith and kin; otherwise it would have been 'all day' with Bruin at the first pass, and no mistake.

"The bear was an animal of note, and called General Jackson, from the fact of his licking up everything that came in his way, and taking 'the responsibility' on all occasions. He was a wicked looking beast, very lean and unamiable in aspect, with hair all standing the wrong way. He had fought some fifty bulls (so they said), always coming out victorious, but that either one of the fifty had been an Attakapas bull, the bills of the perfor-

---

1 Lakes to the north and east of New Orleans.

mances did not say. Had he tackled Attakapas first it is likely his fifty battles would have remained unfought.

"About half past four o'clock the performances commenced.

"The bull was first seen, standing in the cage alone, with head erect, and looking a very monarch in his capacity. At an appointed signal, a cage containing the bear was placed alongside the arena, and an opening being made, bruin stalked into the battle ground—not, however, without sundry stirrings up with a ten foot pole, he being experienced in such matters, and backwards in raising a row.

"Once on the battle-field, both animals stood, like wary champions, eyeing each other, the bear cowering low, with head upturned and fangs exposed, while Attakapas stood wondering, with his eye dilated, lashing his sides with his long and bushy tail, and pawing up the earth in very wrath.

"The bear seemed little inclined to begin the attack, and the bull, standing a moment, made steps first backward and then forward, as if measuring his antagonist, and meditating where to plant a blow. Bruin wouldn't come to the scratch no way, till one of the keepers, with an iron rod, tickled his ribs and made him move. Seeing this, Attakapas took it as a hostile demonstration, and, gathering his strength, dashed savagely at the enemy, catching him on the points of his horns, and doubling him up like a sack of bran against the bars. Bruin 'sung out' at this, and made a dash for his opponent's nose.

"Missing this, the bull turned to the 'about face,' and the bear caught him by the ham, inflicting a ghastly wound. But Attakapas with a kick shook him off, and renewing the attack, went at him again, head on and with a rush. This time he was not so fortunate, for the bear caught him above the eye, burying his fangs in the tough hide, and holding him as in a vice. It was now the bull's turn to 'sing out,' and he did it, bellowing forth with a voice more hideous than that of all the bulls of Bashan.[1] Some minutes stood matters thus, and the cries of the bull, mingled with the hoarse

---

1 From Psalm 22:12. The bulls of Bashan's pasturelands were legendarily strong.

growls of the bear, made hideous music, fit only for a dance of devils. Then came a pause (the bear having relinquished his hold), and for a few minutes it was doubtful whether the fun was not up. But the magic wand of the keeper (the ten foot pole) again stirred up bruin, and at it they went, and with a rush.

"Bruin now tried to fasten on the bull's back, and drove his tusks in him in several places, making the red blood flow like wine from the vats of Luna.[1] But Attakapas was pluck to the back bone, and, catching bruin on the tips of his horns, shuffled him up right merrily, making the fur fly like feathers in a gale of wind. Bruin cried 'Nuff' (in bear language), but the bull followed up his advantage, and, making one furious plunge full at the figure head of the enemy, struck a horn into his eye, burying it there, and dashing the tender organ into darkness and atoms. Blood followed the blow, and poor bruin, blinded, bleeding, and in mortal agony, turned with a howl to leave, but Attakapas caught him in the retreat, and rolled him over like a ball. Over and over again this rolling over was enacted, and finally, after more than an hour, bruin curled himself up on his back, bruised, bloody, and dead beat. The thing was up with California,[2] and Attakapas was declared the victor amidst the applause of the multitude that made the heavens ring."[3]

"There," said he, "can you find anything against Connecticut equal to that?" The Southerner had to admit that he was beat by the Yankee. During all this time, it must not be supposed that the old gent. with the two daughters, and even the young ladies themselves, had been silent. Clotel and they had not only given their opinions as regarded the merits of the discussion, but that sly glance of the eye, which is ever given where the young of both sexes meet, had been freely at work. The American ladies are rather partial to foreigners, and Clotel had the appearance of a fine

---

1 Reference to British historian and essayist Thomas Babington Macaulay (1800–59), "Horatius," 62. Luna, a Roman colony, was known for its vineyards.
2 Allusion to the 1846 "Bear Flag Revolt," in which white American settlers in California, then a part of Mexico, attempted to establish an independent republic.
3 "Sunday Amusements in New Orleans," 114.

Italian. The old gentleman was now near his home, and a whisper from the eldest daughter, who was unmarried but marriageable, induced him to extend to "Mr. Johnson" an invitation to stop and spend a week with the young ladies at their family residence. Clotel excused herself upon various grounds, and at last, to cut short the matter, promised that she would pay them a visit on her return. The arrival of the coach at Lynchburgh separated the young ladies from the Italian gent., and the coach again resumed its journey.

CHAPTER XXIII.

TRUTH STRANGER THAN FICTION.

"Is the poor privilege to turn the key
Upon the captive, freedom? He's as far
From the enjoyment of the earth and air
Who watches o'er the chains, as they who wear." *Byron.*[1]

During certain seasons of the year, all tropical climates are subject to epidemics of a most destructive nature. The inhabitants of New Orleans look with as much certainty for the appearance of the yellow-fever, small-pox, or cholera, in the hot-season, as the Londoner does for fog in the month of November. In the summer of 1831, the people of New Orleans were visited with one of these epidemics. It appeared in a form unusually repulsive and deadly. It seized persons who were in health, without any premonition. Sometimes death was the immediate consequence. The disorder began in the brain, by an oppressive pain accompanied or followed by fever. The patient was devoured with burning thirst. The stomach, distracted by pains, in vain sought relief in efforts to disburden itself. Fiery veins streaked the eye; the face was inflamed, and dyed of a dark dull red colour; the ears from time to time rang painfully. Now mucous secretions surcharged the tongue, and took away the power of speech; now the sick one spoke, but in speaking had a foresight of death. When the violence of the disease approached the heart, the gums were blackened. The sleep, broken, troubled by convulsions, or by frightful visions, was worse than the waking hours; and when the reason sank under a delirium which had its seat in the brain, repose utterly

---

1 George Gordon, Lord Byron, *Don Juan* (1819–24), Canto 10, stanza 68.

forsook the patient's couch. The progress of the heat within was marked by yellowish spots, which spread over the surface of the body. If, then, a happy crisis came not, all hope was gone. Soon the breath infected the air with a fetid odour, the lips were glazed, despair painted itself in the eyes, and sobs, with long intervals of silence, formed the only language. From each side of the mouth spread foam, tinged with black and burnt blood. Blue streaks mingled with the yellow all over the frame. All remedies were useless.[1] This was the Yellow Fever. The disorder spread alarm and confusion throughout the city. On an average, more than 400 died daily. In the midst of disorder and confusion, death heaped victims on victims. Friend followed friend in quick succession. The sick were avoided from the fear of contagion, and for the same reason the dead were left unburied.[2] Nearly 2000 dead bodies lay uncovered in the burial-ground, with only here and there a little lime thrown over them, to prevent the air becoming infected.

The negro, whose home is in a hot climate, was not proof against the disease. Many plantations had to suspend their work for want of slaves to take the places of those carried off by the fever. Henry Morton and wife were among the thirteen thousand swept away by the raging disorder that year. Like too many, Morton had been dealing extensively in lands and stocks; and though apparently in good circumstances was, in reality, deeply involved in debt. Althesa, although as white as most white women in a southern clime, was, as we already know, born a slave. By the laws of all the Southern States the children follow the condition of the mother. If the mother is free the children are free; if a slave, they are slaves. Morton was unacquainted with the laws of the land; and although he had married Althesa, it was a marriage which the law did not recognise; and therefore she whom he thought to be his wife was, in fact, nothing more than his slave. What would have been his feelings had he known this, and also known that his two daughters, Ellen and Jane, were his slaves? Yet such was the fact. After the disappearance of the disease with which Henry Morton had so suddenly been removed, his brother went to New Orleans to give what aid he could in settling up the affairs. James Morton, on his arrival in New Orleans, felt proud of his nieces, and promised

---

1   "*It appeared in a form unusually repulsive … remedies were useless*": John R. Beard, *The Life of Toussaint L'Ouverture*, 214–15. Beard (1800–76) was an English Unitarian minister and educator.

2   "*In the midst of disorder and confusion … were left unburied*": Beard, *Life*, 216.

them a home with his own family in Vermont; little dreaming that his brother had married a slave woman, and that his nieces were slaves. The girls themselves had never heard that their mother had been a slave, and therefore knew nothing of the danger hanging over their heads. An inventory of the property was made out by James Morton, and placed in the hands of the creditors; and the young ladies, with their uncle, were about leaving the city to reside for a few days on the banks of Lake Ponchetain,[1] where they could enjoy a fresh air that the city could not afford. But just as they were about taking the train, an officer arrested the whole party; the young ladies as slaves, and the uncle upon the charge of attempting to conceal the property of his deceased brother. Morton was overwhelmed with horror at the idea of his nieces being claimed as slaves, and asked for time, that he might save them from such a fate. He even offered to mortgage his little farm in Vermont for the amount which young slave women of their ages would fetch. But the creditors pleaded that they were "an extra article," and would sell for more than common slaves; and must, therefore, be sold at auction. They were given up, but neither ate nor slept, nor separated from each other, till they were taken into the New Orleans slave market, where they were offered to the highest bidder.[2] There they stood, trembling, blushing, and weeping; compelled to listen to the grossest language, and shrinking from the rude hands that examined the graceful proportions of their beautiful frames.[3]

After a fierce contest between the bidders, the young ladies were sold, one for 2,300 dollars, and the other for 3,000 dollars. We need not add that had those young girls been sold for mere house servants or field hands, they would not have brought one half the sums they did. The fact that they were the grand-daughters of Thomas Jefferson, no doubt, increased their value in the market. Here were two of the softer sex, accustomed to the fondest indulgence, surrounded by all the refinements of life, and with all the timidity that such a life could produce, bartered away like cattle in Smithfield market.[4] Ellen, the eldest, was sold

---

1 Misspelling of Ponchartrain; see p. 179, note 1.
2 *"ate nor slept, nor separated ... New Orleans slave market"*: Martineau, *Society*, 2:325.
3 *"There they stood, trembling, blushing ... their beautiful frames"*: Child, "The Quadroons," 137.
4 *"accustomed to the fondest indulgence ... refinements of life"*: Child, "The Quadroons," 137. Smithfield is an area of London known for its meat market.

to an old gentleman, who purchased her, as he said, for a house-keeper. The girl was taken to his residence, nine miles from the city. She soon, however, knew for what purpose she had been bought; and an educated and cultivated mind and taste, which made her see and understand how great was her degradation, now armed her hand with the ready means of death. The morning after her arrival, she was found in her chamber, a corpse. She had taken poison.[1] Jane was purchased by a dashing young man, who had just come into the possession of a large fortune. The very appearance of the young Southerner pointed him out as an unprincipled profligate; and the young girl needed no one to tell her of her impending doom. The young maid of fifteen was immediately removed to his country seat, near the junction of the Mississippi river with the sea. This was a most singular spot, remote, in a dense forest spreading over the summit of a cliff that rose abruptly to a great height above the sea; but so grand in its situation, in the desolate sublimity which reigned around, in the reverential murmur of the waves that washed its base, that, though picturesque, it was a forest prison.[2] Here the young lady saw no one, except an old negress who acted as her servant. The smiles with which the young man met her were indignantly spurned. But she was the property of another, and could hope for justice and mercy only through him.

Jane, though only in her fifteenth year, had become strongly attached to Volney Lapuc, a young Frenchman, a student in her father's office. The poverty of the young man, and the youthful age of the girl, had caused their feelings to be kept from the young lady's parents. At the death of his master, Volney had returned to his widowed mother at Mobile, and knew nothing of the misfortune that had befallen his mistress, until he received a letter from her. But how could he ever obtain a sight of her, even if he wished, locked up as she was in her master's mansion? After several days of what her master termed "obstinacy" on her part, the young girl was placed in an upper chamber, and told that that would be her home, until she should yield to her master's wishes. There she remained more than a fortnight, and with the exception of a daily visit from her master, she saw no one but the old negress who waited upon her. One bright moonlight evening as she was

---

1 *"an educated and cultivated mind and taste ... had taken poison"*: "The Woes of Slavery," 186.

2 *"This was a most singular spot ... washed its base"*: "A Peep into an Italian Interior," 244.

seated at the window, she perceived the figure of a man beneath her window. At first, she thought it was her master; but the tall figure of the stranger soon convinced her that it was another. Yes, it was Volney! He had no sooner received her letter, than he set out for New Orleans; and finding on his arrival there, that his mistress had been taken away, resolved to follow her. There he was; but how could she communicate with him? She dared not trust the old negress with her secret, for fear that it might reach her master. Jane wrote a hasty note and threw it out of the window, which was eagerly picked up by the young man, and he soon disappeared in the woods. Night passed away in dreariness to her, and the next morning she viewed the spot beneath her window with the hope of seeing the footsteps of him who had stood there the previous night. Evening returned, and with it the hope of again seeing the man she loved. In this she was not disappointed; for daylight had scarcely disappeared, and the moon once more rising through the tops of the tall trees, when the young man was seen in the same place as on the previous night. He had in his hand a rope ladder. As soon as Jane saw this, she took the sheets from her bed, tore them into strings, tied them together, and let one end down the side of the house. A moment more, and one end of the rope-ladder was in her hand, and she fastened it inside the room. Soon the young maiden was seen descending, and the enthusiastic lover, with his arms extended, waiting to receive his mistress. The planter had been out on an hunting excursion, and returning home, saw his victim as her lover was receiving her in his arms. At this moment the sharp sound of a rifle was heard, and the young man fell weltering in his blood, at the feet of his mistress. Jane fell senseless by his side. For many days she had a confused consciousness of some great agony, but knew not where she was, or by whom surrounded. The slow recovery of her reason settled into the most intense melancholy, which gained at length the compassion even of her cruel master. The beautiful bright eyes, always pleading in expression, were now so heart-piercing in their sadness, that he could not endure their gaze.[1] In a few days the poor girl died of a broken heart, and was buried at night at the back of the garden by the negroes; and no one wept at the grave of her who had been so carefully cherished, and so tenderly beloved.[2]

---

1 *"the sharp sound of a rifle … could not endure"*: Child, "The Quadroons," 139–40.

2 *"no one wept at the grave of her … so tenderly beloved"*: Child, "The Quadroons," 141.

This, reader, is an unvarnished narrative of one doomed by the laws of the Southern States to be a slave. It tells not only its own story of grief, but speaks of a thousand wrongs and woes beside, which never see the light; all the more bitter and dreadful, because no help can relieve, no sympathy can mitigate, and no hope can cheer.[1]

CHAPTER XXIV.

THE ARREST.

"The fearful storm—it threatens lowering,
        Which God in mercy long delays;
Slaves yet may see their masters cowering,
While whole plantations smoke and blaze!" *Carter.*[2]

It was late in the evening when the coach arrived at Richmond, and Clotel once more alighted in her native city. She had intended to seek lodgings somewhere in the outskirts of the town, but the lateness of the hour compelled her to stop at one of the principal hotels for the night. She had scarcely entered the inn, when she recognised among the numerous black servants one to whom she was well known; and her only hope was, that her disguise would keep her from being discovered. The imperturbable calm and entire forgetfulness of self which induced Clotel to visit a place from which she could scarcely hope to escape, to attempt the rescue of a beloved child, demonstrate that over-willingness of woman to carry out the promptings of the finer feelings of her heart. True to woman's nature, she had risked her own liberty for another.

She remained in the hotel during the night, and the next morning, under the plea of illness, she took her breakfast alone. That day the fugitive slave paid a visit to the suburbs of the town, and once more beheld the cottage in which she had spent so many happy hours. It was winter, and the clematis and passion flower were not there; but there were the same walks she had so often pressed with her feet, and the same trees which had so often shaded her as she passed through the garden at the back of the house. Old remembrances rushed upon her memory, and caused her to shed tears freely. Clotel was now in her native-town, and

---

1 "*It tells not only its own story ... hope can cheer*": "Story of a Slave Mother," 186.
2 J.G. Carter, "Ye Sons of Freedom," lines 13–17.

near her daughter; but how could she communicate with her? How could she see her? To have made herself known, would have been a suicidal act; betrayal would have followed, and she arrested. Three days had passed away, and Clotel still remained in the hotel at which she had first put up; and yet she had got no tidings of her child. Unfortunately for Clotel, a disturbance had just broken out amongst the slave population in the state of Virginia, and all strangers were eyed with suspicion.

The evils consequent on slavery are not lessened by the incoming of one or two rays of light. If the slave only becomes aware of his condition, and conscious of the injustice under which he suffers, if he obtains but a faint idea of these things, he will seize the first opportunity to possess himself of what he conceives to belong to him.[1] The infusion of Anglo-Saxon with African blood has created an insurrectionary feeling among the slaves of America hitherto unknown. Aware of their blood connection with their owners, these mulattoes labour under the sense of their personal and social injuries; and tolerate, if they do not encourage in themselves, low and vindictive passions.[2] On the other hand, the slave owners are aware of their critical position, and are ever watchful, always fearing an outbreak among the slaves.

True, the Free States are equally bound with the Slave States to suppress any insurrectionary movement that may take place among the slaves. The Northern freemen are bound by their constitutional obligations to aid the slaveholder in keeping his slaves in their chains. Yet there are, at the time we write, four millions of bond slaves in the United States. The insurrection to which we now refer was headed by a full-blooded negro, who had been born and brought up a slave. He had heard the twang of the driver's whip, and saw the warm blood streaming from the negro's body; he had witnessed the separation of parents and children, and was made aware, by too many proofs, that the slave could expect no justice at the hand of the slave owner.[3] He went by the name of "Nat Turner."[4] He was a preacher amongst the negroes, and distinguished for his eloquence, respected by the whites, and loved and venerated by the negroes.

---

1 *"The evils consequent on slavery ... idea of these things"*: Beard, *Life*, 19.

2 *"labour under the sense of their personal ... vindictive passions"*: Beard, *Life*, 21.

3 *"heard the twang of the driver's whip ... many proofs"*: Beard, *Life*, 27.

4 Nat Turner (1800–31) led a slave rebellion in Southampton County, Virginia, in August 1831. Over 200 people died, including at least 55 white people.

On the discovery of the plan for the outbreak, Turner fled to the swamps, followed by those who had joined in the insurrection. Here the revolted negroes numbered some hundreds, and for a time bade defiance to their oppressors. The Dismal Swamps cover many thousands of acres of wild land, and a dense forest, with wild animals and insects, such as are unknown in any other part of Virginia. Here runaway negroes usually seek a hiding-place, and some have been known to reside here for years. The revolters were joined by one of these. He was a large, tall, full-blooded negro, with a stern and savage countenance; the marks on his face showed that he was from one of the barbarous tribes in Africa, and claimed that country as his native land; his only covering was a girdle around his loins, made of skins of wild beasts which he had killed; his only token of authority among those that he led, was a pair of epaulettes made from the tail of a fox, and tied to his shoulder by a cord. Brought from the coast of Africa when only fifteen years of age to the island of Cuba, he was smuggled from thence into Virginia. He had been two years in the swamps, and considered it his future home. He had met a negro woman who was also a runaway; and, after the fashion of his native land, had gone through the process of oiling her as the marriage ceremony. They had built a cave on a rising mound in the swamp; this was their home. His name was Picquilo.[1] His only weapon was a sword, made from the blade of a scythe, which he had stolen from a neighbouring plantation. His dress, his character, his manners, his mode of fighting, were all in keeping with the early training he had received in the land of his birth. He moved about with the activity of a cat, and neither the thickness of the trees, nor the depth of the water could stop him. He was a bold, turbulent spirit; and from revenge imbrued his hands in the blood of all the whites he could meet. Hunger, thirst, fatigue, and loss of sleep he seemed made to endure as if by peculiarity of constitution. His air was fierce, his step oblique, his look sanguinary.[2] Such was the character of one of the leaders in the Southampton insurrection. All negroes were arrested who were found beyond their master's threshold, and all strange whites watched with a great degree of alacrity.

Such was the position in which Clotel found affairs when she

---

1 No slave named Picquilo took part in Nat Turner's revolt; Brown seems to have invented the character on the basis of the description of the Haitian revolutionary Jean-Jacques Dessalines (1758–1806) in Beard's *The Life of Toussaint L'Ouverture* (1853).

2 "*a bold, turbulent spirit; and from revenge imbrued ... his look sanguinary*": Beard, *Life*, 167–68.

returned to Virginia in search of her Mary. Had not the slave-owners been watchful of strangers, owing to the outbreak, the fugitive
could not have escaped the vigilance of the police; for advertisements, announcing her escape and offering a large reward for her
arrest, had been received in the city previous to her arrival, and the
officers were therefore on the look-out for the runaway slave. It was
on the third day, as the quadroon was seated in her room at the
inn, still in the disguise of a gentleman, that two of the city officers
entered the room, and informed her that they were authorised to
examine all strangers, to assure the authorities that they were not in
league with the revolted negroes. With trembling heart the fugitive
handed the key of her trunk to the officers. To their surprise, they
found nothing but woman's apparel in the box, which raised their
curiosity, and caused a further investigation that resulted in the
arrest of Clotel as a fugitive slave. She was immediately conveyed
to prison, there to await the orders of her master. For many days,
uncheered by the voice of kindness, alone, hopeless, desolate, she
waited for the time to arrive when the chains were to be placed on
her limbs, and she returned to her inhuman and unfeeling owner.[1]

The arrest of the fugitive was announced in all the newspapers,
but created little or no sensation. The inhabitants were too much
engaged in putting down the revolt among the slaves; and although all the odds were against the insurgents, the whites found
it no easy matter, with all their caution. Every day brought news
of fresh outbreaks. Without scruple and without pity, the whites
massacred all blacks found beyond their owners' plantations: the
negroes, in return, set fire to houses, and put those to death who
attempted to escape from the flames. Thus carnage was added to
carnage, and the blood of the whites flowed to avenge the blood
of the blacks. These were the ravages of slavery.[2] No graves were
dug for the negroes; their dead bodies became food for dogs and
vultures, and their bones, partly calcined by the sun, remained
scattered about, as if to mark the mournful fury of servitude and
lust of power.[3] When the slaves were subdued, except a few in the
swamps, bloodhounds were put in this dismal place to hunt out
the remaining revolters. Among the captured negroes was one of
whom we shall hereafter make mention.

---

1 "*For many days, uncheered by the voice of kindness ... she waited*":
   "Pauline," 102.
2 "*Without scruple and without pity ... ravages of slavery*": Beard, *Life*,
   192–93.
3 "*No graves were dug for the negroes ... lust of power*": Beard, *Life*, 193.

CHAPTER XXV.

DEATH IS FREEDOM.

"I asked but freedom, and ye gave
Chains, and the freedom of the grave."—*Snelling.*[1]

There are, in the district of Columbia, several slave prisons, or "negro pens," as they are termed. These prisons are mostly occupied by persons to keep their slaves in, when collecting their gangs together for the New Orleans market. Some of them belong to the government, and one, in particular, is noted for having been the place where a number of free coloured persons have been incarcerated from time to time. In this district is situated the capitol of the United States. Any free coloured persons visiting Washington, if not provided with papers asserting and proving their right to be free, may be arrested and placed in one of these dens. If they succeed in showing that they are free, they are set at liberty, provided they are able to pay the expenses of their arrest and imprisonment; if they cannot pay these expenses, they are sold out. Through this unjust and oppressive law, many persons born in the Free States have been consigned to a life of slavery on the cotton, sugar, or rice plantations of the Southern States. By order of her master, Clotel was removed from Richmond and placed in one of these prisons, to await the sailing of a vessel for New Orleans. The prison in which she was put stands midway between the capitol at Washington and the president's house. Here the fugitive saw nothing but slaves brought in and taken out, to be placed in ships and sent away to the same part of the country to which she herself would soon be compelled to go. She had seen or heard nothing of her daughter while in Richmond, and all hope of seeing her now had fled. If she was carried back to New Orleans, she could expect no mercy from her master.

At the dusk of the evening previous to the day when she was to be sent off, as the old prison was being closed for the night, she suddenly darted past her keeper, and ran for her life. It is not a great distance from the prison to the Long Bridge, which passes from the lower part of the city across the Potomac, to the extensive forests and woodlands of the celebrated Arlington Place, occupied by that

---

1 A rewriting of lines from William J. Snelling's "Osceola," *Dublin University Magazine* 18 (August 1841): 219 ("I asked but freedom— and ye gave/The freedom of the lonely grave"). Snelling (1804–48) was a writer and journalist.

distinguished relative and descendant of the immortal Washington, Mr. George W. Custis. Thither the poor fugitive directed her flight. So unexpected was her escape, that she had quite a number of rods[1] the start before the keeper had secured the other prisoners, and rallied his assistants in pursuit. It was at an hour when, and in a part of the city where, horses could not be readily obtained for the chase; no bloodhounds were at hand to run down the flying woman; and for once it seemed as though there was to be a fair trial of speed and endurance between the slave and the slave-catchers. The keeper and his forces raised the hue and cry on her pathway close behind; but so rapid was the flight along the wide avenue, that the astonished citizens, as they poured forth from their dwellings to learn the cause of alarm, were only able to comprehend the nature of the case in time to fall in with the motley mass in pursuit, (as many a one did that night,) to raise an anxious prayer to heaven, as they refused to join in the pursuit, that the panting fugitive might escape, and the merciless soul dealer for once be disappointed of his prey. And now with the speed of an arrow—having passed the avenue—with the distance between her and her pursuers constantly increasing, this poor hunted female gained the *"Long Bridge,"* as it is called, where interruption seemed improbable, and already did her heart begin to beat high with the hope of success. She had only to pass three-fourths of a mile across the bridge, and she could bury herself in a vast forest, just at the time when the curtain of night would close around her, and protect her from the pursuit of her enemies.

But God by his Providence had otherwise determined. He had determined that an appalling tragedy should be enacted that night, within plain sight of the President's house and the capital of the Union, which should be an evidence wherever it should be known, of the unconquerable love of liberty the heart may inherit; as well as a fresh admonition to the slave dealer, of the cruelty and enormity of his crimes. Just as the pursuers crossed the high draw for the passage of sloops, soon after entering upon the bridge, they beheld three men slowly approaching from the Virginia side. They immediately called to them to arrest the fugitive, whom they proclaimed a runaway slave. True to their Virginian instincts as she came near, they formed in line across the narrow bridge, and prepared to seize her. Seeing escape impossible in that quarter, she stopped suddenly, and turned upon her pursuers. On came the profane and ribald crew, faster than ever, already exulting in her capture, and threatening punishment for her flight. For a moment she looked wildly and anxiously around

---

1 A rod is five and a half yards.

to see if there was no hope of escape. On either hand, far down below, rolled the deep foamy waters of the Potomac, and before and behind the rapidly approaching step and noisy voices of pursuers, showing how vain would be any further effort for freedom. Her resolution was taken. She clasped her *hands* convulsively, and raised *them*, as she at the same time raised her *eyes* towards heaven, and begged for that mercy and compassion *there*, which had been denied her on earth; and then, with a single bound, she vaulted over the railings of the bridge, and sunk for ever beneath the waves of the river![1]

Thus died Clotel, the daughter of Thomas Jefferson, a president of the United States; a man distinguished as the author of the Declaration of American Independence, and one of the first statesmen of that country.

Had Clotel escaped from oppression in any other land, in the disguise in which she fled from the Mississippi to Richmond, and reached the United States, no honour within the gift of the American people would have been too good to have been heaped upon the heroic woman. But she was a slave, and therefore out of the pale of their sympathy. They have tears to shed over Greece and Poland; they have an abundance of sympathy

---

1 "*At the dusk of the evening previous to the day ... waves of the river*": [Seth M. Gates], "Slavery in the District," 1.

for "poor Ireland;" they can furnish a ship of war to convey the Hungarian refugees from a Turkish prison to the "land of the free and home of the brave." They boast that America is the "cradle of liberty;" if it is, I fear they have rocked the child to death. The body of Clotel was picked up from the bank of the river, where it had been washed by the strong current, a hole dug in the sand, and there deposited, without either inquest being held over it, or religious service being performed. Such was the life and such the death of a woman whose virtues and goodness of heart would have done honour to one in a higher station of life, and who, if she had been born in any other land but that of slavery, would have been honoured and loved. A few days after the death of Clotel, the following poem appeared in one of the newspapers:

"Now, rest for the wretched! the long day is past,
And night on yon prison descendeth at last.
Now lock up and bolt! Ha, jailor, look there!
Who flies like a wild bird escaped from the snare?
A woman, a slave—up, out in pursuit,
While linger some gleams of day!
Let thy call ring out!—now a rabble rout
Is at thy heels—speed away!

"A bold race for freedom!—On, fugitive, on!
Heaven help but the right, and thy freedom is won.
How eager she drinks the free air of the plains;
Every limb, every nerve, every fibre she strains;
From Columbia's glorious capitol,
Columbia's daughter flees
To the sanctuary God has given—
The sheltering forest trees.

"Now she treads the Long Bridge—joy lighteth her eye—
Beyond her the dense wood and darkening sky—
Wild hopes thrill her heart as she neareth the shore:
O, despair! there are *men* fast advancing before!
Shame, shame on their manhood! they hear, they heed
The cry, her flight to stay,
And like demon forms with their outstretched arms,
They wait to seize their prey!

"She pauses, she turns! Ah, will she flee back?

Like wolves, her pursuers howl loud on their track;
She lifteth to Heaven one look of despair—
Her anguish breaks forth in one hurried prayer—
Hark! her jailor's yell! like a bloodhound's bay
On the low night wind it sweeps!
Now, death or the chain! to the stream she turns,
And she leaps! O God, she leaps!

"The dark and the cold, yet merciful wave,
Receives to its bosom the form of the slave;
She rises—earth's scenes on her dim vision gleam,
Yet she struggleth not with the strong rushing stream:
And low are the death-cries her woman's heart gives,
As she floats adown the river,
Faint and more faint grows the drowning voice,
And her cries have ceased for ever!

"Now back, jailor, back to thy dungeons, again,
To swing the red lash and rivet the chain!
The form thou would'st fetter—returned to its God;
The universe holdeth no realm of night
More drear than her slavery—
More merciless fiends than here stayed her flight—
Joy! the hunted slave is free!

"That bond woman's corse—let Potomac's proud wave
Go bear it along *by our Washington's grave*,
And heave it high up on that hallowed strand,
To tell of the freedom he won for our land.
A weak woman's corse, by freemen chased down;
Hurrah for our country! hurrah!
To freedom she leaped, through drowning and death—
Hurrah for our country! hurrah!"[1]

---

1 Sarah J. Clarke, "The Escape," 152. The poem would subsequently
   appear under Clarke's pen name, Grace Greenwood, in *Poems*
   (Boston: Ticknor, Reed, and Fields, 1851), where it is entitled "The
   Leap from the Long Bridge." In the 1851 version, the penultimate
   stanza is rewritten and the final stanza is omitted. It has long been
   thought that Brown wrote the final two stanzas himself; in fact,
   he simply copied the 1844 version, italics and all. Greenwood
   (1823–1904) was an author who advocated for social reform.

CHAPTER XXVI.

THE ESCAPE.

"No refuge is found on our unhallowed ground,
    For the wretched in Slavery's manacles bound;
While our star spangled banner in vain boasts to wave
    O'er the land of the free and the home of the brave!"[1]

We left Mary, the daughter of Clotel, in the capacity of a servant in her own father's house, where she had been taken by her mistress for the ostensible purpose of plunging her husband into the depths of humiliation. At first the young girl was treated with great severity; but after finding that Horatio Green had lost all feeling for his child, Mrs. Green's own heart became touched for the offspring of her husband, and she became its friend. Mary had grown still more beautiful, and, like most of her sex in that country, was fast coming to maturity.

    The arrest of Clotel, while trying to rescue her daughter, did not reach the ears of the latter till her mother had been removed from Richmond to Washington. The mother had passed from time to eternity before the daughter knew that she had been in the neighbourhood. Horatio Green was not in Richmond at the time of Clotel's arrest; had he been there, it is not probable but he would have made an effort to save her. She was not his slave, and therefore was beyond his power, even had he been there and inclined to aid her. The revolt amongst the slaves had been brought to an end, and most of the insurgents either put to death or sent out of the state. One, however, remained in prison. He was the slave of Horatio Green, and had been a servant in his master's dwelling. He, too, could boast that his father was an American statesman. His name was George. His mother had been employed as a servant in one of the principal hotels in Washington, where members of Congress usually put up. After George's birth his mother was sold to a slave trader, and he to an agent of Mr. Green, the father of Horatio. George was as white as most white persons. No one would suppose that any African blood coursed through his veins. His hair was straight, soft, fine, and light; his eyes blue, nose prominent, lips thin, his head well formed, forehead high and prominent; and he was often taken

---

1 Edwin A. Atlee, "New Version of the National Song, the Star Spangled Banner," lines 21–24.

for a free white person by those who did know him. This made his condition still more intolerable; for one so white seldom ever receives fair treatment at the hands of his fellow slaves; and the whites usually regard such slaves as persons who, if not often flogged, and otherwise ill treated, to remind them of their condition, would soon "forget" that they were slaves, and "think themselves as good as white folks." George's opportunities were far greater than most slaves. Being in his master's house, and waiting on educated white people, he had become very familiar with the English language. He had heard his master and visitors speak of the down-trodden and oppressed Poles; he heard them talk of going to Greece to fight for Grecian liberty, and against the oppressors of that ill-fated people. George, fired with the love of freedom, and zeal for the cause of his enslaved countrymen, joined the insurgents, and with them had been defeated and captured. He was the only one remaining of these unfortunate people, and he would have been put to death with them but for a circumstance that occurred some weeks before the outbreak. The court house had, by accident, taken fire, and was fast consuming. The engines could not be made to work, and all hope of saving the building seemed at an end. In one of the upper chambers there was a small box containing some valuable deeds belonging to the city; a ladder was placed against the house, leading from the street to the window of the room in which the box stood. The wind blew strong, and swept the flames in that direction. Broad sheets of fire were blown again and again over that part of the building, and then the wind would lift the pall of smoke, which showed that the work of destruction was not yet accomplished. While the doomed building was thus exposed, and before the destroying element had made its final visit, as it did soon after, George was standing by, and hearing that much depended on the contents of the box, and seeing no one disposed to venture through the fiery element to save the treasure, mounted the ladder and made his way to the window, entered the room, and was soon seen descending with the much valued box.[1] Three cheers rent the air as the young slave fell from the ladder when near the ground; the white men took him up in their arms, to see if he had sustained any injury. His hair was burnt, eyebrows closely singed, and his clothes smelt strongly of smoke; but the heroic young slave was unhurt. The city authorities, at

---

1 "*The wind blew strong, and swept the flames ... did soon after*": "The Mother," 2.

their next meeting, passed a vote of thanks to George's master for the lasting benefit that the slave had rendered the public, and commended the poor boy to the special favour of his owner. When George was on trial for participating in the revolt, this "meritorious act," as they were pleased to term it, was brought up in his favour. His trial was put off from session to session, till he had been in prison more than a year. At last, however, he was convicted of high treason, and sentenced to be hanged within ten days of that time. The judge asked the slave if he had anything to say why sentence of death should not be passed on him. George stood for a moment in silence, and then said, "As I cannot speak as I should wish, I will say nothing." "You may say what you please," said the judge. "You had a good master," continued he, "and still you were dissatisfied; you left your master and joined the negroes who were burning our houses and killing our wives." "As you have given me permission to speak," remarked George, "I will tell you why I joined the revolted negroes. I have heard my master read in the Declaration of Independence 'that all men are created free and equal,' and this caused me to inquire of myself why I was a slave. I also heard him talking with some of his visitors about the war with England, and he said, all wars and fightings for freedom were just and right. If so, in what am I wrong? The grievances of which your fathers complained, and which caused the Revolutionary War, were trifling in comparison with the wrongs and sufferings of those who were engaged in the late revolt. Your fathers were never slaves, ours are; your fathers were never bought and sold like cattle, never shut out from the light of knowledge and religion, never subjected to the lash of brutal task-masters. For the crime of having a dark skin, my people suffer the pangs of hunger, the infliction of stripes, and the ignominy of brutal servitude. We are kept in heathenish darkness by laws expressly enacted to make our instruction a criminal offence.[1] What right has one man to the bones, sinews, blood, and nerves of another? Did not one God make us all? You say your fathers fought for freedom—so did we. You tell me that I am to be put to death for violating the laws of the land. Did not the American revolutionists violate the laws when they struck for liberty? They were revolters, but their success made them patriots—we were revolters, and our failure makes us rebels.

---

1 *"trifling in comparison with the wrongs ... a criminal offence"*: William Lloyd Garrison, "Declaration of the National Anti-Slavery Convention," 198.

Had we succeeded, we would have been patriots too. Success makes all the difference. You make merry on the 4th of July; the thunder of cannon and ringing of bells announce it as the birthday of American independence. Yet while these cannons are roaring and bells ringing, one-sixth of the people of this land are in chains and slavery. You boast that this is the 'Land of the Free'; but a traditionary freedom will not save you. It will not do to praise your fathers and build their sepulchres. Worse for you that you have such an inheritance, if you spend it foolishly and are unable to appreciate its worth. Sad if the genius of a true humanity, beholding you with tearful eyes from the mount of vision, shall fold his wings in sorrowing pity, and repeat the strain, 'O land of Washington, how often would I have gathered thy children together, as a hen doth gather her brood under her wings, and ye would not; behold your house is left unto you desolate.'[1] This is all I have to say; I have done." Nearly every one present was melted to tears; even the judge seemed taken by surprise at the intelligence of the young slave. But George was a slave, and an example must be made of him, and therefore he was sentenced. Being employed in the same house with Mary, the daughter of Clotel, George had become attached to her, and the young lovers fondly looked forward to the time when they should be husband and wife.

After George had been sentenced to death, Mary was still more attentive to him, and begged and obtained leave of her mistress to visit him in his cell. The poor girl paid a daily visit to him to whom she had pledged her heart and hand. At one of these meetings, and only four days from the time fixed for the execution, while Mary was seated in George's cell, it occurred to her that she might yet save him from a felon's doom. She revealed to him the secret that was then occupying her thoughts, viz. that George should exchange clothes with her, and thus attempt his escape in disguise. But he would not for a single moment listen to the proposition. Not that he feared detection; but he would not consent to place an innocent and affectionate girl in a position where she might have to suffer for him. Mary pleaded, but in vain—George was inflexible. The poor girl left her lover with a heavy heart, regretting that her scheme had proved unsuccessful.

Towards the close of the next day, Mary again appeared at the prison door for admission, and was soon by the side of him

---

1 "*a traditionary freedom will not save ... left unto you desolate*": Charles Chauncy Shackford (1815–91); quoted in "Shackford's Letters on the War with Mexico," 1.

whom she so ardently loved. While there the clouds which had overhung the city for some hours broke, and the rain fell in torrents amid the most terrific thunder and lightning. In the most persuasive manner possible, Mary again importuned George to avail himself of her assistance to escape from an ignominious death. After assuring him that she, not being the person condemned, would not receive any injury, he at last consented, and they began to exchange apparel. As George was of small stature, and both were white, there was no difficulty in his passing out without detection; and as she usually left the cell weeping, with handkerchief in hand, and sometimes at her face, he had only to adopt this mode and his escape was safe. They had kissed each other, and Mary had told George where he would find a small parcel of provisions which she had placed in a secluded spot, when the prison-keeper opened the door and said, "Come, girl, it is time for you to go." George again embraced Mary, and passed out of the jail. It was already dark, and the street lamps were lighted, so that our hero in his new dress had no dread of detection. The provisions were sought out and found, and poor George was soon on the road towards Canada. But neither of them had once thought of a change of dress for George when he should have escaped, and he had walked but a short distance before he felt that a change of his apparel would facilitate his progress. But he dared not go amongst even his coloured associates for fear of being betrayed. However, he made the best of his way on towards Canada, hiding in the woods during the day, and travelling by the guidance of the North Star at night.

With the poet he could truly say,

> "Star of the North! while blazing day
> Pours round me its full tide of light,
> And hides thy pale but faithful ray,
> I, too, lie hid, and long for night."[1]

One morning, George arrived on the banks of the Ohio river, and found his journey had terminated, unless he could get some one to take him across the river in a secret manner, for he would not be permitted to cross in any of the ferry boats, it being a

---

1 John Pierpont, "The Fugitive Slave's Apostrophe to the North Star," lines 7–10. Pierpont (1785–1866) was a poet, educator, lawyer, and minister who influenced the anti-slavery movement.

penalty for crossing a slave, besides the value of the slave. He concealed himself in the tall grass and weeds near the river, to see if he could embrace an opportunity to cross. He had been in his hiding place but a short time, when he observed a man in a small boat, floating near the shore, evidently fishing. His first impulse was to call out to the man and ask him to take him over to the Ohio side, but the fear that the man was a slaveholder, or one who might possibly arrest him, deterred him from it. The man after rowing and floating about for some time fastened the boat to the root of a tree, and started to a neighbouring farmhouse.

This was George's moment, and he seized it. Running down the bank, he unfastened the boat, jumped in, and with all the expertness of one accustomed to a boat, rowed across the river and landed on the Ohio side.

Being now in a Free State, he thought he might with perfect safety travel on towards Canada. He had, however, gone but a very few miles when he discovered two men on horseback coming behind him. He felt sure that they could not be in pursuit of him, yet he did not wish to be seen by them, so he turned into another road leading to a house near by. The men followed, and were but a short distance from George, when he ran up to a farmhouse, before which was standing a farmer-looking man, in a broad-brimmed hat and straight-collared coat, whom he implored to save him from the "slave-catchers." The farmer told him to go into the barn near by; he entered by the front door, the farmer following, and closing the door behind George, but remaining outside, and gave directions to his hired man as to what should be done with George. The slaveholders by this time had dismounted, and were in front of the barn demanding admittance, and charging the farmer with secreting their slave woman, for George was still in the dress of a woman. The Friend, for the farmer proved to be a member of the Society of Friends,[1] told the slave-owners that if they wished to search his barn, they must first get an officer and a search warrant. While the parties were disputing, the farmer began nailing up the front door, and the hired man served the back door in the same way. The slaveholders, finding that they could not prevail on the Friend to allow them to get the slave, determined to go in search of an officer. One was left to see that the slave did not escape from

---

1 Dissenting Protestants who emphasize personal and direct religious experience; also known as Quakers. Wells Brown, the Ohioan who sheltered Brown during his escape and from whom Brown took his middle and last names, was a Quaker.

the barn, while the other went off at full speed to Mount Pleasant, the nearest town. George was not the slave of either of these men, nor were they in pursuit of him, but they had lost a woman who had been seen in that vicinity, and when they saw poor George in the disguise of a female, and attempting to elude pursuit, they felt sure they were close upon their victim. However, if they had caught him, although he was not their slave, they would have taken him back and placed him in jail, and there he would have remained until his owner arrived.

After an absence of nearly two hours, the slave-owner returned with an officer and found the Friend still driving large nails into the door. In a triumphant tone and with a corresponding gesture, he handed the search-warrant to the Friend, and said, "There, sir, now I will see if I can't get my nigger." "Well," said the Friend, "thou hast gone to work according to law, and thou canst now go into my barn." "Lend me your hammer that I may get the door open," said the slaveholder. "Let me see the warrant again." And after reading it over once more, he said, "I see nothing in this paper which says I must supply thee with tools to open my door; if thou wishest to go in, thou must get a hammer elsewhere." The sheriff said, "I will go to a neighbouring farm and borrow something which will introduce us to Miss Dinah;" and he immediately went in search of tools. In a short time the officer returned, and they commenced an assault and battery upon the barn door, which soon yielded; and in went the slaveholder and officer, and began turning up the hay and using all other means to find the lost property; but, to their astonishment, the slave was not there. After all hope of getting Dinah was gone, the slave-owner in a rage said to the Friend, "My nigger is not here." "I did not tell thee there was any one here." "Yes, but I saw her go in, and you shut the door behind her, and if she was not in the barn, what did you nail the door for?" "Can't I do what I please with my own barn door? Now I will tell thee; thou need trouble thyself no more, for the person thou art after entered the front door and went out at the back door, and is a long way from here by this time. Thou and thy friend must be somewhat fatigued by this time; won't thou go in and take a little dinner with me?" We need not say that this cool invitation of the good Quaker was not accepted by the slaveholders. George in the meantime had been taken to a friend's dwelling some miles away, where, after laying aside his female attire, and being snugly dressed up in a straight collared coat, and pantaloons to match, was again put on the right road towards Canada.

The fugitive now travelled by day, and laid by during night.

After a fatiguing and dreary journey of two weeks, the fugitive arrived in Canada, and took up his abode in the little town of St. Catherine's, and obtained work on the farm of Colonel Street. Here he attended a night-school, and laboured for his employer during the day. The climate was cold, and wages small, yet he was in a land where he was free, and this the young slave prized more than all the gold that could be given to him. Besides doing his best to obtain education for himself, he imparted what he could to those of his fellow-fugitives about him, of whom there were many.

CHAPTER XXVII.

THE MYSTERY.

George, however, did not forget his promise to use all the means in his power to get Mary out of slavery. He, therefore, laboured with all his might to obtain money with which to employ some one to go back to Virginia for Mary. After nearly six months' labour at St. Catherine's, he employed an English missionary to go and see if the girl could be purchased, and at what price. The missionary went accordingly, but returned with the sad intelligence that, on account of Mary's aiding George to escape, the court had compelled Mr. Green to sell her out of the state, and she had been sold to a negro trader, and taken to the New Orleans market. As all hope of getting the girl was now gone, George resolved to quit the American continent for ever. He immediately took passage in a vessel laden with timber, bound for Liverpool, and in five weeks from that time he was standing on the quay of the great English seaport. With little or no education, he found many difficulties in the way of getting a respectable living. However he obtained a situation as porter in a large house in Manchester, where he worked during the day, and took private lessons at night. In this way he laboured for three years, and was then raised to the situation of clerk. George was so white as easily to pass for a white man, and being somewhat ashamed of his African descent, he never once mentioned the fact of his having been a slave. He soon became a partner in the firm that employed him, and was now on the road to wealth.

In the year 1842, just ten years after George Green (for he adopted his master's name) arrived in England, he visited France, and spent some days at Dunkirk. It was towards sunset, on a warm day in the month of October, that Mr. Green, after strolling some distance from the Hotel de Leon, entered a burial ground, and wandered long alone among the silent dead, gazing upon the many green graves and marble tombstones of those who once moved on the theatre of busy life, and whose sounds of gaiety once fell upon the ear of man. All nature around was hushed in silence, and seemed to partake of the general melancholy which hung over the quiet resting-place of departed mortals. After tracing the varied inscriptions which told the characters or conditions of the departed, and viewing the mounds beneath which the dust of mortality slumbered, he had now reached a secluded spot, near to where an aged weeping willow bowed its thick foliage to the ground, as though anxious to hide from the scrutinising gaze of curiosity the grave beneath it. Mr. Green seated himself upon a marble tomb, and began to read Roscoe's *Leo X.*,[1] a copy of which he had under his arm. It was then about twilight, and he had scarcely gone through half a page, when he observed a lady in black, leading a boy, some five years old, up one of the paths; and as the lady's black veil was over her face, he felt somewhat at liberty to eye her more closely. While looking at her, the lady gave a scream, and appeared to be in a fainting position, when Mr. Green sprang from his seat in time to save her from falling to the ground. At this moment, an elderly gentleman was seen approaching with a rapid step, who, from his appearance, was evidently the lady's father, or one intimately connected with her. He came up, and, in a confused manner, asked what was the matter. Mr. Green explained as well as he could. After taking up the smelling bottle which had fallen from her hand, and holding it a short time to her face, she soon began to revive. During all this time the lady's veil had so covered her face, that Mr. Green had not seen it. When she had so far recovered as to be able to raise her head, she again screamed, and fell back into the arms of the old man. It now appeared quite certain, that either the countenance of George Green, or some other object, was the cause of these fits of fainting; and the old gentleman, thinking it was the former, in rather a petulant tone said, "I will thank you, sir, if you will leave us alone." The child whom the lady was leading, had now set up a squall; and amid the death-like appearance of the lady, the harsh look of the old man, and the cries of the boy, Mr. Green left the grounds, and returned to his hotel.

Whilst seated by the window, and looking out upon the crowded

---

1 See p. 67, note 2.

street, with every now and then the strange scene in the grave-yard vividly before him, Mr. Green thought of the book he had been reading, and, remembering that he had left it on the tomb, where he had suddenly dropped it when called to the assistance of the lady, he immediately determined to return in search of it. After a walk of some twenty minutes, he was again over the spot where he had been an hour before, and from which he had been so unceremoniously expelled by the old man. He looked in vain for the book; it was nowhere to be found: nothing save the bouquet which the lady had dropped, and which lay half-buried in the grass from having been trodden upon, indicated that any one had been there that evening. Mr. Green took up the bunch of flowers, and again returned to the hotel.

After passing a sleepless night, and hearing the clock strike six, he dropped into a sweet sleep, from which he did not awake until roused by the rap of a servant, who, entering his room, handed him a note which ran as follows:—"Sir,—I owe you an apology for the inconvenience to which you were subjected last evening, and if you will honour us with your presence to dinner to-day at four o'clock, I shall be most happy to give you due satisfaction. My servant will be in waiting for you at half-past three. I am, sir, your obedient servant, J. Devenant. October 23. To George Green, Esq."

The servant who handed this note to Mr. Green, informed him that the bearer was waiting for a reply. He immediately resolved to accept the invitation, and replied accordingly. Who this person was, and how his name and the hotel where he was stopping had been found out, was indeed a mystery. However, he waited impatiently for the hour when he was to see this new acquaintance, and get the mysterious meeting in the grave-yard solved.

CHAPTER XXVIII.

THE HAPPY MEETING.

> "Man's love is of man's life, a thing apart;
> 'Tis woman's whole existence."—*Byron*.[1]

The clock on a neighbouring church had scarcely ceased striking three, when the servant announced that a carriage had called for Mr. Green. In less than half an hour he was seated in a most sumptuous barouche, drawn by two beautiful iron greys, and rolling

---

1 Byron, *Don Juan*, Canto 1, stanza 194.

along over a splendid gravel road completely shaded by large trees, which appeared to have been the accumulating growth of many centuries. The carriage soon stopped in front of a low villa, and this too was embedded in magnificent trees covered with moss. Mr. Green alighted and was shown into a superb drawing room, the walls of which were hung with fine specimens from the hands of the great Italian painters, and one by a German artist representing a beautiful monkish legend connected with "The Holy Catherine," an illustrious lady of Alexandria.[1] The furniture had an antique and dignified appearance. High backed chairs stood around the room; a venerable mirror stood on the mantle shelf; rich curtains of crimson damask hung in folds at either side of the large windows; and a rich Turkey carpet covered the floor. In the centre stood a table covered with books, in the midst of which was an old-fashioned vase filled with fresh flowers, whose fragrance was exceedingly pleasant. A faint light, together with the quietness of the hour, gave beauty beyond description to the whole scene.

Mr. Green had scarcely seated himself upon the sofa, when the elderly gentleman whom he had met the previous evening made his appearance, followed by the little boy, and introduced himself as Mr. Devenant. A moment more, and a lady—a beautiful brunette—dressed in black, with long curls of a chestnut colour hanging down her cheeks, entered the room. Her eyes were of a dark hazel, and her whole appearance indicated that she was a native of a southern clime. The door at which she entered was opposite to where the two gentlemen were seated. They immediately rose; and Mr. Devenant was in the act of introducing her to Mr. Green, when he observed that the latter had sunk back upon the sofa, and the last word that he remembered to have heard was, "It is her." After this, all was dark and dreamy: how long he remained in this condition it was for another to tell. When he awoke, he found himself stretched upon the sofa, with his boots off, his neckerchief removed, shirt collar unbuttoned, and his head resting upon a pillow. By his side sat the old man, with the smelling bottle in the one hand, and a glass of water in the other, and the little boy standing at the foot of the sofa. As soon as Mr. Green had so far recovered as to be able to speak, he

---

1 "by a German artist representing a beautiful monkish ... lady of Alexandria": "The Translation of St. Catherine," 255. The article is accompanied by an engraving of Heinrich Mücke's 1836 painting of that name, which depicts Catherine being carried through the air by angels.

said, "Where am I, and what does this mean?" "Wait a while," replied the old man, "and I will tell you all." After a lapse of some ten minutes he rose from the sofa, adjusted his apparel, and said, "I am now ready to hear anything you have to say." "You were born in America?" said the old man. "Yes," he replied. "And you were acquainted with a girl named Mary?" continued the old man. "Yes, and I loved her as I can love none other." "The lady whom you met so mysteriously last evening is Mary," replied Mr. Devenant. George Green was silent, but the fountains of mingled grief and joy stole out from beneath his eye-lashes, and glistened like pearls upon his pale and marble-like cheeks.[1] At this juncture the lady again entered the room. Mr. Green sprang from the sofa, and they fell into each other's arms, to the surprise of the old man and little George, and to the amusement of the servants who had crept up one by one, and were hid behind the doors, or loitering in the hall. When they had given vent to their feelings, they resumed their seats, and each in turn related the adventures through which they had passed. "How did you find out my name and address," asked Mr. Green? "After you had left us in the grave-yard, our little George said, 'O, mamma, if there aint a book!' and picked it up and brought it to us. Papa opened it, and said, 'The gentleman's name is written in it, and here is a card of the Hotel de Leon, where I suppose he is stopping.' Papa wished to leave the book, and said it was all a fancy of mine that I had ever seen you before, but I was perfectly convinced that you were my own George Green. Are you married?" "No, I am not." "Then, thank God!" exclaimed Mrs. Devenant. "And are you single now?" inquired Mr. Green. "Yes," she replied. "This is indeed the Lord's doings," said Mr. Green, at the same time bursting into a flood of tears. Mr. Devenant was past the age when men should think upon matrimonial subjects, yet the scene brought vividly before his eyes the days when he was a young man, and had a wife living. After a short interview, the old man called their attention to the dinner, which was then waiting. We need scarcely add, that Mr. Green and Mrs. Devenant did very little towards diminishing the dinner that day.

After dinner the lovers (for such we have to call them) gave their experience from the time that George left the jail dressed in Mary's clothes. Up to that time Mr. Green's was substantially as we have related it. Mrs. Devenant's was as follows:—"The night

---

1 "*the fountains of mingled grief and joy stole out ... marble-like cheeks*": "The Mother," 2.

after you left the prison," said she, "I did not shut my eyes in sleep. The next morning, about eight o'clock, Peter the gardener came to the jail to see if I had been there the night before, and was informed that I had, and that I had left a little after dark. About an hour after, Mr. Green came himself, and I need not say that he was much surprised on finding me there, dressed in your clothes. This was the first tidings they had of your escape." "What did Mr. Green say when he found that I had fled?" "Oh!" continued Mrs. Devenant, "he said to me when no one was near, I hope George will get off, but I fear you will have to suffer in his stead. I told him that if it must be so I was willing to die if you could live." At this moment George Green burst into tears, threw his arms around her neck, and exclaimed, "I am glad I have waited so long, with the hope of meeting you again."

Mrs. Devenant again resumed her story:—"I was kept in jail three days, during which time I was visited by the magistrates, and two of the judges. On the third day I was taken out, and master told me that I was liberated, upon condition that I should be immediately sent out of the state. There happened to be just at the time in the neighbourhood a negro-trader, and he purchased me, and I was taken to New Orleans. On the steam-boat we were kept in a close room, where slaves are usually confined, so that I saw nothing of the passengers on board, or the towns we passed. We arrived at New Orleans, and were all put into the slave-market for sale. I was examined by many persons, but none seemed willing to purchase me, as all thought me too white, and said I would run away and pass as a free white woman. On the second day, while in the slave-market, and while planters and others were examining slaves and making their purchases, I observed a tall young man, with long black hair, eyeing me very closely, and then talking to the trader. I felt sure that my time had now come, but the day closed without my being sold. I did not regret this, for I had heard that foreigners made the worst of masters, and I felt confident that the man who eyed me so closely was not an American.

"The next day was the Sabbath. The bells called the people to the different places of worship. Methodists sang, and Baptists immersed, and Presbyterians sprinkled, and Episcopalians read their prayers, while the ministers of the various sects preached that Christ died for all; yet there were some twenty-five or thirty of us poor creatures confined in the 'Negro Pen,' awaiting the close of the holy Sabbath, and the dawn of another day, to be again taken into the market, there to be examined like so many beasts of burden.[1] I need not tell you with what anxiety we waited for the advent of another day. On Monday we were again brought out and placed in rows to be inspected; and, fortunately for me, I was sold before we had been on the stand an hour. I was purchased by a gentleman residing in the city, for a waiting-maid for his wife, who was just on the eve of starting for Mobile, to pay a visit to a near relation. I was then dressed to suit the situation of a maid-servant; and upon the whole, I thought that, in my new dress, I looked as much the lady as my mistress.

"On the passage to Mobile, who should I see among the passengers but the tall, long-haired man that had eyed me so closely in the slave-market a few days before. His eyes were again on me, and he appeared anxious to speak to me, and I as reluctant to be spoken to. The first evening after leaving New Orleans, soon after twilight had let her curtain down, and pinned it with a star,[2] and while I was seated on the deck of the boat near the ladies' cabin, looking upon the rippled waves, and the reflection of the moon upon the sea, all at once I saw the tall young man standing by my side. I immediately rose from my seat, and was in the act of returning to the cabin, when he in a broken accent said, 'Stop a moment; I wish to have a word with you. I am your friend.' I stopped and looked him full in the face, and he said, 'I saw you some days since in the slave-market, and I intended to have purchased you to save you from the condition of a slave. I called on Monday, but you had been sold and had left the market. I inquired and learned who the purchaser was, and that you had to go to Mobile, so I resolved to follow you. If you are willing I will try and buy you from your present owner, and you shall be free.' Although this was said in an honest and off-hand manner, I could not believe the man to be sincere in what he said. 'Why should you wish to set *me* free?' I asked. 'I had an only sister,' he replied, 'who died three years ago in France, and you are so much like her that had I not known of her death, I would most certainly have taken you for her.' 'However much I may resemble your sister, you are aware that I am not her, and why take so much interest in one whom you never saw before?' 'The love,' said he, 'which I had for my sister is transferred to you.' I had all along suspected that

---

1   *"The bells called the people to the different places ... and Presbyterians sprinkled"*: "Pauline," 102.

2   *"twilight had let ... with a star"*: much-circulated misquotation of a couplet from McDonald Clarke's "Death in Disguise" (1833).

the man was a knave, and this profession of love confirmed me in my former belief, and I turned away and left him.

"The next day, while standing in the cabin and looking through the window, the French gentleman (for such he was) came to the window while walking on the guards, and again commenced as on the previous evening. He took from his pocket a bit of paper and put it into my hand, at the same time saying, 'Take this, it may some day be of service to you; remember it is from a friend,' and left me instantly. I unfolded the paper, and found it to be a 100 dollars bank note, on the United States Branch Bank, at Philadelphia. My first impulse was to give it to my mistress, but, upon a second thought, I resolved to seek an opportunity, and to return the hundred dollars to the stranger.

"Therefore I looked for him, but in vain; and had almost given up the idea of seeing him again, when he passed me on the guards of the boat and walked towards the stem of the vessel. It being now dark, I approached him and offered the money to him. He declined, saying at the same time, 'I gave it to you— keep it.' 'I do not want it,' I said. 'Now,' said he, 'you had better give your consent for me to purchase you, and you shall go with me to France.' 'But you cannot buy me now,' I replied, 'for my master is in New Orleans, and he purchased me not to sell, but to retain in his own family.' 'Would you rather remain with your present mistress than be free?' 'No,' said I. 'Then fly with me to-night; we shall be in Mobile in two hours from this, and when the passengers are going on shore, you can take my arm, and you can escape unobserved. The trader who brought you to New Orleans exhibited to me a certificate of your good character, and one from the minister of the church to which you were attached in Virginia; and upon the faith of these assurances, and the love I bear you, I promise before high heaven that I will marry you as soon as it can be done.' This solemn promise, coupled with what had already transpired, gave me confidence in the man; and rash as the act may seem, I determined in an instant to go with him. My mistress had been put under the charge of the captain; and as it would be past ten o'clock when the steamer would land, she accepted an invitation of the captain to remain on board with several other ladies till morning. I dressed myself in my best clothes, and put a veil over my face, and was ready on the landing of the boat. Surrounded by a number of passengers, we descended the stage leading to the wharf, and were soon lost in the crowd that thronged the quay. As we went on shore we encountered several persons announcing the names of hotels, the starting of boats for the interior, and vessels bound for Europe. Among these was the ship Utica, Captain Pell, bound for Havre. 'Now,' said Mr. Devenant, 'this is our chance.' The ship was to sail at twelve o'clock that night, at high tide; and following the men who were seeking passengers, we went immediately on board. Devenant told the captain of the ship that I was his sister, and for such we passed during the voyage. At the hour of twelve the Utica set sail, and we were soon out at sea.

"The morning after we left Mobile, Devenant met me as I came from my state-room, and embraced me for the first time. I loved him, but it was only that affection which we have for one who has done us a lasting favour: it was the love of gratitude rather than that of the heart. We were five weeks on the sea, and yet the passage did not seem long, for Devenant was so kind. On our arrival at Havre we were married and came to Dunkirk, and I have resided here ever since."

At the close of this narrative, the clock struck ten, when the old man, who was accustomed to retire at an early hour, rose to take leave, saying at the same time, "I hope you will remain with us to-night." Mr. Green would fain have excused himself, on the ground that they would expect him and wait at the hotel, but a look from the lady told him to accept the invitation. The old man was the father of Mrs. Devenant's deceased husband, as you will no doubt long since have supposed. A fortnight from the day on which they met in the graveyard, Mr. Green and Mrs. Devenant were joined in holy wedlock; so that George and Mary, who had loved each other so ardently in their younger days, were now husband and wife.

A celebrated writer has justly said of woman, "A woman's whole life is a history of the affections. The heart is her world; it is there her ambition strives for empire; it is there her avarice seeks for hidden treasures. She sends forth her sympathies on adventure; she embarks her whole soul in the traffic of affection; and, if shipwrecked, her case is hopeless, for it is a bankruptcy of the heart."[1]

Mary had every reason to believe that she would never see George again; and although she confesses that the love she bore him was never transferred to her first husband, we can scarcely find fault with her for marrying Mr. Devenant. But the adherence of George Green to the resolution never to marry, unless to his Mary, is, indeed, a rare instance of the fidelity of man in

---

1 Washington Irving, "The Broken Heart," 1:108.

the matter of love. We can but blush for our country's shame when we recal to mind the fact, that while George and Mary Green, and numbers of other fugitives from American slavery, can receive protection from any of the governments of Europe, they cannot return to their native land without becoming slaves.

CHAPTER XXIX.

CONCLUSION.

My narrative has now come to a close. I may be asked, and no doubt shall, Are the various incidents and scenes related founded in truth? I answer, Yes. I have personally participated in many of those scenes. Some of the narratives I have derived from other sources; many from the lips of those who, like myself, have run away from the land of bondage. Having been for nearly nine years employed on Lake Erie, I had many opportunities for helping the escape of fugitives, who, in return for the assistance they received, made me the depositary of their sufferings and wrongs. Of their relations I have made free use. To Mrs. Child, of New York, I am indebted for part of a short story. American Abolitionist journals are another source from whence some of the characters appearing in my narrative are taken. All these combined have made up my story. Having thus acknowledged my resources, I invite the attention of my readers to the following statement, from which I leave them to draw their own conclusions:—"It is estimated that in the United States, members of the Methodist church own 219,363 slaves; members of the Baptist church own 226,000 slaves; members of the Episcopalian church own 88,000 slaves; members of the Presbyterian church own 77,000 slaves; members of all other churches own 50,000 slaves; in all, 660,563 slaves owned by members of the Christian church in this pious democratic republic!" May these facts be pondered over by British Christians, and at the next anniversaries of the various religious denominations in London may their influence be seen and felt! The religious bodies of American Christians will send their delegates to these meetings. Let British feeling be publicly manifested. Let British sympathy express itself in tender sorrow for the condition of my unhappy race. Let it be understood, unequivocally understood, that no fellowship can be held with slaveholders professing the same common Christianity as yourselves. And until this stain from America's otherwise fair escutcheon be wiped away, let no Christian association be maintained with those who traffic in the blood and bones of those whom God has made of one flesh as yourselves. Finally, let the voice of the whole British nation be heard across the Atlantic, and throughout the length and breadth of the land of the Pilgrim Fathers, beseeching their descendants, as they value *the* common salvation, which knows no distinction between the bond and the free, to proclaim the Year of Jubilee. Then shall the "earth indeed yield her increase, and God, even our own God, shall bless us; and all the ends of the earth shall fear Him."[1]

---

1 Psalm 67:6.

Appendix A: Contemporary Reviews

[The few surviving reviews of *Clotel* indicate the tension between what Brown hoped to accomplish and what the examples of Frederick Douglass's *Narrative of the Life of Frederick Douglass* (1845) and Harriet Beecher Stowe's *Uncle Tom's Cabin* (1852) had led at least some readers to expect. The reviewer for the *Hereford Times* observes that in *Clotel* one does not find Douglass's "vivid imagination, deep pathos, and wealth of language" (Appendix A1); neither does one find, according to the reviewer for the *London Eastern Star*, "the thrilling power, the easy humour, or the graphic description" of Stowe (Appendix A3). What *does* one find, if not the gradual, continuous unfolding of a world in which one can be absorbed? "[M]uch variety," writes the reviewer for the *Bristol Mercury*, for the narrative repeatedly "diverges into different branches, in which fresh sets of characters are introduced" (Appendix A6). If "artistically treated"—if developed fluidly and at length—the material in *Clotel* could have filled "a three volume novel," writes the reviewer for the *Anti-Slavery Advocate* (Appendix A4). Instead, "conciseness, amounting almost to abruptness, is the character of the work." Like many of *Clotel*'s subsequent readers, the reviewers were unprepared for the book's wild leaps, dashes of humor, and conflations of fiction and fact, not because they were unfamiliar with such things but because they were not used to encountering them in the literature of abolitionism.

In the reviews that follow, brackets indicate extracts from the text of *Clotel* that are not reproduced in full here.]

1. *"Clotel," Hereford Times* (17 December 1853): 12

The name of Mr. William Wells Brown, the fugitive from American slavery, has become so well known through his lectures on that infamous system, during the last four years, in various parts of this country, that anything from his pen possesses an *a priori* claim to attention. As a man of colour whose public addresses have given another signal refutation to the slaveholders' calumny that the negro race are incapable of anything above forced toil, Mr. Brown occupies a position in public esteem only second to that of his powerful-minded compatriot, Frederick Douglass. Without Mr. Douglass's vivid imagination, deep pathos, and wealth of language, Mr. Brown has achieved not less honour by the clearness of his statements, his generally happy choice of language, and the calm power of his appeals to the reason of his auditors. When we add that the men who have thus. nobly vindicated the capacity for, as well as the right of their injured race to, freedom, are self-educated—Douglass having only begun to cultivate his great natural powers when a man, at his escape from slavery, and Brown having been ignorant even of the alphabet up to twenty years of age—we need say no more to justify their high place in the esteem and the sympathy of all true lovers of freedom and progress. As a specimen of Mr. Brown's power of public address, we may point to his lucid and powerful lecture on Monday night (reported in our 6th page), while the neat little book before us is not less pleasing evidence that he knows how to wield the pen of a ready writer.[1]

"Clotel" is a tale, made up (as we learn from the preface) chiefly from incidents in which Mr. Brown was either an actor or an eye-witness. It records the life of a daughter of the late President Jefferson, who, upon her father's death, suffered all the horrors of a system which he so eloquently denounced, yet from which he left his own child unguarded. In that case, the greater part of the crime must be put down to the account of the executors of the President, who, of course, knew or cared nothing about his child except as she was a marketable chattel; but the traffic is often dyed in an infinitely deeper guilt than theirs. In the case of Mr. Brown himself, his uncle was the "master" who sold him, his sisters, and his mother; while every hour American fathers pollute that sacred title by selling their own children like cattle. The profligacy which this infernal system produces among the slaveholders themselves is appalling: the female slave may be sister or daughter to her master; the law knows no such relationship in a slave, but requires implicit obedience from her, on pain of death, if her tyrant choose to sacrifice her market value by killing her. These "peculiar" features of the "peculiar institution of the south" are working out its punishment. The large infusion of Anglo-Saxon blood among the slaves has made them all the more difficult to keep down. As Mr. Brown remarks, it is that element which has produced the insurrectionary movements of late years;

---

1 "Slavery in the United States," *Hereford Times*, 17 December 1853, 6.

and we do not doubt that a half-breed Tell[1] will some day avenge the wrongs of his maternal ancestors upon their corrupters and oppressors. If the "chivalry" of the south continue deaf to the calls of both justice and mercy, it would be but prudent for them to get rid of slavery as a measure of personal safety.

In "Clotel," the writer has touched lightly upon his dreadful subject, yet, writing upon a matter of which he has had such painful experience, he could hardly fail to be interesting. His portraitures of character, especially the slaveholding parson, his excellent daughter, and Carlton, disgusted with religion because it is perverted by hypocrites to sanction slavery, are each graphically drawn. Some of his sketches are drily humorous, witness the stage-coach discussion between the Massachusetts clergyman and his Louisianian friend. We had marked half-a-dozen passages for extract, but can only find room for one:

> ["She had seen or heard nothing of her daughter while in Richmond ... who, if she had been born in any other land but that of slavery, would have been honoured and loved." (p. 191)]

2. *"Clotel," Pennsylvania Freeman* (29 December 1853): 207

We find, in our English exchanges, warmly commendatory notices of a narrative of slave life in the United States, just published in London, with the above title. It is from the pen of Wm. W. Brown, and though presented in the garb of fiction, it is largely composed of facts which have come within the range of his personal experience, or under his observation, or which he learned directly from other fugitives from the Patriarchal Paradise of Slavery, during several years' service on the underground railroad.

The heroine of the tale is a daughter of President Jefferson, doomed to slavery, like so many other children of proud Virginian fathers, by her maternity.

Her history, through a changeful and eventful life, to a tragic death, is traced with a skill and tact that interweaves with it many thrilling and important incidents of slave life. The London *Morning Advertiser* styles it a "tale of deep and lasting interest,

---

1 According to legend, William Tell, a fourteenth-century Swiss folk hero, assassinated a tyrant.

calculated to impress the most heedless, and give renewed vigor to the sacred cause of universal freedom," and adds of it:

"What the genius of Mrs. Stowe has accomplished by *Uncle Tom*, that of William Wells Brown, though marked by different qualities and incidents, will accomplish most certainly by the tale of *Clotel*, which, like the other, is only too true."

We trust that we shall soon see it on this side the ocean. Mr. Brown has many friends here who will welcome it cordially, and the public mind has not been so sated with "Uncle Tom" literature, that it will refuse more.

3. "W.W. Brown's New Work," *National Anti-Slavery Standard* (31 December 1853): 128

From The (London) Eastern Star

America would soon cease to be a slaveholding country if she gave birth to many such men as Wm. Wells Brown. We should hear no more of those insurmountable obstacles to the case of Abolition which are now said to exist. We should hear nothing of the dangers to America which would arise from a complete emancipation of her slaves. We should near nothing of the *right* which one man has to keep his fellow man in hopeless servitude—in cruel debasing bondage. On the contrary, we should find that the instincts of self-preservation alone would impel every slave-owner to give a practical proof of his belief in the equality of the human race. He would no longer dare to look down upon those whose skin was darker than his own; he would no longer plead that as an apology for crimes more horrible than any that have ever stained the page of world-history; cowardice would give him wisdom; terror would teach him truth. Truth which he denied to justice he would give to fear. He would tread no more upon the worm when he found that it had the power to turn and sting him. Ministers of the Gospel would not either, as at present, degrade their holy calling, and blaspheme God's word, by defending the relations of master and slave. They would read the Holy Word in another spirit, and give different interpretation to that which they now labour so industriously to pervert and falsify. Wm. Wells Brown is no ordinary man. Born and bred a slave, exposed to all the oppression and cruelty which fall to the lot of his race—bought, sold, and bartered as a chattel—torn from those near and dear to him, without hope of meeting again in this world—tasked as a beast of burden, and treated with even less consideration, he has nobly asserted his claim to be recognized as a member of the great human family. He has flung aside the fetters which cruelty had placed upon his limbs, and the still stronger fetters with which ignorance had imprisoned his mind and he now stands erect, independent, a free man among freemen, earning an honourable subsistence by his talents and his industry. If every slave possessed the determination, energy, boldness, and perseverance which distinguish William Wells Brown, the labours of the Abolitionist might cease at once. No despotism could constrain, no tyranny could bind, no cruelty could subdue the spirit of resistance which would be aroused. Emancipation would be granted not as being likely to lead to the disruption of society, to the extinction of trade, and to the confiscation of property, but as the only means by which these and even deeper evils could be avoided. Slavery, we repeat, would cease for ever.

The book before us appears to have been written for the purpose of proving—if any additional proof were needed—that the incidents which the authoress of "Uncle Tom's Cabin"[1] has related in that admirable work are no mere inventions of fancy, but actual occurrences, the counterparts of which are to be met with in the daily scenes of slave life. The author has imagined, perhaps, and we think with justice, a book written by one who has himself tasted of the horrors he describes, by one who has taken part in the ghastly scenes which he delineates, would be more convincing than any vindication, any appeal to facts, any arguments put forth by those who are necessarily compelled to receive their information from others. Accordingly, "Clotel" is a reproduction of many of the events in the author's life, bound together by the lightest possible thread of fiction, more for the purpose of giving a connected form to the narrative than of investing it with the interest of imaginative incident. Those, therefore, who expect to find in its pages the thrilling power, the easy humour, or the graphic description of Mrs. Stowe, will be disappointed. But to all who may still entertain doubts as to the truthfulness of the pictures of slave life which that authoress has drawn; to all who may wish to accumulate evidence of the capacity of the human mind, even under the worst circumstances, to elevate itself above the influences which tend to darken and debase it; to all who wish freedom to the captive negro, and who hail with delight any fresh evidence of his power to appreciate

---

1 Harriet Beecher Stowe (1811–96).

and to obtain it, "Clotel" will be welcomed as a remarkable and an interesting book. Mr. Brown writes with ease and fluency; he does not pretend to possess those finished graces of style which belong to the writers of fiction; but he expresses himself in a clear, intelligible, manly manner, oftentimes writing with considerable force, when more than ordinarily aroused by the recollection of his wrongs and the wrongs of his race. There is a dash, too, of humour in many parts of the work which we could scarcely have expected from one who has suffered so much, and which relieves the more painful portions of the narrative. The following extracts afford fair evidence of the author's style and powers. We cordially recommend "Clotel" to all our readers.

["Thousands of dollars change hands during a passage from Louisville or St. Louis to New Orleans ... and the passengers went to the hotels, and the slaves to the market." (pp. 83–86)]

["A mob was collected together, and a Lynch Court was held ... the same fate awaited them if they should prove rebellious to their owners." (pp. 88–89)]

4. "Clotel," Anti-Slavery Advocate 2 (January 1854): 125

This little narrative occupies less than 200 pages, but it offers to the reader's attention a quantity of incident quite remarkable in these days of book-spinning. It is not too much to say that the book contains material amply sufficient, if artistically treated, to fill a three volume novel.

It is founded on fact—or rather woven out of many facts, some of which have already appeared in print, and some we have ourselves heard from the lips of the writer when detailing his own experience, or that of other slaves and fugitives. The remark that truth is often stranger than fiction is never more true than in connexion with American slavery. The "peculiar institution" has given rise to scenes of anguish, of endurance, and of noble daring on the one hand, of despotism and revenge on the other, unsurpassed in the records of romance.

The chief character in the tale is Clotel, a daughter of Thomas Jefferson, afterwards President of the United States, and author of the celebrated "Declaration of Independence," one of the noblest announcements of human freedom ever penned. We may well exclaim, alas for consistency! when we find such a man holding slaves, some of them his own children, and leaving them in bondage at his death. These facts are known to be true, though this tale does not pretend to literal truth.

Clotel and her sister Althesa, with their mother, are exhibited on the auction-stand in the city of Richmond, Virginia, and sold to the highest bidder. On this subject our author remarks:

> ["No one forfeits his or her character or standing in society ... from others the loud hysteric laugh, denoting still deeper agony." (p. 96)]

Althesa and her mother become the property of a slave speculator for the southern market, but Clotel is purchased at a high price by a young man whose affections have been won by her beauty and amiability, and whom she loves with all the strength of her young heart. Her lot is therefore apparently a happy one. Horatio Green marries the lovely quadroon girl, and they reside in a charming cottage near Richmond, blessed by true affection, and in due time by the birth of a daughter.

But poor Clotel holds her happiness by a precarious tenure. Gifted with beauty and sensibility, formed to be an ornament of society, descended from a wealthy and influential family,—all this avails her nothing. Society contemptuously shuts its door in her face, the law gives no binding sanction to her marriage, and ambition lures her husband into circles which she cannot enter. His gradual absorption in political life, his engagement with the daughter of a wealthy patron, and consequent estrangement from Clotel, with the sad tale of their final separation, are told with great feeling, although in few words; for conciseness, amounting almost to abruptness, is the character of the work.

He marries Gertrude, but his first affections remain with Clotel, who, however, will hold no communication with him. Circumstances arouse the suspicions of his white wife, who contrives to have Clotel sold out of the State, and the child brought up as a menial and drudge under the father's roof.

We shall not follow Clotel through her life as a slave in Vicksburgh, her escape to Cincinati disguised in men's clothes, her return to Richmond to search for her daughter, her capture and imprisonment there, her escape and tragic end.

The thread of her adventures is frequently interrupted by details of the fortunes of her mother and sister, by characteristic sketches of masters, mistresses, and slaves, and by valuable genuine extracts from American newspapers. One of the richest *morceaus*[1] in the book is the sermon of Snyder the missionary, from the text, "All things whatsoever ye would that men should do unto you, do ye even so to them," and the subsequent criticisms of his sable auditors:—

> ["'Well,' said Joe, after the three white men were out of hearing ... 'thar was more den what Snyder lets us hear.'" (pp. 106–07)]

With this extract we must take leave of the little volume, hoping that many of our readers will turn to its pages and judge for themselves.

Some grammatical errors have escaped notice, which we trust will be corrected in a subsequent edition. And the matter would frequently have been rendered clearer by being broken into paragraphs. But the heart of the book is sound.

The tale is preceded by a memoir of the author, who has so bravely struggled with difficulties, worked his way upwards, and won for himself education, respectability, and independence.

5. "*Clotel*," *Tait's Edinburgh Magazine* 21 (January 1854): 57–58

The narrative of "Clotel" might almost serve as a key to "Uncle Tom's Cabin." It abounds in the delineation of actual scenes as striking and as appalling as any in the romance of Mrs. Stowe, and is a remarkable and truthful illustration of the horrors of the slave system, and its infernal operation upon the character of the whites engaged in it. We shall quote one scene as a sample of the work. The daughters of the President Jefferson, the writer of the American Declaration of Independence, are put up to auction, along with their mother.

> ["Clotel was the last, and, as was expected, commanded a higher price ... whose ministers preach that slavery is a God-ordained institution." (pp. 79–80)]

The reader must not look for great dramatic power, nor much of the romance-writer's craft, in this production of a fugitive slave; but as the work of an eye-witness of the events described, it has a value peculiarly its own. The life of the author, prefixed

---

1 Morsels.

to the story of "Clotel," is one of the most curious and characteristic pieces of biography which has appeared for some time.

6. *"Clotel," Bristol Mercury* (28 January 1854): 6

Another contribution to the "Uncle Tom" department of our
literature,[1] emanating from the pen of William Wells Brown, a
"fugitive slave," whose life furnishes one among the many striking instances of the miseries, anomalousness, and abominable
injustice of the system which is the opprobrium of the great republic of the west. The little volume narrates the fortunes of two
slave girls and their mother, the former being the offspring of
Jefferson, the celebrated President of the United States, who, says
the writer, "is not the only American statesman who has spoken
high-sounding words in favour of freedom, and then left his own
children to die slaves" (p. 146). The members of this little family
are sold into separate bondage, and the tale in consequence diverges into different branches, in which fresh sets of characters
are introduced. Clotel the heroine—one of the daughters—lives
for a time with a young master, to whom she bears a devoted
affection, but he outrages her feelings by marrying another, and
she is afterwards sold. Eventually having run away from a lustful
owner, she drowns herself rather than suffer recapture. From the
number of persons introduced the reader will find much variety
in the narrative, which is written with simple yet graphic power.
The author vouches for the truth of the incidents and scenes
contained in the work, and the writing has all the semblance of
reality. In particular the volume strongly illustrates the social
evils springing from the gross immorality to which "the peculiar
institution" conduces. We extract one or two passages—

> ["With the growing population of slaves in the South-
> ern States of America ... immoral condition of the
> relation of master and slave in the United States of
> America." (p. 73)]

Althesa, the sister of Clotel, had been married to a young physician named Morton, who, however, through ignorance of the
laws, neglected to emancipate her. They were both swept off by
yellow fever, and the fate of their children is told as follows—

---

1 Referring to Stowe's *Uncle Tom's Cabin.*

["Henry Morton and wife were among the thirteen thousand swept away ... no one wept at the grave of her who had been so carefully cherished, and so tenderly beloved." (pp. 183–86)]

7. [William Lloyd Garrison,] "New Work by William Wells Brown," *Liberator* (3 February 1854): 19

A fugitive slave successfully turning author—giving spirited sketches of men and things in the old world, as well as of the hideous system of tyranny from which he has made his escape, so as to excite the interest and extort the admiration of highly cultivated minds—is a surprising event even in this age of wonders. "That a man," says the London *Weekly News and Chronicle*, referring to Mr. Brown's "Three Years in Europe," "who was a slave for the first twenty years of his life, and who has never had a day's schooling, should produce such a book as this, cannot but astonish those who speak disparagingly of the African race." Of the present work, "Clotel," the English journals speak in terms of the warmest commendation. For a copy of it, we are greatly obliged to the author; and, having read it, we wish it might be reprinted in this country, believing it would find many readers. While the Declaration of Independence is preserved, the memory of Thomas Jefferson, its author, will be cherished, for the clear recognition it makes of the natural equality of mankind, and the inalienable right of every human being to freedom and the pursuit of happiness. But it will also be to his eternal disgrace that he lived and died a slave-holder, emancipating none of his slaves at his death, and, it is well understood, leaving some of his own children to be sold to the slave speculators, and thus to drag out a miserable life of servitude. Of the last, "Clotel" was one—beautiful, intelligent, captivating.[1]

["The appearance of Clotel on the auction block created a deep sensation ... whose ministers preach that slavery is a God-ordained institution!" pp. 79–80]

"Clotel" is sold into various hands, and experiences the painful vicissitudes to which one in her condition is ever liable, till at

---

1 Several early nineteenth-century newspaper articles contain the assertion that some of Thomas Jefferson's children were sold at auction and spent their lives as slaves (Appendix B1). Clotel was obviously not one of those children.

length, about to be transported to New Orleans, as her prison in Washington was being closed for the night, she suddenly darted past her keeper, and ran for her life towards the famous "Long Bridge," which spans the Potomac from the lower part of the city; but, being hemmed in by her pursuers, and seeing escape impossible, she vaulted over the railings of the bridge, and sunk forever beneath the waters of the Potomac.

Mr. Brown has skillfully embodied in his affecting tale numerous well-authenticated occurrences, which have transpired at the South within a comparatively short period—all calculated to intensify the moral indignation of the world against American slavery.

Appendix B: Slave-Auction Scenes

[In *My Southern Home* (1880), Brown's narrator casts his memory back before the war and recalls that when abolitionists wanted to make their textual attacks on slavery "stronger" they would emphasize not only that men, women, and children were continually sold at auction but that "many of the slaves were as white as those who offered them for sale." And as Brown knew very well, if abolitionists wanted to make their attacks even stronger than that, they had an iconic scenario at their disposal: the spectacle of a beautiful, cultivated, white-appearing woman being sold into sexual slavery. In *Clotel*, four such women are auctioned off: Clotel and Althesa in Richmond and Althesa's daughters Ellen and Jane in New Orleans. In his descriptions of those sales, Brown borrows language from three earlier descriptions of slave-auction scenes: a newspaper article entitled "An Auction" (Appendix B2), a passage in Harriet Martineau's *Society in America*, and a passage in Lydia Maria Child's "The Quadroons." As that recycling should suggest, Brown's aim is not to innovate but to capitalize—not to do something new with an established convention but to put that convention to work. The passages below are meant to suggest the kind of work that the spectacle of the "fancy girl" auction—a spectacle that the historian Joseph Roach has described as being "as American as baseball"—was capable of doing.[1] Joining the author of the "Declaration of Independence" to an enslaved woman's body; turning the credentials of elite white women into the marketable features of expensive female slaves; marking, at the climax of a series of sales of "black" people to "white" people, the point at which that racial distinction disappears; linking philanthropy to pornography; evoking the secret spirit of consumerism—in all these ways and more, representations of the sale of fair-skinned women were capable of making strong, troubling claims on the consciousnesses of Brown's contemporaries.]

---

1   Joseph Roach, *Cities of the Dead: Circum-Atlantic Performance* (New York: Columbia UP, 1996), 220.

1. From [William Lloyd Garrison,] "A Scene at New Orleans," *Liberator* (21 September 1838): 152

SALE OF A DAUGHTER OF THO'S JEFFERSON.
'GOING FOR A THOUSAND DOLLARS! WHO BIDS!'
'Going! going! gone! Who's the buyer?'

The following fact was related in our hearing, by the writer, Dr. GAYLORD[1] of Sodus, at the Wayne County Anti-Slavery Society's meeting, at Palmyra, last June. At our request, he has now furnished it for publication. Read it, fellow citizens, and ponder. If a daughter of THOMAS JEFFERSON may be sold at auction, what security can you, or any of us, have, that *our* daughters may not, one day, be sold in the same manner? COLOR IS NO PROTECTION. *"Bleached or unbleached!"* says Gov. M'Duffie![2] 'CLEAR WHITE *complexion'*—say the slave advertisements!

From the Friend of Man

MR. GOODELL,[3]—My apology for not furnishing you with an earlier communication, in regard to the following fact, must be found in my having been absent to the "far West," for several weeks, whence I have just returned.

Gladly, Mr. Editor, would I draw the mantle of oblivion over a transaction disclosing so dark a spot on the moral escutcheon of the man, whose name stands enrolled so high on the archives of our proud republic, did I not believe, that like the faithful delineations on our sacred pages, of the sin of David,[4] and other eminently great men, it should descend on record, as a solemn beacon, not only to excite disgust and warning against the crime, but also to awaken the lovers of our country, of morality, humanity, and religion, to see the *natural results* connected with the

---

1 Dr. Levi Gaylord (1794–1852), of Sodus, New York, was an abolitionist and temperance activist.
2 In an 1835 speech to the South Carolina legislature, Governor George McDuffie (1790–1851) declared that if the slaves, "bleached or unbleached," were freed, "[n]o rational man would consent to live in" the South.
3 The abolitionist William Goodell (1792–1878) was the editor of the *Friend of Man*, published in Utica, New York, from 1836 to 1842.
4 Adultery. David committed adultery with Bathsheba (2 Samuel 11).

"*practical operations*" of slavery—and hoping, also, that it may assist in prostrating the power of lawless passion, and legalized cruelty; and in preventing similar scenes of disgrace from being either enacted or tolerated, by high or low, as they frequently are, to the burning shame of our beloved country.

In a recent conversation with Mr. OTIS REYNOLDS,[1] a gentleman from *St. Louis, Missouri,* himself a practical, as well as theoretical supporter of slavery, in our discussion of the subject, Mr. Reynolds endeavored to find an apology for the "domestic institution" of the South, by assuming, as a fact, the alleged inferiority of the colored race.

I replied, that it was currently reported here, that the "best blood of Virginia, flowed in the veins of the slaves;" and the argument therefore could have no force, in regard to the amalgamated portion of the slaves.[2] Said he, with much emphasis,

"That's true; I saw myself, the DAUGHTER of THOMAS JEFFERSON SOLD in New Orleans, for ONE THOUSAND DOLLARS." ...

The authenticity of the above fact, rests on the sober testimony of a southern man, whose credibility is unquestioned, in the presence of some respectable merchants of our village, whose names can be given, if necessary; and as it may be highly important to the full [exposure] of a system, in which amalgamation and an utter disregard to the claims of consanguinity and domestic ties, are perfectly commonplace, it is my deliberate opinion, that such astounding facts should be spread before the community, to awaken them to the repulsive workings of that system of wrongs and wretchedness, which has so long been the foulest blot on the fair fame of our republic.

> Very respectfully, yours,
> LEVI GAYLORD.

Sodus, August 13, 1838.

---

1 Otis Reynolds was a St. Louis-based steamboat captain; in the late 1820s, when captaining the steamboat *Enterprise*, he had employed Brown as a waiter.

2 In *Letters on Slavery* (Lexington, KY: Skillman, 1833), the Rev. John D. Paxton had written that "[m]any mulattoes know that the blood of the first families in the south runs in their veins" (34).

2. H.S.D., "An Auction," *National Anti-Slavery Standard* (20 March 1845): 165

From the Liberty Press

While traveling at the south, a short time since, one day, as I was passing through a noted city, my attention was arrested by a concourse of people upon the public square. At first I queried as to the cause, but beholding a liberty pole in their midst, with a long flag of stripes and stars unfurled by the breeze, and remembering that it was the thirtieth anniversary of a celebrated battle, fought on that very ground, I was not long in deciding that they had met to commemorate the event, and sing the prowess of American arms.[1] But judge of my surprise, when, alighting from my horse, and crowding my way to the centre of the group, I soon satisfied myself that it was to be a southern auction. Here is quite a contrast, thought I, an auction to *sell* the liberty of one or more native born citizens, on the very ground, where our fathers spilt their blood in a struggle to *defend* their liberties! And as I had never witnessed the sale of a human being, I thought I would stop until it took place.

There being no one within the ring around the stand, I thought I would inquire the cause of the sale. Turning to a man in black, with rather a calculating mien, I was promptly informed that a merchant of the city had failed in business. The stranger said the merchant owed him a large amount, and he had attached his property, and "among other things, his beautiful domestic." He said the owner had been to great expense to educate her, and had rendered her every way interesting; and with emphasis, he added, "that slave shall now be mine."

Soon I saw two men coming through the crowd, attended by a female. They entered the ring around the stand. The sequel showed them to be the auctioneer, the unfortunate merchant, and the more unfortunate young lady, for slave she could not be. The auctioneer stepped upon the stand and ordered her to follow. She dropped her head upon her heaving bosom, but she moved not. Neither did she weep—her emotion was too deep for tears. The merchant stood near me. I attentively watched his countenance. 'Twas that of a father for the loss of an only daugh-

---

1 The "noted city" is New Orleans and the date is 8 January 1845, the thirtieth anniversary of the Battle of New Orleans, the last major battle of the War of 1812.

ter. Daughter he had not; but I understood that he had intended to adopt her, who, instead of being now free, was doomed to perpetual slavery. He appeared to have a humane heart. With tears in his eyes he said, "Helen, you must obey—I can protect you no longer." I could bear no more—my heart struggled to free itself from the human form. I turned my eyes upwards—the flag lay listlessly by the pole, for not a breeze had leave to stir. I thought I could almost see the spirits of the liberty martyrs, whose blood had once stained that soil, and hear them sigh over the now desecrated spot.

I turned around and saw two veterans of that eventful day, tottering over their staves a few feet from me. They had come from one of the free States to spend that anniversary on the ground of the spilt blood of their brothers. While they looked upon the scene before them, tear answered to tear. With shriveled hands uplifted toward heaven, the elder broke the silence by exclaiming, "O, my country! my country! How fallen! Has the angel of liberty taken her departure forever? O, weeps she not over crushed humanity?"

I turned to look for the doomed. She stood upon the auction stand. In stature, she was of the middle size. Slim and delicately built. Her skin was lighter than many a Northern *brunette*. And her features were round, with thin lips. She was the most fair albino that I ever saw. Indeed, many thought no black blood coursed in her veins. Now despair sat on her countenance. O! I shall never forget that look. "Good heavens!" ejaculated one of the two aged fathers, as he beheld the features of Helen, "is that beautiful lady to be sold?"

Then fell upon my ear the auctioneer's cry, "How much is said for this beautiful, healthy slave girl—a real albino—a fancy girl for any gentleman? (!) How much? How much? Who bids?" "Five hundred dollars," "eight hundred," "one thousand," were soon bid by different purchasers. The last was made by the friends of the merchant, as they wished to assist him to retain her. At first no one seemed disposed to raise the bid. The crier then read from a paper in his hand, "She is intelligent, well informed, easy to communicate, a first rate instructress." "Who raises the bid?" This had the desired effect. "Twelve hundred"—"fourteen"—"sixteen," quickly followed. He read again—"She is a devoted Christian, sustains the best of morals, and is perfectly trusty." This raised the bids to two thousand dollars, at which she was struck off to the gentleman in favor of whom was the prosecution. Here closed one of the darkest scenes in the book of time.

This was a Southern auction—an auction at which the bones, muscles, sinews, blood and nerves of a young lady of nineteen, sold for one thousand dollars; her improved intellect, for six hundred more; and her Christianity—the person of Christ in his follower, for four hundred more.[1]

It is but just to remark, that the above sale never took place to our knowledge. But no thanks to slaveholders nor the system of American Slavery, that it has not. They have all the elements, and all that is lacking is the suitable circumstances.

3. "Slave Auction Scene," *Anti-Slavery Reporter* (1 December 1846): 194–95

In the winter of 1840 and 41, having business in Western Virginia, where the peculiar institution flourishes in its mildest form (be it remembered at this time I was opposed to anti-slavery principles), December 28th, I found myself at Martinsburg, the county seat of Berkley. About 10 o'clock of the aforesaid day, I observed a crowd congregated in the public square, in front of a suspicious-looking building, which had very much the appearance of a jail, as it proved to be. On inquiry of my landlord concerning the cause of the meeting, he said it was "a hiring"—in other words a negro sale—as I afterwards found that a number were hired for life. I walked down to the market, and to obtain a better view, I mounted a large wagon in the street, directly opposite to the stand of the auctioneer, who had commenced his work. He was a large man, dressed in aristocratic style, with a profusion of ruffles, gold finger rings, watch seals, and last, and not least, a large whip, called by drivers "a loaded whip." The hiring I understood to be of a number of slaves of a certain estate who were hired out from year to year to the highest bidder, for the benefit of the heirs. These sales take place between Christmas and New Year, the holidays, quite a recreation for the slaves who are to change masters.

After a number had been disposed of in this way, the crier announced that he would offer for sale six slaves. He then put up two, father and son. The old man was nearly sixty years of age, a cripple; the son was about twenty-three, a perfect specimen of man. There were present two Georgia soul-drivers, who bid eight hundred dollars for both. When the crier remarked it was a small bid for both, the Georgian replied, he would give eight hundred

---

1 For Brown's rewriting of this narrative, see pp. 79–80.

without the old man, as he was of no account. The young man gave the bidder a look that would have shamed the devil; the old man wept bitterly. The son sold at the bid, and the father was sold for sixty dollars to an old farmer who had never kept a slave in his life. Thus father and son were separated. The next case was that of a girl, fifteen years of age. (These slaves had been hired out to different individuals the past year.) She was brought, crying, upon the stand. With an oath he bid her to stop her "blubbering," and then proceeded with the sale. After enumerating her qualities, he stated that the prospect was good for an *increase of the property*, saying which, the brutal wretch placed his whip beneath her apron, and raised it above her head, exhibiting to the enlightened multitude, the spectacle of a girl fifteen years old, far advanced in pregnancy! She was sold for one hundred and fifty dollars.

The next case was that of a young white woman, sixteen years old, with a young child. I say *white* woman, because the auctioneer said, she was only one-eighth black, and I have seen many of the fair girls of Ohio who could not boast of as fair complexion, or as good figure or features. She came upon the stand with her infant in her arms, in the deepest misery. A gentleman, who had taken his seat beside me, observing that I was very interested, remarked he thought I was a stranger in that country. I answered that I was. "These things look odd to you?" "They do." Said he, "You see that man in the crowd," pointing to one within a few paces of the stand—"that is Dr. C. He hired that girl last year, and that child is his!" The Georgian bid three hundred dollars; some one bid four; the Georgian bid four fifty; the girl cast a piercing glance at the crowd, her eyes rested on Dr. C. who instantly averted his face. She gazed one moment, then burst into a torrent of tears. She was knocked off to the Georgian. Thus the fiend saw his child and its mother sold into Southern bondage. My God! thought I, is it possible? *I was cured of my pro-slavery principles.*—*Cincinnati Herald*

4. From "The Case of Two Slave Girls," *Christian Watchman* (2 November 1848): 2

New York, Oct. 27, 1848

The papers of last Monday morning announced that a public meeting would be held in the evening, at the Broadway Tabernacle, for the purpose of raising funds to redeem from slavery two Christian mulatto girls, who would otherwise in a few days be sold by their present owner, in Virginia, to a southern owner, where their condition would be worse even than that of slavery. The announcement drew a crowd to the Tabernacle. The two girls in question, with four brothers, were of that party of slaves who attempted to escape from the District of Columbia, in the schooner Pearl. They are daughters of an old man by the name of Edmonson, are members of the Methodist Episcopal church, have attractive manners and persons, and are valued at $2250.[1]

Rev. Henry W. Beecher, of Brooklyn, arose, and with no little emotion addressed the attentive audience in a most forcible and eloquent speech which was received with thunders of applause....[2]

After considering ... preliminary questions he came to the case before his audience; and said he,

Fellow-citizens, do you know that all that goes to make a man, except his deathless love of liberty, goes to make him a better slave. The strength of limb, the roundness of muscle, mind, tender affections, sympathy, all this is so much fat laid upon the ribs of Slavery. Here, at the North, to be of comely presence is considered a blessing; there, at the South, so much money is made of it in the market. A slave will bring all the more for being such a fine-looking man. I droop to think what abominable use is made of such a recommendation, if the slave chances to be a woman. That which excites among us the profoundest respect goes there to augment her value—not as a wife, not as a sister—but for purposes from the bare idea of which the virtuous soul revolts. In the slave girl, beauty, refinement, is not a matter of respect, but of profit. And suppose you add thrift, skill, intelligence. Here, at the North, we take all this as so much added to the man; but there, the more there is of thrift, of skill, of intelligence, of enterprise, the higher price in the market. And then, if in addition to all, he is only docile; if he will be a planning machine, and not a running-away machine, he is the very perfection of a slave. There are great advantages in Slavery, but nimble legs are a great drawback upon its profitableness. If a slave has all these excellent properties and no love of Liberty, there is nothing else to be desired. Yes, there is. What is it? What else can you desire?—When you bring him on the stand, he goes up to $600. You describe his physical perfections; he touches $650. He

---

1 After being freed by means of this "auction," Mary Edmonson (1832–53) and Emily Edmonson (1835–95) participated in several mock slave auctions at abolitionist meetings. They entered Oberlin College together in 1853.

2 Henry Ward Beecher (1813–87), the brother of Harriet Beecher Stowe, was an influential abolitionist clergyman.

is intelligent, skillful, docile—he goes up to $700. Then add, he is a pious member of the Methodist Episcopal Church in good and regular standing, and $800, $900, $1,000 is bid. [Tremendous excitement in the audience.]

In the course of his address Mr. B. introduced the letter of Bruin & Hill, the slave dealers, in which they agree to detain the girls a certain number of days for a certain sum of money paid in hand. After commenting on the letter, Mr. B. says: "Would to God Shakspeare were still living! Two words of such a letter would have suggested to him the most powerful drama ever written. This Bruin is a man. Satan has entrapped him—not entrapped, such as he walk willingly into his toils—he has been beguiled to say, and put it in writing, that he has purchased a man's daughters and refuses to let their own father have them."

In concluding his appeal Mr. Beecher said:

"And now, please to imagine your daughters or sisters in bondage. Suppose them so comely that no price less than three thousand dollars would purchase them: suppose all this, and act as you would act then. Look at this poor old man. His sons are long ago sold as slaves to labor on the southern plantations. His daughters, unless we can do something to detain them, must go too, to a worse fate. But I trust in God and I trust in you that it shall not be heard from New York that an appeal like this was made in vain, and that you will make it heard that these girls, must not, shall not be slaves—that they shall be free."

Other persons beside Mr. B. spoke on this interesting and exciting occasion. The result was that the desired sum was raised, and the two girls are now enjoying their freedom. It is evident that occurrences like this are doing very much to open the eyes of this community to the horrors of slavery, particularly those horrors connected with that fate to which these beautiful mulattoes would have been consigned. The lighter complexion of the female offspring of these girls would have been sure to entail on them a like destiny.

5. From "Visit to a Slave Auction," *Frederick Douglass' Paper* (2 February 1855): 2

Editorial Correspondence of the Utica Herald

NEW ORLEANS

I have just returned from a Slave Auction. The more prominent beauties of the "Institution" are perpetually thrusting themselves upon one, "will he, nill he."[1] I as little dreamed two hours ago, of attending a "negro auction" as I did of taking a trip to the moon. Let me tell you how it came about. I was sauntering along St. Louis street, (in the "French part,") when I observed a crowd of negroes composed of men, women and children, marching under the escort of a white man towards the St. Louis Hotel.—A moment afterwards, I observed another gang going in the same direction, and soon after a third. I had the curiosity to follow them, and as I entered the Rotunda of the Hotel, observed, I should presume, no less than one hundred and fifty negroes ranged in front of the different auctioneers' stands. Operations had not yet commenced. Fresh "lots" of negroes were constantly coming in, and the various "dealers" were making examinations of the different "articles" on exhibition. The immense Rotunda—an elegant and most fashionable affair—was thronged with speculators, buyers, dealers, and lookers on. Some were smoking their Havanas—some were taking their toddies—some were reading their morning papers—and some were chattering on politics, the money market and the weather. The auctioneers were slowly walking to and fro upon their elevated rostrums like men who appreciate their importance, and occasionally stooping to answer an inquiry from a customer. The laugh—the joke—the stinging repartee—the sunny smile—the cordial greeting of friends—the courteous auctioneers—the elegant hall—the flash of fashion, and the atmosphere of gentility pervading the gay throng—how unlike the horrors of my gloomy imaginings. Yet what amazing callousness!

The clock strikes twelve! A change comes over the spirit of the scene. The *batons* of the auctioneers brought down against the solid marble, act with the potency of magic upon the babbling throng. Four auctioneers in four several sections of the Rotunda, hammering away with frightful volubility and still more frightful gesticulation, at four several parcels of human "chattels." These four gentlemen are shouting at the top of their voices, alternately in French and English, as if each made a point of striving to drown the voice of the others. But the gentleman on my right seems to carry off the honors, both as respects strength of lungs and rapidity of utterance. I wish, dear reader, you were standing near me, for I can give you but a very indifferent daguerreotype of the efforts of this popular stump orator. He is now engaged in hauling upon the "block" a feeble negro woman

---

1 Haphazardly (whether one wills it or not).

with a sad and sickly countenance. Having placed her in the proper position with rather more expedition than gentleness, with commendable candor he informs the spectators that "this girl" (she is aged at least forty) "is always *pretending* to be sick, and does not therefore warrant her." He sells her, however, at a low figure—some $400—and the next instant her place is supplied by a fine looking bright eyed young mulatto woman, with an infant *almost perfectly white* in her arms. He informs his patrons that "this girl is named ANN, aged twenty two, and free from the diseases and vices designated by law;" and proceeds alternately in French and English, somewhat thus: "How much for this girl? *Quant donnez me pour cette Esclave?* How much do I hear for this splendid girl? Five hundred—*Cinque cents*; seven hundred—*six cents* [sic]. Gentlemen, look at this girl! Good nurse and seamstress.—Do I hear one thousand? One thousand is offered—one thousand—going—going—sold to Cash, one thousand." Next is sold for $1200 a plantation hand named JIM; then a "boy," aged about 50, named TOM, for $1000; then two "boys"—mulattoes—"first rate coopers," for $1500 each; then a "family" composed of a mother and four children,—the latter all mulattoes—for $2500. Our eloquent friend having disposed of his entire lot, proceeded without hardly a moment's interruption to sell a lot of real estate, &c.

The three other gentlemen auctioneers were driving on an equally flourishing, tho' not quite so rapid, trade. One of them, a very handsome, youngish looking man—was devoting himself exclusively to the sale of young mulatto women. On the block at the time I approached his stand was one of the most beautiful young women I ever saw.—She was aged about 16 years, was dressed in a cheap striped woolen gown, and bare headed. *I could not discover a single trace of the African about her features.* She was much whiter than the average of Northern white women, her form was graceful in the extreme, and she carried in her head a pair of eyes that pierced one through and through. Unlike many of her fellow captives, she seemed fully sensible of her degraded position, and shrank with true maiden timidity from the impudent stare of the hard featured throng about her. Sensitive Reader! What do you think became of that beautiful girl? She was struck off for $1250 to one of the most lecherous-looking old brutes I ever set eyes on. GOD shield the helpless victim of that bad man's power—it may be, ere now, that bad man's—lust! ...

And these scenes in the Rotunda of the most fashionable Hotel in the city! The air is soft and balmy, and the day is as beautiful as ever gladdened the heart of man. The golden sunshine, streaming through the crystal dome, bathes the spacious hall in a flood of radiance. Above, around this mart of human souls, a gay and giddy throng are holding joyous revelry. The great Hotel is thronged with wealth and beauty, and the music of piano and guitar are blending with the still sweeter music of glad voices. Above the din of the hot and dusty street, and above the hoarser din of the mart below, is heard the loud laugh and heartfelt glee of the apostles of pleasure. Gay equipages are drawing up before the stately pile, and "fair women and brave men" are proudly disappearing through its portals to swell the throng. Within these sumptuous halls—amid that gay and gleeful throng—amid that flash of beauty, fashion and wealth, where so many splendors are gathered together—who would dream that under the same broad dome, and in the effulgence of the same golden sunlight—crime, and sin, and despair, were holding high revel? Who would dream that the former drew their sustenance from the latter?

Appendix C: The Aesthetic of Attractions

[The *Oxford English Dictionary* tells us that by 1829 the word "attraction" had acquired the meaning of a "thing or feature which draws people by appealing to their desires, tastes, etc., *esp.* any interesting or amusing exhibition which 'draws' crowds." The world of William Wells Brown—the rapidly modernizing cultural world of cities like Boston, New York, and London, disseminated along newly efficient pathways of transportation and communication into the backcountries of the US and Great Britain—was awash in exhibitions of this kind. The abolitionist editor Gamaliel Bailey (1807–59) reports that in New York's Bowery Theater thousands of lower-class men and women responded to a medley of overblown skits and spectacles with noisy cheers and laughter; in Mechanics' Hall, hundreds of middle-class men and women responded in much the same way to the discontinuous hyperboles of a minstrel show (Appendix C1). Shoppers at one of the large new department stores in Manhattan were presented with a dazzling array of objects to choose from, or simply luxuriate amidst, according to the *New York Evening Post*—and if that grew old, they could always check out the third-floor clock museum or take in on-site diorama exhibitions and minstrel shows (Appendix C2). After making a splash in the US, John Banvard's three-mile-wide (or so he said) painting of scenes along the Mississippi River became a sensation in England as well, thanks not only to the variety of objects, incidents, and scenes that appeared as it passed from spool to spool, but also to the diversified accompaniments that Banvard (1815–91), as master of ceremonies, energetically supplied (Appendix C3). Even a temperance lecture in a Boston church could be, as the journalist George Washington Bungay (1818–92) testifies, pyrotechnically entertaining (Appendix C4). All of these types of attractions appealed to Brown—he staged over-the-top theatrical performances, borrowed from minstrel humor and song, supported Christmas-season abolitionist bazaars, exhibited a panorama, and aspired to be the kind of lecturer that Bungay describes—and all of them contributed to the shaping of *Clotel*.]

1. From [Gamaliel Bailey,] "Popular Amusements in New York," *National Era* (15 April 1847): 3

The popular amusements of our great cities present a subject of the most profound interest. I do not believe that our philosophers and reformers have by any means given this subject that attention, either in sort or degree, which it merits. It is very true that the drama has had its intelligent and enthusiastic apostles; and it cannot be denied that, on the other hand, the theatre—from the days when the *elite* of the imperial city rushed to her Coliseum,[1] and

> "The buzz of eager nations ran,
> In murmur'd pity or loud roar'd applause,
> As man was slaughtered by his fellow-man"[2]—

down to last week, when a great Thespian athlete murdered Shakspeare at the Park[3]—has been the object of all sorts of anathema. It seems to me, however, that the modes in which so many thousands of human being contrive to amuse themselves night after night, are worthy of a somewhat more considerate regard than that which manifests itself by puffs in the papers and blasts from the pulpit. Boldly striking out, the other evening, into those densely populated regions which lie between Centre street and the East River—

> "A filthy purlieu of a port,
> Where Hebrew slop-sellers,
> And cheating chop-sellers,
> And trulls and tars resort"[4]—

encountering many strange sights and smells in my progress I found myself at length in front of the Bowery Theatre. Crossing

---

1   The Colosseum, completed in 80 CE, was the major site of public spectacles in imperial Rome.

2   From George Gordon, Lord Byron, *Childe Harold's Pilgrimage* (1812–17), 4.139–41.

3   The Park Theater, completed in 1798, had been the most respectable theater in New York City. By the 1840s, however, it had begun competing with popular lower-class entertainment venues by presenting melodramas and blackface performances.

4   From "The Vaults of St. Michan's," *Dublin Penny Journal*, 25 August 1832, 70.

the vestibule, from which the policemen then on duty were just then ejecting an intoxicated ruffian, I entered the vast amphitheatre, and was perfectly amazed by the spectacle spread out before me. A sea of heads stretched itself out on the right and left, and away to the orchestra-box, immediately in front of the stage, and gallery above gallery, up to the lofty dome, presented a dense mass of human beings. There could not have been less than between three or four thousand persons present, of all ages, and infinite variety of condition. The great majority of those in the boxes appeared to be of the middling class of shopkeepers, mechanics, and small tradesmen. There was great good order throughout the house, but a terrible munching of apples and pea-nuts; and the densely packed pit appeared to be in a state of profuse perspiration, from the evident anxiety to get rid of all superfluous clothing. I confess I awaited the rising of the curtain with a good deal of interest, for it was really worth something to learn for one's self the staple of that entertainment which had attracted such a vast congregation. At length the curtain was drawn. Some half dozen sturdy vagabonds, with tinseled inexpressibles,[1] and immense helmets on their heads, were seated around a table, on which appeared a number of empty champagne bottles. "Comrades, let us drink once more!" shouted one of the fellows, raising a tin cup to his lips. His associates made show of obedience, the audience regarding the scene with the profoundest attention. The principal vagabond—whose swaggering gait and a peculiar thickness of speech betokened recent libations more potent than those in which he had just indulged on the stage—then informed his auditors that he was determined to woo the "Naiad Queen." This declaration quite alarmed the other chaps with helmets and tinsel, and they shouted, "Oh! don't think of such a thing!" "I go!" exclaimed the swaggering hero; "who follows?" But none of his friends evinced any inclination to share his adventures; and at last, after several "parting drinks," in which his faithful associates most cordially joined him, off he started, accompanied only by his affectionate servant, a miserable scarecrow, dressed like a clown, whose grimaces put the pit in an ecstasy. In the next scene, the knight and his attendant arrived at the scene of his romantic adventures—a cavern on the banks of the Rhine, which was represented by a few pieces of board, painted black for rocks, a strip of blue muslin stretched across the entrance being the river. An attenuated female figure, with a

---

1 Underwear.

very long nose and very scant drapery, then made her appearance on one of the rocks overhanging the river; and the knight, whose tongue was becoming thicker every moment, making a desperate plunge towards the mouth of the cavern, poured out a rhapsody of which not six words were entirely audible, though the boxes lauded it with a thundering round of applause. The creature on the rock shook her head, and, sustained by a wire, glided downward to the centre of the stage, where she disappeared through a trap-door, behind the blue muslin, the audience testifying their delight and astonishment in quite a vociferous manner. But the knight was not thus to be foiled, for he instantly clambered up the rocks, and, after politely waving his hand to the audience, boldly leaped after the nymph in scant drapery, and, scrambling away on all-fours, was out of sight in a moment. Meantime, his poor servant, the clown, who had been quite dumb from fear or astonishment, now uttered a piteous cry, which elicited general laughter. A biped, in buffalo skin, armed with a club, and wearing a hideous mask, now rushed on the stage, and between him and the clown a fierce encounter took place, amid excited cheers from all parts of the theatre. At length the monster, who got rather the worst of it, disappeared through a trap-door, whilst the clown, pulling a flask from his pocket, seated himself on the stage, and, bowing to the audience, informed them that "he believed he was now fairly entitled to a private drink;" to which the audience—not to be outdone in politeness—at once responded in a universal guffaw. The next scene opened with the "Bath of Beauty," as it was facetiously styled in the bills, in which some eighteen or twenty female anatomies sprawled about the stage in a style utterly graceless in every sense of the term. Into this delectable gathering the knight now pursued the nymph in scant drapery, when he in his turn encountered the monster. Another terrific combat—great shouts from the galleries and pit—great scampering of all the female anatomies—a great hubbub in the orchestra, and the curtain fell on the first act. I then left the theatre, quite oppressed by the melancholy reflections which the strange, sad spectacle had naturally excited....

A few evenings since, I was enlightened on a point with regard to which I felt much curiosity. I was a good deal at a loss to know whether the disciples of those religious teachers who denounce the drama in any shape, indulged in any public amusements; and, if they did, what those amusements were. Passing the "Mechanics' Hall," in Broadway, I saw, by the light of two magnificent lamps, a large placard, announcing that "Christy's

Minstrels" were performing within; and, being informed that they had been attracting overflowing houses for two months past, I entered, in order to judge of their quality.[1] The hall, capable of seating eight hundred persons, was crowded to excess, and, as usual, no thought of providing for its ventilation having entered the mind of the architect, the effluvium was oppressive in the extreme. On a platform at the end of the hall were seated six young men, with their faces blackened and who were now shouting in full chorus the classic melody of "Dandy Jim of the Caroline!"[2] These were the Minstrels! I looked around on the audience. It was composed chiefly of highly respectable citizens, who would have regarded it as worse than bankruptcy to be seen within the walls of a theatre! Yet here they were, with their wives and daughters, enjoying for a whole evening a vulgar caricature of a class of their fellow-men whose sad lot surely demanded the tear of Christian sympathy, rather than the loud laughter of the fool! Yes, there they sat, these intellectual, evangelical, theatre-hating, Presbyterian, Dutch Reformed Christians, encoring the doggerel slang of these delectable minstrels, and applauding till the roof rang again the performance of one of them, who, in female apparel, danced before them with vulgar and indecent gestures!

None of my readers, I trust, will regard this passing notice of the popular amusements of this great metropolis out of place in the "National Era," a journal which seeks, in a large and liberal Christian spirit, the improvement and elevation of our race.[3] My object is to show that the tendency of these amusements is to dissipate and degrade our fellow-men; and that mere denunciation will not remedy the evil.... But fear not a disquisition. I desire only to make a suggestion. Why should not Christian philanthropy provide in our large cities well-devised and well-conducted plac-

---

1   E.P. Christy's minstrel troupe performed at Mechanics' Hall, on Broadway near Grand, from 1847 to 1857.

2   "Dandy Jim of Caroline," in which a man brags about his attractiveness to women, was one of the best-known minstrel songs of the 1840s. An abolitionist song set to its tune, "A Song for Freedom," appears in Brown's *The Anti-Slavery Harp* (Boston: Marsh, 1848) and in *The Escape* (Boston: Wallcut, 1858); it is possible that Brown wrote the revised lyrics.

3   The *National Era*, which was edited by Bailey, is now best known for its wildly popular serialization of Harriet Beecher Stowe's *Uncle Tom's Cabin* in 1851–52.

es of popular amusement? Why should not the refining and humanizing influences of music, painting, natural philosophy, and the drama, be combined, under the management of Christian men, and rendered available to the people, in properly-conducted public halls, to which the prices of admission would be as low as possible? I know that, in Glasgow, the great manufacturing metropolis of Great Britain, concerts for the people have been given on Saturday evenings, with the happiest results. Is not this subject, at all events, worthy of serious attention? For myself, I cannot behold thousands of my fellow-men, night after night, subjected to the demoralizing influences of the present system of popular amusement without some concern, and an earnest desire to see some effort made to effect a reform.

2. "Mechanical Museum—Lafayette Bazaar," *New York Evening Post* (22 December 1847): 2

This wonderful and unique establishment is at all hours crowded with visitors.[1] Citizens resort here to purchase what they can nowhere else find; travellers, to see what nowhere else can be seen; strangers, to gaze in astonishment at the wonderful variety, taste, and elegance displayed in the merchandise of the Bazaar. It better repays an hour's visit, than half the places of amusement in the city; and yet the spacious saloons are free to all. Each article is tastefully arranged in a neat show case, on which is marked the price of all the articles within, from six cents to almost any amount—one case containing cheap articles, to suit one class, another for another, while the best and most costly articles are found in another. Here, especially, of all places in the city, does Santa Claus hold his levees. Such an infinite variety of bonbons, toys, jouets,[2] and children's amusements we never before saw collected together. Not alone to the young does the Bazaar offer its attractions. "Children of a larger growth" will here find articles to please the fancy and gratify the taste in almost infinite variety.

---

1 Lafayette Bazaar, on the corner of Broadway and Liberty, was one of the large new stores that helped to transform New York City shopping into a leisure experience. Well-dressed African-American men stood outside its doors handing out playbill-like catalogs of items for sale, and the price tags, by eliminating the need for conversation with shopkeepers, made shopping a more interior, fantasy-rich event.

2 Toys.

Beautiful and expensive mantle and table ornaments of endless variety, just imported from Paris, toilet articles, dressing cases, fancy boxes and baskets, jewelry, vases, fortune tables—in short, almost every thing useful or ornamental, rich or plain, extravagantly dear, or wondrously cheap can here be found in perfection. A vast variety of confectionery is here to be found, and many a happy young heart will be made to leap for joy the coming Christmas from the treasures here obtained.

Beside this there are several wonderful clocks in the mechanical museum in the 3rd story, one of which contains an automaton singing bird, another a rope dancer; these alone are more than worth the price of admission; and then too, there are, during the afternoon and evening, dioramic views, and a band of negro minstrels. These Bazaars, though somewhat novel among us, are common in Paris and London. They afford a pleasant lounge, and offer facilities for purchasers not elsewhere obtained.

3. From "Banvard's Panorama of the Mississippi and Missouri Rivers," *Illustrated London News* (9 December 1848): 364

This is just the season for prodigies; and, opportunely enough, a painting of this class was opened on Monday for exhibition at the Egyptian Hall, in Piccadilly. The picture is stated to be painted on three miles of canvass, exhibiting a view of country of 3000 miles in length, extending on the Missouri and Mississippi rivers, through the very heart of America, to the city of New Orleans. We must take the artist's voucher for the dimensions of his work; but we can answer for its having occupied nearly two mortal hours in unrolling from off cylinders, on Saturday night last, when a private view was given of the pictorial wonder. It is shown in what is termed the "dioramic" fashion, with the aid of strong gas light; the picture being inclosed in a sort of dark proscenium; and the apartment in which the audience is seated is alike darkened. Upon a platform in front is seated Mr. Banvard,[1] who explains the localities, as the picture moves, and relieves his narrative with Jonathanisms[2] and jokes, poetry and patter, which delight his audience mightily; and a piano-forte is incidentally invoked, to relieve the narrative monotony.

---

1   The New York-born John Banvard was the best-known panorama painter of his day.

2   "Jonathan" was a nickname for Americans; Jonathanisms were idiomatic American expressions.

The painter, in his catalogue, modestly tells us that he does not exhibit this painting as a work of art, but as a correct representation of the country it portrays; and its high reputation at home is based upon its remarkable accuracy and truthfulness to nature. The picture has much of these characteristics; here and there bits are very effectively painted, but the majority is of the level of scene-work; though, on this account, the better fitted for exhibition by artificial light. The river scenery is of greater variety than might have been expected; and its flatness is relieved by many episodal groups which illustrate the manners, customs, and modes of life, of the dwellers on the banks. Now and then, we have the incident of a steamer upset by "snags," and left a useless log upon the waters; and then, a well-freighted vessel, steaming in all the pride of a river race, with a wonderful prodigality of steam and human life, imparts great animation to the scene. Then we have bluffs, bars, islands, rocks and mounds, points and cliffs, without number, and of fantastic varieties of form; encampments and war-dances; hunting-grounds and burial-places; prairies with their giant grasses, perchance burning to the very horizon; log cabins and villages, sometimes nestling in natural amphitheatres, and at others perched upon the rock tops; and a great variety is imparted to the Exhibition by showing it under different influences, as night and daybreak, moonlight and coming storm. The principal places on the rivers are St. Louis, a French-built town, with a host of steamboats and river-craft, "bound to all points of the boatable waters of the Mississippi;" next is Cairo, which, from its geographical position, and the immense range of navigable rivers, all centering at this point, is destined to become one of the largest inland cities in the United States.... Memphis is beautifully situated, but does not justify its grand name. President's Island shows cotton plantations, with slaves at work, not forgetting the planters' mansions, "the negro quarters," and the cypresses, the pride of the southern forests. Natchez is romantically placed on a very high bluff, and is much the largest town in the State of Mississippi; the upper town being 300 feet above the river level. Baton Rouge is now the capital of Louisiana: from thence, the river below, to New Orleans, is lined with splendid sugar plantations, and what is generally termed the "Coast"—a strip of land on either side of the river, extending back to the cypress swamps, about two miles. It raises nearly all the tropical fruits—oranges, figs, olives, and the like; and is protected from inundations by an embankment of earth of six or eight feet in height, called a levee. Behind the levee we see extensive sugar-fields, noble mansions, beautiful gardens, large sugar-houses, groups of negro quarters, lofty churches, splendid villas, presenting in all, one of the finest views in the United States. The picture-journey terminates with New Orleans. This is the great commercial emporium of the south, situated on the *eastern* shore of the river, in a bend so deep and sinuous, that the sun rises to the inhabitants of the city over the *opposite* shore. The harbor presents an area of many acres, covered with all the grotesque variety of flat-boats, keel-boats, and water-craft of every description, which line the upper part of the shore. Steamboats rounding to, or sweeping away, cast their long horizontal streams of smoke behind them. Sloops, schooners, brigs, and ships occupy the wharves, arranged below each other, in the order of their size, showing a forest of masts; and the whole, seen in the bright coloring of the brilliant sun and sky of the climate, presents a splendid spectacle.

4. From George Washington Bungay, *Crayon Sketches and Off-Hand Takings* (1852), 61

Everybody said, "Let us go to the great meeting at Tremont Temple, this evening, and hear Philip S. White, the distinguished champion of the temperance reform."[1] At the appointed hour, that magnificent forum was filled with the wealth, beauty, talent, and moral worth of Boston. The immense building was brilliant-ly illuminated, as though the sun had risen behind the orchestra and concentrated its rays within the walls of the Temple. On the platform were some of the *elite* and *literati* of society,—authors, orators, and philanthropists. After the usual preliminaries, at the commencement of the exercises, skilful fingers touched the magic keys of the mammoth organ, and we were pleasantly en-tertained with sweet strains of delightful melody. Sometimes it seemed as if a choir of soft-voiced maidens was enclosed behind those golden columns, singing such rich, lute-like airs that an-gels, on their mission of mercy, might have mistaken that place for the gate of heaven. Then the heavy bass would roll like a wave of thunder through the large hall, startling the charmed hearers to a sense of the fact that they were still under the clouds.

As the music subsided, a tall, portly man, on the mellow side of fifty, arose to address the audience. "Is that the man who stood at the head of the Order of the Sons of Temperance?" is the general inquiry. "It is," was the response. The "observed of all observers"

---

1 Philip S. White (b. 1807) was a Kentucky-born lawyer and temperance activist. The extract is an account of his 1849 lecture at Boston's Baptist Tremont Temple.

on this occasion, is a person of good mould, somewhat bald, but makes up that deficiency by a luxurious growth of whiskers, which become his face as feathers do an eagle. He has a large, aquiline, Bardolphian[1] nose, dark eyes, and a wide mouth, indicative of eloquence and good nature. He commences in a conversational pitch of voice; face dull and passionless as marble; has spoken ten minutes without *saying any thing*, and the sanguine expectations of the people are sadly disappointed. The hearers bow their heads like bulrushes, and some would leave the meeting but that they *hope* for better things. He is not quite so prosy now as he was fifteen minutes ago. His voice is deeper and clearer, his utterance more rapid and distinct, and his face shines as though it had been freshly oiled. There is a resurrection now among the bowed heads; he has just made a thrilling appeal, which moved the audience like a shock from an electric battery. Now he relates a tale of pity, which is drawing tears from eyes "unused to weep." Now he surprises his attentive hearers with an unanticipated stroke of humor, which makes them laugh until they shake the tear-drops from their cheeks. All are glad they came now, for the orator is in his happiest mood, his blood is up, and his tongue as free as the pen of a ready writer. He throws light on the question by the coruscations of his attic wit;[2] drives home a truth by solid argument, and clinches it by a quotation from Scripture; convulses the auditory by using a ludicrous comparison; convinces them by presenting sober-faced statistics; entertains them by relating an appropriate anecdote, and fires their indignation against the traffic, while the rum-dealers present shake in their shoes. He warns the drinkers with a voice which arouses them like a clap of thunder through a speaking-trumpet. In a word, his sparkling satire, keen wit, eloquent declamation, happy comparisons, classical allusions, rib-cracking fun, and heart-melting pathos, render him one of the most efficient public speakers in America.[3]

---

1 Red, like the nose of the drunkard Bardolph in Shakespeare's *Henry IV.*
2 Attica, a region of ancient Greece whose principal city was Athens, was associated with the most refined forms of eloquence and humor.
3 Brown plagiarizes from this passage in a mini-biography of the black minister Singleton Jones in *The Rising Son* (1874) where he writes, "When in the pulpit, [Jones] throws light on the subject by the coruscations of his wit, drives home a truth by solid argument, and clinches it by a quotation from Scripture, and a thrilling and pointed appeal which moves his audience like a shock from an electric battery" (531).

Appendix D: Brown and His Audiences

[In a letter written shortly after meeting Brown, the Irish abolitionist Richard D. Webb (1805–72) described his new acquaintance as "an upright, downright, straightforward fellow.... He is excellent company, full of anecdote, has graphic and dramatic powers of no mean order, and a keen appreciation of character."[1] Nowhere are those qualities more fully on display than in the transcripts of Brown's lectures. Like most other black abolitionists, Brown presented, when necessary, a sobriety and dignity; unlike most other black abolitionists, he also offered, when his audiences seemed receptive to it, free-wheeling entertainment. In the first of the excerpts below, a reporter for the sensationalist, anti-abolitionist *New York Herald* offers, at the end of a mostly disparaging account of the American Anti-Slavery Society's annual meeting, an admiring description of Brown's resuscitation of a low-spirited and somewhat surly crowd (Appendix D1). In Norfolk, England, before a large, enraptured audience, Brown narrates the story of the escape of William and Ellen Craft from slavery—a story that he would fictionalize in *Clotel*— with so many theatrical flourishes that it is as if he is thinking about turning it into a play (Appendix D2). Back in the United States, at another annual abolitionist gathering, he showcases his comic timing in a pair of anecdotes about racism in New York City restaurants (Appendix D3). Finally, in the midst of a speech insisting that black and white Americans are capable of living together, he uses a comic story about his white relatives in Kentucky to indicate not only how deeply white and black lives are intertwined, but how pleasurable that intertwining can be (Appendix D4).]

1. From "The Anniversaries," *New York Herald* (9 May 1849): 1

Before the speaking commenced ... those assembled with their umbrellas between their legs, were engaged in discussing a variety of topics—the most prominent of which was the probable duration of slavery in the United States, the magnanimity of England in freeing her West India colonies, the affairs of Canada, of Europe

---

1 "Foreign Correspondences," *National Anti-Slavery Standard*, 13 September 1849, 63.

and of the universe in general. The conversation was suddenly interrupted by a hemming and coughing emanating from one end of the room, a tolerably good indication that somebody was going to sing. In a moment or two the indications ceased, and our friend Brown, the refugee slave, who would not allow his friends to contribute for his release a sum to be paid to his master, equal to his value in the slave market, gave vent to his inspirations, and entertained the company with the following song:—

> Fling out the Anti-slavery flag
> On every swelling breeze;
> And let its folds wave o'er the land,
> And o'er the raging seas,
> Till all beneath the standard sheet,
> With new allegiance bow;
> And pledge themselves to onward bear
> The emblem of their vow.
>
> Fling out the Anti-Slavery flag,
> And let it onward wave
> Till it shall float o'er every clime,
> And liberate the slave;
> Till, like a meteor flashing far,
> It bursts with glorious light,
> And with its Heaven-born rays dispels
> The gloom of sorrow's night.
>
> Fling out the Anti-Slavery flag,
> And let it not be furled,
> Till like a planet of the skies,
> It sweeps around the world.
> And when each poor degraded slave,
> Is gathered near and far;
> O, fix it on the azure arch,
> As hope's eternal star....[1]

[Brown] then spoke.—He said he appeared before them as a refugee slave, one who had fled from slavery in Missouri, where his master now lives, to the North, for liberty. He had no doubt

---

1   The lyrics of "Fling Out the Anti-Slavery Flag," which Brown apparently wrote, had recently appeared in Brown's *The Anti-Slavery Harp* (Boston: Marsh, 1848), 22. They were sung to the tune of "Auld Lang Syne."

that his master, who now lives in St. Louis, would be happy of his return back; but he did not think he would oblige him. (Laughter.) In fact he thought he would decline all the polite invitations which his master might extend to him to return. (Laughter.) Well, he appeared before the audience, not only as a refugee slave, but also as the son of a slave-holder. Indeed it has been asserted, that he is related to the present President of the United States, but however that may be, or however related he may be to the slaveholders, by the tenderest ties of blood, he would not on that account refrain from saying what he experienced of the horrors of slavery. The gashes which he bears on his back have made too great an impression on him to allow his doing so. He then said he would read a few choice gems from the St. Louis *Republican*.

VOICE—Have you got the paper?

No, but it is edited by a Mr. Charles, whom I knew very well, for I worked for him, and he whipped me like smoke. (Laughter.) The impressions which he made on my back, have made an impression of him on my memory. Much has been said against the church, but if it did not aid, and abet, and promote slavery, no attack would be made upon it. The abolitionists are called infidels, but give him the infidelity of the abolitionists, which knocks the fetters from the slave, in preference to the Christianity of the church, which fastens them on his limbs. (Applause.) Go to the South—see Theological Institutes selling slaves, and breeding slaves, for the purpose of raising funds wherewith to make ministers. When I lived down South, and my master—and here let me give you a description of my old master, for he made an impression on me which I would like to make upon you—he was a whining, praying, complaining, psalm-singing man, who ordered me, every evening at nine o'clock, to go down to the "niggers," and call them to prayers. (Laughter.) Every night he called them in, and the influence which the master had, in putting them all asleep, by prayer, was remarkable. He possessed a magnetic power, which Sunderland could not touch.[1] (Laughter.) Well, Saturday was always fixed for reading the Bible, and at every verse he would tell the niggers to ask him the meaning of any passage which they did not understand. He was extremely proud of being asked; for he was proud of being thought an expounder of the Bible. Well, he never asked him the explanation of any passage but once, and then he applied to him to know the meaning of that passage of scripture "Whatever he would that others would do unto you, you do to them?" "Why," said

1 LaRoy Sunderland (1804–85) was a minister, abolitionist, and mesmerist.

he, "Where did you hear that? I never read it to you." (Laughter.) "I got it in the city," I replied. "Just like the City," said he; "You can never send a servant to the city, but he is spoiled." (Renewed Laughter.) "Now, mind you, Sambo," said he, "I'll explain this to you, but never ask me such a question again." (Roars of laughter.) "Well," said he, "Sambo, if you were my master, and I were your slave, would you not like me to do all that you desired me to do?" "Well," said I, "I guess I would." (Loud laughter.) No, he never read that page of the Bible to me, but he was very proud of reading and explaining that part of scripture which says "Servants, obey your masters." (More laughter, in which all present joined heartily.) It has been said, that masters and mistresses are kind to their slaves; but he has had striking evidence— (laughter)—that such is not the fact. He continued in this strain for some minutes longer, and concluded by singing:—

> The fetters galled my weary soul—
> A soul that seemed but thrown away;
> I spurned the tyrant's base control,
> Resolved at last the man to play.—
> > The hounds are baying on my track;
> > O Christian! will you send me back?

> I felt the stripes, the lash I saw,
> Red, dripping with a father's gore;
> And, worst of all, their lawless law,
> The insults that my mother bore!
> > The hounds are baying on my track;
> > O Christian! will you send me back?

> Where human law o'errules Divine,
> Beneath the sheriff's hammer fell
> My wife and babes—I call them mine—
> And where they suffer, who can tell?
> > The hounds are baying on my track;
> > O Christian! will you send me back?

> I seek a home where man is man,
> If such there is upon this earth,
> To draw my kindred, if I can,
> Around its free, though humble hearth.
> > The hounds are baying on my track;
> > O Christian! will you send me back?[1]

---

1 Elizur Wright, "The Fugitive Slave to the Christian," lines 1–24.

The meeting then adjourned, to meet again this morning and remain in session all day.

2. From "Address from W.W. Brown, an Escaped Slave," *Norfolk News*, 4 May 1850, 3

Within the last 18 months ... said the lecturer, two slaves, a black man, and his wife, who was a white woman, have made their escape from Georgia.[1] They had long talked about trying to make their escape, and they had thought of many plans, but all had failed. Finally, however, just a year ago last Christmas, as the slaves in that part of the country have, at that time, a few days' holiday, these slaves resolved to make another attempt. The plan was laid by the woman; and I know there is a common saying, that if there is anything bad, anything mischievous on foot, a woman is sure to be at the bottom of it; but it is a poor tool that will not cut both ways, and I think that if there is anything clever on foot, ten chances to one but a woman is at the bottom of that too. Well, this woman lays the plan for their future happiness. The husband, who was a good mechanic, after working early and late for several years, had found himself in the possession of about £25, and on one occasion he sits down in the night to count his money, and to talk to his wife about escaping. "Let me lay the plan," said his wife; "you know I am white enough to pass unsuspected, and that I might have made my escape years ago if I had been willing to go without you?"—"Yes." "And you know I resolved that I never would leave you in slavery, but would rather suffer with you than do that?"—"Yes." "Well, now, my plan is this—you have often said I can act the lady as my mistress?"—"Yes." "Now I think myself that I could act the gentleman too, as well as my master; so you purchase for me a suit of gentleman's clothing, and I will dress as a gentleman; I will then take the railway train as a gentleman going to a free state, and you can accompany me as my servant." The husband comes to the conclusion that his wife's plan is a good one; but at last he hesitates, and remarks—"But when you are called upon to register your name at the hotel, what will you do—you can neither read nor write, you know not A from B?" "Let us see"—replied the wife—"is it not the right hand they write with?"—"Yes." "Then I will bind it in a poultice and put it in a sling, and say

---

1 The "two slaves" are William and Ellen Craft, Brown's friends and lecture partners.

it is sore."—"Ah," objects the husband again, "but you would not be able to look the white people in the face, as white people look at each other, because you have been brought up to be afraid of them; what would you do if a slave holder were to come up to you and look you in the face?" "Oh," said the wife, "you purchase me a pair of spectacles, and then I can look at them well enough I think." So the spectacles are purchased, the hand is put in a sling, and leave is obtained of the masters for them to go into the country and be there four days. They go to the station at six o'clock in the morning on the 20th of December, 1848. It is dark. The slave slips into one of the Jim Crow pens or carriages, which are set aside for slaves to ride in, and the lady, who assumes the name of "W. Johnson, Esq.," books herself and servant for a southern port, and takes her tickets. But what is to be done? the ticket for one is on yellow paper, and the other on white, and the lady, though calling herself "Esquire," cannot tell which is which! After a moment's hesitation, however, she turns to the servant and says, "keep your place in the carriage, and when they come for your ticket, tell them to come to your master for it, and I will hand them both, and there will then be no need of reading them." Off they start, but they had not travelled more than 100 miles, when a real slave holder, with his two daughters, takes his seat in the same carriage with Mr. Johnson, and after the usual American fashion, commences an inquiry about our friend's residence and his delicate state of health, and observes that he appears as though he had better be in bed, and in answer to a pressing inquiry as to what was the matter with him, Mr. Johnson tells the gentleman that he is troubled with "Inflammatory Rheumatism." Well, they travel together for a very considerable distance, and during the time, the eldest daughter scrutinizes Mr. Johnson most peculiarly, and at length, after she has had some conversation with her father, the latter slips out of the carriage and goes to speak to Mr. Johnson's servant. Calling him aside, the gentleman observes, "Well, my boy, your master tells me he is from Michigan." "Yes, Sir." "And how many more such boys as you has he?" "About 40, Sir." "Oh, indeed, a pretty wealthy man then?" "Yes, Sir." "He is a good looking fellow, I think?" "Yes, Sir, the ladies says so." "He is not married, is he?" "No, Sir." "That's enough," replied the gentleman, and then hurries back to report progress to the eldest daughter, "that every thing is right." By and bye they approach the place at which the gentleman resides, and he extends an invitation to Mr. Johnson. "You had better," he says, "stop two or three weeks, and make my place your home, you and your servant; you are not well enough to travel further; my wife will give you a hearty welcome, and my daughters will be delighted, and you will then go on with a lighter heart." And while the father is putting in his plea, and urging Mr. Johnson to stop, the daughter thinks that a single word from her will give it a little impetus, and so she says in a very fascinating style, "Oh, yes, Mr. Johnson, you had better stop, we shall be so pleased." But Mr. Johnson thinks that that is no place for him to stop, and it is finally settled that he will stay a short time with them, if ever he comes that way again. Well, Mr. Johnson and his servant arrive at the city of Philadelphia. There I become acquainted with them; they travel with me for seven months; and they now reside in the city of Boston, Massachusetts. They were actually in a free state before their masters knew where they were. I shall never forget their being introduced to a meeting at Boston, when an audience, much larger than this, resolved that the man and woman should never be carried back, though the constitution gave the slaveholder the right of coming after them. [Cheers.] ... With respect to himself, he remarked, that he had heard that his master now said, "he would not have him again, for he was good for nothing." That put him in mind of the man who caught a rabbit alive, and while he was carrying it home under his arm, he said frequently to it; "I'll make a good pot pie of you, I have had some of you fellows before, and I know you make a capital pot pie." Before the man arrived home, however, the rabbit sprung from under his arm and ran off. The man endeavoured to retake it, but as he was unsuccessful, he contented himself by ejaculating, "Ah, well, I'm glad you are gone; a tough old thing like you would be good for nothing; it would take more butter to cook you than you are worth." [Considerable laughter.] After dwelling for some time on his love for his fellow bondmen, and on the fact that it was education, sobriety, and intellectual pursuits that would aid them most in overthrowing slavery, Mr. Brown alluded to what had been done by Great Britain on behalf of slaves. The acts of the people of this country, he observed in conclusion, in abolishing slavery in their own West Indies, and towards putting down the African slave trade, have given them a home in the hearts of the coloured population of the United States; and when slavery shall be abolished, the disenthralled slaves will raise their arms to heaven and thank the British people for what they have done in the great cause of universal freedom. Mr. Brown then resumed his seat amid great cheering....

The thanks of the meeting were then presented, by the chairman, to the lecturer, who briefly acknowledged the kindness which he had received from the people of Norwich; and concluded by singing in true negro style, amid great cheering, a song, composed by himself, and called "The Escape," in which the leading circumstances attendant upon his own flight from slavery were briefly recorded. Portraits of "William Johnson, Esq.," "Narratives of Mr. Brown's Experiences," and song books, bearing the title of "The Anti-slavery Harp,"[1] were announced for sale, on the platform and at the door, and the meeting then broke up, a very large number of persons rushing to purchase one or more of these publications.

3. From "Third Anniversary of the New York Anti-Slavery Society," *National Anti-Slavery Standard* (16 May 1856): 4

I saw in a newspaper published in my town, St. Louis—for I happen to have come from among the "border ruffians" (laughter)—an editorial announcement that a man who owned a slave there, a short time since, had caused that slave to be branded upon the right cheek with the words "slave for life," and the editor spends a great deal of invective and indignation upon this owner of the slave, saying that the slave was a good servant and had committed no offence to merit such treatment. The crime of this victim was, being born with a white skin, for the editor tells us that he had straight hair and would pass for a white man. Being white, it was easy for him to escape, and hence the necessity of branding these words on his cheek, so as to prevent his running away. Perhaps, too, he had too much Anglo-Saxon blood in him to be a submissive slave, as Theodore Parker would say.[2]

Such are the workings of slavery. A slave must always be made to know his place; if it were not so, he could not be kept in his chains. We see the effects of slavery everywhere throughout the North. I saw an illustration of it to-day in your own city. A very nice-looking coloured lady, a stranger in this city, no doubt, who was not aware that on the Sixth Avenue they have cars expressly for coloured people, entered a car that stopped to take in some

---

1 See p. 243, note 2.
2 Theodore Parker (1810–60) was a Transcendentalist minister and abolitionist who believed that "Anglo-Saxon blood" was exceptionally vigorous.

other ladies. She was rudely thrust from the platform by the conductor and told that that was not the car for her to ride in. She was considerably lighter in complexion than myself, and perhaps as white as some that were seated in the car.

Some year and a half ago, I landed in this city from a British steamer, having just left England, after having been abroad in different countries in Europe for a number of years, where I was never once reminded that I was a coloured person, so that I had quite forgotten the distinction of caste that existed in democratic America. I walked into an eating-house. I had scarcely got my hat off when the proprietor told me I could not eat there. Said I, "I have got a good appetite, and if you will give me a trial, I rather think I will convince you that I can." "But," said he, "it is not allowable." I did not know what to make of it; I had been away five years, and had forgotten the great power of slavery over the North. I felt insulted. I walked into another eating-house. The proprietor asked me what I wanted. I said I wanted my dinner. "You can't get it here; we don't accommodate niggers." That was twice I was insulted. I went into a third, with a like result. I then went and stood by a lamp post for some five minutes. I thought of the nineteen years I had worked as a slave; I thought of the glorious Declaration of Independence; I looked around me and saw no less than seven steeples of churches; and I resolved I would have my dinner in the city of New York (applause). I went to another restaurant. I made up my mind what I would do. I saw a vacant plate at a table; I took aim at it. I pulled back the chair, and sat down, turned over the plate, and stuck my knife in something. I was agitated, and did not know what it was, until I got it on my plate, when I found it was a big pickle (laughter). At any rate I went to work at it. The waiter stared at me. Said I, "Boy, get me something to eat." He stared again, walked to the proprietor, and said something to him, came back, and helped me. When I got through my dinner, I went up to the bar, and handed the proprietor a dollar. He took it, and then said, "You have got the greatest impudence of any nigger I have seen for a great while (laughter); and if it hadn't been that I didn't want to disturb my people sitting at the table, I would have taken you up from that table a little the quickest." "Well, sir," said I, "if you had, you would have taken the table cloth, dishes and all with me. Now, sir, look at me; whenever I come into your dining saloon, the best thing you can do is let me have what I want to eat quietly. You keep house for the accommodation of the public; I claim to be one of the public."

Some twenty days after that, I was about to start for Boston; I hadn't time to go to that saloon, so I went to a confectionary establishment, and thought I would do with a little pastry. I walked in; a young woman, who attended, came up and said she, "Can't accommodate you, sir." I paid no attention to her, but picked up a knife, and pitched into a piece of pie. Said she, "We can't accommodate you, sir." Said I, "This is very good pastry" (laughter). Then said she, "We don't accommodate niggers." Said I, "Did you make this?" (Laughter.) I finished my piece of pie, and then a second piece. By and by another lady came to me, and said, "Sir, we don't accommodate niggers." Said I, "You give very good accommodations; I shall always patronize you." I finished my third piece of pie, and asked for a glass of soda water. Says she, "Just leave my place, and I will charge you nothing." Said I, "Madam, I expect to pay wherever I get accommodation, but I can't pay for this until you give me a glass of soda water." So I took a chair and sat down, saying I was in no hurry; for I concluded to wait and go on the next train. As soon as she saw I was determined to stay, she said, "You may have your soda water." I drank it and walked out. Now that grated very hard on my feelings, after being away so long, and forgetting almost everything about the way coloured people were treated in this country.

4. From "Speech of William Wells Brown," *National Anti-Slavery Standard* (26 May 1860): 4

Now, continued Mr. Brown, I say that there is no justice for the coloured man in this country. Every particle of pity is for the white man. Talk with a man about the slave or the abolition of slavery, and he begins to pity the white man; he has no pity for the black man. If he prays, he does it as Dr. Blagden did in Boston, at a Union meeting.[1] He prayed, "Oh Lord, bless our country, our whole country, and especially the Southern half of our country" (laughter). It reminded me of an anecdote that I heard when I was in the South. Two men owned an old and blind black man, whom they kept in a shop turning out table-legs, bedstead-legs, &c. One of the men was pious, the other a great sinner. Well, the cholera came along, and the pious man wanted to sell out his half of the slave to the other, but he would not buy, and he

---

1 George Washington Blagden (1802–84), pro-slavery pastor of Boston's Old South Church.

asked more for his half than the pious man would give; so he determined he would put up a prayer to Heaven, and he prayed, "Oh Lord, protect my family and house from the cholera; protect my neighbors, all my relations, and especially my half of Sam!" (Much merriment.)

Now, Mr. Chairman, just as the condition of the coloured man in this country begins to improve, and his prospects to look more encouraging, the white people are trying to get rid of him. Mr. Wade, a Republican, says he is tired of hearing so much said about the equality of the negro. Another Republican says he wants the coloured people sent off to South America, New Mexico, or somewhere else. Another gets up and says that he is willing to give his vote for money to send the negroes out of the country to Africa. Now, my friends, let me say, on behalf of the coloured people, that we are not going to Africa—we are not going to leave this country at all (applause). The slaveholders have mixed the Anglo-Saxon blood with ours, so that even in the pro-slavery cities of New York and Philadelphia coloured men and women ride in the cars and omnibuses, and are so light that they are mistaken for white people, while the white man is so dark that he is sometimes taken for a negro (laughter). In 1844, Henry Clay, in one of his letters, said that slavery was to be abolished by the inevitable law of population. Some one asked him what he meant, and he said, "amalgamation, as carried on in the slave States." It is fearful to think of or look at; but it is doing a work at the South at the present time, and we throw upon the slaveocracy of the South the responsibility of the whole system of illegitimate amalgamation that exists in this country.

I say the black people are not going to leave the United States. We are connected with the South by the tenderest ties of nature. The free coloured people of the North are connected with the slaves of the South. Many of the free coloured people of the North, especially the fugitive slaves, are connected with the slaveholders of the South. They look into the Southern States, and they see there their white relatives as slaveholders. I met a good friend of mine yesterday, who came from the South about the time I did, and one of the first questions he asked me was, how my white relatives in Lexington prospered since I came away (laughter); and I asked after his white relatives. He wanted to know how my cousin William was, who is our Minister Plenipotentiary to the Court of Spain. The Hon. William Preston married my cousin Fanny (laughter). If you had been there, and heard us talking about our relatives, you would have thought that I was just from the United States Senate, for he knew very well that my relatives were among the first in the State of Kentucky. My cousin Bob Wickliffe—the Wickliffe family is a very aristocratic family in Kentucky—died a few months since, worth, it is said, five millions. My cousin Charles A. Wickliffe was Postmaster-General under John Tyler (laughter). Probably many of you don't know anything about John Tyler, he filled such a small niche in our country's history, but certainly you must have heard of my cousin Charles (great merriment).[1]

Now, Mr. Chairman, and ladies and gentlemen, I do not look upon these white relatives of mine with as much pleasure as you would think, perhaps; but still, they are my relatives (laughter). Sometimes, you know, we find ourselves related to some people that we don't care much about (renewed laughter). But I say, here we are. We are connected with the slaves and the slaveholders by the tenderest ties of nature; and if this country wants me to run away and leave my white relatives, I can't do it (great merriment). If they want to drive me away from my black relatives, I shall stay here and labor for their emancipation (loud applause).

---

1   The references are to the politician William Preston (1816–87), his wife Margaret Wickliffe Preston (1819–98), the politician Robert Wickliffe (1774–1859), the politician Charles Wickliffe (1788–1869), and John Tyler (1790–1862), the tenth president of the United States.

Appendix E: Plagiarism

[In both academic and mass-cultural contexts, the word *plagiarism* comes trailing clouds of scandal that can be suffocatingly thick. It is tempting, accordingly, to define Brown's covert use of other people's writing as something other than plagiarism, to describe it as being more like sampling, collage, or editing. To do so, however, is to concede, implicitly, that unmarked copying is essentially wrong, when in fact it depends on who copies, how they copy, when and where they copy, and why. It is also to overlook the fact that Brown's contemporaries would unquestionably have described the unmarked copying in *Clotel* as plagiarism and that plagiarism was, in mid-nineteenth-century Anglo-American culture, scandalous. The passages below, drawn from the voluminous archive of mid-nineteenth-century discussions, are intended, first of all, to evoke the degree of that scandalousness. Once one knows how venomous the attacks on plagiarists like Samuel Taylor Coleridge (1772–1834) and Benjamin Disraeli (1804–81) were and how explicitly Brown had been warned, several months before the publication of *Clotel*, against enveloping himself—and, by association, other black abolitionists—in a plagiarism scandal, it becomes hard to believe that Brown was unaware of the risks he was running. As the passages below are also meant to suggest, however, some of Brown's contemporaries conceived of the practice of making texts out of other texts in more nuanced ways. There was, in other words, some space for movement within the discourse on plagiarism, even though that discourse consisted mostly of expressions of horror and scorn. Either because he was aware of that space and imaginatively operated within it or because he was convinced that the benefits outweighed the potential costs, Brown plagiarized, throughout his career, on an astonishing, unparalleled scale. Even if one can quite easily think of reasons why he might have chosen to use other people's language in the way that he did—to recirculate the most energizing bits and pieces of the abolitionist archive, say, or to participate in the public sphere without being fully invested in, and therefore exposed by, that participation—there is, in the end, something fundamentally mysterious about his attraction to plagiarism, his fascination with textual worlds in which hundreds of voices secretly sing.]

1. From [James Frederick Ferrier,] "The Plagiarisms of S.T. Coleridge," *Blackwood's Magazine* 47 (March 1840): 299

We have now done with our subject. We have set forth and argued the case of Coleridge's plagiarism, precisely as we should have done that of any other person who had carried them on to the same extent. By this we mean to say, that we have accorded to him—on the plea of peculiar habits, or peculiar intellectual conformation—no privilege, or immunity, or indulgence, which we would not equally have accorded to any plagiarist of the most methodical ways and of the most common clay. And in acting thus, we think we have acted rightly. For why should a man, who has been *more* highly gifted than his fellows, be therefore held *less* amenable than they to the laws which ought to bind all human beings, and regulate their relations and their dealings with one another? It is high time that *genius* should cease to be pleaded as an excuse for deviations from the plain path of rectitude, or be held up as a precedent which the leading men of future generations may avail themselves of, should they be inclined to depart from the strict standards of propriety and truth.

That Coleridge was tempted into this course by vanity, by the paltry desire of applause, or by any direct intention to defraud others of their due, we do not believe: this never was believed, and never will be believed. But still he *was* seduced into it—God knows how: he *did* defraud others of their due, and therefore we have considered it necessary to expose his proceedings, and to vindicate the rights of his victims. Perhaps we might have dwelt more than we have done upon what many may consider the extenuating circumstances of his case—we mean his moral and intellectual conformation, originally very peculiar, and further modified by the effects of immoderate opium-taking.[1] But this would only take us out of one painful subject into another still more distressing. We therefore say no more. Our purpose will have been answered, should any future author who may covet his neighbour's Pegasus or prose-nag,[2] and conceive that the high authority of Coleridge may, to a certain extent, justify him in making free with them, be deterred from doing so by the ex-

---

1 Coleridge was known to be a habitual user of opium.
2 Winged or ordinary horse; Ferrier (1808–64), a Scottish metaphysical writer, is comparing the plagiarism of both poetic and prosaic writing to horse-theft.

ample we have now put forth *in terrorem*.[1] Let all men know and consider that plagiarism, like murder, sooner or later *will out*.[2]

2. From "Plagiarism," *New-York Mirror* (15 January 1842): 18

A writer in an influential morning paper is battering a popular poet with charges of plagiarism. This is a kind of attack which we think will not do. It is an imputation which is popularly thought to be fatal to the reputation of an author; but it may be observed that those who have been thoroughly conversant with literature, and in the habit of thinking carefully about it, have generally attached little or no importance to the charge. Goethe[3] laughed it to scorn; he said that the notion requiring a man to write only out of the resources of his own mind would end in meagerness and poverty of composition, and that it was an author's duty to use all that was suggested to him from any quarter. Montaigne[4] came to the same result by a metaphysical process: he says that what one mind perceives upon the prompting of another is as truly the perception and the property of that mind as of his who first saw it. "If I see," he remarks, "the same truth that Plato[5] saw, it is as much according to Montaigne as it is according to Plato." These opinions, as philosophical views, strike us as being extreme, for they go the length of denying any merit to invention. We rest the defense on narrower ground. We say that the grounds on which the literary reputations of past times have been made up, the basis on which the fame of all great authors rests, require that the praise of modern writers should be measured by the merit that appears upon the face of their pages, without reference to the sources whence the notions may have been drawn. Of course we do not include the case of a bald copying from a predecessor; in such a case it is not a question of merit, but to whom the authorship belongs. What we mean is, that if an author borrows from others, and sets the borrowed matter so well that it has in his book a character and beauty which it had not in the original, and sufficient to give the new work an independent popularity of its own, it is proper that he should have all the praise that the inherent spirit of the whole

---

1 In order to strike fear in others (Latin).
2 Allusion to Geoffrey Chaucer, "The Nun's Priest's Tale."
3 Johann Wolfgang von Goethe (1749–1832) was a German writer.
4 Michel de Montaigne (1533–92) was an influential French essayist.
5 Plato (c. 427–347 BCE) was a Greek philosopher.

performance calls for; and this, because in settling the reputation of Shakspeare, Milton,[1] and all other great writers, the world has not thrown out the plagiarisms, but judged them according to what appeared on their pages.... As we pass up along the backward chain of authors we find invention retreating before us indefinitely, till at the head of the line we catch Prometheus[2] stealing all the fire of inspiration from heaven. The fact is, that in all cases the praise of a thing is due not to the first faint conceiver of it, but to the last complete applier of it. This is recognized in the grosser arts; twenty men thought of steamboats, but Fulton[3] is the inventor of the steamboat, because he first set a steamboat a-going; the rest were dreamers; inventors mentally but not inventors in the art. Of all arts, Dr. Paley[4] has said with admirable truth, "He only discovers who proves;" and of literature we say, he that combines so as to produce a new effect, creates. We hold, therefore, that to condemn a poet for borrowing the elements of a detached thought or image is to mistake the true character of literary invention.

3. Untitled Article, *Caledonian Mercury* (18 November 1852): 2

In another column we have given from the *Globe* an exposure of a very glaring piece of plagiarism committed by Mr. Disraeli[5] upon Mons. Thiers,[6] Mr. Disraeli being convicted of having stolen bodily the finest passage in his eulogium on the Duke of Wellington[7] delivered the other day in the House of Commons, from an eulogium on Marshal Gouvion de St. Cyr,[8] delivered by Mons. Thiers in the year 1829, and republished in the *Morning*

---

1 John Milton (1608–74) was an English poet.
2 In Greek mythology, the deity who stole fire from Mount Olympus and gave it to humans.
3 Robert Fulton (1765–1815) developed the first commercially successful steamboat.
4 William Paley (1743–1805) was a utilitarian English theologian.
5 Benjamin Disraeli (1804–81) was an English novelist and politician who rose in the 1860s to the position of prime minister.
6 Marie Joseph Louis Adolphe Thiers (1797–1877) was a French politician and historian.
7 Arthur Wellesley, first Duke of Wellington (1759–1852) was an English politician and soldier. He led the defeat of Napoleon at Waterloo in 1815.
8 Laurent de Gouvion Saint-Cyr (1764–1830) was a French military commander.

Chronicle of 1st July 1848. The conviction is complete, and we are really sorry for it. The crime of Mr. Disraeli is not merely the highest literary crime which it is possible to commit, but it is the only literary crime which is never to be forgiven. It stands recorded against the convicted offender, and prevents him in all time coming from getting credit for being the real author of any production which he may in future give to the world as his own, in which the existence of any merit may be recognized. If Mr. Disraeli at any future time shall make a fine speech upon any side of any question—and he can make good speeches on all sides of all questions—he must be content to be asked the question "Where have you stolen that?" Now, the great pity is, that a gentleman of real ability and of real eloquence, should have placed himself in a position so disadvantageous to himself—but the deed is done—and his best friends can have no confidence that the finest passages which appear in his speeches are of his own making—while his enemies will believe that he never rises above mediocrity, except when he steals his neighbour's thunder—and in reference to that Hebrew extraction,[1] of which the Chancellor of the Exchequer[2] is in the way of boasting, there will be plenty of sneering allusions to people who enrich themselves with borrowed jewels.

4. From Untitled Article, *London Times* (22 November 1852): 4

An awful clatter has been raised about an alleged piece of appropriation by no less a personage than the Chancellor of the Exchequer.[3] Last Monday, in virtue of his office, he had to move some resolutions with regard to the public funeral; and in doing so he made a speech which might, perhaps, be rather more elaborate than suited the occasion, but was still much admired, and, what is more, made a very deep impression. It was speedily discovered that one passage in it was almost identical with a quotation that appeared four years ago in one of our morning contemporaries. This, of course, was a grand discovery. A shout of "stop thief!" was raised, and a whole pack of jealous *litterateurs* were immediately on the scent of their offending, and perhaps too successful, brother.... For our part, the thing appeared so

---

1   Disraeli's ancestors on his father's side were Italian Sephardic Jews.
2   Disraeli was then serving as chancellor of the exchequer, a British cabinet position equivalent to the secretary of the treasury.
3   I.e, Disraeli.

trivial, that we were only sorry a speech which we had read with pleasure should be liable to any exception whatever. It was evident that Mr. Disraeli had adopted a practice deliberately recommended and extensively practiced by no less an authority than Cicero[1]—viz., storing in the memory a variety of "topics" or common-places, and producing them whenever matter might be wanting, or the thread of the speech lost for the moment. The passage in question, describing the peculiar difficulties and excellences of military genius, is exactly such a topic as Cicero meant, and is one which even now, after this terrible exposure, our younger readers might do well to store in their memory. As for plagiarism, there is not a great orator or poet who has not been a plagiarist, and that on a very extensive scale. The calendar would include every author worth reading since the world began.

5. From "Stop Thief!" *Fife Herald* (25 November 1852): 3

[H]ow fallen is this famous Chancellor now, and irrecoverably fallen! The detection of his enormous literary plagiarism of last week has sapped the very foundation on which all his influence and fame rested, whilst the fact that he robbed a Frenchman to do honour to Wellington, shows both head and heart to have been alike empty. No mere politician could stand up against the consequences of such a discovery. It would have damaged even a Castlereagh;[2] and altogether damned a Peel.[3] How much more must it annihilate D'Israeli, who is a statesman simply because he was a literary man, and for whom literary genius alone procured his present post of Chancellor of the Exchequer.

Instead of exulting with party glee over the irretrievable disgrace which Mr. D'Israeli has brought down upon himself, we mourn over it as a scandal and an injury to literature. This literary suicide affects the whole literary order, and causes every member of it to hang his head in grief and shame. Yet the crime will admit of no such apology as the *Times* of Monday urges, and urges, probably, because the *Times* itself was not the policeman

---

1 Marcus Tullius Cicero (106–43 BCE) was a Roman philosopher and orator.
2 Robert Stewart, Lord Castlereagh (1769–1822) was an Irish and British statesman.
3 Robert Peel (1788–1850) was a British statesman who had served as prime minister.

that made the discovery, otherwise the Thunderer[1] would not have checked a single volley. Mr. D'Israeli, pleads the *Times*, has a remarkable memory. He remembered the French paragraphs. Yes: no doubt of it; by why did he not also remember that they were not his own? Why did he give them as his own, and thus pilfer, instead of quote, them? ...

That the shameless plagiarism which has surprised and disgusted the whole country is the first literary theft perpetrated by Mr. D'Israeli, no one believes. Suspicion is afoot; and we have little doubt that, in a short time, the goods of many injured authors and orators will be detected in his possession. We ourselves, pretending to no uncommon power of discrimination, and with unexcited suspicions, have long wondered at this curious fact about Mr. D'Israeli's writings and speeches—that their abundant and decisive talent is unstamped and unindented by individuality. He may have carefully obliterated the names of the men to whom they properly belong, and marked them with his own; but no image of his is upon them, nor does anything about the material prove it to be of native manufacture.

6. From William Wells Brown, "Letter from William W. Brown," *Frederick Douglass' Paper* (10 June 1853): 1

DEAR MR. GARRISON:—I forward to you, by this day's mail, the papers containing accounts of the great meeting held in Exeter Hall last night. No meeting during this anniversary has caused so much talk and excitement as this gathering. No time could possibly have been more appropriate for such a meeting than the present. *Uncle Tom's Cabin has come down upon the dark abodes of slavery like a mornings sunlight, unfolding to view its enormities in a manner which has fastened all eyes upon the "peculiar Institution," and awakening sympathy in hearts that never before felt for the slave, had Exeter Hall been capable of holding fifty thousand instead of five thousand, it would no doubt have been filled to its utmost capacity....

We copy the above letter from the Liberator, because we are always glad to lay anything from Mr. Brown before our readers. His letter is very prettily expressed; but he will pardon us if we suspect that his vicinage to *Mr. D'Israeli* has not been, in all respects, to his advantage. The sentence which we have taken the liberty to mark above, so resembles certain lines which occur in a "Call", published nearly a year ago, by *"the Rochester ladies'*

---

1 Nickname for the *London Times*.

Anti-Slavery Society,"[1] that we fear friend Brown has, like some other *literary* men, mistaken the beautiful sentiment of another for the creation of his own fancy! The lines to which we refer are as follows; and we think them enough alike to be twins: *"'*Uncle Tom's Cabin,*' by Mrs. Harriet Beecher Stowe, has come down upon the dark abodes of human bondage like the morning sunlight, unfolding to view the enormities of slavery in a manner which has fastened all eyes upon them, and awakened sympathy for the slave in hearts unused to feel."[2]

7. From Thomas Montgomery, *Literary Societies, Their Uses and Abuses* (1853), 14–15

Plagiarism! What a *plaguy* ugly word! "The act of purloining another man's literary works, or introducing passages from another man's writings, and putting them off as one's own; literary theft."—*Webster*.[3] I feel that this vice is so low, so contemptible that I can scarcely touch it. Go and steal another man's hat, steal his coat, steal his shoes, and you will be safely housed in the Penitentiary. Can you hope then, to be guiltless when you steal his brains? See that pale and weary student, toiling by the faint flickering of the midnight lamp. After the most laborious efforts, the most intense and exhausting strivings, he succeeds in chiselling a beautiful figure from the rock of truth. Stamping it with his name, which he trusts now shall be immortal, he places it upon its pedestal, and exposes it to public view and admiration. In the darkness of the midnight hour, that splendid work of art is taken down, the name of the maker concealed or defaced, another's name engraved upon it, and thus mutilated, thus basely stolen, in another locality, it is exhibited to the world. What should be the punishment of such a butcher, of such a thief? None greater or less than of him who is a plagiarist. The young writer longs for literary glory; the young speaker pants for the sickly breath of popular applause; and unwilling, or unable to secure it by the exercise of his own original powers in the only legitimate way, puts forth his hand to the forbidden tree, plucks the fatal fruit, is intoxicated for a moment, then sickens and dies.

---

1 The secretary of the Rochester (NY) Ladies' Anti-Slavery Society was Frederick Douglass' close friend Julia Griffiths (1811–95).
2 The editorial commentary in the second paragraph of this excerpt was written by Douglass.
3 Noah Webster (1758–1843) was an American lexicographer.

8. From "Plagiarism: Especially That of Coleridge," *Eclectic Magazine* 32 (August 1854): 485

Every great poet has at one time or another been accused of being a great thief. The old Greek mythology, which concealed an overflowing wisdom in its poetic fables, and in the passions and adventures of its gods and goddesses—things merely fanciful or grotesque to the vulgar, but full of deep meaning for the inner circle of souls—prefigured the idea of plagiarism by representing Hermes as the Inventor of the Lyre and the God of Thieves. It must be confessed that, in most cases, when a charge of plagiarism has been fixed upon a great author, the proof has been easy. But what does it signify? The mighty masters of song are none the less mighty for an occasional peccadillo of this kind. Perfect originality is impossible, unless it be the originality of the maniac. Every writer is of necessity indebted to his contemporaries and his predecessors. He lives in the great ocean of human thought, and could not think if there had not been no thinkers before him. If Shakspere had been left in his childhood on a desert island, and had remained there all his life, he might have been an Orson[1] or a Robinson Crusoe,[2] but he never could have written or even imagined his immortal plays. If there had been no mathematics before the days of Newton,[3] he would never have discovered the law of gravitation. It is only when an inferior author takes the thoughts and the *ipsissima verba*[4] of great writers, and passes off the plunder as his own property, that the charge of plagiarism is worth entertaining. Sensible men attach but little importance to it in the case of those who have genius enough of their own to entitle them to stand in the first rank, and who would remain immeasurably rich without the misappropriation of other people's ideas. He who purloins a pennyworth of literary old iron, and converts it, in the furnace of his mind, to finely tempered steel, worth a hundred thousand times the amount, is not to be condemned in a literary point of view, but to be lauded.

---

1 A character in the early modern French romance *Valentine and Orson* who was abandoned in the woods as a boy and grew up in a bear's den.

2 The protagonist of Daniel Defoe's *Robinson Crusoe* (1719), who was shipwrecked on an uninhabited island.

3 Isaac Newton (1643–1727) was an English physicist and mathematician.

4 The precise words (Latin).

The charge of plagiarism falls to the ground in such cases, and is of no account. It must be remembered, too, that there is a kind of plagiarism which is quite involuntary and unconscious. The echo of another man's wisdom or wit may remain in the mind long after all remembrance has been lost of the source whence it was derived. Besides, as Coleridge remarked, "There are such things as fountains in the world;" and it must not be imagined that every stream which is seen flowing "comes from a perforation made in another man's tank."[1]

---

1 The quotation is from Coleridge's Preface to "Christabel" (1816).

Select Bibliography

Published Works by Williams Wells Brown

The American Fugitive in Europe; Sketches of People and Places Abroad. Boston: Jewett, 1855.

The Anti-Slavery Harp. Boston: Marsh, 1848.

The Black Man: His Antecedents, His Genius, and His Achievements. New York: Hamilton, 1863.

Clotel; or, the President's Daughter. London: Partridge and Oakey, 1853.

Clotelle: A Tale of the Southern States. Boston: Redpath, 1864.

Clotelle: or, The Colored Heroine. Boston: Lee and Sheppard, 1867.

A Description of William Wells Brown's Original Panoramic Views of the Scenes in the Life of an American Slave. London: Gilpin, 1850.

The Escape; or, A Leap for Freedom. Boston: Wallcut, 1858.

A Lecture Delivered before the Female Anti-Slavery Society of Salem. Boston: Massachusetts Anti-Slavery Society, 1847.

Memoir of William Wells Brown. Boston: Anti-Slavery Office, 1859.

Miralda; or, the Beautiful Quadroon. In *The Weekly Anglo-African,* 1 December 1860–16 March 1861.

My Southern Home; or, The South and Its People. Boston: A.G. Brown, 1880.

Narrative of the Life of William W. Brown, a Fugitive Slave. Boston: Anti-Slavery Office, 1847.

Narrative of the Life of William W. Brown, an American Slave. London: Gilpin, 1849.

The Negro in the American Rebellion: His Heroism and His Fidelity. Boston: Lee and Sheppard, 1867.

The Rising Son; or, The Antecedents and Advancement of the Colored Race. Boston: A.G. Brown, 1874.

St. Domingo: Its Revolution and Its Patriots. Boston: Marsh, 1855.

Three Years in Europe; or, Places I Have Seen and People I Have Met. London: Gilpin, 1852.

"A True Story of Slave Life." *Anti-Slavery Advocate* 3 (December 1852): 23.

Biographies

Farrison, William Edward. *William Wells Brown: Author and Reformer.* Chicago: U of Chicago P, 1969.

Greenspan, Ezra. *William Wells Brown: An African American Life.* New York: Norton, 2014.

Critical Studies of Brown and *Clotel*

Carpio, Glenda. *Laughing Fit to Kill: Black Humor in the Fictions of Slavery.* New York: Oxford UP, 2008.

Chakkalakal, Tess. *Novel Bondage: Slavery, Marriage, and Freedom in Nineteenth-Century America.* Urbana: U of Illinois P, 2011.

Cohen, Lara Langer. "Notes from the State of Saint Domingue: The Practice of Citation in *Clotel*." In *Early African American Print Culture*, edited by Lara Langer Cohen and Jordan Alexander Stein, 161–77. Philadelphia: U of Pennsylvania P, 2012.

Coleman, Dawn. *Preaching and the Rise of the American Novel.* Columbus: Ohio State UP, 2013.

duCille, Ann. "Where in the World Is William Wells Brown? Thomas Jefferson, Sally Hemings, and the DNA of African-American Literary History." *American Literary History* 12 (Autumn 2000): 443–62.

Ernest, John. *Resistance and Reformation in Nineteenth-Century African-American Literature: Brown, Wilson, Jacobs, Delany, Douglass, and Harper.* Jackson: UP of Mississippi, 1995.

Fabi, M. Giulia. *Passing and the Rise of the African American Novel.* Urbana: U of Illinois P, 2001.

Gilmore, Paul. "'De Genewine Artekil': William Wells Brown, Blackface Minstrelsy, and Abolitionism." *American Literature* 69 (1997): 743–80.

Loughran, Trish. *The Republic in Print: Print Culture in the Age of U.S. Nation Building, 1770–1870.* New York: Columbia UP, 2007.

Reid-Pharr, Robert. *Conjugal Union: The Body, the House, and the Black American.* New York: Oxford UP, 1999.

Sanborn, Geoffrey. *Plagiarama! William Wells Brown and the Aesthetics of Attractions.* New York: Columbia UP, 2016.

Stadler, Gustavus. *Troubling Minds: The Cultural Politics of Genius in the United States, 1840–1890.* Minneapolis: U of Minnesota P, 2006.

Wilson, Ivy G. *Specters of Democracy: Blackness and the Aesthetics of Politics in the Antebellum U.S.* New York: Oxford UP, 2011.

Sources for Plagiarized Passages in *Clotel*

Note: The database where each source was located is listed at the end of the entry.

Allen, George. *Resistance to Slavery Every Man's Duty.* Boston: Crosby and Nichols, 1847. *Google Books.*

Baines, Edward. "Testimony and Appeal on the Effects of Total Abstinence." *British Friend* (January 1853): 10. *Google Books.*

Beard, John R. *The Life of Toussaint L'Ouverture, The Negro Patriot of Hayti.* London: Ingram, Cooke, 1853. *Google Books.*

Bowditch, William I. *Slavery and the Constitution.* Boston: Wallcut, 1849. *Google Books.*

"Charlotte Corday." *Eclectic Magazine* 17 (June 1849): 275–76. *Google Books.*

Child, Lydia Maria. "The Quadroons." *The Liberty Bell,* edited by Maria Weston Chapman, 115–41. Boston: Massachusetts Anti-Slavery Fair, 1842. *Google Books.*

"Christianized Sensibility vs. Christianity." *New York Evangelist,* 15 April 1847, 58. *American Periodicals Series.*

"Curious Funeral Service." *Albany Evening Journal,* 5 May 1845, 2. *America's Historical Newspapers.*

[de Kroyft, Helen.] "Beautiful Letter." *North Star,* 8 August 1848, 4. *America's Historical Newspapers.*

"The Dismal Swamp." *New York Commercial Advertiser,* 7 July 1848, 1. *America's Historical Newspapers.*

"Emancipation in Maryland." *Liberator,* 15 August 1845, 130. *Slavery and Anti-Slavery.*

"The Free Colored Veterans." *New Orleans Daily Picayune,* 9 January 1851, 2. *America's Historical Newspapers.*

Garrison, William Lloyd. *An Address, Delivered Before the Free People of Color, in Philadelphia, New-York, and Other Cities, During the Month of June, 1831.* Boston: Foster, 1831. *Slavery and Anti-Slavery.*

——. "Declaration of the National Anti-Slavery Convention." *Liberator,* 14 December 1833, 198. *Slavery and Anti-Slavery.*

[Gates, Seth M.] "Slavery in the District." *New York Evangelist,* 8 September 1842, 1. *American Periodicals Series.*

Gleanings from Pious Authors. Edited by James Montgomery. 1846; repr. Philadelphia: Longstreth, 1855. *Google Books.*

[Grimké, Sarah.] *An Address to Free Colored Americans.* New York: Dorr, 1837. *Slavery and Anti-Slavery.*

H.S.D. "An Auction." *National Anti-Slavery Standard,* 20 March 1845, 165. *Slavery and Anti-Slavery.*

Hughes, Benjamin F. *Eulogium on the Life and Character of William Wilberforce.* New York: Office of *The Emancipator,* 1833. *Slavery and Anti-Slavery.*

"Hunting Robbers with Bloodhounds." *Utica Daily Observer,* 25 September 1848, 1. *Old Fulton NY Postcards.*

[Hutson, William F.] "The *History of the Girondists." Southern Presbyterian Review* 2 (1848): 387–413. *Google Books.*

"Lucy Stone." *Anti-Slavery Advocate* 1 (January 1853): 29. *Slavery and Abolition.*

Martineau, Harriet. *Society in America.* 3 vols. London: Saunders and Otley, 1837. *Google Books.*

Maxcy, Milton. *An Oration, Delivered in the Dutch Church in Schenectady.* Albany, NY: Whiting, 1803. *Google Books.*

McDonogh, John. *Letter of John McDonogh, on African Colonization.* New Orleans: Commercial Bulletin, 1842. *Slavery and Anti-Slavery.*

"The Mother." *Albany Evening Journal,* 10 January 1849, 2. *Old Fulton NY Postcards.*

Palfrey, John G. *Papers on the Slave Power.* Boston: Merrill, Cobb, 1846. *Slavery and Anti-Slavery.*

Patton, William Weston. *Slavery, the Bible, Infidelity: Pro-slavery Interpretations of the Bible.* Hartford: Burleigh, 1847. *Google Books.*

"Pauline." *Anti-Slavery Reporter,* 1 July 1846, 102–03. *Slavery and Anti-Slavery.*

"A Peep into an Italian Interior." *Chambers' Edinburgh Journal* (16 April 1852): 241–45. *Google Books.*

"Prospects of Slavery." *Liberator,* 29 April 1853, 65. *America's Historical Newspapers.*

Purvis, Robert. *A Tribute to the Memory of Thomas Shipley.* Philadelphia: Merrihew and Gunn, 1836. *Slavery and Anti-Slavery.*

Scoble, John. "American Slavery." *Anti-Slavery Reporter,* 1 July 1846, 97. *Slavery and Anti-Slavery.*

"Sentimental." *Water-Cure Journal,* 1 June 1849, 165. *American Periodicals Series.*

"Shackford's Letters on the War with Mexico." *North Star,* 10 March 1848, 1. *Slavery and Anti-Slavery.*

"Shocking Affair—Desperate Courage of a Slave." *Liberator*, 11 May 1849, 76. *Slavery and Anti-Slavery.*

"Smart Boy." *Rural Repository.* 6 June 1846, 111. *Google Books.*

Stevens, Thaddeus. "The Slavery Question." *National Era*, 7 March 1850, 37. *Slavery and Anti-Slavery.*

Stewart, Alvan. *A Legal Argument Before the Supreme Court of the State of New Jersey.* New York: Finch and Weed, 1845. *Google Books.*

"Story of a Slave Mother." *Pennsylvania Freeman*, 18 November 1852, 186. *Slavery and Anti-Slavery.*

Sunderland, LaRoy. *Anti-Slavery Manual.* 3rd ed. New York: Benedict, 1839. *Slavery and Anti-Slavery.*

[Thornwell, James.] "The Religious Instruction of the Black Population." *Southern Presbyterian Review* 1 (December 1847): 89–120. *Google Books.*

Tillinghast, W. "Chattel and Wages Laborers." *Liberator*, 20 April 1849, 61. *America's Historical Newspapers.*

"The Translation of St. Catherine." *People's Journal* 2 (1847): 255. *Google Books.*

"Views of the Benevolent Society of Alexandria." *Alexandria Gazette*, 22 June 1827, 2. *America's Historical Newspapers.*

"A Visit to a Kennel of Blood-hounds, Kept for the Purpose of Hunting Slaves." *London Nonconformist*, 29 December 1847, 912. *Access Newspaper Archive.*

[Welch, Jane S.] "Jairus's Daughter." *New England Offering* 1 (August 1848): 108. *Google Books.*

Weld, Theodore. *American Slavery as It Is.* New York: American Anti-Slavery Society, 1839. *Google Books.*

——. *The Bible Against Slavery.* New York: American Anti-Slavery Society, 1838. *Google Books.*

Whittier, John Greenleaf. "The Great Slave Market." *Emancipator and Republican*, 23 November 1843, 120. *America's Historical Newspapers.*

"The Woes of Slavery." *Pennsylvania Freeman*, 18 November 1852, 186. *Slavery and Anti-Slavery.*

"Worshippers of Mammon." *Anti-Slavery Bugle*, 10 April 1846, 4. *Chronicling America.*

Sources for Quotations in *Clotel*

Arzelia. "The Slave Auction—A Fact." *Friend of Virtue*, 1 October 1847, 302. *Slavery and Anti-Slavery.*

Atlee, Edwin A. "New Version of the National Song, The Star Spangled Banner." *Liberator*, 13 September 1844, 146. *Slavery and Anti-Slavery*.

Badger, P.S. "The Wife." *Weekly Messenger*, 16 November 1842, 411. *American Periodicals Series*.

Bailey, Margaret. "The Blind Slave Boy." In *The Liberty Minstrel*, edited by George W. Clark, 37–39. New York: Leavitt and Alden, 1845. *Slavery and Anti-Slavery*.

Burleigh, William H. "A Summer Morning in the Country." In *Voices of the True-Hearted*, 150. Philadelphia: M'Kim, 1846. *Google Books*.

Carter, Mrs. J.G. "Ye Sons of Freedom." In *The Liberty Minstrel*, edited by George W. Clark, 121–25. New York: Leavitt and Alden, 1845. *Slavery and Anti-Slavery*.

Chandler, Margaret. "The Bereaved Father." In *The Liberty Minstrel*, edited by George W. Clark, 11. New York: Leavitt and Alden, 1845. *Slavery and Anti-Slavery*.

Clarke, Sarah J. [Grace Greenwood]. "The Escape." *Liberator*, 20 September 1844, 152. *Slavery and Anti-Slavery*.

"Clerical Blasphemy." *Pennsylvania Freeman*, 12 July 1838, 3. Quoted in Bowditch, *Slavery*, 1.

Coleridge, Samuel Taylor. "The Ballad of the Dark Ladie." Quoted in Child, "The Quadroons," 115.

———. "*Eros aei lalethros etairos.*" Quoted in Child, "The Quadroons," 123.

"A Doctrine of Devils." *Liberator*, 16 January 1836, 10. Quoted in Bowditch, *Slavery*, 62.

"Ecclesiastical Action." *Emancipator*, 9 May 1839, 8. Quoted in Bowditch, *Slavery*, 62.

Edwin. "Our Own 'Slave Trade.'" *Genius of Universal Emancipation* 4 (May 1825): 128. *Slavery and Anti-Slavery*.

"The Flying Slave." In *The Liberty Minstrel*, edited by George W. Clark, 179. New York: Leavitt and Alden, 1845. *Slavery and Anti-Slavery*.

Frean, Thomas. "A Parody on 'Massachusetts vs. South Carolina.'" In "Pro-Slavery," *National Anti-Slavery Standard*, 20 March 1845, 165. *Slavery and Anti-Slavery*.

Garrison, William Lloyd. *Letter to Louis Kossuth*. Boston: Wallcut, 1852. *Slavery and Anti-Slavery*.

Gillies, Mary Leman. "Alone." *Eclectic Magazine of Foreign Literature* 10 (March 1847): 427. *Google Books*.

Goodell, William. *The American Slave Code in Theory and Practice*. New York: American and Foreign Anti-Slavery Society, 1853. *Google Books*.

"Horrible Murders by Negroes." *New Orleans Times-Picayune*, 9 June 1842, 2. *America's Historical Newspapers.*

"Hurrah for the Nineteenth Century!" *Liberator*, 17 November 1843, 182. *Slavery and Anti-Slavery.*

"I Am Monarch of Nought I Survey." In *The Liberty Minstrel*, edited by George W. Clark, 18–19. New York: Leavitt and Alden, 1845. *Slavery and Anti-Slavery.*

"An Incident at the South." *Liberator*, 9 February 1849, 23. *Slavery and Anti-Slavery.*

Irving, Washington. "The Broken Heart." In *The Sketch-Book of Geoffrey Crayon*, 1:108. 2 vols. London: Murray, 1821. *Google Books.*

Jaques, D.H. "Your Brother Is a Slave." In *The Signal of Liberty*, 10 February 1845, 1. *Slavery and Anti-Slavery.*

Key, Thomas G. "My Little Nig." *Liberator*, 27 December 1844, 208. *Slavery and Anti-Slavery.*

"Love Thy Neighbor." *Liberator*, 9 August 1850, 128. *Slavery and Anti-Slavery.*

Lowell, James Russell. "Are Ye Truly Free?" In *The Liberty Minstrel*, edited by George W. Clark, 126–27. New York: Leavitt and Alden, 1845. *Slavery and Anti-Slavery.*

"Macon." *Macon Weekly Telegraph*, 27 November 1838, 2. Quoted in Bowditch, *Slavery*, 103.

"Missionary Hymn, for the South." In *Voices of the True-Hearted*, 159–60. Philadelphia: M'Kim, 1846. *Google Books.*

Moore, Thomas. "To the Lord Viscount Forbes." In *Poetical Works*. London: Longman, 1850. *Google Books.*

"Negro Dogs." *Sumter County* (AL) *Whig*, 6 November 1845. Quoted in Bowditch, *Slavery*, 101.

Nell, William Cooper. *Services of Colored Americans, in the Wars of 1776 and 1812*. Boston: Prentiss and Sawyer, 1851. *Slavery and Anti-Slavery.*

"Notice." *Madison* (LA) *Journal*, 26 November 1847. Quoted in Bowditch, *Slavery*, 101.

"Phlebotomy—Amalgamation!" *Liberator*, 20 March 1846, 46. *Slavery and Anti-Slavery.*

"Phoebe Morel." In *Five Hundred Thousand Strokes for Freedom*, edited by Wilson Armistead, 321. London: Cash, 1853. *Google Books.*

Pierpont, John. "The Fugitive Slave's Apostrophe to the North Star." In *The Liberty Bell*, edited by George W. Clark, 75–80. Boston: American Anti-Slavery Society, 1839. *Google Books.*

"Quite a Blunder." *Emancipator and Republican*, 16 August 1849, 1. *American Periodicals Series.*

Simpson, J. Mac C. "The Slaveholder's Rest." *Liberator,* 23 November 1849, 188. *Slavery and Anti-Slavery.*

"Spirit of Colonization." *Liberator,* 20 July 1849, 113. *Slavery and Anti-Slavery.*

"Sunday Amusements in New Orleans." *New York Weekly Herald,* 9 April 1853, 114. *America's Historical Newspapers.*

Walker, Jonathan. *A Brief View of American Chattelized Humanity.* Boston, 1846. *Slavery and Anti-Slavery.*

Waterston, Robert C. "Freedom's Banner." In *Anti-Slavery Melodies,* edited by Jairus Lincoln, 72. Hingham: Gill, 1843. *Slavery and Anti-Slavery.*

Whittier, John Greenleaf. "Clerical Oppressors." In *Poems,* 145–46. Boston: Mussey, 1850. *Google Books.*

——. "The Farewell of a Virginia Slave Mother to Her Daughters." In *The Liberty Minstrel,* edited by George W. Clark, 5–7. New York: Leavitt and Alden, 1845. *Slavery and Anti-Slavery.*

——. "Our Countrymen in Chains." In *The Liberty Minstrel,* edited by George W. Clark, 76–77. New York: Leavitt and Alden, 1845. *Slavery and Anti-Slavery.*

——. "Stanzas for the Times." In *Poems,* 150–52. Boston: Mussey, 1850. *Google Books.*

Wright, Elizur. "The Fugitive Slave to the Christian." In *The Liberty Minstrel,* edited by George W. Clark, 34–36. New York: Leavitt and Alden, 1845. *Slavery and Anti-Slavery.*

From the Publisher

A name never says it all, but the word "Broadview" expresses a good deal of the philosophy behind our company. We are open to a broad range of academic approaches and political viewpoints. We pay attention to the broad impact book publishing and book printing has in the wider world; we began using recycled stock more than a decade ago, and for some years now we have used 100% recycled paper for most titles. Our publishing program is internationally oriented and broad-ranging. Our individual titles often appeal to a broad readership too; many are of interest as much to general readers as to academics and students.

Founded in 1985, Broadview remains a fully independent company owned by its shareholders—not an imprint or subsidiary of a larger multinational.

For the most accurate information on our books (including information on pricing, editions, and formats) please visit our website at www.broadviewpress.com. Our print books and ebooks are also available for sale on our site.

On the Broadview website we also offer several goods that are not books—among them the Broadview coffee mug, the Broadview beer stein (inscribed with a line from Geoffrey Chaucer's *Canterbury Tales*), the Broadview fridge magnets (your choice of philosophical or literary), and a range of T-shirts (made from combinations of hemp, bamboo, and/or high-quality pima cotton, with no child labor, sweatshop labor, or environmental degradation involved in their manufacture).

All these goods are available through the "merchandise" section of the Broadview website. When you buy Broadview goods you can support other goods too.

broadview press
www.broadviewpress.com